SPLIT SECOND

Douglas E. Richards

Paragon Press

This book is a work of fiction. The characters, incidents, and dialogues are products of the author's imagination and are not to be construed as real. Any resemblance to actual events or persons, living or dead, is entirely coincidental.

Published by Paragon Press, 2015

E-mail the author at doug@san.rr.com

Friend him on Facebook at Douglas E. Richards Author

Visit the author's website at www.douglaserichards.com

First Edition

PART ONE
Breakthrough

Split Second (noun):
1. a fraction of a second.
2. an infinitesimal amount of time.

—Dictionary.com

"The past cannot remember the past. The future can't generate the future. The cutting edge of this instant right here and now is always nothing less than the totality of everything there is."

—Robert Pirsig

1

Jenna Morrison kissed her sister, Amber, goodbye, ignoring the shrieks of tiny Sophia, who was swaddled so completely in a baby blanket that her actual presence could not be confirmed by eye, as though she had fallen into a cottony-soft, mint-green black hole. The swaddling did nothing, however, to lessen Sophia's eardrum-searing screams, honed by evolution to be exceedingly irritating and impossible to ignore.

Amber patted Sophia's back gently, holding her close, hoping that the need for a burp was causing this unholy racket and shooting her sister a look of apology and helplessness. The baby's timing couldn't have been worse.

"Thanks for coming, Jen," said Amber. "You're a life saver."

"Are you kidding?" said Jenna, a little louder than usual to be heard over her niece's shrieks. "I wouldn't have missed this for the world. I got to see you. Bond with Sophia. Not to mention getting a baby fix. I should thank *you*."

"You truly are the best," said Amber, unable to keep the sadness at her sister's departure, and the mounting panic Jenna knew she was feeling, from her expression.

But who could blame her for feeling panicked? Becoming a mother at twenty was one thing, but having the father disappear within two months of the birth was another, and would freak out just about anyone, regardless of their intestinal fortitude.

Jenna had flown out from San Diego as soon as possible after Amber had learned she would be raising a baby on her own, to help with Sophia and give Amber moral support, at least for a week. The visit had been a good one, and she was convinced her sister was beginning to regain her emotional stability, although regaining it fully could well take months or even years.

But it was extremely encouraging that not only did Amber not show any signs of postpartum depression, she was one of those moms who seemed to glow from within, basking in motherhood and drowning in the soothing oxytocin that was released by the infant's tireless efforts to suck the nipples right from her body.

Jenna would have liked to stay longer, but she was in the middle of a relentlessly challenging PhD program in genetics and needed to get back to her life. And also back to her fiancé, Nathan Wexler.

"You take care of yourself," said Jenna earnestly. "And remember, don't let *anything* keep you down. Everyone has bad days. But you have a great life ahead of you. I know it. Sophia has no idea just how lucky she is."

Amber nodded as a tear formed in the corner of one eye. Jenna kissed the mint-green blanket, pressing her lips into the material so the screaming baby could feel the weight of them on the back of her head, and then let herself into the back of the waiting cab without saying another word.

As the cab made its way to O'Hare, Jenna reflected on life. She wouldn't wish what had happened to her sister on anyone, but babies were undeniably adorable, and many women had thrived as single mothers. And Jenna had been surprised to learn that she had a strong motherhood instinct as well, just waiting for the sight of a baby to reveal itself.

When would she and Nathan begin having a family? she wondered. And how many children would they have?

Nathan Wexler was a brilliant physicist and mathematician, and while she wasn't nearly at his level—who was?—she was considered gifted herself. Both of their lives were sure to be demanding, and fulfilling, for as far into the future as they could imagine.

They had agreed they wanted to have kids at some point, but they had only discussed parenthood in the vaguest of generalities. True, they had plenty of time. After all, Nathan might be twenty-nine, but she was only twenty-six. But would they *ever* decide the time was right? In between careers and intellectual pursuits that might change the world—a possibility that was especially likely for Nathan.

After all, they hadn't even managed to get around to making their unofficial marriage official. They had been living together now for eighteen months and already thought of themselves as husband and wife, but Jenna's interest in stealing time from other passions to make this happen was vanishingly small. And a quickie Vegas wedding was out, as well, since Nathan's family would never forgive them.

So they needed to find a venue. Plan out a ceremony. Invite guests.

She shuddered. She would rather sit on a mound of fire ants.

Jenna wondered how long it would take for her and Nathan to get around to tying the knot. And if they couldn't seem to find the time to plan a wedding, would they *ever* get around to having kids? Maybe not.

Just a year earlier, she and Nathan had watched an old movie called *Idiocracy*, which they found quite humorous and often bitingly brilliant, but which had also struck a nerve. The movie's premise was that humanity was on course, not to evolve toward greatness, but to *devolve* into idiocy.

And this point was made quite effectively. A narrator pointed out that the process of natural selection once ensured that the strongest, smartest, or fastest reproduced in the greatest numbers. But now, in the case of human society, with no natural predators to thin the herd, evolution didn't reward those with the most intelligence, but simply those who reproduced the most.

The movie then demonstrated this premise by showing scenes of illiterate slobs who would screw anything that moved, including various relatives, and who seemed to think chucking chairs at each other at the slightest provocation was the height of good sport. The film showed these people reproducing with total abandon, like rabbits with a sex addiction.

Why? For lack of anything else to do with their time. Because they were impulsive and not bright enough to even understand the importance of birth control. And because the more kids they had, the bigger the welfare checks and food stamp handouts they received.

This was contrasted with a scene in which two prissy, high-IQ professionals were discussing having children. They both agreed that having children was an important decision and that they needed to wait for the right time, since child bearing wasn't something that should be rushed into. Ultimately, they died childless.

The moral: the dimwitted and impulsive might not be able to hold a job or learn algebra, but they sure knew how to screw each other—and reproduce like crazy.

The movie took place many generations in the future, after which this reverse evolution had run its inevitable course, resulting in a society largely composed of morons.

A comedy, yes, and while the accuracy of this premise was still being debated in scientific circles, it was hard for Jenna to fault its logic.

She was brilliant, while her sister was far less so, and far more impulsive. She wondered how many children Amber would have. And if she and her super-genius husband would ever have *any*.

Jenna was greeted at Lindbergh Field in San Diego by a beaming but bleary-eyed Nathan Wexler, who looked the same as he had looked during their Skype calls all week—as though he were allergic to sleep.

After a long embrace, and when her luggage finally arrived at the carousel in an airport known for the slowness of its luggage retrieval, Wexler began the drive back to their small rental home in La Jolla, where he was by far the youngest full professor in the physics department of the University of California, San Diego, having already produced groundbreaking work in several areas of physics and mathematics.

Wexler peppered Jenna with questions about her visit with her sister and her view of Amber's mental health on the way home, even though they had discussed this during their daily calls. When they arrived, he produced a bottle of expensive red wine and two elegant, oversized crystal glass goblets, and filled them up with a sparkle in his eye.

"Welcome back," he said as he poured.

Jenna was impressed. It took a special occasion for them to use anything other than plastic cups. She and Nathan were both wearing old jeans and T-shirts, of like mind that comfort was more important than style, and fine wine in a fine crystal goblet seemed too fancy for their current attire.

It was nearing midnight and she was exhausted. In just minutes Sunday night would officially change into Monday morning, although this had occurred hours earlier in Chicago and her body was still on this time. Nathan appeared to be even more exhausted than she was, but he also had a triumphant glow about him, like he had recently won a lottery.

They had never been apart for this long since they had moved in together, so maybe this separation had affected him more than either had expected. "You know you don't have to get me drunk to have your way with me, right?" she said, the corners of her mouth turning up into a wry smile.

What was he waiting for? They should be tearing each other's clothes off by now. Sometimes exhaustion, especially mental exhaustion, led to epic sex. The more the brain was taken out of the equation, allowing primitive, primal instinct to run the show, the better.

"Good to know," he replied, returning her smile. "But this isn't about getting you drunk. If it was, I would have poured the usual. You know. From the giant carton of wine in the fridge."

"Yeah. Last week was a good year for wine," she replied with a grin.

"I trust you noticed that this came from an actual bottle. With an actual cork, made from, you know, cork."

"Impressive," she said. She raised her eyebrows. "Miss me that much?"

"Of course I missed you," said Wexler. "But I have to admit, this is for something else." He paused. "You'll never guess."

"You got a huge raise?" said Jenna.

"No, I wasn't asking you to *guess*. I was saying that, *literally*, you could live to be a thousand and would never guess."

Jenna laughed. He was a bit quirky, but given his intellect, far less than one might expect. And he was funny and loving and so fast on the uptake that it was dizzying.

She had always hated dumb guys. When she met Nathan, despite having been the valedictorian of her high school and earning a near perfect SAT score, she had suddenly become the slow one. Discussions with him were exhilarating.

But it had to be difficult for him. To be so far ahead of everyone else. Even the best brains in the physics department couldn't measure up. And if brilliant people were slow by comparison, how much patience did he need to bear people who were average?

Jenna had no doubt that having the chance to be stimulated intellectually by a mental giant was worth putting up with some quirks. And this was, after all, par for the course. She had seen a movie about Stephen Hawking and how his wife had not only put up with the quirks of the super intelligent, but with a man whose entire body was paralyzed. Well, all except for his penis, which enabled them to have three children, although the thought picture of how this was accomplished wasn't something on which she liked to dwell.

The Hawking situation had been a thousand times more difficult than anything *she* had to deal with. Nathan was just fashion-impaired, absentminded, and too literal sometimes. He talked to himself under his breath fairly frequently, and often couldn't remember where he had left stuff, as though his mind was too powerful to dwell on the mundane. All traits she now found endearing.

"Okay, so if I'll never guess, how about you telling me," she said, raising her glass.

"I thought you'd never ask," he replied with a grin. "I had an epiphany the day you left and have been working on it around the clock. Astonishing really. I stumbled across some esoteric mathematics that had never been found to have any real-world applications, and suddenly I had an insight that allowed me to come up with something truly remarkable."

"How remarkable?"

"You're about to drink wine that didn't come out of a box, remarkable. Possible *Nobel Prize* remarkable. I haven't begun to determine if there are any real-world applications, but on theoretical grounds this could be a huge breakthrough. Immense. I'm not saying it's on the level of general relativity, but once it's fleshed out, you never know. And even if it doesn't quite reach the level of importance of relativity, I think it will be just as surprising to the world as this was when Einstein first presented it. And maybe as revolutionary."

"And you've been working on this the entire week?"

He nodded.

This explained his lack of sleep, she realized. When he was in the throes of a major idea, he would work on it around the clock until he collapsed from exhaustion. "How is it that you never said a word about this when we Skyped?"

"Well, you were dealing with a crisis, and I wanted to make this week about you and your sister. Besides, I was never sure I wasn't hallucinating the entire thing. I'm still not."

"You're killing me. Are you going to tell me what you've found?"

Wexler smiled. "I don't know," he said, teasing her. "Maybe I should wait until I'm absolutely certain. I still need to finish triple checking the calculations and logic, and have this vetted by the best minds I know, just to be sure I don't embarrass myself. It's possible that I've missed something big."

"We both know *that's* unlikely."

"I appreciate your faith," said Wexler sheepishly. "But in this case, the complexities of the math and logic dwarf anything I've ever done. This makes string theory look as simple as addition. I've already written Dan Walsh, telling him what I think I've discovered, and asking him to clear the decks for a bit so he can be a second set of eyes on it, to check for accuracy."

Dan Walsh was a physicist at nearby UCLA and had been a close friend of Nathan Wexler for years.

"Okay," said Jenna. "This is very cute and all, Nathan. I like how you're trying to build the suspense. But enough already. I'm at the edge of my seat. Really."

She set the goblet of wine down on a nearby end table. "So out with it. Spill. I'm not going to drink to a breakthrough discovery until I at least know the gist of what it is."

Wexler tapped the screen of his cell phone and a drum roll issued from the speaker.

"Really?" said Jenna, laughing. Apparently, the wine wasn't the only thing he had prepared for this moment. "I had no idea you were this theatrical."

"There's a lot you don't know about me," he replied with a broad smile as the drum roll continued to loop in a repeating pattern.

The front door shot open and three men burst through the threshold and into their small home, as though cued by the drum roll.

For just a moment Jenna thought they might be part of the show, but something about their look, their seriousness, squelched this notion, and gave her an unmistakable sense that these men were highly dangerous. And Nathan's reaction—his mouth dropping open and his eyes almost exploding from their sockets—made their uninvited status a certainty.

She didn't know who these men were, or why they had stormed into their home, but one thing was certain—they were highly skilled. Not only had they managed to unlock the door without a sound, but had somehow deactivated the alarm that Nathan had set as well.

What in the hell was going on?

The men stood their ground, silently, waiting for the two scientists to digest their presence.

"Who are you?" whispered Nathan Wexler in alarm to the trio of intruders. "And what are you doing here?"

2

Jenna knew immediately the men were not there to rob them. A team this good would have set their sights on a far more valuable prize. A mansion or an art museum. But certainly not the small house they were renting.

"Dr. Wexler," said the tallest of the three, nodding at Nathan. "Miss Morrison. Sorry about the intrusion. But I'm afraid you need to come with us. If you cooperate," he continued, "I can promise that you won't be harmed."

The man's two companions, a short, stocky black man, and a pale blond who looked to be of German ancestry, remained silent and alert.

"Who are you?" repeated Wexler. "And what is this about?"

"This is about the discovery you just made. I need to bring you to someone who wants to discuss it with you."

"How do you have any idea of what discoveries I might have just made?"

"Look, my mission parameters are very tight. I've already disclosed more than I should have. My job is to bring you in, gently, but ask you to put off all questions until you meet with my boss. Apparently, any discussion I might have with you is above my pay grade."

"And if we refuse?" said Jenna.

The man shook his head while his two colleagues maintained a calm but hardened look. "I'm afraid I can't take no for an answer."

Jenna's mind raced. The man hadn't made an explicit threat, nor had he drawn a gun. But then again, he didn't have to. She had no doubt that just one of these men, unarmed, could probably best her and Nathan if they both had machine guns in their hands.

What had Nathan discovered? How did they know about it so quickly? And Nathan had said his discovery was largely theoretical, with unclear real-world applications, so why the intense interest?

"We'll be leaving in a moment," said the gang's spokesman. "Apologies again, but we first need to take care of a few things."

He nodded toward his two companions who began to carry out what were obviously pre-planned tasks. The blond made his way to Wexler's desktop computer and produced a small screwdriver, expertly dismantling the computer and removing the hard drive in less than a minute.

His colleague searched the house for several minutes and returned holding Wexler's laptop. "I've confirmed that he only has the one desktop and one laptop, as per our intel," he reported. "I've also removed all of our bugs."

The tall man nodded while Jenna's heart leaped to her throat. They had been bugged? For how long? And why?

But if this was about Nathan's recent discovery, she reasoned, he had only spoken of it out loud minutes earlier. They couldn't possibly have carried out an operation with this little notice. The conclusion was inescapable. Along with the bugs, they must have been monitoring Nathan's phone and computers as well. Nathan had told her that he had sent an e-mail about his discovery to Dan Walsh recently. This must have set the wheels of this raid on their home in motion.

The tall man lifted a phone to his face. No 3D image hovered in the space before him, which meant he had purposely kept the call audio-only. "I trust you've copied everything in Wexler's cloud storage account, correct?" he said into the phone.

He listened to the response, which must have been an affirmative. "Great. Go ahead and wipe the account, then," he ordered, and then ended the call.

He turned to the two scientists. "I'm afraid I need you to give me your phones," he said, holding out his hand.

Jenna glanced at Nathan. He blew out a long breath and nodded, handing the tall spokesman his phone, and Jenna followed suit. Once this was done, the man gestured toward the front door, ignoring

Jenna's laptop that was still packed in her carry-on luggage. She was somehow certain that these men knew her laptop was there, but had no interest in any of her work.

"I'd love to be civilized," said the tall intruder, clearly the group's leader and spokesman. "So can I count on the two of you not to scream or attract attention? These actions won't change a thing, and I'm sure you'd prefer not to be gagged. We'll be gone before anyone can intervene or call the cops." He shrugged. "And to be honest, even if they do, it won't matter."

He said it with such a total air of certainty that it was impossible for Jenna not to believe him.

3

The La Jolla night sky was cloudless, as usual, and the display of stars would have been awe-inspiring under normal circumstances. As it was, Jenna fought to calm herself and become a dispassionate and clinical observer and thinker.

The physical and mental exhaustion she had been feeling had been obliterated by repeated surges of adrenaline and she was hyper-alert as the group of five rounded the block, stopping before a semi. The truck was small for an eighteen-wheeler, but it was still an *eighteen-wheeler*, a fish out of water in a residential neighborhood. It dominated the street like the rare moving vans that would visit the neighborhood every few years.

As if the night hadn't been surreal enough, the truck had the words *Hostess Cakes* emblazoned in blue on both sides. Several red hearts were arrayed around this logo, and large images of cupcakes, Ho Hos, and Twinkies adorned the outside of the vehicle. While the sky was moonless, the star field was just bright enough for her to make out these decorations, as well as the truck's license plate, which she memorized.

Another man was already seated in the driver's seat of the cab, apparently waiting for his three colleagues to return. The back of the truck was open and dimly illuminated, and they were led up a ramp and inside.

Three more men were waiting there, sitting against one wall, and nods were exchanged as their two colleagues came into view in the back of the truck.

Wexler turned to the short, stocky man beside him and arched one eyebrow. "Sure you brought enough men?" he said sarcastically.

"Yeah, this is total overkill," admitted the man with a shrug. "I'll give you that. But take this as a compliment, Dr. Wexler. It's a measure of your importance."

The shorter man, clearly the team's second-in-command, motioned for them to take a seat on the wall opposite his three associates, and they complied. He parked Wexler's hard drive and laptop beside him, and he and his blond partner sat next to their colleagues on the wall opposite the two prisoners as well. Seconds later the truck's engine roared to life and the large vehicle pulled away from the curb, beginning its mysterious journey.

Heavy equipment of unknown type was stacked against the back wall of the windowless trailer and strapped tight, and each of their captors had large nylon duffel bags resting beside them. Jenna had no idea what was inside these bags, but it wasn't a shipment of Twinkies or Ho Hos, of that she was certain. She guessed weaponry of some kind, although their captors had yet to point a gun in their direction and continued to try to maintain the illusion that their cooperation was voluntary.

Jenna stared at the stocky man and forced a smile. "Surely you can tell us *something*," she said. "I get that your boss wants to control the discussion with Dr. Wexler. But what's the harm in telling us where we're going? I mean, we *are* American citizens, after all, and you're military, right?"

The man smiled and shook his head. "Nice try. You can assume anything you'd like. But I still can't tell you anything more. But rest easy. You won't be harmed, and answers are only a few hours away."

Jenna frowned at this response, but also realized her attempt had not been entirely futile. At least they had a sense that their journey in the back of a semi would be a relatively short one.

The truck made a number of turns as it worked its way out of residential areas. Within ten minutes they accelerated up what must have surely been a freeway onramp, and less than an hour later they began climbing steadily. While there were a number of mountains and mountain ranges near San Diego, after twenty minutes of steadily increasing elevation their current location was clear. Only one mountain was this tall and this close: Palomar.

Palomar Mountain State Park was only about sixty miles northeast of San Diego, although winding one's way up a mountain with an elevation of over six thousand feet was slow going, so the trip could take as long as ninety minutes to two hours. The park was densely wooded with oak trees and any number of conifers, including pine, cedar, and fir, as well as large numbers of ferns.

The mountain's chief claim to fame, stationed near its top, was the Palomar Observatory, home to the Hale Telescope, for many decades considered the most important telescope in the world.

After five additional minutes of slowly winding up the corkscrew road, the driver slammed on the brakes, and the inhabitants of the trailer were all jerked several feet toward the cab, fighting to regain their balance and find a handhold on one of the straps hanging down from the walls.

"Change of plans," said a disembodied male voice, one that was tense and agitated, no doubt the driver communicating via some kind of speaker system. "Our forward car spotted an assault team a mile ahead. They'll try to hold them off while we backtrack down the mountain. We can't rule out that we'll run into a flanking team behind us, so prepare for imminent action. We're calling in reinforcements."

The reaction inside the trailer was immediate and frenzied. The men removed compact submachine guns and numerous clips the size of cigarette cartons from their nylon duffels and readied themselves for a possible assault. Several of them voiced variations of the phrase, "what the fuck?" with great agitation, as the truck reversed course, hurtling dangerously back along the narrow road that corkscrewed down the mountain. The residents of the back of the truck all clutched straps and hung on for dear life, but were still thrown this way and that with considerable force.

"What is going on?" demanded Jenna, unable to control her frayed nerves any longer, her words screeched out more than spoken.

"Don't know," said the man in charge as he continued to prepare for whatever might be coming. "We know there's a rival group out there. But there is no way they could know about this op. No way," he repeated in dismay. "This was supposed to be routine. A milk run. Our large force of men and spotter car were just standard precautions. We weren't expecting any trouble."

"That's very comforting," grunted Wexler, clutching at a strap he shared with Jenna as the truck continued careening down the mountain.

Then, from out of nowhere, their small stretch of Palomar Mountain State Park became a *war zone*.

The driver slammed on the brakes once again, almost yanking Jenna's arm from its socket as she fought to retain her grip on the handhold, as horrifying sounds of explosions and heavy gunfire filled the trailer. The forces on the braking Hostess delivery truck became too great for it to hold its line, and it fishtailed. The trailer slammed over onto its side and left the road, shearing away from the cab and sliding down a steep slope.

Inside the trailer, bodies flew in every direction, and the machinery at the back of the trailer tore loose from its bonds and collided randomly with the inhabitants. After ten or fifteen seconds of this, the sliding trailer slammed into a line of evenly spaced tree trunks and came to a rest against them, on its side and at a thirty-five-degree angle.

The trailer's light had been extinguished immediately during the slide, and they had been tumbled in absolute darkness, as though stuffed inside a massive clothes dryer filled with heavy objects.

As gunfire continued to rain around them, one of their captors managed to produce a glow stick and crack it open, and two others soon followed suit, providing enough illumination for Jenna to take stock. She had several minor cuts and abrasions but was largely unscathed. Two of their five captors were unconscious, and from the blood leaking from their heads, were most likely dead.

And both of Nathan's legs had been broken!

He was alive, but something heavy had crashed into his lower body with incredible force. He was groaning in agony, his legs splayed in awkward positions. A bone poked through his lower right leg, which was bleeding profusely.

She slid over and put her hands under his head, lifting it slightly, as tears rolled down her face. The sound of machine gun fire continued to echo through the trailer.

"How bad is it?" asked Nathan, his voice thin and reedy.

Jenna was glad Nathan had known enough not to look at his legs himself, which might have sent him reeling into shock. "Not so bad," she lied through her tears. "Nothing a few good doctors can't patch up good as new," she added, forcing a smile.

She had to keep him as relaxed as possible. Keep his mindset positive.

While she spoke, their three remaining captors, all of them more or less healthy, had affixed sophisticated night vision goggles to their faces, pulled, no doubt, from their mysterious bags. "McFadden, you're with me," said one of the men, who immediately slid toward the trailer door, with someone who must have been McFadden following.

The door had been designed to slide up and down, but now had to be forced from left to right in the capsized trailer. "Simkin," barked the man now in charge, as both he and McFadden pulled the door open enough for them to leave, "you stay here and watch our guests. And don't forget the stakes we're playing for," he added grimly.

Just as the two men exited the trailer there was another burst of gunfire, at point-blank range, and Jenna had no doubt they had been ambushed as they tried to leave.

Seconds later a voice called into the truck. "Simkin," it said. "I only want to relieve you of Dr. Wexler. There is no need for you to die. Lay down your arms and I'll leave you in peace."

Simkin didn't reply, but his eyes frantically surveyed the tumbled contents of the trailer. In seconds he found what he was looking for, Wexler's hard drive and laptop, and put several bursts of automatic fire into each of them, ensuring that not even the best forensic computer specialist on Earth could get anything useful from them.

Upon hearing these shots, the men outside moved in and began firing at him.

But instead of returning fire, Simkin did the unexpected. *The unthinkable.*

As bullets tore into his body, he reached out and yanked at Jenna, sending her sliding away from the man she loved, and in the same motion, with his other hand, he pointed his weapon at Wexler's head.

Then, as his last act before finally succumbing to death, the man named Simkin sent a burst of rounds into the magnificent brain of Dr. Nathan Wexler, instantly and totally obliterating one of the greatest minds in history.

4

Jenna Morrison heard a bloodcurdling scream and realized a moment later that it was coming from her own mouth.

The two intruders slid along the smooth trailer wall until they were directly in front of where Jenna had been moments earlier, surveying the carnage.

Simkin and Nathan Wexler were both dead, although Wexler's head was a bloody pulp, unrecognizable, turning him into nothing but a torso and a pair of bloody, shattered legs. Crimson liquid had sprayed everywhere and puddles collected at various locations in the trailer, drawn there by the inexorable pull of gravity.

"*God-dammit!*" shrieked one of the men, sounding almost as anguished as Jenna, who had only avoided vomiting because she had nothing in her stomach. "*Fuck!*"

"Jenna, come with me," said one of the men, turning to her. "I'll protect you."

Her eyes were unfocused and she made no sign of comprehension.

"Jenna, come on! *Jenna*," he repeated for a third time. "Snap out of it!"

The man's words were incomprehensible to her. She felt numb, paralyzed, and it seemed as though she was hearing everything through ten miles of cotton, including the never-ending barrage of gunfire going on in the woods outside. Her mind and her psyche were unable to process Nathan's barbaric and sudden death.

Just that morning she had been with her sister and niece in Chicago. Only hours ago with Nathan in her cozy home in La Jolla.

And now?

Now she was in the bowels of *hell*. In the middle of a war zone. In a beautiful state park in California that might as well have been Afghanistan or Iran.

Nathan was dead! Just like that. The love of her life. With his mighty intellect spread all over the back of a *cupcake* truck. How could this be happening?

She only gradually became aware that the world had taken on a green glow, several seconds after the man who had spoken to her had finished affixing night vision goggles to her head, his actions having failed to register with her at all.

"Jenna, come on!" he implored once again. "God-dammit!" He slapped her in the face, hard. "*Come on!* Getting yourself killed won't bring back Dr. Wexler," he said, slapping her a second time.

This time the pain finally registered and she was sparked back to reality once again. His last sentence now drilled into her returning consciousness.

He was *right*. She couldn't bring Nathan back. But she could find out what this was all about and why it had happened. She could, *somehow*, make sure those responsible roasted in hell.

"My name is Andy," said her rescuer, having looked into her eyes and realizing his slaps had pulled her back from the abyss. "Andy Cavnar. I'll make sure you're safe from these bastards. But you have to come with me."

She allowed the man to pull her toward the exit, letting her eyes focus for the first time, surprised by just how vivid the neon green world appeared through the night vision headset.

They slid out of the truck with Cavnar's partner in tow. She vaguely became aware of the ferocious whipping of helicopter blades thundering through the cool night air. She realized a moment later that the large aircraft responsible was hovering above the treetops, not twenty-five yards away, showing up with surprising clarity in her goggles.

Cavnar rushed her away from the trailer, but they were still on uneven, acutely sloped terrain, and Jenna collapsed to the ground, unable to fight off a bout of dizziness that had suddenly engulfed her.

Dizziness that saved her life.

Four men were now sliding down ropes that had dropped from the helicopter, firing as they did so, spraying the area she was in at chest height. One of her two escorts was nearly torn in half as she hugged the cool, pinecone-strewn ground, while Andy Cavnar fell to the forest floor beside her, shot in the leg.

Even before the four rappellers touched the ground they were engaged from behind, giving Cavnar a reprieve and Jenna the few seconds she needed to regain her senses, and her equilibrium.

Cavnar fired at the four men, now caught in a crossfire, as another group of four began to descend from the helicopter. He paused for a moment, shoving his partner's compact submachine gun into Jenna's hands. "Go!" he commanded. "Run!"

Jenna took a deep breath and clutched tightly at the weapon. Crouching low, driven by adrenaline and a stronger survival instinct than she had guessed she possessed, she half-ran, half-skidded down the wooded slope as quickly as she could, while Cavnar brought his gun into the battle once again.

Jenna turned every so often to look over her shoulder. The gunfire had become sporadic, as though the two forces had annihilated each other, with no one left standing. One of the dying combatants had managed to put a bullet into the helicopter and it was belching black smoke, forced to limp away so it wouldn't crash into the trees and burst into a fireball.

After five minutes of racing down the slope she arrived at the road, having traveled from one of its corkscrew turns to a lower one. Bats were darting about everywhere, their hidden lives revealed to her night vision equipment. Normally this would have freaked her out beyond measure, but after what she had just gone through she could spare no adrenaline or fear for these nocturnal animals, who were no doubt feasting on insects and were careful to avoid humans. At least she hoped.

After she had walked along the pavement for twenty minutes headlights suddenly emerged from a higher elevation. Without thinking she closed her eyes and rushed to the middle of the road, parking herself there with her right arm fully extended in front of her face, her palm facing the oncoming vehicle. If the driver was paying any kind of attention, he or she would stop. If not, she would be road kill.

Sure enough, the driver saw her with plenty of room to spare and brought the car to an abrupt halt in front of her.

She pulled off the night vision apparatus and ran to the driver's side of the car. The driver was a chubby man in his early thirties, already going bald. She raised her automatic weapon and pointed it at him, pushing away all feelings of guilt. "Get out!" she demanded, loudly enough to be heard clearly through the closed window.

The driver looked at her in horror and disbelief, but there was no denying the reality of the submachine gun in her hands, nor the cuts and blood spatter that adorned her body.

"Now!" screamed Jenna as the driver continued to hesitate, paralyzed by fear. One part of her mind remained purely clinical, taking note of how quickly the survival instinct could turn an otherwise civilized scientist like her into a barbarian. It was remarkable, and horrifying.

The man stumbled out of the car with his hands up.

"I'm not going to hurt you," she said as calmly as she could manage. "But I do need to borrow your car. It's a matter of life and death. Believe it or not, I'm a victim, not a perpetrator."

The man appeared to not believe this for a moment, but remained silent. He was likely praying for his life, she guessed, even if he had been an atheist moments before.

"Give me your phone," said Jenna.

He handed it to her and she shoved it into the front pocket of her jeans.

"I can't have you calling the cops just yet," she explained. "But I promise you you'll be okay. I'll call one of your close contacts in three or four hours and tell them where to find you, and where I've left your car. Like I said, I just need to borrow it."

She handed him the night vision goggles. "Here," she said. "Use these until sunrise."

She was happy that she didn't have to leave this poor guy stranded in total darkness. At least that was *something*.

She wondered if any more cars would be passing by at this time of the morning, and if so, if the displaced driver would try to copy her gambit and flag one of them down. She doubted it. Right now he would want to lie low until the morning light and then assess his situation. He wasn't nearly as desperate as she was. Staring into approaching headlights to stop an oncoming car wasn't for the faint of heart.

She made the balding man walk ten feet away with the goggles in his hand before she entered his car and adjusted the seat and mirrors. She lowered the window a few inches. "I am really, really sorry about this," she said. "But I promise you, you'll get your car back soon."

And with that, Jenna Morrison powered the window fully closed again, stepped on the gas, and shot off into the darkness.

5

Jenna focused on hurtling down the mountain as quickly as the laws of physics and the narrow, twisty roads would allow, which at least demanded her rapt attention, leaving her less time to dwell on her predicament or dredge up horrifying images of Nathan with his legs ruined and his head all but torn from his shoulders.

She had been exposed to the aftermath of endless gun battles in movies, of course—who hadn't?—but she was surprised to learn that movie gore didn't even come close to the utter devastation of the real thing. The caliber and power of modern weapons all but disintegrated the target, something movies didn't properly convey. Thankfully.

Even though she needed to marshal all of her concentration to keep from flying off the road for the second time in under an hour, she still burst into tears several times before she reached the bottom.

Finally, using the last remaining vestiges of a powerful will that had been tested beyond its breaking point, she managed to push Nathan from her mind and find a way to begin to concentrate on the problem at hand.

Who were the men who had ambushed the Hostess truck? Were they trying to rescue her and Nathan?

On the surface, it would appear that way. Simkin had not shot wildly, but with hideous purpose. Andy Cavnar, on the other hand, had tried to protect her. Had paused in a gun battle to make sure she ran to safety.

So what now? Go to the police? Homeland security? The press?

All of these places?

Maybe. But first things first. She needed to return home. Because there was only one thing of which she was certain. This all had been triggered by Nathan's discovery. Simkin had destroyed the data on

Nathan's computers rather than let someone else have it. And then he had destroyed the creator of this data as well, just as completely.

Prior to this they had sucked out every file Nathan had stored in his cloud account, and then annihilated this account as well.

They had been very thorough. But what they didn't know was that Nathan would never store something this important in the cloud. It was one of his quirks. He was a bit paranoid. He was thought of as the up-and-coming whiz kid. A brash boy genius. And while, at twenty-nine, he was hardly a boy, he was also far more accomplished than this age would suggest, and there were many who resented his success. And most of the scientists in his line of work were brilliant hackers. So he refused to take any chances with the cloud. He did back up his most important files every night—just not to cyberspace like most people.

Jenna had thought this precaution was just one of his quirks, but perhaps this behavior was more prudent than she had realized.

Any work Nathan thought was original, and especially work he thought was groundbreaking, was stored locally and password protected. He routinely saved a copy to the hard drive of his desktop, and a backup to one other location, to a flash drive hidden inside the house. An expensive model, capable of wireless downloads, so Nathan wouldn't have to shove it into a computer port. The flash drive served as a sort of private cloud storage outside of the cloud. Convenient, but not requiring him to dip even a toe into cyberspace.

He had programmed the drive so that if three incorrect passwords were entered in a row, all data would be wiped clean. Even Jenna didn't know the password. Unfortunately, she suspected that someone with financial resources and determination could eventually find a way to circumvent Nathan's safeguards.

She wasn't about to take this chance. Not given what had happened. So her first order of business was to retrieve the drive. She could turn it over later to experts, who could also find a way to get at the data, and she would discover what had been so important—what had ended Nathan's life and destroyed her own. She wouldn't rest until she knew.

California was still bathed in blackness when she arrived at her house—*their* house—the location of a joyous reunion just hours before, but now a painful reminder of all she had lost.

She entered the master bedroom, fighting back tears once again. Resting on Nathan's dresser was a toy commonly called Newton's cradle. Named after the peerless physicist, this device consisted of five gleaming silver balls, hanging down in a line between two suspending bars. The device was a favorite of physicists, demonstrating conservation of momentum and energy. When the ball at one end was lifted and released, it would strike the stationary spheres with a distinctive clicking sound, transmitting a force through them that would push the last one upward, which would then pendulum down again, repeating this action in the opposite direction. This would continue through multiple cycles until heat and friction had bled the system of energy.

But Nathan had modified this apparatus, incorporating a flash drive into its base. Jenna carefully removed the tiny stick, roughly the size of her thumb, not surprisingly, since these storage units were also commonly referred to as *thumb drives*. These devices could have been downsized further, but the tinier an object the easier it was to lose, so this size had become fairly standard.

Jenna rushed out of the bedroom, lost in thought, trying to determine her next move. But after taking two steps into her living room she stopped abruptly, gasping in horror.

An intruder was standing inside the front door, patiently waiting for her to return from the bedroom. Not a cop. Like the others that night, he was lean and gave off an aura of deadly professionalism.

Either their original abductors had left one man behind to watch the house, and he had seen her arrive, or one of the two sides in this clash had had the presence of mind to rush someone here after learning she had escaped, just in case she returned.

Unlike the initial group of three intruders, this man wasted no time in raising a gun and pointing it at her with a menacing intensity. His eyes widened in excitement when he spied the flash drive in her hand.

"Bingo!" he said happily. "Who says long shots don't pay off?"

"*What do you want with me?*" screamed Jenna at the top of her lungs, as the calm rationality to which she had been trying to cling shattered. *"Leave me alone!"*

"All I want is that thumb drive. Give it to me. Once I verify I can open it, you're free to go. Is it password protected?"

Jenna nodded yes, taking deep breaths as she fought off alternating emotions of fury and loss that threatened to cause a total meltdown.

"Do you know the password?"

Jenna blinked rapidly, as if she didn't comprehend the question.

"*Do you know the password?*" the intruder barked impatiently.

"Of course," she lied as her mind began functioning properly once again, not a moment too soon.

He held out his hand. "Give me the stick. And the password. And I promise you'll be left alone. Forever."

She didn't reply for several seconds as she searched frantically for a way out.

"This is the best deal you're going to get, believe me."

In a burst of inspiration, Jenna seized on a plan. It was desperate, for sure, but no more so than *she* was, and it was likely the only chance she had.

"Why on earth would I ever trust you?" she asked, buying a few seconds of distraction while she moved two steps closer to a nearby end table.

Before the intruder could answer she arrived at the table and quickly snatched up the large goblet of wine she had set there hours earlier, just before Nathan had playfully triggered a drum roll, her last positive memory before she was dragged through all nine circles of hell.

"Back off!" she screamed, extending the flash drive over the pool of red liquid so it was all but touching it. "I drop this in and the data is gone forever. It's the last copy, and the only man who knows what's on here is dead."

The intruder couldn't keep the panic from his face as his prize hung precariously above the elegant crystal glass.

Jenna could read the recognition of the situation in his eyes. He had been badly outmaneuvered. He had decided to try to get the password from her, to simplify his life, rather than shoot her and take the drive. But now he was screwed. She had created her very own dead-man's switch. If he shot her now the memory stick would fall into the wine and be destroyed.

The truth was she wasn't certain about this. For all she knew the drive was waterproof. But even if this was the case, would it be able to survive *alcohol* as well? She didn't know, and fortunately, the intruder seemed to have accepted her semi-bluff without question.

"Toss your gun and car keys over to me," she demanded, pressing her advantage. "Now! Or I'll drop it in," she finished, nodding toward the tiny stick in her right hand. Her left hand, which held the large crystal wineglass, had a slight tremor as it was, and the man had to fear the wine might splash upwards and ruin the drive by accident.

"I'll do it," she warned again.

"Look, give me the drive," said the intruder as calmly as he could. "If you destroy it," he added, his upper lip curling into a snarl, "I will kill you. Guaranteed."

He raised the gun higher and extended it toward her head to emphasize the point.

"But if you give it to me," he continued as pleasantly as he could, "I'll let you go. I won't hurt you. I promise."

"A promise from you means *nothing* to me!" spat Jenna through clenched teeth. "After what I've seen tonight, I think you'll kill me the second you get this. So I have absolutely nothing to lose." She raised her eyebrows. "Can you say the same?"

The man looked uncertain.

Jenna's expression hardened even further. "You have thirty seconds to toss your keys and gun over here. If you don't, I'll destroy your prize, and you can explain what happened to your boss."

She could tell from his sick expression that she had him. And he never took his eyes off her hands, which were still shaking enough to make him fear that an accident might occur at any time.

"You're down to twenty seconds," said Jenna. "I *will* do it, even knowing you'll kill me. You think that *scares* me? The love of my life was just murdered in front of my eyes. I've lost *everything* tonight! At this point, I don't have much reason to live. I almost hope you don't do what I ask, so I can destroy this drive and have you put me out of my misery."

Jenna said these words so convincingly that even she wasn't sure how much of this was a bluff and how much was reality.

She paused for a few more seconds. "Ten," she said simply. "Nine. Eight. Seven—"

"Wait!" said the man facing her, panic sweeping over his features. "Say I let you go. How do I know you won't destroy the drive the second you're gone?"

"You don't," said Jenna. "You'll have to take my word for it."

"Do I *have* your word?"

Jenna nodded. "You do. I'm as interested in knowing what's on it as you are. So you lose this round. You give up your gun and keys and let me leave. But the information you're after lives. And given how resourceful you and your gang of thugs seem to be, I'm sure you can still catch me and retrieve it, right?"

"You make an interesting proposition. But if I'm going to let you leave here, I need your word on one more thing. I need you to keep whatever you find on that drive privileged information. You can't let it become widely known."

"Why not?"

"Think whatever you'd like about me, but trust me on this. It would be bad for *everyone*. My guess is that only a few people in the world are capable of understanding what's on there anyway. But treat the information with total respect, even if you have no idea what it means. Like it was a simple recipe for a hydrogen bomb."

Jenna's eyes widened. "Is it a catastrophic explosive?"

He shook his head. "No. Nothing like that. But trust me, it would be *bad* if it got out. Do you believe me?"

She stared deeply into his eyes, and for some reason she did. Perhaps the picture was getting a tiny bit clearer. Both groups wanted

Nathan's discovery for themselves, but would do anything to make sure no one *else* got it.

"Tell me what's on the drive," she said.

He shook his head. "I can't. I'm not supposed to give you any information. Not even what I've already told you. I only did because you've put me in an impossible bind here, and I'm forced to make decisions on the fly. So promise me you won't destroy the drive, and you'll keep its contents privileged, and I'll let you go. Push me any further and I'll destroy it myself."

"Okay. I believe you. Whatever is on here is dangerous, and I'll take precautions. I'll treat it like the recipe for the bomb. What you said."

And she would, she realized. At least until she achieved a full understanding of the situation. Then she would make her own assessment of whether this discovery warranted absolute darkness or the brightest of sunshine.

Jenna was fifteen feet away from him. Without saying a word or coming any closer, he tossed his gun and keys gently toward her. They landed on her soft beige carpet a few steps away.

"Now your phone," she said, realizing she couldn't leave him the ability to make calls.

Anger spread over his face, but he tossed his phone at her feet as well.

"Now get in the coat closet and shut the door while I gather all this up," she demanded, not about to lower her guard while in his view and take the chance he might rush her.

He shook his head in disbelief and shot her a look that could have melted lead. He obviously wasn't used to being ordered around in this way by someone who should be helpless against him. It was a ridiculous situation, but she didn't have time to contemplate the utterly surreal nature of holding off a ruthless assassin, and turning him into her slave, armed only with a glass of wine.

"Closet!" she repeated, and after glaring at her for another moment he finally did as she asked.

Jenna gathered up the gun, phone, and keys and shoved them into her pockets.

"There's a door to the garage through the kitchen," she shouted so he could hear her inside the closet. "Meet me in the garage in one minute. If you don't show in two, I'm going to destroy the data and drive out of here."

She found her purse and grabbed her wallet. She rushed to the garage and popped open the empty trunk of their white four-door sedan, a 2018 Hyundai Sonata that Nathan had driven just hours earlier to return her from the airport. It was relatively inexpensive but was heavy and sturdily built, which would serve her needs well.

By the time her uninvited guest walked into the garage, she was as far away from the trunk as possible, kneeling down, with the glass of wine on the floor before her, still holding the thumb drive less than an inch above the red liquid.

"Get in the trunk and close it from the inside," she ordered.

"No fucking way! You've lost your fucking mind!"

"I don't think so. Because now I have your gun. So do what I say, or I'll not only destroy the drive, but put enough holes in you to turn you into a *sieve*. I've been shooting since I was eight," she lied. "My father was a cop," she added, also a fabrication.

"You'd better hope I'm not the one who finds you," he spat, and then lowered himself into the Sonata's trunk. Once inside, one of his arms reached up and found a way to lower the lid. Finally, there was a telltale click, indicating it was fully locked.

Jenna rushed outside to the car she had stolen on Palomar Mountain. The Sonata was serving as a prison, and even if it weren't, she felt safer taking a car that, at least for the moment, no one knew was connected to her.

She took the driver's seat, shoved the flash drive into her pocket, and drank down the full glass of wine in one prolonged gulp, wishing for just a moment that she had the entire bottle with which to calm her raw, exposed nerves, and drown her sorrows.

6

Lee Cargill was bleary-eyed and pissed off. More than pissed off. Seething. *Enraged.*

He paced in a cavernous room filled with heavy equipment, part of a spacious facility that the Army Corps of Engineers had dug out under the peak of Palomar Mountain during the construction of the Hale Telescope in 1935, complete with meeting rooms and lodging. It had been constructed in parallel with the Hale Observatory so the construction work could go largely unnoticed.

God-dammit! fumed Cargill.

He loved the Palomar facility. It was ideally located near the top of a scenic mountain. Not only was the facility itself spacious and well laid out, but at night he and his people often ventured outside to enjoy the fresh air and a star field that blazed with an amazing light, which was the very reason it had been chosen to be the home of what had once been the most impressive telescope ever built.

But now everything had been blown to hell. "Fuck you, Edgar Knight!" he shouted to an empty room.

Just as Cargill's shout finished reverberating around the walls, his second-in-command, Joe Allen, entered the room with an expression as grim as his own. "The third team we sent in has reported back," he said.

"*And?*" barked Cargill impatiently.

"Almost everyone is dead. On both sides. Every member of our initial extraction team was killed. And every member of the teams we sent in response to their alarm. Only the helo pilot survived, and his bird was badly damaged. Luckily, he managed to get it out of there. Can you fucking imagine? If that thing had gone down, fire or no fire, we'd have a headache the size of Texas."

"We already have *that*," snapped Cargill. "But yes, it would have been even bigger." He paused. "You're certain no one else survived?"

"We think Jenna Morrison may have, but we aren't positive. Some of the bodies were pretty unrecognizable."

"*Really?*" shouted Cargill. "Wasn't she the only female? That should be a big fucking clue, right?"

Joe Allen swallowed hard. "No female bodies found yet," he said. "She could be alive, or she could be dead but not yet found. Maybe she was wounded and managed to leave the scene. We're still combing the woods."

"Recognize anyone on their side?"

"Not yet."

"How do we know *everyone* from their side was killed?"

"We got counts of what the teams were up against, and the dead body count matches what we expected."

"But in the heat of battle, who knows if one or more of the enemy was miscounted. So we can't be sure none of them escaped. And we can't be sure they don't have Jenna Morrison."

"True, but that won't help them. Nathan Wexler and all traces of his work are gone. You could interrogate Einstein's wife all you wanted, but you wouldn't get any new insights into general relativity."

"Thanks for that revelation, Joe. Because I didn't know that. I'm that fucking stupid." He shook his head, incensed. "This has to be the work of Edgar Knight. Has to be. To think I called that prick my friend. I can't fucking wait until my next report to the president. We lost good men. Irreplaceable men. Knight should never have known about this base. He split off from us before we moved here, and I know he wasn't aware this facility even existed, which is one of the reasons I chose it."

"We have a mole. It's the only explanation."

"No kidding," said Cargill. "One who must have been with us from the beginning. Biding his time. Knight knew we were here but figured a direct attack on this base would almost surely fail. He must have decided to keep his powder dry, to piggyback off of our superior intelligence capabilities and wait for us to discover something that would be a game-changer."

Allen nodded. "Which we just did."

"We were monitoring Wexler," said Cargill in disgust, "and Knight was monitoring *us*."

He turned away, his eyes blazing. "So now I can't trust anyone, can I? How do I know *you* aren't working for Edgar Knight for Christ's sake?"

"Come on, Lee. We've known each other for too long. You know me. You know this isn't true."

Cargill's features softened. "I know that, Joe. I do. But I'm frazzled. And I *thought* I knew everyone on this team. But apparently I don't."

"So what now?"

"We have to evacuate and find a new base. This base should be impregnable, and isn't easy to sneak up on, so I doubt we're in any immediate danger. But I'll never underestimate Edgar Knight again." Cargill scowled. "But, obviously, our first priority has to be rooting out the man, or men, who have infiltrated our organization. Until we do that, changing headquarters, or anything else we do for that matter, won't mean shit."

7

Jenna drove to La Jolla Country Day high school and parked in the center of its minotaur maze of buildings and connecting lots. Only a few cars were present anywhere, left there overnight for unknown reasons. It was now just after four in the morning.

She turned off the lights, shut her eyes, and struggled to come up with a plan of action. But her mind refused.

She had been exhausted after arriving home near midnight—two a.m. Chicago time—but it had now been almost twenty-four hours since she had last slept. Her body had produced rivers of adrenaline for the past several hours, but the effect was wearing off and she was crashing hard.

She almost melted into the seat of the car, waging a futile struggle to stay awake but drifting quickly into a fitful sleep. Her eyes shot open less than an hour later and she shook her head vigorously to bring herself fully back to consciousness.

But even this nap, short as it was, was a godsend, and she now found she was able to remain awake and concentrate once again. She didn't need a full-length mirror to know she looked as though she had been through a war, which she *had* been, and was covered in cuts, bruises, and blood, most of it not her own.

So now what?

Think! she demanded of herself.

What should she do?

She decided to first take inventory. The only useful items in her wallet were two twenties, an ATM card, and a credit card, but she decided that she couldn't risk using the credit card until she knew what she was up against.

Her own cell phone had been confiscated but she now had two others, one belonging to a chubby driver on Palomar Mountain and one to a man she had sealed in the trunk of her car.

And she had two guns. A compact submachine gun and a semiautomatic pistol.

First order of business, she decided, was to get more money. She drove to a nearby ATM and withdrew five hundred from savings, the maximum her bank would allow with one transaction. She then gassed up the car at a station that was open all night before returning to the high school parking lot to continue planning.

It was now nearly five thirty. The sun would be coming up in less than an hour. How soon before the owner of the car she was in managed to call in a report?

Should she beat him to the punch and go to the police herself? The men who had taken her and Nathan didn't seem too troubled by the prospect of the local police being alerted that they were being abducted. The spokesman of the kidnapping squad had specifically said so, and she had believed him.

So did these men have the cops in their pockets?

She couldn't rule it out. Whoever had taken them, and whoever had then tried to intervene with an ambush, were almost certainly in positions of power—or at least whoever was backing them was. Possibly even *legitimate* power. The kind of people who could have great influence with the police.

So going to the cops might be playing right into their hands. She imagined sitting in a station while a friendly detective left for a moment to get coffee, only to secretly alert her abductors that the woman they had been looking for had arrived, as they had anticipated.

She shuddered at the thought.

And even if the cops were clean, or couldn't be influenced by either group, would she pull up to the station in a *stolen car*?

And if she did, what would she report?

If she told them the truth they would think she was a lunatic. They would never believe her story.

And for good reason. She didn't believe her story either. And she had *lived* it.

She could produce the weapons and cell phones she had taken, but that might just suggest she was deranged and dangerous. This *could* work, but could just as easily backfire. Badly.

So what *would* happen if she told the truth, described her and Nathan's abduction and subsequent events? If they didn't take her a thousand percent seriously they might not get around to checking her house for some time. When they did, they'd either find a man in the trunk of her car, who surely would claim she was a madwoman who had assaulted him, or, if he had escaped, a home with no signs of forced entry, and aside from a dismantled computer, all jewelry and other valuables still there. No sign of any struggle. And no sign of Nathan.

So what then? They would tell her that she was free to file a missing persons report. That after forty-eight hours or so, if he didn't turn up, they would begin to look into it.

There were other variations of this she could conceive. The carnage on Palomar could come to light, but even so Nathan wouldn't be recognizable, and his phone and wallet weren't on his corpse to identify him. And if the Hostess truck was found, federal agencies would push the local cops aside, anyway, shutting them out of the case.

If Palomar Mountain did come into play, how long before the driver she had accosted described the crazed commando woman who had threatened him with a submachine gun? Hell, if this were to happen she could well become the chief *suspect* in Nathan's murder—when the authorities finally got around to figuring out that he was dead.

While all this was going on, the people working with trunk-man would be after her. And her identity and whereabouts would be logged into the police system, which she wouldn't trust to protect her.

So best case nothing would happen for days.

Worst case, this would blow up in her face.

So the cops were definitely out. And the more she thought about it, the more she realized they would be out even if none of her reasoning were true, and they genuinely believed her and tried to help from the start.

Because they'd be hopelessly out of their league. Going to them would be like counting on a golden retriever puppy to protect her from a pack of wolves.

So where could she turn?

After several more minutes of thought, she came up with a way forward. Not great, but under the circumstances anything that wasn't absolutely disastrous was inspired.

She would hire a private detective. The most bad-ass detective she could find. Those looking for her might easily manage to put out notices to police forces, having them be on the lookout for her and shaping reality in any way they saw fit.

But a private detective would be well out of this loop. Far safer. Far more anonymous.

But she couldn't stay in La Jolla. That would be just asking for trouble.

In a flash of insight it became clear where she needed to go, and what she needed to do.

If she couldn't immediately unlock the thumb drive, she could at least learn the gist of Nathan's discovery. He had only told one person: Dan Walsh. In the e-mail that had almost certainly set this firestorm in motion.

But she would need to meet with Dan in person. She had to assume his phone and computer were bugged. She needed to know what he knew, and alert him to the probable danger he was in.

She decided she would recruit a private investigator first. One located in LA, and thus much closer to the UCLA campus and Nathan's physicist friend.

It took thirty minutes of frantic searching through the Web, through dozens and dozens of agencies, but she finally found a man who seemed perfect for her needs, a man named Aaron Blake, and scoured his website for an additional five minutes.

He was a highly decorated ex-Army Ranger, seventy-fifth regiment, who had served within various counter-terrorism groups in Yemen, Somali, and Iraq. Jenna Googled the 75th Ranger Regiment and learned this was an elite special operations force headquartered at Fort Benning, Georgia, and tasked with a variety of special operations missions.

Impressive, to say the least.

Only three months earlier, Blake had left the service and hung up his shingle in LA as a private investigator. He listed his qualifications, which were impressive, but most importantly to Jenna, he could handle himself in a gunfight and under extreme pressure, something that seemed likely given the events of the past six hours.

He couldn't be more ideal for what she was looking for. Maybe her luck was beginning to change.

Finally with a plan in mind, Jenna Morrison took a deep breath, started her stolen car, and began the drive that would lead her to a face-to-face meeting with an ex-Army Ranger.

Now all she had to do was get him to believe her story.

8

Aaron Blake drummed the fingers of his left hand on his desk while he continued to read Internet primers on his monitor, instructing him on how to publicize his business, how to use social media effectively, and ten tips for enhanced search engine optimization, which would help his name rise to the top when anyone searched for a private investigator in LA.

He had a keen mind for detective work, which he had proven repeatedly in his past life in the military. He had always done very well in school, and was especially proud of his reasoning skills. He had a knack for asking the right question. For observation. For reconstructing complex histories from meager clues. His brothers-in-arms could not have been more complimentary of his skills in this regard.

But skills as a detective weren't enough to launch a successful PI practice. Not if no one knew you existed. And until you built a reputation, no one would. And this required business and publicity skills, not detective skills.

If you were the best chess player in the world, you would eventually be recognized as such. You'd have to start at satellite tournaments, true, but if you kept beating others you'd soon take your place at the top of the pecking order.

But you could be the best writer, or the best accountant, or the best PI, and flounder forever if you didn't know how to promote yourself. If only the PI world held tournaments, where practitioners of the art could compete against one another for glory and bragging rights.

Since this wasn't possible, Blake knew it might take a long time for him to build a thriving practice. So he had begun by setting up office in his apartment, a tiny efficiency, not much bigger than an actual office would be. And while nothing reeked of small-time, of failure, more than being forced to work and sleep out of the same tiny residence, he had to start somewhere. And at least the apartment complex was in a respectable neighborhood and presented well, with rows of pricey but magnificent King Palms arrayed around the grounds, several pools, and a large fountain near the entry gate.

Plus, he was lucky that his resumé spoke for itself, so the trappings of success weren't as important as they would be in other businesses. He was counting on his background, and then his results, to keep him in demand until he could move to a real office.

So far almost all of his clients had been men and women wanting to catch their spouses in the act of cheating—or learn if any money was parked in offshore accounts during divorce proceedings.

Cheating spouse cases were not only boring, routine, and voyeuristic, they were painfully cliché. A few times he had taken on more interesting cases, but this was all too rare.

Once a wealthy suburbanite had been robbed of an heirloom, one of limited economic value but great personal value. When it became clear the police were going to do nothing about it, he had paid big money for Blake to investigate and catch the thief, which Blake did, in a display of detective work that would have impressed Sherlock Holmes.

Blake could only hope that as his reputation grew the number of interesting cases that came his way would rise dramatically. And he had finally managed to schedule some appointments with law firms in the area, which often needed investigatory work done in conjunction with certain cases. He had high hopes that offering his services free of charge, on a trial bases, until the lawyers were satisfied that he was as good as he said he was, would eventually pay big dividends.

But he desperately needed for this to happen quickly. Not because he cared about the money, but because there was nothing he hated more than inactivity, than boredom. He had become an adrenaline junkie in the military. He wasn't a sadist. And he despised the necessity to kill. But if killing one man could save hundreds, Blake was able to make peace with this equation.

And while he hated killing, hunting for a man, battling a man, matching wits and skills with another man when their lives were both on the line, provided the ultimate competition. And thus the ultimate rush.

Every contest was sudden death, requiring superhuman focus and superhuman effort. It was reminiscent of the Old West, where no gunslinger could ever be taken lightly, regardless of appearance, since every gunslinger still alive had never once been bested, by definition.

Ernest Hemingway had said, "There is no hunting like the hunting of man, and those who have hunted armed men long enough and liked it, never care for anything else thereafter."

Blake realized he was beginning to live this famous quote and took it as a personal warning. He began to fear the rush was growing too great, becoming too addictive. He feared he was approaching the point of no return. That he would never be able to lead a normal life, and that he would take on more and more risk to get his fix, inevitably resulting in an early death.

But while the fear of spinning out of control was one catalyst in his decision to leave the military, frustration at politicians, and the lack of understanding demonstrated by many in the West, was the final straw. At least indirectly.

The *direct* cause of his decision had been the deaths of his two closest friends. Deaths he had witnessed. Deaths that had been totally unnecessary.

His team had been ordered on a raid by the powers that be in Washington DC, one that had been absolutely pointless, and they had been shackled with rules of engagement so crippling that failure and loss of life were all but assured. The friends he had lost were his brothers-in-arms. He was willing to die for them, and they for him. They had been as close to him as only those who had bonded in war could possibly be.

It wasn't just their loss, which had been crushing, that had finally driven him over the edge.

It was the futility of it all.

How many thousands of men had America lost fighting the advance of barbaric hordes of Islamic extremists, only to have politicians who had no understanding of the military and little of world politics give back all gains? How many times had politicians, elected solely on charisma and domestic policy expertise, made tragic blunders, totally *avoidable* tragic blunders, leaving the soldiers in the field to twist in the winds of political expediency?

Spilling blood to protect the homeland was one thing. But spilling blood, only to then vacate hard-won gains on a whim and leave a vacuum that ended up making the problem far worse, was another.

It made Blake physically ill.

Hiding one's head in the sand and ignoring reality wasn't going to make the problem go away. And it was maddening how often the civilized world allowed itself to be duped by barbarians with no ethics or morals. By savages who would do *anything* for their cause. Literally, *anything*. They placed no value on human life, and no act, no matter how savage or despicable, was off limits, including genocide.

Many in the West, compassionate but misguided, were determined to bend over backwards to understand the extremists, to empathize with them.

But there was no understanding an ideology this rabid, this diseased. Who could understand a woman who would strap a bomb on a child and send him or her into a crowded square?

These extremists had been brainwashed by a sick, close-minded, hateful ideology. Some in the West believed that poverty was responsible, that America was somehow at fault for hoarding so much of the world's resources. But many of the extremists were well-off, as Bin Laden had been. And hundreds of millions of people around the world lived in squalor, but had never resorted to sawing off heads and burning men alive.

But while the West often failed to understand the motivations of these extremists, the *extremists* understood the motivations of the West only too well. They found the West soft. Gullible. Stupid. Its media easily manipulated.

So their snipers would hide behind women and children, using them as human shields, picking off soldiers. And this wasn't a one-off phenomenon, but a deliberate strategy. Richard Kemp, commander of British forces in Afghanistan, had written in a formal report that, "The Taliban's use of women to shield gunmen as they engage NATO forces is now so normal it is deemed barely worthy of comment."

If an American soldier was too decent to shoot through these helpless human shields he would die. If he did defend himself and a civilian was killed, this would appear on news programs around the world as yet another example of the cruelty and overzealous nature of the American military, of the barbarity of the American soldier, emphasizing the plight of the poor freedom fighters whose countries they were invading.

This wasn't to say that some American soldiers weren't sadists. Some were. it was inevitable. And this wasn't to say that mistakes were never made, that atrocities never occurred, coming from the American side. Innocent civilians were killed, each and every occurrence a horror.

But to suggest this was systemic, to suggest the Western forces were no better, and possibly worse, than the ruthless extremists, or that the West had brought this on themselves, made Blake's blood boil. The Americans often went to great lengths, and even risked their own lives, to limit civilian casualties. While the very *mission* of the extremists was to wipe out as many Western women and children as possible, billions if they could.

Still, there were those who continued to believe that one man's terrorist was another man's freedom fighter, even with respect to groups as despicable as the Taliban. The same Taliban who willfully destroyed sixth-century statues of Buddha carved into the side of a cliff. The same Taliban the United Nations reported routinely committed systematic massacres against civilians.

And those who fought with every ounce of strength for women's rights in America would somehow overlook the atrocities the Taliban committed against their own women. Treating them as possessions, prohibiting them from showing their faces, from walking in public without a male relative to escort them. And executing female *children* for the unforgivable crime of attending school.

Yes, nothing was totally black-and-white. Yes, there were good and bad actors in every large group of people. But those who suggested an equivalency between the actions of the West and the extremists made Blake so furious he couldn't see straight.

So he had left it all behind. For his sanity. For his life. To come down off his adrenaline addiction. To find a way to feel alive without need of life-and-death stakes. To never again have to suffer the death of brothers.

And not to have to take orders from politicians who couldn't see Islamic extremism for the despicable ideology it was, an ideology immune to reason, its adherents showing a level of barbarity and intolerance *incomprehensible* in the West.

So Blake had decided it was time for a course correction. And even though spying on unfaithful spouses wasn't exactly what he had in mind, it was probably good for him, just as cold turkey, painful though it was, was necessary for a junkie to cleanse his system.

Aaron Blake breathed a deep sigh and brushed these thoughts to the side, returning to the task of learning how to run a business. But just as he did so, Myla, his personal digital assistant, alerted him in a pleasant, feminine voice that a woman was approaching his door.

He checked the time. It was a little before eight in the morning.

Interesting.

As he watched the woman approach on his monitor he realized this wouldn't be just another cheating spouse assignment. More like a *beating* spouse assignment. Judging from this young woman's appearance, her husband had done quite a number on her.

Sad, and tragic, but he suspected there was little he could do in such a situation. This was a case probably best left to cops, although he cautioned himself from jumping to conclusions.

Perhaps there was more to this than met the eye.

He watched as the woman on the monitor took a deep breath and pressed the doorbell.

9

"Thank God you're here," said the visitor when Blake answered the door. "I'm sorry to bother you before regular hours."

"Don't be," he replied with a warm smile as he gestured her inside. "I'm an early riser. And in this line of work regular hours don't exist. Besides," he said, making a show of looking her up and down, "you don't look to be in any condition to be patient."

He motioned her to take a chair before his all-glass desk, chosen because glass tended to make the room look bigger, which he sorely needed. He had done everything possible to make his living room office-like, rather than apartment-like, and there were no couches or other furniture, and no television. The main room led to a kitchen and bedroom, and this was the extent of it.

"I'm Jenna," said the woman, extending her hand. "Jenna Morrison."

"Nice to meet you," he said, shaking her hand. "Aaron Blake."

She had short brown hair and matching eyes, and while she was more plain than pretty, she was fit and had a perfect complexion. He judged her to be in her twenties, and despite wearing jeans and a T-shirt and looking far worse for wear, there was something attractive about her. He judged her to be about five foot five, only two inches shorter than his own underwhelming height.

"What can I do for you, Ms. Morrison?" he asked.

"Jenna."

"Jenna," he amended.

She took a deep breath, and he could tell she was searching for a place to begin. "I'm in a hurry, but it's critical that you believe me and don't think I'm crazy. So I'm going to take this one step at a time."

He nodded. "Go right ahead."

"I am engaged to, and living with, one of the most brilliant minds of our time. A physicist at UCSD named Nathan Wexler, who has already contributed some major work to the field."

She paused. "Before I go on any further, I want you to verify what I've just said. Look up Nathan. Go on the UCSD website. Go on his Facebook page, where you can see us together, see that we're engaged and living together."

Blake smiled warmly. "No need. I'm prepared to take your word for it."

She shook her head. "No. I need you to do this. My story is going to sound crazy, and I want to establish my credentials, so to speak, before I go any further."

Blake stared into her eyes, intrigued.

She waited in silence as he surfed the Web and confirmed her information.

"Okay," he said after several minutes had passed. "I accept that you're Jenna Morrison and the truth of your relationship with Nathan Wexler. Also, it's clear that Dr. Wexler is quite the genius. So why don't you tell me what this is all about."

His visitor began, explaining she had been in Chicago for a week with her sister, during which time her fiancé had made a major breakthrough, the nature of which she had yet to learn. And then she proceeded to tell her tale, which he interrupted for questions or clarifications, but infrequently.

Blake decided Jenna Morrison had been correct: her tale *did* sound ridiculous. And yet she spoke with detail and assurance. And her intelligence and reasoning power were impossible to miss.

But criminal psychopaths could be brilliant and utterly convincing. Could weave rich tapestries of lies.

On the other hand, this girl's story was *too* rich of a tapestry. If she had murdered Nathan Wexler, why complicate things so much, make up wrinkles that were so simple to disprove?

"When you first began," said Blake when she had finished, "you told me you *are* living with Nathan Wexler. Present tense. If he's dead, as you say, why weren't you using past tense?"

"I didn't want you to have any preconceptions. If you knew he was dead from the start, you'd absorb what I told you in a different light. I didn't want that."

Blake nodded. Very shrewd of her. "And you don't even have a guess as to what he might have discovered?"

"No. But as I said, there is one man who knows, at least the gist."

"Dr. Dan Walsh at UCLA?"

"Correct. And we need to find a way to warn him he's in danger. If he's even still alive."

Blake studied her face carefully.

"Look," she said, impatience showing for the first time. "Do you believe me? Will you help me?"

His every instinct told him this Jenna Morrison was something special. Some people melted under pressure and some reacted to its squeeze by turning into diamond, becoming battle hardened. He was all but certain this girl fell into the latter camp.

While she occasionally allowed the severe emotional pain she was feeling to show in her eyes, she didn't have the bearing of a beaten wife. She had a fire about her. An easy intelligence. A self-confidence and competence. For someone who had been through hell, this was quite impressive.

"Your story is definitely out there," he said. "But you already knew that. And you haven't given me any reason to doubt its veracity." He rubbed his chin in thought. "You said you confiscated the cell phones of two men. Can I see them?"

Jenna shook her head. "No. I tossed them in San Diego. I realized as I began the drive here that they could be used to track me. I promised the poor guy I stranded on Palomar that I would call one of his friends and tell them where to find his car, but I decided I couldn't. At least not yet."

"A wise decision," said Blake in genuine admiration. Her reasoning from start to finish had been impeccable. Each individual move she had made, by itself, was unremarkable, even obvious in hindsight, but it was his experience that very few civilians, when thrust into a nightmare the way she had been, would have had the presence of mind to unerringly navigate the precisely correct path.

"What about the weapons you say you, ah . . . acquired?" he asked. If she had gotten rid of these, also, this would cast considerable doubt as to the truth of her story. "Can I see them?"

"Absolutely," she replied immediately. "They're in the trunk of my car. Well, you know, the car I drove here."

"You really know how to use a trunk," said Blake wryly. "Most women just use them to carry groceries or luggage. It's the rare women who understands their utility for storing weapons and trapping dangerous intruders."

Jenna smiled, the first time since Nathan's death, and led Blake to her car, parked in a visitor's spot near his apartment. She popped open the trunk.

Blake recognized the SMG inside immediately—an MP5, favored by US Special Forces. Interesting. Not the sort of weapon a Jenna Morrison could get her hands on. It would be easier for her to murder Nathan Wexler than to acquire one of these. The automatic pistol was also one used by the US military.

He shut the trunk.

"Check the license plate," she said. "You can confirm it's not registered to Jenna Morrison or Nathan Wexler. And it's a plate that will definitely be reported stolen before too long."

Blake nodded. He had planned to do just that. He took a photo of the plate with his phone and led her back inside.

"As I said," he began when they resumed their positions, one in front and one behind his desk, "you've given me no reason to doubt you. And based on the weapons you showed me, every reason to believe you. Which means Dr. Walsh may be in trouble, as you've said."

He rubbed his chin once again for several long seconds. "Myla," he said finally to his personal digital assistant, "what are the formal hours of the UCLA physics department today?"

"Eight thirty to five," responded the feminine computer voice.

Blake glanced at his watch. It was eight forty. He turned to Jenna. "I'm going to call him. Make sure he's . . . well, that he's alive."

"Don't you have to assume he and his phone are bugged?" said Jenna.

"Yes. But don't worry, I won't give anything away. I'm going to put this on speaker, but don't say anything. If anyone is tapping in, I don't want them to recognize your voice."

He had Myla place the call, which was answered on the second ring. "Physics department," said a cheerful female voice.

"Dan Walsh please."

"Whom may I say is calling?"

"Tell him Randi Schatz. And that it's *extremely* important."

After less than a minute delay the line was picked up. "Dan Walsh," said a male voice.

Is that him? mouthed Blake.

Jenna nodded.

"Hi, Dr. Walsh. My name is Randi Schatz. I'm an inventor, and I've come up with some software that can simplify the analysis of advanced mathematics. I'd love to schedule an appointment and demonstrate it for you."

"Thanks, but I'm not interested," said Walsh abruptly, hanging up on him.

Blake couldn't blame him. No one appreciated being bothered by a solicitor who got him to the phone under false pretenses, especially this early in the morning. But Blake had no choice. If the call was being bugged, he needed it to appear as legitimate as possible. Had he hung up after verifying Walsh was alive and at work, this would have raised the eyebrows of anyone listening.

"Nicely done," said Jenna. "You're hired," she added, not that this had ever been in question, but it was her way of saying she was beginning to appreciate his skills. "It's a relief to know Dan is alive. But we have to warn him to make sure he stays that way."

"I agree. But I don't think he's in much danger at the moment. We've been assuming they know Nathan sent an e-mail to Walsh with a summary of what he'd discovered. But if this were enough to trigger the kind of all-out response against Walsh that was triggered against Nathan, it would have happened by now. The groups you described don't play around. Which isn't to say they aren't monitoring him. But we should have time."

"Okay," said Jenna. "I guess that makes sense."

She paused for a moment and then sighed. "I should tell you that I can't pay you much upfront. Five hundred is all I have on me. But I have more than enough in savings. And Nathan had a million dollar life insurance policy," she added, her eyes becoming moist again from this reminder of how he had been snuffed out in his prime, in a single, unthinkable instant. "His parents told him it was a good idea," she explained, her voice barely above a whisper. "At his age and health, it only cost him twenty-two bucks a month."

Blake waited silently as Jenna managed to blink back tears.

"So I don't even want to know your rate," she continued, her voice regaining strength. "Whatever it is, I'll pay it."

"Fair enough," said Blake, who knew that if her story panned out he would be willing to pay *her* to be in on it. A case that was likely to be as immensely important as it was challenging. One that would get his juices flowing. And one that didn't require him to film a businessman screwing his secretary.

"But just so we're on the same page, Jenna, what do you see as the goals of this investigation?"

She answered without hesitation. "Learn who these men are and why Nathan was so important to them. Learn what Nathan discovered. Make sure the men who did this are *punished*," she said bitterly, fire gleaming in her eyes. "Make sure Dan Walsh stays safe. And make sure I stay alive and out of jail for grand theft auto."

"Excellent," said Blake. "You have a very clear grasp of what we need to accomplish."

He stared deeply into her brown eyes and nodded reassuringly. "And you've come to the right man. I promise you I'll get to the bottom of this. If it's the last thing I ever do."

10

The loud, grating buzz of the alarm clock near Jenna Morrison's head finally managed to awaken her from what had been the most profoundly deep sleep of her life, after more than a minute of trying. She managed to slam her hand into the off button on the clock, still disoriented as pain signals arrived from multiple locations on her now-rested body. It took a few seconds for her to remember the previous night, but the numerous scrapes and bruises that now demanded to be recognized made this an easier task.

She had set the clock to go off at noon, giving her almost exactly three hours of concentrated sleep, which had left her more refreshed than she had expected.

She wallowed in the horror and sadness of Nathan's brutal death for several minutes before finally managing to push this from her mind. She would mourn properly when this was over, but right now she didn't have the luxury of severe depression and paralysis.

After telling her story to Aaron Blake earlier that morning she had once again hit a physical and mental brick wall. An hour nap in a high school parking lot had rejuvenated her enough to keep it together while bringing Blake up to speed, but exhaustion had caught up with her again, and with a vengeance. Blake had kindly offered to let her sleep in his bed while he worked.

So she had taken a quick shower and donned a blue robe he had loaned her, which served its purpose despite being too large. Blake had then insisted that he needed to do a load of laundry and would include her jeans and shirt, since these were in as desperate a need of cleaning as she had been.

Jenna smiled as she noticed her clothing beside the bed, clean and neatly folded. She changed back into her own clothes as she continued to shake off the fog of sleep.

She had a great feeling about Aaron Blake. He had told her she'd come to the right man, and her instincts told her this was definitely the case. He seemed bright and competent. Even better, he had been eminently reasonable, asking all the right questions and coming to all the right conclusions.

For the most part he looked like a regular guy. The men who had been at her house had presented a more formidable appearance, but Blake's combat credentials spoke for themselves.

He was on the short side, maybe five foot seven or five foot eight, maximum, and although he probably had a wiry strength, she had somehow expected bulging muscles, fighting to burst their way through his shirt, and an intense aura of a highly trained combat veteran who had seen more death than the Grim Reaper. Instead, he had a lithe frame and seemed friendly and relaxed, about as dangerous as a tax accountant.

Blake was at his desk, studying his computer monitor, when she exited the tiny bedroom.

"How's it going?" she said hopefully.

He shot her an odd look, which she had trouble interpreting, but it was almost as though he were studying her, evaluating her all over again. She had thought he had gotten that out of his system during their initial conversation, but perhaps not.

"I'm not so sure," he said tentatively. He waved his hand toward the chair in front of his desk. "Have a seat."

Jenna lowered herself into the chair and looked at Blake questioningly.

"I've done some routine checking," he began. "Just to put check marks in boxes. For instance, I called UCSD a few hours ago to confirm that Nathan didn't show up for work."

"*Of course* he didn't. He was *murdered*. What's going on? Were you just *pretending* to believe me?"

"No. I believe you. But investigations aren't all about brilliant Sherlock Holmes type deductions and flashy intuitive leaps. They are also about routine grunt work and the thorough checking of all facts. It's critical to never take *anything* at face value."

"Okay," she said, not entirely mollified. "It's your show. So you spent a minute and confirmed Nathan wasn't at work."

"That's right," replied Blake. He raised his eyebrows. "But I also learned that he had sent an e-mail at seven-thirty this morning to several members of his department, explaining that he wouldn't be in for a few weeks. Seems he had a family emergency to attend to."

Jenna shook her head. "Impossible! Obviously, the e-mail didn't come from him. You do realize it must have been sent by whoever kidnapped us last night. They must have figured, why attract more attention than necessary? Better if no one knows that Nathan is dead."

Blake nodded. "I expressed surprise and asked if they were sure the e-mail had come from Nathan, and wasn't just a practical joke. The woman I spoke with checked the message again, and said it was definitely from him. It was sent from his e-mail address and the greeting and sign-off were vintage Nathan."

"Which means nothing. These men have been monitoring his e-mails, so they would know his style well enough to mimic him."

"Yes. That is very true. I'm not saying I've drawn any definitive conclusions. I'm just reporting what I found."

"Go on," said Jenna.

"I checked the license plate number of the Hostess truck you gave me. Either you got it wrong or the plates were doctored. Either way, this plate number doesn't exist."

Blake paused to let this sink in. "My time in the military allowed me to establish a number of connections with high level people in the intelligence community. So I asked a friend of mine, Sylvia Tagert, to pull some strings and get me the footage from dozens of street cameras that cover your neighborhood. Footage from eleven to one last night."

Jenna knew what was coming. "And you didn't find a single Hostess truck anywhere, is that what you're going to tell me?"

Blake nodded.

"So we're dealing with some very formidable people. We already knew that. And they clean up after themselves. I'm guessing in our digital world it wouldn't take much effort to alter the data stream captured by street cameras, provided you were high level enough to have access." She paused. "But my story is looking more and more like a fabrication, isn't it? So now what? Change your mind? Think I'm crazy, after all?"

Blake shook his head. "No. I think what you think—that this is a demonstration of what we're up against. Obviously, I'd be lying if I said this doesn't increase the chances that you're deceiving me in some way. But what is intriguing about this, assuming your story is a hundred percent accurate, is what it says about the capabilities, and savvy, of the groups involved. If you hadn't managed to escape, no one would be looking for Nathan. At least not for a while. And even after you escaped, if you didn't happen to take an M5 SMG with you, no one would believe your story."

Jenna wasn't familiar with the initials SMG, but from context their meaning as an abbreviation for *submachine gun* was obvious. "Good point," she said. "The men after me didn't know I had it. And I left both guns in the car when I returned to my house for Nathan's flash drive. In hindsight, I should have brought the damn SMG."

"Ever fired a gun?"

Jenna shook her head.

"Then you were far better off holding your assailant at bay with a glass of wine."

"If they had known I had the M5, I'll bet you they would have found some magical way to discredit me. Maybe report that a woman matching my description had robbed a private home and stolen one, or something like that. Making sure to plant seeds of doubt in the minds of anyone I might approach."

"There's more," said Blake with a frown. "Right after you went to sleep I called the local police station. I told them I was a PI and had gotten wind of a BOLO on Jenna Morrison. I reported that I thought I might have seen you."

Jenna's eyes narrowed. "BOLO?"

"Sorry. *Be on the lookout.* You told me you came here and not to the cops because you worried the groups after you might have law enforcement in their pockets. I thought this idea was worth a quick experiment. My call was nothing more than a fishing expedition. I had no reason to expect there really was a BOLO out for you. But the detective I spoke with was *very* interested, and certainly didn't correct me."

"Shit!" said Jenna. "So now they're looking for me in LA?"

"No. I used my cell in a mode that makes it untraceable and told them I was calling from San Diego—which is where they expect you to be. But there's more. I told them I saw you in the stolen car, to which the detective replied, 'What stolen car?'"

"Just perfect," she said sarcastically, shaking her head in disgust. "So they're hunting for me, despite not having any official reason to be doing so."

"Exactly. Which suggests that you were right. Whoever is behind this can wield the police like so many pawns."

Jenna felt ill once again. It was all so . . . diabolical. She had been right. Had she gone to the cops she'd be in the hands of the men who wanted her already. And if Andy Cavnar hadn't handed her a submachine gun on Palomar Mountain, everyone would think she was a raving lunatic.

"I should also tell you that about an hour ago," continued Blake, "I went out and bought a fabric cover for your car. One that hides everything, its make, model, color, and license plates. I parked my car on the street and moved yours to my designated spot, and then covered it."

Jenna was impressed. This was a simple but effective strategy to ensure the police never identified the stolen car. "Thanks, Aaron," she said sincerely.

"You're welcome. That car is the only link to you. When the groups after you figure that out, they'll pull out all stops to find it."

Jenna tilted her head in thought. "Speaking of cars, shouldn't we consider going back to my house as soon as we can? If that guy is still in the trunk of my car, you could interrogate him. Find out everything he knows."

"That ship probably sailed before you even arrived here," said Blake. "The guy you bested is part of a team. When he didn't check in, or his team leader couldn't reach him, they'd have sent someone to your house to investigate. So he's long out of your trunk, and by now they have so many cameras pointing at your house a ghost couldn't get in undetected."

"I really blew it, didn't I?" she said miserably. "I should have made him tell me what this was all about when I had the chance."

"Not at all. You were freaked out, you had no weapons or combat training, and you were busy holding off a seasoned killer with a bluff. You didn't know what end was up, or when more of his team might be arriving. And you believed him when he refused to tell you anything more and insisted that you'd pushed him to his limits. You're being too hard on yourself. The fact that you figured out a way to turn the tables on him was brilliant."

"Thanks," whispered Jenna, but his words didn't help. Nathan was gone and she had blown her best chance to get to the truth. Maybe her *only* chance.

"So what now?" she asked, self-disgust still written all over her face.

"I'd like to take a drive to Palomar Mountain. Recon the site and gather evidence. And let's see just how good these guys really are at cleaning up after themselves."

She had a visceral aversion to the idea of retracing her path of the night before, of revisiting the site of Nathan's death, but she pushed through it. Of course that's what they needed to do. What detective would take a case without first visiting the crime scene?

"Okay," said Jenna softly. "Palomar Mountain it is."

"Before you commit, I should mention that it would be safer if I went alone and you stayed here. I just thought that since we want to get a handle on this quickly, going together will allow us to get to know each other better and discuss the case. But if you'd rather not take this risk, I understand. Are you *certain* you want to come?"

Jenna desperately wanted to take the out Blake was offering, but instead focused on turning her feelings of sorrow into a more useful emotion: Hate. A transformation that did the trick almost immediately. "I did mention that these assholes murdered the love of my life, right?" she replied in a guttural growl, wearing an expression intense enough to intimidate the hardest of men.

One corner of Blake's mouth turned up in just the hint of a smile. "I'll take that as a yes," he said simply.

He made a show of looking her up and down once again. "But before you go anywhere we need to change your appearance. Every cop in the area is on the lookout for you. So while I was out getting the car cover, I picked up a long blonde wig."

As he said this he lifted a glossy white paper bag and set it on his desk. The word "Macy's" was printed at the bottom of the bag and a giant red star above this.

"How long a wig are we talking about?" asked Jenna suspiciously.

"Halfway down your back."

Jenna made a face but remained silent.

"I'm sure it won't be your favorite," acknowledged Blake, "but this way we avoid dying your hair, and you won't have to duck down every time we pass a cop." He paused. "Would I be right in assuming you aren't big on makeup or jewelry? Or was your appearance when you arrived on my doorstep not typical for you?"

"No. You'd be correct," said Jenna. Her ears were pierced but she rarely wore earrings. "My engagement ring is the only jewelry I usually wear, and little or no makeup most of the time."

"So we'll do the opposite. Don't wear the ring. Leave it here or put it in your pocket. And I bought a few pairs of large hoop earrings," he said, nodding toward the Macy's bag. "I also got some vivid blue eyeshadow I want you to apply—liberally."

"Great," said Jenna, rolling her eyes. "This just keeps on getting better and better. Good thing we don't have time for me to get a boob job," she added wryly

Blake laughed. "There is one last thing I took care of while I was out running . . . errands," he said, serious once again. "I was able to find a business supply store that carries the same brand of flash drive Nathan used. I bought three of them. I saved large files on each, so they don't appear empty, and then password protected them the best I could."

"Outstanding," said Jenna admiringly, her mood improving immediately. This guy seemed to think of everything. Maybe if she would have slept longer he'd have the entire case wrapped up by now.

Blake rooted in a desk drawer for several seconds and produced a pen. He removed the cap to reveal a tiny, chiseled blue tip. "This is standard issue equipment in my line of work," he explained. "It contains ink that will only show up under UV light. Ink that's waterproof and very permanent. Use it to mark Nathan's thumb drive so we'll be able to distinguish it from the others," he finished, handing her the pen.

Jenna removed the memory stick from her pocket and carefully drew an X on one end. Blake produced a tiny UV flashlight from another drawer, a blue steel cylinder not much bigger than a roll of quarters, and turned it on the flash drive. Sure enough, the invisible X immediately made its presence known.

"So I hide the real thumb drive and put one of your decoys in my pocket instead, right?"

"Exactly. You'll most likely never need a decoy," said Blake, "but you never know."

"Why did you buy three of them?"

"One for you. One for me to keep. And one that I'll hide in this apartment."

Jenna thought about this a moment. "In case they somehow manage to connect you to me and search the place, right?"

"Yes. If a rabid dog is looking for a bone, it's probably safer to give him one. It's highly unlikely something like this will come to pass. But why not?"

"I couldn't agree more," said Jenna. She held Nathan's flash drive out in front of her face. "So where should I hide the real thing?"

"I don't know. But you need to decide this for yourself. It doesn't have to be this second, but when you figure it out, I'll make sure to leave you alone for however long it takes."

Jenna shook her head. "No. I want you in the loop. If something happens to me, I don't want to risk Nathan's discovery being lost to the world."

Blake nodded. "I think that's wise. But are you really willing to trust me with something this important?"

"The fact that you even asked me tells me that I can," she said.

She knew there was a small risk she had misread Aaron Blake, but she had such a positive feeling about him she decided it was very small. Given recent history, the chances were considerably greater that she would be killed, and she was not going to let Nathan's discovery die with her.

"So pretend this is *your* flash drive," continued Jenna. "Where would you hide it?"

"I wouldn't," he said simply. "Not yet. I'd recommend finding out what's on it first."

"And you know how to do that?"

"I don't. But I have a friend who does. More than a friend. A guy named Greg Soyer. We served together in the military three years ago. I'm not sure you can truly understand how much going through hell with another man cements a permanent bond. A friendship beyond friendship. He saved my ass during an anti-terror operation, and I saved his twice. It goes without saying that I still trust him with my life."

"Okay," said Jenna. "I'm sold. If you trust him, I trust him. And you're sure he can access Nathan's discovery?"

"Positive. He left the military years ago. But he's as skilled as anyone I've ever known with a computer. And speaks fluent Arabic."

"That must have come in handy."

"Very. But if you met him and didn't know, you'd never guess his military background in a million years. Seems like the sweetest, softest guy you'll ever meet. A blond-haired, blue-eyed Jewish kid who grew up on the not-so-mean streets of Billings, Montana. Double majored in computer science and Middle Eastern studies at Princeton."

"Great," said Jenna. "I've been playing defense. But maybe with your friend's help, I can begin going on offense. So how do we get him involved?"

"He lives in Orange County, so he's more or less on the way to Palomar Mountain."

"When do you want to head out?"

"Immediately. There is no time to waste. I don't think Dan Walsh is in immediate danger, like I said, but we need to know what he knows sooner rather than later. So after we visit Greg and recon last night's ambush site, connecting with Walsh should be our next priority. During your nap I learned he teaches a night class on Mondays, and I worked out a plan to squirrel him away from any surveillance. I won't need to be at UCLA until about seven this evening. If we leave right now, we should have a cushion of a few hours, but you never know what might come up."

Jenna rose. "I'm ready whenever you are."

She picked up the Macy's bag, making another face as though the bag had been used to clean up after a large pet dog. "I'll make myself, um . . . pretty," she said, rolling her eyes once again, "while we're on the road."

"Great," said Blake, making his way the short distance to his kitchen. He removed a box of granola bars from a pantry. "And once you've changed into your Halloween costume," he added with a broad grin, waving the box in his hand, "lunch is on me."

11

"We'll be at Greg's house in just a few minutes," announced Blake as they waited for a stoplight to turn green.

Jenna looked around. For several miles now they had passed an eclectic mixture of auto repair shops, special interest boutiques, small restaurants, and numerous furniture stores, and the dense throng of commercial outlets didn't seem to be thinning.

She raised her eyebrows. "Does your friend live in a futon store? Because this seems like the furniture district, not a residential one."

"You would think so, wouldn't you?" replied Blake. "See that strip mall ahead?" he said, pointing.

Jenna craned her neck and nodded.

"You can't see it from here, but there's a canyon running behind it, which boxes in this section of real estate. There are a few fairly isolated houses up that hill," he said, nodding up ahead and to their left, "that are situated above the canyon. They're old and on the small side. Fifteen to eighteen hundred square feet, ranch style."

"Meaning just a single story, right?"

"Right. This isn't a residential district, as you've pointed out, but these few homes were grandfathered in. Greg grew up in Montana. He loves Southern California but hates the congestion. In Montana there's nothing but wide open spaces, ranches, and homes with huge acreage around them. In Orange County, on the other hand, you can spend two million on a track home with a yard the size of a postage stamp, and so close to your neighbors on all sides that when one of them scratches their ass you think they're in the room with you."

Jenna made a face. "Wow, that's a thought picture I really didn't need to have."

"Sorry," he said in amusement. "So Greg found one of the few homes around here he could afford that was somewhat isolated, and had a view—at least of a canyon. The house is old and not open and expansive like modern homes, and doesn't let in as much light. But the interior is modern, and the kitchen is huge. He also built an office for himself off the back of house, larger than the master bedroom, and he put in a large sliding glass door so he gets lots of sunlight and can go outside and ponder nature when he wants a break."

While they conversed, Blake left the main road and headed up the hill he had pointed out, taking a narrow, winding stretch of pavement that led to his friend's home. Minutes later they arrived and exited the car.

As Blake had suggested, Soyer's home was small, dark, and antiquated. And while isolation could be an attractive feature, in Jenna's opinion the property was a little on the creepy side, as though it were the residence of a grizzled old hermit, or an Appalachian family with a rusted, broken-down pickup truck on the lawn. This, despite the fact that all she could see, other than the house, was Soyer's white Mercedes in the driveway and a sizable, well-maintained expanse of dark green grass.

They rang the bell and the door was thrown open immediately.

"Aaron!" said Greg Soyer cheerfully as he shook hands with his friend, a handshake that ended in a hearty bear hug.

"What's it been, three weeks?" said Blake as Soyer ushered his two guests inside.

Once again, Blake's description had been spot on. The inside was brighter than seemed possible, and the furniture and limestone flooring was light colored as well, to counteract the dark, depressing exterior.

"All I know," said Soyer, "is that it's been *too* long."

The computer expert turned toward Jenna. "Please tell me that you're dating this guy."

She shook her head, trying not to let the stress and tragedy she had been feeling show. "Sorry, but I'm afraid not."

Blake looked slightly embarrassed. "Greg here is dying for me to get into a relationship so we can double date," he explained. A smile spread slowly across his face. He stared at his friend and arched a eyebrow. "You didn't tell me that Alisa had moved in."

"Yeah? What gave you that idea?"

"Are you kidding?" said Blake, gesturing toward the narrow entrance into the family room. "You don't have to be a private detective to figure this one out. Either your couch just gave birth to a litter of throw pillows, or you have a woman living here."

"You caught me," admitted Soyer with a broad grin. He turned to Jenna. "But I've been rude enough. " He extended his hand. "Greg Soyer," he said, introducing himself.

Jenna shook the offered hand and opened her mouth to reply, but Blake beat her to the punch. "She's a client," he explained. "So for purposes of anonymity, let's just say she's Jane Smith."

Soyer rolled his eyes. "Nice to meet you, Jane," he said.

"You too," she replied pleasantly, unable to keep herself from touching one of the turquoise hoop earrings that seemed intent on pulling her earlobes to the ground, something the heavy blonde wig was also trying to do to her head. All in all, Blake's purchases couldn't have disguised her any better. Even she didn't recognize the overdone blonde she saw in the mirror, a person she hoped to never have to see again.

"Can I get you two anything to drink?" said their host.

"Thanks, Greg," said Blake. "I'd love a bottle of water. But I'm afraid we can only stay a few minutes. I assume Alisa is at work?"

Soyer nodded.

"Didn't mean to barge in on you like this, but I had reasons for not calling ahead."

"Always great to see you, no matter what the circumstances," said Soyer as he led them from the family room through a small open door into the kitchen. On the opposite side of the kitchen another small door was open, revealing a dining room and an elegant glass and marble table. Although modern kitchens weren't as closed off as this one, it was unusually large, and the appliances and cabinetry were modern and state-of-the-art. "But how did you know I'd be home?"

"Didn't," replied Blake. "But I knew you left the military so you could be a consultant. So you could sit around in your pajamas all day playing with your computer. Where else would you be?"

"Hah! That's where you're wrong, Aaron. Sometimes I trade my pajamas for swim trunks and do my work by the pool."

Blake laughed. "Yeah, if you wanted to do that, you'd be living in *my* complex, not your hillbilly shack."

"You do know this cost me almost eight hundred thousand dollars, right?"

"Just means they have a higher caliber of hobo in Southern California."

Soyer laughed. "So what can I do for you, Aaron?" he said warmly, handing his friend a bottle of water and Jenna a diet Peach Snapple, which had been her selection.

"Jane here has a flash drive that is password protected," said Blake. "We need someone to retrieve the file the password is protecting. But we can't take any risk the file will be compromised under any circumstances."

"Since she's Jane Smith, I assume you'd rather I didn't read what's on it, correct?"

"You know I trust you with my life," said Blake. "But I think it would be better all around if you didn't."

Blake's demeanor became deadly serious. "Before you agree to help, though, I have to tell you that there are men with spec ops level training who will kill without a second thought to get what's on that stick. If I knew anything more that might be helpful, like who these men might be, or what is on that drive, I would tell you. But where it counts, you know what I know."

Soyer considered. "Which is why you didn't call or text. So there is no recent electronic link between us."

Blake nodded.

"How big do you think this will end up being?"

"Given everything I know, which is very limited, my gut tells me huge. Enormous. The drive would be a hot potato if it contained financial records for the mob, for example, but this information could only take down a few mobsters. I think this has far larger ramifications than that. I think it's important on the level of a massive government cover-up, affecting thousands. Maybe more. I don't think that's what it is, but I'm trying to give you a sense of scale."

"Then how can I say no?" said Soyer.

"Easily. This isn't your problem. You've served your country and fellow man. If you'd rather not help us, it won't change my high opinion of you in the slightest."

"Understood. But I'm in. I'll be sure to watch my back, just in case. So tell me exactly what you want me to do."

"Ideally, if you could break in, find the file, and then give it this password," said Blake, handing Soyer a piece of paper containing a password he and Jenna had both memorized, "I'd be grateful."

Jenna produced the marked memory stick and gave it to Soyer. "Are you sure you can do this?" she asked. "If three incorrect passwords are entered, it will wipe the data, so there is no tolerance for guesses."

"Let me take a look," said Soyer.

He led them to his spacious office, an add-on at the back of his house, and to his advanced desktop computer. He carefully inserted the flash drive into a port and then manipulated a mouse, keyboard, and touch screen at a pace too quick for the eye to follow. Finally, he paused on a screen full of what looked like indecipherable gibberish.

He studied the words and symbols for almost a minute and then turned to face Jenna. "I can beat this," he said with conviction. "I'm sure of it. This isn't all that secure in the scheme of things. This is the equivalent of installing a dead-bolt lock on your door. It'll keep out your average criminal, but not a pro."

"Great," replied Jenna. "Nath—um, the person who protected this information—didn't expect for it to be found. I was even surprised he bothered with a password. I know the protection on his hard drive was much more rigorous."

"Well, lucky for us, this isn't. I could do this in a matter of minutes. But if you want zero chance of hitting a self-destruct sequence, I'll have to take the long way around. First, I'll have to hack in and build a wall around the file, one that will withstand any command to erase the data. That way, I can muck around at the password end of things without fear of it being wiped. And if there are hidden traps or if I make a mistake, it'll be safe as well."

"Thanks, Greg," said Blake. He took a deep breath. "I owe you one."

"At *least* one," said Soyer with a twinkle in his eye.

Jenna was ignoring the banter between them, staring off into space in a world of her own. Her conscience was troubling her. She had been selfish. Until Blake had brought it up, she hadn't really thought about how much they were endangering this man. The memory stick could well turn out to be Pandora's box. Wherever it went, death and destruction might follow. Relentlessly. Inevitably.

She had to take care to limit the number of innocent people exposed to this danger. She had already spread the plague by including Blake. The problem was that she and Blake alone didn't have the skills to get to the data. So if they wanted to know what was on the drive, they would have to expose someone else.

At least Soyer was highly trained, and Blake had been a step ahead of her, making certain to minimize any trail between them and his friend.

Was there anything that could be done to help ensure Soyer's safety? The safety of all three parties now involved?

The answer came to her almost immediately. If her brain had been hitting on all cylinders, she would have thought of it before. The leverage she had was obvious, and should be highly effective against all involved players. Leverage that might be the only thing that would keep them alive.

She turned her attention back to the two men just in time to hear Blake apologize for their need to rush off. He began walking toward the door, gesturing for her to follow.

"Wait," she said, stopping in her tracks and facing both men. "One last thing. The men who are after the file on this drive are willing to do anything to get it. Which puts us all at risk. But I'm pretty sure they'd also do anything to make sure no one *else* gets it."

Both men exchanged glances. "Go on," said Blake.

"I think the threat of wide disclosure can be a powerful deterrent. Might be enough to keep us alive if we're discovered."

Blake looked impressed. "You might be right," he said. "Greg, after you've burrowed in and uncovered the file, I assume you can rig up a dead-man's switch, right? So if any of us aren't alive to enter a code each week, whatever is on the drive gets sent all over the world. Maybe like an out-of-control pop-up ad, sent primarily to the press and university physics departments."

"No problem."

Jenna chewed on her lower lip, a thoughtful expression on her face. "No. Whoever is after this information might have a good reason for not wanting it to get out. So we can't do this, not until we know more about what's going on."

She turned to the baby-faced computer expert. "Why don't you set it up, but without the dead-man's switch. So put the file in the cloud, with protection as unbreakable as you can make it, and have it set for wide distribution. But only if we *actively* make that happen."

"You got it," said Soyer.

"But if we get into trouble," said Jenna, "we can still *say* we have a dead-man's switch. Doesn't cost us anything to bluff."

"I don't know who you really are, Jane," said Soyer in admiration, "but I like the way you think."

12

"Your friend seems like a great guy," said Jenna when they were on the highway once again, now heading directly to Palomar Mountain.

"Thanks. And sorry that he's trying to fix us up. He's annoyed with me for not dating more. He thinks it's unhealthy." He smiled sheepishly. "Just might be, at that," he admitted. "But for the moment, I want to put all of my energy into building a thriving agency."

"So why did you leave the military?" asked Jenna. "And don't answer if you'd rather not. It *is* a very personal question."

Blake answered, but not with the vitriol he felt. He just said the powers that be had trouble making up their minds, the terrorists were even more despicable than civilians could comprehend, which most would be surprised was possible, and that he had lost his two closest friends. But he also took a few minutes to describe some of his experiences, in bloodless, generic terms, and skills he had developed, so she would know more about his capabilities.

After ten minutes he insisted he had said enough about himself, and it was time to learn more about the case.

Jenna briefly provided her own background, something she hadn't done until this point.

"It's still hard to imagine you're just twenty-six," he said when she had finished. "You seem too savvy for a twenty-six-year-old."

"I get that a lot," she said with a sigh. "Not the savvy part, but the disbelief at how young I am."

"Well it can't be your appearance, because you don't *look* any older."

"Thanks," she said. "So that's about it. I spend most of my days on the UCSD campus. I take grad courses, read the genetics literature, and conduct experiments. Oh yeah," she said, "I'm also a teaching assistant for a freshman biology course."

"Sounds pretty demanding, actually," said Blake.

They drove in silence for several more seconds. "I know your wound is still pretty raw," he said gently, "but it's critical that we spend some time talking about Nathan. Are you ready for that?"

"Go ahead," said Jenna, impressed with Blake's sensitivity, which made her like him even more.

"Did Nathan teach also?"

"Only one course each year," she said. "He had plenty of grants, and became a full professor two years ago, at the age of twenty-seven. When most physicists are just getting their PhDs."

"What was he like?"

"Wonderful," she said, determined to discuss this in an emotionally detached state. She had leaked too many tears already. "Generous and funny. Thoughtful, but absentminded. Might order an amazing personalized cake for your birthday and Mylar balloons, and then totally forget to pick them up. And he was brilliant, of course."

"You are too, aren't you? I know you have to be pretty bright to be getting a PhD in genetics at UCSD. But I have the feeling you're even brighter than most in this program."

Jenna sighed. "Well, at the risk of seeming immodest, that is probably true. But I'm special-needs compared to Nathan. His mind was in another realm. I've always loved bright people. But at the same time, I can't stand intellectual snobs. You know, the type of people who look down their noses at anything mainstream, because they're way too smart for that. The type who have to say everything as pretentiously as possible, using the most obscure vocabulary every chance they get."

Blake nodded but kept his eyes on the road.

"Don't get me wrong," continued Jenna, "I have nothing against people with good working vocabularies. I'd like to think I have one. And sometimes a less common word needs to be used to convey a nuance, or achieve a necessary level of precision. But if something can be said simply, it should be. Using big words isn't impressive. Getting points across simply, succinctly, but with great clarity *is*."

She paused and the flicker of a smile played across her face. "It's like that famous quote, 'If I would have had more time, I'd have written you a shorter letter.'"

"Never heard that one before," said Blake. "But I like it. And I know the type. I've always believed that someone truly brilliant wouldn't feel the need to show off." He grinned. "You know, would simply use the word *use,* rather than utilize the word *utilize.*"

Jenna laughed. "*Exactly.* That's my exact point. The truly brilliant can be subtle about it. Nathan was the *opposite* of an intellectual snob. He never put on intellectual airs. He was down-to-earth in every way, and so was his language, although he could dazzle when speaking formally or when he required the highest levels of precision. He had nothing to prove. So if you met him at a party and knew nothing about his background, you'd think he was just a regular guy. But before too long you'd begin to see it. The wit. The depth of thinking. The speed of assimilating a new situation. The way he could choose words to make the mundane seem magical."

She stopped as the ache inside became nearly unbearable.

They sat in silence for several minutes, and Blake knew enough to let her regroup. He continued on toward Palomar, scanning the road ahead for cops since he was heavy on the gas pedal by nature.

"Go ahead, Aaron," said Jenna finally. "I'm good now."

Blake waited a few more seconds and then said, "Okay, Nathan's discovery is at the crux of what's happening. I know you have no idea what it is. But it might be helpful if you told me what problems he was working on."

"As far as I could tell, he was working on everything and nothing. His job was basically to imagine the universe, imagine physics and mathematics that no one had ever imagined before. He soaked up all fields of math and physics like a sponge. And he enjoyed creating math that wasn't tethered to the real world. Really crazy stuff. I think they call it abstract math. What he created was usually beyond me, even conceptually."

She reached up and absently touched the smooth steel hoop hanging from her left earlobe once again, still not used to wearing this kind of earring. "Lately, he dabbled a lot in dark matter and dark energy theory. If I were a betting woman, I'd guess the discovery had something to do with this."

"And you know what these fields are all about?"

"More or less."

Jenna allowed herself a brief smile. "Mostly less," she admitted. "I did read several books on cosmology and physics for the lay person, so Nathan could at least discuss his work with me. At least in generalities. And no one could make complicated concepts understandable the way he could."

"Great. I'm ready to be educated."

"I really don't know all that much."

"Not much is a lot more than I know at this point."

Jenna smiled. She gathered her thoughts and tried to recall how Nathan had first explained this subject matter to her. "Here's the gist: up until the 1970s and '80s, physicists thought they had a pretty good handle on matter and energy, and knew exactly how to detect these things. For the most part, matter was something visible, something we could see. Even if a hunk of matter was in a dark cave, so we couldn't see it with our eyes, or if certain matter didn't radiate in the visible spectrum at all, we could still detect it with other forms of electromagnetic radiation. We could view it with UV light, or bounce radar or radio waves off of it. We could heat it up with microwaves."

"Are you saying this isn't the case with dark matter?"

"That's right. The word *dark* is a misnomer, since it implies that lack of light is the problem, that if you could just shine a flashlight on dark matter you could see it. But this stuff can't be detected by our current science. Period. Not by our eyes or any of our instruments. When Harry Potter was under his invisibility cloak, you could still feel him if you ran into him. Not so with dark matter. Like a ghost, it goes right through regular matter. Scientists have set up dark matter detectors deep underground, to minimize interference, but after years there is no definitive proof that they've detected even a single particle of it."

Blake squinted in confusion. "Then how the hell do we even know it exists?"

"Because it still exerts a gravitational force. Apparently, it has a profound influence on the movements of galaxies and galaxy clusters." She arched an eyebrow. "Any guesses how much of the universe is composed of this stuff? How much of our universe is totally invisible to us?"

Blake shook his head.

"Twenty-five percent. But this number is misleading, because there is something else that physicists discovered, in 1998. Dark energy. Turns out that while dark matter is an attractive force within and between galaxies, dark energy is a repulsive force. We know it's there because the universe is expanding far faster than it has any right to. The teams who first discovered this won a Nobel Prize for it in 2011. To say that this was an astonishing result is an understatement. Nathan told me it would be like releasing an apple at chest height, expecting it to crash to the ground, only to watch it rise to the ceiling instead. Chalk another one up to the universe for having some good tricks up its sleeve."

Jenna paused for a moment to let this sink in. "Nathan tells me that dark matter and dark energy are right up there with the most incredible discoveries of the millennium," she continued. "Most cosmologists agree that dark matter and dark energy make up ninety-five percent of the universe. The parts we can detect, the hundreds of billions of galaxies filled with hundreds of billions of stars and planets, represent only *five percent* of the total. Five percent!"

"Do scientists have any idea what dark energy is?"

"Two theories are most popular. The first is that it's a manifestation of something called zero point energy. Long story, but quantum physics has shown there is an energy field that exists everywhere, including the vacuum of space, called the zero point field. The energy produced is too fleeting for us to tap, but it's there. The problem with this one is that the zero point field has been calculated as being nearly infinite. Dark energy's affect on the universe is incomprehensibly immense, but if the zero point field were responsible, some scientists believe it would be even stronger."

"And the second theory?" said Blake, appearing to be genuinely fascinated.

"Well, there are four fundamental forces in nature that we know of. Electromagnetism, which everyone knows about. The weak nuclear force, which makes possible the fusion that powers the sun. And the strong nuclear force, which basically holds the nuclei of atoms together."

"I'll take your word for it," said Blake dryly.

Jenna winced. "I'm going into too much unneeded detail, aren't I?" she said. "Sorry. Nathan can make this stuff a lot more interesting than I can."

"No, no," said Blake. "You're doing great. Please go on."

"Okay. I was going to say that gravity can be considered the fourth fundamental force, although it is something like a trillion trillion times weaker than any of the others."

"Gravity is the *weakest* force?"

"Yeah. I was surprised when Nathan first explained this to me, but it's obvious. We tend to think it's all powerful because we live on a massive ball of matter, and in a universe filled with enormous quantities of gravity-producing stars and planets. But if you think about it, a one-ounce magnet can lift a paperclip from the ground. Despite the fact that the gravity produced by the *entire Earth* is trying to hold it down. Six thousand trillion tons of mass being counteracted by a tiny magnet."

"That's how much the Earth weighs?"

Jenna nodded.

"Wow. That must have been *some* scale."

Jenna smiled. "So let me get back to your question. The second theory is that dark energy is a *fifth* type of fundamental force. One that was previously unknown. One physicists have dubbed *quintessence*, a force that exists throughout the universe in something called the quintessence field. I'm not sure how this is different from the zero point field, but it is all-pervasive as well."

"So the *quint* in quintessence means five, right? Like quintuplets?"

"Yes. Actually, modern physicists stole the word from the ancient Greeks. The ancients didn't know about the four fundamental forces we know about, of course. But they believed that everything was made up of a combination of four types of elements, four types of matter: earth, air, fire, and water. And this belief was widespread in a number of different cultures. But the ancients often included a fifth element, which they believed filled the universe beyond Earth. They called this element quintessence. Also called *ether* in ancient Greece, and *akasha* in India."

"And in modern English, of course," said Blake, "*quintessence*, and *quintessential*, means the most perfect example of something. The most pure and essential essence."

"Exactly," said Jenna. She was coming to appreciate that Aaron Blake was far more than just a bad-ass commando. Like Nathan, he didn't feel the need to flaunt his depth and intelligence, but it was there.

"Very interesting stuff," said Blake.

"Thanks. But I'm afraid that's all I know."

They were nearing the mountain and Blake pulled off the road and into a gas station, wanting to fill the tank so they wouldn't have to bother for the return trip. He bought a large orange Gatorade and Jenna bought a twenty ounce bottle of, fittingly enough, Palomar Mountain Spring Water, and they resumed their journey, and their conversation.

"Could it be that Nathan discovered what dark energy really is?" asked Blake after he swallowed a large mouthful of orange liquid.

"Yes. I guess it's possible."

"What if he found a way to harness this energy? That would have to be the holy grail."

"Absolutely. The energy is everywhere. Finding a way to use it would usher in an absolute revolution. Early man had no concept of electricity and no way to tap it. Think about how much harnessing this previously invisible source of energy changed civilization. This would do the same. And then some."

"So maybe that's what's on your flash drive."

She shook her head. "Can't be. Nathan told me he wasn't sure of the real world uses for his discovery. If he learned how to do this the practical applications would be obvious, and immense. Nathan told me that physicists were making some progress identifying this energy, but he was certain there would never be a way to use it. You could tap in—maybe—but even if you managed this, Nathan's calculations, and those of others, showed you'd never be able to control it. It would be all or nothing. Drinking from a fire hose. Tap it and the *minimum* energy you would release would be more than enough to vaporize the Earth, possibly the entire solar system."

Blake nodded, clearly disappointed, and continued driving in silence, finally beginning the ascent up the mountain.

In Jenna's opinion, while this had been a necessary exercise, they were right back where they started. Scratching their heads.

"I know you were in the back of a semi," said Blake finally, changing the subject, "without any windows. But any guesses where your truck left the road?"

"I'd say about fifteen or twenty minutes up the mountain from where we are now."

"Okay, but let's both start searching for it in five or ten minutes, just to be sure."

"Don't worry, I'll be able to find it on my own. You can keep your eyes on the road. Believe me, when an eighteen-wheeler becomes a toboggan, the aftermath is impossible to miss."

Fifteen minutes later they heard the unmistakable sound of chainsaws ripping through the otherwise still air. Blake turned to Jenna and raised an eyebrow. "That's interesting."

As they came closer to the source of the intermittent roar, Jenna continued to study the downward sloping side of the road, while Blake's eyes were constantly on the move.

Moments later his eyes stopped moving and focused on the physical pavement ahead. His instincts told him something wasn't right, but it took a few seconds for him to put his finger on what: the approaching section of road appeared just the slightest shade lighter than the rest of the pavement they had been traversing.

Someone had scrubbed it. And for this to be even a little bit noticeable they must have used industrial strength power washers, obliterating any skid marks from any semis that may have braked so hard their cargo compartments had fishtailed into the woods.

Blake slowed as he approached this stretch of road and followed Jenna's line of sight. Six men appeared on the slope below. Four of the men were hustling about—one with a rake, several with chain saws, and one shoving brush into a heavy nylon sack—while two of the men appeared to be taking a break, their eyes turned up toward the road.

A large swath of the forest, from the roadside down to where these men were positioned, had been laid bare, with several of the felled trees still in evidence. Each man wore a bright yellow shirt and white hard-hat, and they had patches on their arms, green-bordered shields with the silhouette of a pine tree and the words *Forest Service, US Department of Agriculture* stitched inside.

"No!" shrieked Jenna as they passed. "This is where we went off the road. It has to be. I swear to you, every word I told you was the truth. But these bastards just destroyed the evidence I was going to show you."

"These *bastards* are all the evidence I need," said Blake as the men receded behind them. "Just incredible!" he added in awe. "They scrubbed the road, airlifted a Hostess truck out of here, and cleared the area since *last night*. I thought I might have overblown the situation with Greg, but now I don't think so. What in the world are we dealing with?"

Blake saw the despondent look on Jenna's face and winced. "Sorry. Not trying to make this situation worse. But like I said in my apart—office—anyone capable of sanitizing the scene you described would have to be absolute magicians. They must wield enormous resources."

"So you don't think those guys are really with the Forest Service?"

"The two who were watching the road definitely aren't. The others may be legitimate, but I think the odds are good they're military.

Or at least they *were*—not sure who they're working for now. The military trains all kinds of specialists. Men who can construct floating bridges in a single night half a football field long, strong enough for heavy artillery to cross. Men who can build tunnels, or even underground facilities, faster than you'd believe possible. And men who can clear woodlands."

"So this is about the worst development we could ever hope for," said Jenna.

Just as she said this, Blake spotted one of the periodic turnouts in the road, which he was rapidly approaching. "Maybe," he said as he began braking. "But maybe not. If I play my cards right," he added with determination, "this might turn out to be a blessing in disguise."

13

Blake pulled onto the turnout and killed the ignition. "Wait here," he said to Jenna. "Face away from the road and appear to be, you know . . . communing with nature. I'll try to be back within an hour."

"An hour?" repeated Jenna worriedly.

Blake nodded. "My guess is that I can get to a vantage point that looks out on the men we saw in fifteen to twenty minutes," he said. "I'll take a video of them and snap some photos. I have a friend who can run their faces through a database."

"Aren't you going to need a really good telephoto camera for that?"

Blake laughed. He reached well over onto her side of the car and popped open the glove compartment. He removed a small but mighty Nikon telephoto camera that reeked of expense and sophisticated electronics.

He returned his arms and torso to his side of the car and gripped the door handle, preparing to exit. "As far as I know," he said, "this camera can only film cheating spouses screwing co-workers or hookers. But I've always theorized it might be able to film people who still have their clothes on." He raised his eyebrows. "I guess there's only one way to find out."

Jenna's face wrinkled up in disgust. "Ewww," she said as she thought further about this seamy aspect of a private detective's life.

"Yeah," he said in agreement. "Ewww is right." He paused. "So my plan is to get the shots I need and then remain in place for fifteen or twenty minutes in the hope I get lucky."

"Lucky how?"

"Maybe one of them will stray from the herd. Doubtful, but you never know."

"And if one does, you'll go after him?"

"Yes. This probably won't happen, but if it did, we could hit the jackpot. I'm not sure what these men know, but it's bound to be a hell of a lot more than *we* do. At minimum, whatever I could learn would at least suggest other directions of inquiry. It's a long shot, but worth an extra fifteen minutes."

"I assume you're well armed," said Jenna.

Blake smiled. "I'm probably setting off metal detectors as far away as Lindbergh Field even as we speak," he said.

Jenna stared worriedly into his eyes for several seconds. She continued to be convinced that this man was very special. Not nearly as brilliant as Nathan had been, of course, but very sharp. She had already developed an affection for him, and while she wasn't into metaphysics, if people really did posses auras, his was nothing but positive.

"Be careful, Aaron," she said.

He nodded and opened the car door. "You know it."

Jenna followed his figure as he rushed down the slope, but in less than a minute he was completely out of sight.

"Good luck," she whispered inside the empty car. "And come back soon."

14

Blake hustled down the mountain at as close to a run as he could manage given the slope of the terrain and the often dense foliage. He could still hear the faint sound of chain saws off in the distance, although less and less frequently as the job was likely nearing completion. Now it was probably only a matter of carving the main trunks of the felled trees into smaller pieces for easier removal.

The faster he could find a good vantage point and get the images he needed, the faster he could return to Jenna Morrison. He should have left her at his apartment. He had expected, at minimum, to be able to examine tread marks and a trail of crushed vegetation and small trees the trailer had surely sheared on its slide down the hill, like a butter knife of the gods. He had thought it likely that the trailer would still be at its final destination, held in place by several thick trunks that had refused to buckle.

While he knew there was a possibility the Hostess truck had been extricated from the site, he could never have expected a scrub this comprehensive, this fast. Nor that he would be forced to leave Jenna alone as he was doing now. Maybe his skills were already getting dull. Maybe too many divorce cases had softened him, muddled his instincts.

Well, he had better sharpen up quickly. Whatever he was involved with was big. Important. And it would likely provide the adrenaline rush he craved, even though he knew this was something he should be avoiding.

As an added bonus, he liked Jenna Morrison quite a bit, which was a rarity, since so many of his clients he found despicable. If there was a God, he sure had a sense of humor. When Blake had wished for a more challenging assignment, he was pretty sure he wasn't asking for one *this* challenging.

The forest was cool and the air crisp and refreshing. Uncountable needles and pine-cones littered the firm ground, and the smell of sap and pine filled his nostrils.

At last he came to his destination: a cut in the trees created by a twenty-foot wall of rock, bereft of most vegetation, sticking out like a knee through torn green slacks. He had seen this jagged wall from the road as he was passing the chain saw crew, being sure to glance up the slope as well as down. His sniper training had served him well, allowing him to assess possible vantage points in only a glance.

He lowered himself to the landing above the rock face and peered over the edge and down the slope. The road was thirty yards distant and the men he was after twenty yards farther still. All six men remained where they had been, tiny in the distance but well within range of his camera.

He used the Nikon as a spotting scope, dialing up full magnification and clicking any number of still photos, making sure to catch each of their faces in at least one shot. After he thought he had reached his goal he filmed in video mode for thirty seconds.

Perfect. He had all the footage he needed.

Blake considered staying put in the hope that one of the men might peel away, as planned, but given the terrain and the distance to his quarry, even if this happened it would take him too long to take advantage. He sighed. It had been a long shot anyway. Time to return to Jenna.

The underbrush rustled directly behind him!

Blake wheeled around, his hand instinctively reaching for his gun, but before he could draw he realized someone had a bead on him at point-blank range and he wouldn't have a chance if he completed the move.

Blake knew his skills had deteriorated, but not this much. Any man who could sneak up on him this effectively had to be very good. There was an art to moving through a forest like a wraith, not snapping a single twig or displacing a single pine-cone. If his assailant hadn't spooked a small animal hidden in the underbrush—which was simply bad luck for him and unavoidable—he could have tapped

Blake on the shoulder before he would have known he was being stalked.

Blake shot his arms into the air in a show of surrender. "What's going on," he blubbered fearfully, trying to channel an innocent civilian who would be wetting his pants at this point. "You can have my money. Take it. Just don't hurt me."

The man hesitated. "Who are you and what are you doing?"

"My name is Don Barnes," said Blake, the wheels in his head turning at a furious pace. He had always done his best thinking under pressure, which had saved his life on any number of occasions.

He nodded toward the Nikon still in his hand. "I'm a birdwatcher. Please. I'll give you my money. My ATM code. Anything! I don't want to make any trouble."

"Birdwatcher, my ass!" snapped the man.

Blake knew the man must be a scout, working with the crew down below to be sure no one spied on them or sniped at them from above. The fact that Blake was now in the precisely perfect spot for either endeavor was too great a coincidence for this guy to buy. Still, the longer he could play the innocent rube, the longer he could instill some doubt, some hesitation in his adversary, the more chance the man might became lulled by Blake's harmless appearance and dismiss him as a true threat.

"You have five seconds to tell me who you really are."

"I'm a *birdwatcher*," pleaded Blake, half hysterically. "Really. My club put out a bulletin. There have been some spottings of—" he hesitated, realizing that there was probably no subject he knew less about than birds. "In this area here," he added, pointing in the exact opposite direction from which the man's comrades were finishing up their work, to cover for his hesitation and in the hope of sowing as much doubt about his motives as possible.

The gunman rolled his eyes. "Spottings of what?" he said. "You didn't finish."

"I've never had a gun pointed at me," said Blake, stalling for time so he could manufacture some exotic sounding bird name. "So I'm pretty stressed out. I was going to say spottings of Blue-tailed Russian Warblers. Very rare."

The man removed a phone from his pocket. "George," he said, obviously addressing his PDA, "is there a species of bird named the Blue Tailed Russian Warbler?"

"There are over seventy species of warbler," broadcast the phone seconds later. "But none are referred to by this name."

Blake blew out a long breath and lowered his arms slowly to his sides. "Fucking Google," he muttered, although he knew he only had himself to blame. The old him would have thought quickly enough to realize he didn't know squat about birds and wouldn't have walked into this landmine. He should have kept it generic. He should have just said he was looking for rare birds. Period. What an idiot. Not that his ruse would have worked for long anyway.

"Toss me your wallet," said the assailant. "Carefully."

The man caught the leather Frisbee Blake sent his way and opened it hastily. Blake's PI identification was framed neatly inside a windowed compartment, impossible to miss. "Birdwatcher, private detective, pretty much the same thing, huh Aaron?"

Blake didn't respond.

"Draw your gun with two fingers and toss it over to me."

Blake considered pretending he didn't have a gun, but even the lamest of private investigator's would be carrying, so there wasn't much point to the attempt. And if he cooperated the man would be less likely to suspect he had another gun in an ankle holster.

"So what are you doing here?" said the man after Blake had tossed him his Sig Sauer nine millimeter handgun. "Wait, hold on," he added, removing his phone from a pocket and performing a few quick manipulations. When he was finished he dropped the phone gently on a cushion of brown pine needles near his feet. "What are you doing here?" he repeated.

"I office nearby," replied Blake, impressed that the man was savvy enough to have begun recording him so he could detect even the slightest changes to Blake's story during subsequent interrogations. "I was here late last night and saw a truck slide off the road. And today all traces of it are gone. Since I've never seen a Forestry Service crew respond to anything this quickly, I was curious. I'm between clients, and I'm trying to keep my skills sharp." Blake shrugged. "And I love hiking. So two birds with one stone sort of thing," he added, realizing as he said it that this was possibly the only thing he knew about birds: apparently, it was always better to save ammunition while killing them.

"Sure," said the man as he tossed the wallet back to Blake. "Why don't I believe you? She went and hired a PI, that's what she did. Very good," he added appreciatively.

Blake remained silent.

"You're working for Jenna Morrison, aren't you?"

Blake put on a confused expression. "I have no idea who that is."

The man drew his arm out to full extension, the gun still pointed at Blake's head. "The next lie I hear will be your last. Got it? You'll be able to search for your Russian Warbler in the afterlife."

The man's face turned to granite. "I say again, You're working for Jenna Morrison, aren't you?"

Blake gulped. "*Yes,*" he croaked, doing his best to emulate a shivering bunny nearing a nervous breakdown. "Okay, okay. I'll tell you what happened. I have a practice near the Mexican border in San Diego. This chick walks in, crazier than a loon, ranting and raving about all hell breaking loose on this mountain last night. I didn't believe her for a second, of course. A real nutcase. But I'm new to this. I've only been doing divorce cases, and she insisted she'd pay me a small fortune. So I humored her."

"Where is she?" he said severely.

Blake shook his head as the kernel of a plan began to form in his mind. "I don't know," he whispered, his eyes wide with fear. "She was driving a Ford Fusion. A blue one. She paid me five hundred in cash to come up here and find evidence of a fucking Hostess cupcake truck. But she wouldn't tell me where she was staying. She didn't trust me. Said I should investigate and then she'd find me to tell me what she wanted me to do next. That's all I know. I swear it!"

"I'm not buying it. So you have five seconds to tell me something I can use. Four. Three—"

A surge of triumph swept through Blake. He had set the hook as deep as he had hoped.

"Okay!" he shouted, trying to force a tear to his eye. He couldn't quite manage, but he hoped he looked properly freaked out and vulnerable. "I took some photos of her car as she left. Including a close-up of her license plate."

The man considered. "Another bluff? To buy you some time?"

"No!" he pleaded. "I took the pictures with this," he said, holding up the powerful black camera. "Really. See for yourself."

He held out the Nikon. Just as the assailant was about to take it, he let it go. The man was insanely fast, instinctively catching the strap before the camera hit the ground, but as he did so Blake executed a roundhouse kick that caught the man's gun with precision, sending it flying into the woods. In a continuation of the same motion, Blake rolled to his left and drew his backup gun from his ankle holster.

"Freeze!" he shouted at the man, who now dropped the camera. "Hands up!"

The man did as he was told.

Blake recovered his Sig Sauer and camera from the ground and took several quick steps backwards, putting additional distance between himself and a man no doubt well-versed in hand-to-hand combat. He returned his backup gun to his ankle holster, his eyes and gun never wavering from his target.

"Very good," said the man. "You got me to underestimate you. I won't do that again. Obvious military training. Jenna Morrison chose well."

"Now *I'm* going to ask the questions," said Blake.

His voice, which he had kept meek and fearful during his attempts at deception, now conveyed nothing but competence and self-assurance. "And if *you* lie, I'm not going to kill you. I'm going to *maim* you. Take out parts you need, one by one. Kneecaps. Testicles." He shrugged. "But don't worry, nothing you'll miss *too* much."

Blake paused to let his bluff sink in. "What's your name?"

"Justin Hone."

"Sure it is. I guess now it's your turn. Toss me your wallet."

The man did as ordered.

Other than a driver's license the man had nothing to indicate who he might work for, or even if he was military or civilian, not that Blake had any doubt in this regard. "Seems we aren't really being honest with each other. Says here your name is Mark Argent."

Blake paused, not expecting a reply and not getting one. "So who are you, Mark Argent? And what is this all about?"

"First, you should know my threat to kill you was only a bluff. I would never have really done it."

"Easy to say when the gun is on the other foot, isn't it? But you haven't answered my question."

"You don't know what you're dealing with."

"No kidding," said Blake, rolling his eyes. "Which is why I'm asking you: what am I dealing with?"

"I'm with a government organization that doesn't officially exist. One that is only known to those who are a part of it, and the president. Not even the Chairman of the Joint Chiefs has been read in. We have virtually unlimited resources. You can't win."

"I have familiarity with Black Ops. You aren't invincible."

"Yeah, well we're blacker than Black Ops. Compared to us, a standard Black Ops group is about as stealthy as the Mickey Mouse Club."

"So what are you saying, that you're like Sector Seven? Men in fucking black?"

The man sighed. "Look, I'm going to level with you. Jenna Morrison's story is true, which after all you've seen and experienced here I'm sure you've figured out. She had a rough time of it last night. We picked up her and her fiancé, but we meant them no harm. We treated them well. The job was to deliver them to the top guy and let him explain the situation."

"Then why did you murder Nathan Wexler in cold blood?" demanded Blake.

Argent looked genuinely confused. "Is that what she said happened?"

"Are you saying it didn't?" said Blake.

"I don't know. I wasn't there. No one on the exfil team survived. So I don't know what went down. But the orders were to bring them in with zero damage. Nathan Wexler was hugely important." He paused. "But it was all a horrible misunderstanding. We weren't expecting an attack. If you take me to Jenna Morrison, I can explain everything. I'm not your enemy," he said evenly.

Blake considered. Every word Argent had just said could be a lie. Or it could all be true. Or anything in between. After all, in the same situation, he had not hesitated to lie as convincingly as he could. So was this a ruse? To buy time until he could turn the tables?

So what now? Argent knew his real name. He could leave the man in the woods, unconscious. But given the capabilities of this group, leaving someone alive who knew his name was the equivalent of suicide. So was it a choice between homicide and suicide?

Blake shook his head. It didn't matter. He wasn't about to kill Argent in cold blood, even if this was the smartest play. He would have to take him prisoner. Assume the man was telling the truth and let him explain things to Jenna. The risks of this strategy were high, since trying to control a man as highly trained as Argent was asking for trouble, but he had no other choice.

"Drop it!" screamed a voice ten feet behind him. "Now!"

Shit! thought Blake. Was there anyone who wasn't able to glide through the woods without making a sound?

He let the Sig Sauer fall from his hands and to the ground for a *second* time and turned to face this new threat. As expected, the newcomer had a gun pointed at his chest, this one fitted with a sleek silencer.

"Rourk," said Argent, his voice reflecting relief. "I expected you sooner. But better late than never."

"Sorry," said the man named Rourk. "You were already at gunpoint when I arrived. But when I heard you mention Jenna Morrison,

I thought I'd wait a few more seconds to see if your friend here would say anything interesting."

Then, without another word, Rourk calmly pulled the trigger of his gun twice in rapid succession.

Blake stumbled forward, his head reeling, not able to believe that after all he had survived overseas, his death would occur on a beautiful mountain in California.

15

Blake clutched at his chest as two separate realizations penetrated his skull: his hands remained dry and were not turning blood-red in color. And Mark Argent had collapsed to the ground behind him.

Blake wheeled around as blood poured from two holes in *Argent's* chest and the man's eyes fluttered closed for the last time. Blake was unscathed. Rourk had shifted the gun a few degrees just before he fired and had hit Argent instead.

Blake turned back to Rourk, obviously not quite the comrade Argent had been hoping for.

"So I missed the first part of your conversation with Argent," said the killer calmly. "Who are you, and how do you know Jenna Morrison?"

At this point, Blake saw no reason to lie. So he told him that he was a PI representing her, and Rourk didn't bother demanding to see Blake's wallet as Argent had done.

Rourk punched a number into his cell phone, by hand, which was almost unheard of, and waited for an answer.

"Rourk here," he began when someone came on the line. "I'm still on Palomar Mountain. But Jenna Morrison hired a PI and he was snooping around out here. I have him, but I was forced to kill Mark Argent."

Rourk listened to a brief response from whomever he had called and then continued. "I'm alone with the PI. For now. But the rest of the team will be checking up on us in no time. I doubt my cover will hold for long under the circumstances. I recommend leaving the area and using my captive to get to the girl. And we'll still have one of our men on the inside, in case we need him."

There was a pause of several seconds as Rourk listened intently. "Roger that," he said finally, ending the connection.

He nodded to Blake, still holding the phone in his left hand while his gun hand remained extended. "Let's go. Take me to Jenna Morrison right now."

Blake had no idea who this man was or what was going on. He had seen that not even the key players *themselves* knew what team anyone was really on, not without a scorecard. So if Rourk threatened to kill him, this could well be a bluff. By the same token, if Rourk pretended to be his best friend, this could be a ruse as well.

There was no way to know.

What he did know was that Rourk was willing to kill in ice-cold blood, as he had demonstrated minutes earlier. So while Blake had been prepared to play it out a bit further with Argent, whose blood was now nourishing the trees, he needed to make a move on Rourk, no matter how risky. And the sooner he did so, the more likely he could catch him off guard.

Blake took a deep mental breath. "I can take you to Jenna. But I'm betting you don't really need her."

"Yeah? And what do you think I need?"

"It's better if I *show* you."

"Show me what?"

"I'm going to reach into my pocket. Very slowly. I'll bring it out with two fingers. Just don't shoot me."

Not waiting for permission, Blake reached into his front pocket with great care and removed his decoy flash drive, watching Rourk's body language as he did so. The man's reaction wasn't subtle. If he had been a dog, there would be a puddle of drool beneath him.

"I see you recognize this," said Blake. "It has the only copy of Nathan Wexler's work in existence. Jenna gave it to me. She also told me the password. Interested?"

"And if I am?" said Rourk evenly.

"I just want your word you'll leave the girl in peace. We both know you don't really want her. Just this thumb drive. So let's go to a computer. I'll tell you the password. You verify that it works and then let me go." Blake paused. "Deal?"

Blake waved the memory stick back and forth as he spoke and noted with great interest that Rourk never once took his eyes from it. If it were a stopwatch the man would have been hypnotized by now.

"Deal," said Rourk. He motioned up the mountain. "Lead on."

"As a show of good faith, I'll even let you hold on to the drive."

Without waiting for an answer, Blake flung the memory stick in Rourk's direction as hard as he could, so forcefully it landed a full ten yards behind its presumed target. Rourk couldn't help but turn and follow its path, focusing on where it would land so he wouldn't risk losing it in the dense undergrowth.

The instant he turned to follow the drive, Blake rolled to the ground, pulled his backup gun from his ankle holster for the second time in minutes, and came up firing, hitting Rourk in the left forearm just moments after the flash drive had landed behind him. Rourk's phone went flying and he dived behind a wide trunk for cover.

"God-dammit!" he thundered as he hit the ground, further aggravating his wounded arm.

Blake could have shot his adversary in the head, but refused to kill him, even though it was arguably justified, until he knew all of the players and their motivations. The man had killed Argent, but Argent could have been the devil in disguise for all Blake knew, and Rourk's action could well have saved his life.

But now he had forced Rourk to make a choice, as he had intended. The man could retrieve his prized flash drive lower down the slope. Or leave it and go after Blake, who was armed and clearly lethal.

It was as easy a choice as he had expected. Rourk still had his gun, but had little chance of hitting Blake, who was now planted behind a nearby tree trunk. Instead, Rourk picked his way toward where the flash drive had landed, taking a pinball path between trees to shield him from further fire as he worked his way toward his goal.

As soon as Blake was sure of Rourk's intent, he retrieved the man's fallen phone and beat a hasty retreat up the slope, putting distance and as many trees as he could between himself and his prior captor.

16

Aaron Blake was in excellent shape but was still out of breath by the time he reached the car, having sprinted uphill for eight minutes over uneven terrain.

"Duck down," he instructed Jenna as he entered and took the wheel.

"What happened?"

Blake told her as he began driving down the mountain, clinging to a speed just a few miles over the limit, fighting back his adrenaline-fueled need to break the sound barrier. The fight-or-flight instinct perfected by evolution demanded that flight take place at the fastest possible speed, not at a veritable crawl. But the people after him didn't know what car he drove, and screaming down the mountain like he was on fire would give them a giant hint.

Jenna shook her head in dismay after he had finished recounting what had happened. "Why am I having a déjà vu experience?" she said miserably. How many times was she going to be racing down Palomar Mountain, fearing for her life?

"So what are the chances we get off this mountain alive?" she asked.

"Excellent," said Blake, his breath and heart rate rapidly returning to normal.

"How do you figure?"

"The parties after us are in conflict with each other. And I've seen that their loyalties are questionable. It's a messy situation, which is good for us. We're up against a boat filled with quality oarsmen, but they're not all rowing in the same direction. I don't think—"

Blake stopped abruptly as they shot around a turn and approached the stretch of road at which the men with Forest Service patches and hard hats were lurking. He took in the scene in a few practiced glances. Two of the men remained where they had been, but four others were now on the other side of the road, climbing up the slope and fanning out.

"Duck down lower," he instructed, not wanting to risk that one of the four might happen to glance down at the road and into their car. He then relaxed his own features, turning himself into the picture of calm contentment for anyone observing.

"Okay, we're clear," he said less than a minute later, signaling Jenna that she no longer needed to fold her head into her lap. "I think we're out of the woods now."

Jenna thought about pointing out that this idiom probably wasn't ideal when one was actually very much *in* the woods, but decided not to.

"As I was saying," continued Blake, glancing at his rearview mirror every few seconds, "I like our chances of getting off this mountain alive, and even slipping away without incident. These guys will find their fallen comrade soon, but only Rourk knows we were here. And when it comes to the murder of Mark Argent, Rourk is in possession of a smoking gun, almost literally, so he has to get the hell out of here and avoid his former comrades. Since he also thinks he has the real thumb drive, there's no way he'll try to come after us right now. He'll be racing to bring the memory stick back to his boss."

Once again, Jenna was impressed with the speed and quality of his analysis, especially given the pressure they were under.

"How long until they break the password and realize the flash drive is a decoy?" asked Jenna.

"First he has to get it back to his boss, which could take a while. The password isn't all that solid but will still take *some* time to break. I'm guessing we'll have several hours, at minimum, before he cares about us again."

Jenna nodded.

Blake removed a phone from his pocket and handed it to her. "This is Rourk's phone. Copy all the names and numbers you can from it, and then throw it into the woods so we can't be tracked."

Jenna examined the phone for several minutes. "I've never seen a model like this. Must be disposable, because there is no data of any kind here. It's not that his contact list is encrypted, it's that I'm pretty sure it doesn't even exist."

Blake frowned. "Before Greg Soyer set up my phone to be untraceable, I used these burner phones myself. But I've never seen this exact breed before. Probably custom. I'm not entirely surprised, since Rourk entered the number he called by hand, which he wouldn't need to do with even the most basic conventional phone." He paused. "But if it's like most burners, it will at least automatically save the last number dialed. See if you can find it."

Jenna bent to this task immediately. "Got it!" she said less than a minute later.

"Outstanding," said Blake. He handed her his own phone. "Enter the number in here for me."

She worked his phone for a brief period and then announced that she was finished, handing it back to him. She then lowered the window and sent Rourk's phone flying into the trees.

Blake checked the time on the car's dash. "We don't have as much cushion as we did, but we still should be able to make it to UCLA in time to get Dan Walsh."

Jenna sighed. "True. Unless missiles start to, you know, rain down from the sky toward your car. Or there's a division of tanks waiting for us at the bottom of the mountain."

"Right," said Blake with a tight smile. "If either of those things happen, it might make us a minute or two late."

He turned toward Jenna and caught her eye. "One purpose in coming up here was to verify your story. Well, I can now say, without a doubt, that this has been accomplished. So I believe every word you've told me. You are not crazy, Jenna Morrison. This entire situation is absolutely *batshit* crazy, but you're not."

Even though these words had been a show of support, they served to bring back feelings of depression and loss. "Yeah. I only wish I *were* crazy. I wish I could wake up from a temporary insanity to find that the past twenty-four hours never really happened."

Jenna looked away for several seconds and gathered herself. "I'd love to know if Greg has managed to bypass Nathan's password yet," she said.

"Yeah, me too. I wish there was a way to find out short of visiting him again, which we really don't have time for now."

Jenna nodded. It was impossible not to take instant communications for granted, but this was a relatively new development in human history. With Blake refusing to call or text Soyer, she was being given a taste of what the Dark Ages must have been like. If you wanted to learn the status of a friend who lived a hundred miles away, the only way to do it was to walk, run, or hope you had a horse.

Blake checked the time once again. "We'll need to stop at my apartment. I'll have just enough time to shower and gather a few things I'll need before we'll have to leave again to get Dr. Walsh."

"Are you sure we should go forward with this? Why contaminate anyone else?"

"He's already a part of this."

"Yes. But you said yourself that if they wanted to kill him or take him they would have already done it. And I'm like Typhoid Mary. The kiss of death. If he ends up dead because of me, I'll never be able to forgive myself."

Blake sighed. "It's possible you're right. It's possible contacting him will change his status, will suddenly make him a target. But if we ignore him, don't warn him, he's at their mercy. He won't even know they're out there. And what if he takes what's in Nathan's e-mail and works on it himself? He is a top physicist, right? So they could decide at any moment to take him out. At least if we bring him into the fray, he'll have a chance."

Jenna's eyes narrowed in thought, but she didn't respond.

"Also," continued Blake, "we're going to need someone to explain Nathan's work to us once Greg Soyer uncovers it. And probably its significance. When Einstein came out with general relativity, I heard that even a lot of the world's top physicists didn't understand the math, or the full implications. But you know more about this than I do. Do you think you'll be able to grasp what's on that drive? Because I know I won't have a clue."

Jenna frowned. "No. You're right. I've seen some of the papers Nathan wrote, and I'd understand them better if they were in Sanskrit."

"So we'll ultimately have to bring somebody in. Endanger *someone*. If we don't, we'll never truly understand what this is all about. And how do we know failing to get to the bottom of this won't jeopardize thousands of other lives? Since Dr. Walsh is already endangered, it makes sense to go to him."

"You're right," she said begrudgingly. "I don't like it, but you're absolutely right." She blew out a long breath. "Let's go pay a visit to UCLA."

17

Dan Walsh walked the short distance from his office to Kendall Hall, where his quantum electrodynamics class met from seven thirty to nine. He only taught one night class, on Mondays, but he didn't mind it. Most of the time he would just hang out on campus, have dinner with colleagues, and get some extra work done beforehand.

Besides, he liked the early evening. The air was cool, there wasn't the usual kicked-anthill frenzy of students to dodge—a health hazard for someone often lost in thought—and the noise from the ever-present heavy construction equipment was finally quieted.

UCLA was the second oldest college in the California system, founded in 1919, and it had been growing ever since. It now had the largest enrollment of any school in the state, at well over forty thousand students, and the eclectic mixture of architecture reflected different periods of expansion and construction, and included faded red brick buildings, elaborate parking structures, an extensive sculpture garden, modern fountains, and stunning sorority and fraternity houses. In fact, the Westwood campus was so often in a state of flux, some joked UCLA actually stood for *Under Construction Like Always*.

Walsh had just turned thirty-four, and while his career was going relatively well, he had grown worried. Unlike wine, physicists and mathematicians tended to get worse with age. This wasn't always the case, but often flashes of true, dazzling insight required young, daring minds, not hampered in their attempts at thinking outside of the box by having been *inside* the box too long. Not overly poisoned by conventional wisdom or fear of peer ridicule.

Einstein was the classic example. Unable to get a job at a university, at the tender age of twenty-six he published four papers that formed the basis of much of modern physics, shattering previous conceptions of space, time, mass, and energy: four papers so important they had been dubbed his *Annus mirabilis* papers, from the Latin for *extraordinary year*, which most English speakers preferred to translate into *miracle year*.

Walsh was beginning to resign himself to the idea that he would produce solid work and have a successful career, but he would never do more than polish and extend the insights of the truly great. He hadn't given up yet, but he also had to be realistic about it.

But if you couldn't *be* Einstein, being a close friend and colleague of the great man wasn't a bad fate. And if Walsh's sense of Nathan Wexler's potential was accurate, he would be able to tell his spellbound grandchildren someday about his friendship with the leading thinker of his century.

On the other hand, if he wanted to have children, let alone grandchildren, he had some work to do. He was still single, but this was something he was hoping to change within a few years, at the latest. In fact, there was a girl in one of his graduate classes whom he really liked, and he sensed she liked him back. They really seemed to click.

And while this might just be the cliché attraction that many students were fabled to feel toward their professors—although this seemed to work better for literature professors than for those teaching physics—he didn't care. She was twenty-five, so it wasn't as though he was robbing the cradle, and he wouldn't make the slightest overture toward her until she was no longer in his class.

But this didn't stop him from fantasizing about her. It never ceased to amaze him the power of the sex drive. No matter how intelligent and rational a person was otherwise, the sex drive was controlled by more primitive regions, and could turn the most brilliant man on Earth into an animal, flirting with disaster in pursuit of physical gratification, even when he knew in his rational mind that this was nothing but a trick played on him by his incorrigible limbic system.

Walsh entered Kendall Hall and passed a dozen locked doors, including two lecture halls with a seating capacity of many hundreds. In the corridor in front of one of the lecture halls a student in his thirties was sitting with this back to the wall, reading a book, but Walsh didn't recognize him and didn't feel the need to interrupt.

He was fifteen or twenty minutes early, as was his habit. He entered the room that would house his class of twenty-two graduate students and made his way to the front, where a chalkboard spanned the entire wall.

He set his backpack down on the long table and prepared to fill the board with equations prior to the arrival of his students.

Walsh spotted a tablet computer someone had left on the table at the front of the room. It was hard to miss, as it was still on and very bright. Given that this must have been left by someone in the previous class, which had ended an hour earlier, he was surprised it was still glowing, having not gone into hibernation or run out of juice.

As he walked over to scoop it up, he was startled to find the top half of the screen displayed a photo of Jenna Morrison, Nathan Wexler's fiancée. It was unmistakably her.

What in the world?

One didn't need his math genius to know that the odds this random tablet would be displaying a photo of Jenna Morrison were virtually zero. Which suggested this was anything but random.

His eyes narrowed in worry and confusion as he read the bold text below the photo.

Dan, it's Jenna. This is not a joke. Don't say anything out loud, as it's possible you're being bugged. Please scroll over and read my message.

Walsh looked around the room, which was still empty, wondering if he were on a hidden-camera television show, of if someone would jump out and tell him he was the subject of an experiment being conducted by the psychology department. When neither occurred, he glanced back at the tablet as though it were an unstable explosive.

He studied Jenna's photo again and finally, reluctantly, slid his hand on the screen to scroll over to the next page. He took a deep breath and read:

Dan, sorry to hit you with what must look like a charade, but I'm in trouble and I need your help. Just so you can be sure it's really me, the last time Nathan and I got together with you, you had just seen

Guardians of the Galaxy *on television and you told me you couldn't get the song "Hooked on a Feeling" out of your head.*

Regardless of what you may have heard, Nathan is dead, savagely murdered last night by unknown parties.

"What?" whispered Walsh out loud. That was *absurd*. Nathan wasn't *dead*. What kind of sick game was this?

On the other hand, that damn song *had* been stuck in his head the last time he had seen Jenna, which he had confided to her while Nathan was out of the room taking a call. And he hadn't actually seen Nathan in person for weeks.

He looked down at the tablet once more and continued reading.

The only thing I know for certain is that his death, and subsequent events I will tell you about in person, were somehow triggered by a discovery he made recently. He didn't have the chance to tell me what it was about before he was killed, but he did mention he had sent an e-mail summary of the discovery to you, hoping you'd act as a second set of eyes for him. I'm convinced this e-mail was intercepted, which is what set everything in motion.

Walsh paused to consider. Even more so than the "Hooked on a Feeling" thing, the accurate description of Nathan's recent e-mail to him was persuasive evidence that Jenna Morrison really had written this message.

Given the seemingly unlimited resources of the teams of men involved—yes, teams—something about Nathan's discovery is of extreme importance. I managed to escape these men, but I know for certain they'll spare no effort to find me, so even if you weren't bugged or under surveillance before, you are now.

I'm working with a private investigator. He's helping me compose this message right now, and he came up with this plan to extricate you from prying eyes. He'll be the one who will leave this tablet at your desk, since I can't risk being recognized by whoever is watching you.

He also plans to park himself in the hall to make sure that you're the first to arrive in the classroom, so no one else will see this tablet. He had planned to give this to you in person, but I thought it would be less intimidating for you to read it alone, and you once told me you always arrive to your classes fifteen or twenty minutes before your students, so I thought this would be the best way forward.

When you're done reading this message, scroll over again to find a picture of me and my new PI partner together. I'm wearing a hideous blonde wig, by the way. I included this so you'll be able to recognize him, *and know that he really is a friend.*

Nathan is dead and his hard drive has been destroyed. But his work was preserved on a single flash drive that I now have, protected by a password that I don't know. This is why I'm being hunted. Until I talk to you, I have no idea what might be on it, what Nathan discovered, and why people are willing to do anything to get it.

So I need to get you away from UCLA without being seen. I assume that you keep an e-mail archive in the cloud and can retrieve Nathan's recent message once you're clear. But first, remove and pocket the sim card from your phone, so you don't lose your data and settings, and put the phone deep within your backpack. Then leave the phone and backpack in the classroom. Assuming the phone is being monitored or tracked, anyone stalking you will think you're still there.

But to buy us extra time, it would be great if your students stuck around, even with you gone. If they leave right away, anyone watching the building might want to investigate. So write on the board that you had to take a call and will be back in forty-five minutes. Then assign them a reading while you're gone.

But please hurry.

Once you've done this, go to the men's room at the northernmost corner of the building. My partner will be there waiting for you.

Thanks, Dan. I know you might doubt this crazy message, but please consider this: if you do what I've asked and this turns out to be a farce, you've wasted a bit of class time and life goes on. But if you choose to ignore this message and it is real, the impact is far more dire. Please! Write on the board and get the hell out of there. I'll fill you in on the rest when I see you.

18

Blake felt like an idiot standing next to three urinals and staring at the bathroom door. He glanced at his phone and saw that it was now seven twenty, ten minutes before the scheduled start of Walsh's class. The physicist had arrived early to prepare and pre-fill the blackboards as Jenna had insisted would be the case.

He should have found the tablet and read the message in minutes, meaning if he didn't arrive at the men's room soon he probably wasn't coming. Or else something had gone horribly wrong. Blake had a plan B, but he hoped like hell he wouldn't need to use it.

The bathroom door creaked slowly ajar and Blake rolled on the balls of his feet in anticipation.

Dan Walsh entered, a stern, apprehensive expression on his face. Blake caught his eye and put a finger to his lips, signaling for silence. He removed an electronic box, about the size of a package of cigarettes, and waved it a few inches from the physicist, scanning him from head to toe. The indicator light remained green throughout.

Blake powered off the device. "You're clean," he said. "We're all but positive you're being watched. And I suspect you're also being bugged, although I wasn't sure if they would bug your phone or your wallet. Either way works, since these are items you tend to keep with you at all times." He paused. "Did you put your phone deep inside your backpack like I asked?"

Walsh nodded. "Yes. Why does that matter?"

"Assuming it's bugged, the backpack should make reception horrible, so they won't be able to hear exact words."

"I see," said Walsh. "So when my students are talking about what I wrote on the chalkboard, they'll only hear chatter, not content."

"Exactly," said Blake.

"Impressive," said the physicist.

Blake extended a hand. "My name is Aaron Blake, by the way. Welcome to the ah . . . bathroom, Dr. Walsh. Thank you for believing Jenna's message."

"Nice to meet you, Mr. Blake. At least I think it is."

Blake smiled. "Please, Dr. Walsh, call me Aaron."

"Okay, if you call me Dan."

"It's a deal."

"So I suppose you'd rather leave the premises first and tell me what the hell this is all about later."

"You got it," said Blake. He was really beginning to like working with scientists. They were logical and quick on the uptake.

"So what's the plan?" asked Walsh.

"I assume you're familiar with the tunnels under this school, right?"

The physicist nodded slowly. "Yes. Of course."

"Whoever is watching you will be watching the exit door of this building. Only one is open at this hour. Imagine their surprise when you disappear without ever using it."

The possibility of using a tunnel was the first thing Blake had checked when he was coming up with his strategy. A number of institutions of higher learning, built nearly a century or more earlier, possessed systems of subterranean tunnels between buildings, and UCLA was no exception. He was delighted to find that a comprehensive search of the Web was quickly able to reveal a wealth of information about the system here.

UCLA's steam tunnels were a labyrinth of cement conduits three stories underground. The system circulated steam produced at a plant near the Ronald Reagan Medical Center, housed communications lines and pipes for cold water, and linked most of the major buildings on campus. Although access points were well hidden, adventurous students had made it their mission to breach the tunnels for many decades, and for the last few, to post maps and entry portal locations on the Web.

Blake gestured toward the far end of the men's room, which housed a small supply closet. "One of many entrances is through there," he said. "I've taken the liberty of busting the lock while I was waiting for you to arrive."

"How thoughtful," noted Walsh, following Blake as he opened the door to the closet. Blake had already pushed aside several bottles of cleanser to free a trap door, which he had also left open.

"I'll go first," said Blake, lowering himself onto a steel ladder that was entirely vertical. He descended a few rungs to give Walsh room to follow and then stopped.

Walsh's face curled up in distaste but he followed suit, and they soon completed their descent. The tunnels were occasionally punctuated by dim lightbulbs, but were still eerily dark, dank, and claustrophobic.

"Follow me," whispered Blake, so his voice wouldn't echo and make the entire venture even creepier than it was already. He unfolded a map he had printed earlier, with the route he intended to take drawn in red marker, and shined a penlight on it.

They took several offshoots, sometimes traversing through tunnels that could only take them single file, crammed with pipes, wires, and steel cables. The wider tunnels were decorated by graffiti, and Blake felt like an archeologist visiting a prehistoric cave. Except that instead of rough drawings of animals and spears, the drawings here were of male and female genitals, along with a multitude of Greek letters signifying various fraternities, and messages as creative as, "Joe Hempel was here," some with dates indicating they had been written as early as the 1940s.

Sections of the tunnels became quite warm, but this was short-lived as they continued moving at a rapid pace. At one point they entered a huge cavern—the damp insides of a walled-in bridge below the center of campus, where "Welcome to Hell" was scrawled on the ceiling in block letters.

They emerged near a parking lot minutes later, through a door that was strategically covered by a large shrubbery. Blake had broken open the lock before he had traveled to Kendall Hall.

"Wait here," he told the physicist, leaving him in darkness even greater than the inside of the tunnels. He reconned the area to make sure they were clear of any surveillance, and then returned.

"All good?" asked Walsh when Blake was beside him once again.

Blake nodded. "The coast is clear. So let's visit Jenna Morrison and find out what this is all about."

19

Dan Walsh hugged Jenna briefly and then slid into the backseat of Blake's car, parked in a nearby lot. Jenna had been waiting anxiously for the two to finish their trek through the catacombs of UCLA.

Finally—finally!—they would be getting a glimpse of the truth. Jenna hoped this would be a giant leap forward in their ability to make whoever was responsible for Nathan's death pay for his crimes.

"Sorry to pull you into this, Dan," said Jenna. "But we didn't really have much choice. Thank you so much for responding to my message."

"Of course," said Walsh. "But you should know, Nathan wasn't murdered last night. What makes you think he was?"

A tear came to Jenna's eye, which she wiped away with the back of her hand. "I saw him die, Dan," she said softly. "I was right next to him. He was shot point-blank in the head. With no possibility of mistake."

Walsh looked both confused and horrified. "I am so sorry," he whispered.

He paused for several seconds and then shook his head. "I can't even begin to digest a loss this enormous," he said. "Nathan was a good friend and colleague. And he was destined for greatness, making this tragedy all the worse. I still can't believe it," he muttered, looking as though he had just taken a fist to the gut.

Jenna nodded and blinked back tears.

She had to stop this! she told herself. She had to compartmentalize this loss and not get maudlin every time it was driven home to her. "Thanks, Dan. But we need to postpone our mourning," she said, as much to convince herself of this as to convince him. "When this is over, we'll have a proper funeral and proper eulogies. But we can't afford to dwell on this right now."

Before Walsh could respond, Blake broke in. "Sorry, Dan, but I have to ask: what made you so sure Nathan *wasn't* dead?"

"I've exchanged two e-mails with him today. The last one just a few hours ago."

Jenna shook her head in disgust. "It was a decoy," she explained. "Someone pretending to be Nathan."

"Well, whoever it was, he was very convincing. Knew things I thought only Nathan knew."

"The men behind this are insidious," said Jenna in disgust.

"But extremely competent," added Blake.

"Whoever responded to my message knew a lot of the same math Nathan did," said Walsh. "I had been stuck on a problem with tensorial derivatives, which no one is better at solving than Nathan. I laid out the problem in my e-mail and the reply got me un-stuck. There aren't all that many people running around who could have helped me."

Jenna sighed. "They wouldn't be after Nathan's work if they didn't understand its implications. Which means they must have some top physicists working with them. One of these impersonated Nathan."

"Speaking of Nathan's work," said Blake, "I can't tell you how much I need to know what's in that e-mail. To say I've never been more curious about anything in my life would be an understatement."

"I could just summarize it for you," offered Walsh.

"No," said Blake. "I'd appreciate it if you'd read it to us. I want to hear it for the first time from Nathan's perspective, word for word."

Not taking his eyes from the road, Blake thrust his arm toward the backseat behind him. A tablet computer was in his hand. "Use this to access the Internet," he said. "It can't be traced to us."

Walsh quickly found the relevant site in the cloud, entered his user name and password, and retrieved the e-mail from his archives.

"Here it is," announced Walsh. "I'll read it slowly," he added, and then, clearing his throat, began:

Dan. How's life? I hope you are well. As you'll be able to see from the time stamp when you get this, I'm writing at two in the morning.

Why? Because I just completed work on a discovery that came to me from out of nowhere and crystallized in less than a week. I just dotted the last i and crossed the last t an hour ago, and I've checked and rechecked this for days now. Despite the late hour (or early hour, depending on your perspective) I couldn't contain myself. I'm dying to tell at least one other person about this, even if you won't read this until you awaken. I'm not sure this is how most people spend their Saturday nights (or Sunday mornings) but this works for me.

So let me begin at the beginning. Jenna left town for a week to visit her sister (long story), and the next day I awoke to a eureka moment. Maybe I dreamed about it, or maybe it was some kind of divine intervention, but I've been working around the clock to develop it ever since.

It's staggering really. Although you aren't expert in all the areas of mathematics I used to complete it, you're more expert than I am in two disciplines I used, five-dimensional manifold topology and hyperbolic knot invariants. I've quadruple checked everything, and I'm certain there are no flaws in the areas of math I'm most experienced in, but there is a very slight chance I missed something in your areas of expertise. So I was hoping you could read the final write-up and give it your blessing before I try to make history. In exchange, I will invite you to Stockholm when I collect my Nobel Prize. *(just kidding, I'm not that egotistical—which is one of the things that make me so great :)).*

But jokes aside, if you confirm I didn't make any errors, I'm certain this theory will turn out to be sound. Profoundly sound. I have the confidence in this that Einstein had in relativity, even before it was confirmed experimentally, when he famously said the theory was just too beautiful to be false.

I'm dying to send the paper to you this second, but I'd rather it not hit cyberspace. I know I'm somewhat paranoid, but theoretical physicists like us have a license to be a bit eccentric. And I work hard at not being too normal, for fear of failing to live up to expectations.

Anyway, I know you have a night class on Mondays, so I'll plan to drive up to see you Monday before noon, and hand-deliver a paper copy of my work. Eyes-only, of course. You can't breathe a single word of this to anyone until I publish. I can only imagine what a shock, what a tidal wave of media coverage, this will cause when I finally put it out there.

I would drive up later today, but Jenna is returning home this evening, and I plan to meet her at the airport with bells on. So I'll go over the theory one last time, buy some expensive wine to celebrate my discovery with Jenna, and see you on Monday. If you're as enthusiastic as I expect you to be, this visit could well last into Tuesday."

"Hold on a moment," said Blake, interrupting the recitation. "Nathan obviously didn't visit you today as planned. I assume he canceled on you in one of those bogus messages you got. What excuse were you given?"

"The person posing as Nathan wrote this morning and said he had found a flaw in his new theory. He said he was going to attempt to correct it, but he wasn't very hopeful, and if he did visit it wouldn't be for at least a few more weeks."

Blake nodded and exchanged glances with Jenna. "Nice," he said appreciatively. "They found a way to cancel Nathan's visit, discredit his work, and put you off for a few weeks, all in one fell swoop. Not only does this convince you Nathan is alive, but it ensures you don't try to follow up on his theory." Blake shook his head. "I know these guys are ruthless assholes, but it's hard not to appreciate their skills."

"Is this when you wrote back and asked for help with your work?" asked Jenna.

"Not until a few hours later, but yes. And you're both going to find this interesting. As part of the reply, whoever was posing as Nathan told me Jenna's computer had been infected with the mother of all viruses. The virus had invaded her contact list and was periodically sending out lethal, infected messages to her friends. He told me that I should change my settings to block any incoming messages from Jenna Morrison's e-mail address, until further notice."

Jenna's face wrinkled up in confusion. "That doesn't make sense," she said. "If they were monitoring you, they'd *want* us to connect, so you could lead them to me."

"Remember," said Blake, "there are two groups involved here. Maybe this is an effort by one of them to try to prevent the *other* from finding you."

"Maybe," said Jenna.

"Should I continue reading the message?" asked Walsh.

"By all means," said Blake.

The physicist turned back toward the tablet in his hands and took up where he had left off:

"*Part of me wants to wait to spring this on you in person, but there is no way I can contain myself. If I don't at least tell someone the punch line,* I'm pretty much going to *explode. But even though I'll ruin some of the surprise, the actual work contains plenty more. I think you'll be astonished by how the math all fits together and by the underlying assumptions and logic. So here it is. The broad overview, just to whet your appetite.*

Drum roll please (wow, that just gave me an idea for a gag I can do when Jenna gets back).

Are you sitting down?

We've both contributed to the finding that the quintessence field can't be tamed. Not that we could ever find a way to even dip a single toe into it, but if we could, we agreed that this would destroy the Earth, at minimum, and would likely punch a hole in space-time and create a stable black hole.

Turns out we were wrong about that. Dark energy can be tapped into, and all of this crazy energy can be bottled and used after all. But only by using it at right angles to the four dimensions of space and time. By driving the energy usage through a fifth dimension.

My calculations have convinced me that you can tap into the quintessence field, and instead of releasing these incredible energies thermally and kinetically, you can harness them safely. But only to accomplish a single thing: send matter back in time.

There, I said it.

To repeat, it should be fairly straightforward to tap into the dark energy field to send matter, transdimensionally, back through time—without any explosion or other untoward effects. All of the energy drives the time travel, with none left over to cause any havoc. It will be absolutely safe. I'm certain of this.

The first stable platform for which this occurs is at T minus .00004515 seconds, or 45.15 microseconds. I am all but positive I will be able to use this theory to, with minimal trouble really, tap into the dark energy field and send matter back precisely this amount of time, and this amount of time only: 45.15 microseconds.

Just to be crystal clear and avoid any possible confusion, I am not saying I can send matter back in time hundreds or thousands of years—but that this matter can only remain in the past for forty-five microseconds. I am saying I can only send matter back to forty-five microseconds ago.

One interesting aspect of this work is that it appears I should be able to go back even farther, at 45.15 microsecond intervals exactly.

Why this interval? I don't know, but the math here is beautiful, and this is what the results are. I'm only 95% certain of this *right now, but I think I'll be able to firm this up soon and be able to state it with absolute certainty as well.*

If this is true, going back five thousand of these intervals will be just as easy as going back one. But there is one final catch. After going back a bit over ten thousand of these 45.15 microsecond steps, when you reach about a half-second into the past, you're done. No power in the universe can take something back any further.

This falls out of the equations as a barrier that's as absolute as the speed of light. I can't say why this ultimate limit is what it is any more than I can explain why the speed of light limit happens to be 186,283 miles per second.

When you see the theory you will appreciate how revolutionary it really is. It will open up all kinds of theoretical avenues, and will be a totally new window on reality, like relativity and quantum physics before it.

I haven't had a lot of time to think of practical applications as I've been consumed with perfecting the theory, but quantum physics didn't have any practical applications either—until it became the heart and soul of all modern computers and electronic technology.

If this allowed one to send a stock tip or a lottery number back even an hour, the practical implications would be obvious. But a half-second doesn't give you enough time to act on any information.

At the moment, all I'm certain of is the feasibility—the fairly straightforward feasibility—of sending something back exactly 45.15 microseconds. I'd say the blink of an eye, but I looked it up, and it turns out that an eye blink takes almost eight thousand times longer. So this will be challenging to work with. Even designing experiments will be challenging, but I'm assuming I'll figure it out. *And this will provide me with a tool that will enable me to answer so many questions.*

Do we live in a block universe? Is Hawking's chronology protection conjecture correct? How will gravity affect the transference? Does time branch, or is there only a single timeline? And these few profound questions—answerable questions!—are just off the top of my head.

So that's it for now. I'm pretty fried, and I'm about to become unconscious whether I want to or not. So I'm not going to reread this to see if it makes any sense. If it doesn't, just know that we'll have many, many hours to discuss all of this, beginning Monday when I see you at UCLA.

I hope all is well. Can't wait to have a second pair of eyes (connected to that massive brain of yours, of course) look this over.

Nathan.

Walsh stopped reading and there was an extended silence in the car. Jenna's mouth had fallen open halfway through the recitation and had remained there. Blake was just as stunned by the revelations in Nathan Wexler's e-mail as was Jenna, but was forced to keep some of his focus on the road.

"What in the world?" said a wild-eyed Jenna Morrison. "This is beyond extraordinary!" But a few seconds later her expression turned pensive. "But at the same time, what about it could possibly be important enough to *kill* for? Nathan was right. Going back in time far less than the blink of an eye is useless."

"Apparently not," said Blake grimly. "We must be missing something. Something big."

"Well, we'd better figure it out," said Jenna with a sigh. "And we'd better do it quickly."

PART 2
Mystery

Yesterday is history.
Tomorrow is a mystery.
But today is a gift.
That's why they call it the present.

—Unknown

"The Moving Finger writes; and, having writ,
moves on: nor all thy piety nor wit
shall lure it back to cancel half a line,
nor all thy tears wash out a word of it."

—Omar Khayyam

20

Lee Cargill waited impatiently for Joe Allen to arrive, repeatedly delaying the departure of his private jet.

What the hell was keeping him?

Cargill had wanted to arrive in DC in time to catch some quality sleep before his private meeting with Alex Janney, President of the United States.

Cargill checked the time once again and cursed loudly. Finally, ten minutes later, Allen arrived, expressed apologies for his tardiness, and was ushered onto the plane for an immediate takeoff.

The Gulfstream accelerated along the runway and streaked relentlessly to thirty thousand feet before leveling off. While the jet was on the extravagant side, considerable work had been done to give Cargill the cover of a wealthy tech entrepreneur, running a private company called Q5 Enterprises, so a military jet was out of the question.

The plane seated twelve people in such spacious luxury that first-class passengers on commercial flights were like peasants crammed into a third world bus by comparison. But for this trip, Lee Cargill and Joe Allen were the only passengers. The pilot was in the cabin, which had been made totally soundproof so Cargill could carry out business during flights without privacy concerns.

After they had leveled off, Allen began his report. "We found our mole," he reported, but with less enthusiasm than Cargill would have expected, and an instant later he found out why as Allen added, "but I'm afraid we still have one left."

Allen was seated in a cushioned captain's chair that he had swiveled to face the one Cargill was in, a small table between them. If not for the round windows and thirty-thousand-foot drop below them, the meeting could well be taking place in an expensive apartment or an executive lounge.

"One thing at a time," said Cargill. "First, who is the mole you found?"

"Jack Rourk."

"You're positive?"

"Absolutely."

Cargill thought about this. Jack Rourk was a good man. At least this is what he had believed a second earlier. "And your evidence?" he said.

"I realized after the team disposed of Mark Argent's body that they hadn't recovered his phone. So I pinged it. I found it about ten feet away from where he was shot, hidden in a mat of pine needles. He had set it to audio recording, so we have a record of everything that was said."

Allen produced a black custom cell phone, a little worse for wear, and handed it to Cargill. It was the same custom phone Rourk had been issued. While it was an untraceable, no frills variety, it still contained a camera and retained the ability to take audio and video recordings.

"I know you'll want to listen to this yourself," said Allen, "but let me give you the shorthand version. Seems that Mark Argent spotted a guy surveilling our clean-up crew on Palomar Mountain. Argent held him at gunpoint. The guy claimed to be a private detective, working for Jenna Morrison. Which means she *did* get off the mountain alive, after all. He may have been attempting to capture one of our crew. A more charitable interpretation is that he was there to examine what he thought of as a crime scene."

"What's his name?"

"Don't know. Argent never used it, at least after he started recording."

Cargill frowned. "Go on."

"The PI had a camera on him. He claimed Jenna Morrison kept her whereabouts secret, even from him, but he claimed his camera had footage on it that would lead Argent to the girl. But when he was handing over the camera he somehow got the drop on Argent. Not sure exactly how it happened, but he took control."

Cargill nodded thoughtfully. This was a surprise. Like all the men on the team, Argent was top drawer.

"Not much later, Rourk arrived on the scene," continued Allen. "Argent thought he was there to help him." He blew out a long breath. "Until Rourk shot him to death."

Cargill's stomach tightened. Argent's death was bad enough, but a death caused by a *betrayal* was even worse. "You're positive the PI didn't shoot him?"

"Positive," said Allen. "First, Rourk made the PI drop his gun, and was holding him at gunpoint. And just in case there was any doubt remaining, Rourk later called in a report to a superior, who I'm assuming was Edgar Knight. Rourk admitted in his report that he had been, in his own words, 'forced to kill Argent.'"

Allen gave Cargill a few seconds to digest this and then continued. "Rourk also requested to come in, and reminded Knight that they still had one man on the inside."

"Exact words?" said Cargill.

"Yes."

"So he never said the name of our second mole?"

"I'm afraid not."

"Would it have been too much to ask for Rourk to use his partner's fucking name?" thundered Cargill in frustration.

Allen swallowed hard. "On the bright side, at least we know exactly what we're up against. Instead of thinking Rourk was the last of Knight's moles, or wondering if we were infected with several others, now we know the score."

Cargill nodded. "Yes, at least we have that."

"Unfortunately, you're going to like this next part even less," said Allen.

"Are you going to tell me, or just warn me?"

"Rourk was after Jenna Morrison," began Allen, wincing uncomfortably at having to be the bearer of even worse news. "But the PI told Rourk he was carrying a flash drive, which he claimed the girl had given him. One with Dr. Wexler's recent work on it. And now Rourk has it."

Cargill felt as though his heart were being squeezed in a vise. Could it be?

He considered this further and then shook his head. "I think it's fifty-fifty that the PI was bluffing," he said finally. "Our intel was certain that no trace of Wexler's work remained."

On the other hand, thought Cargill, even as he said this, garbage in, garbage out. Why should he trust his intel any more than he could trust his team? He had been told Wexler's work had only been backed up on a single hard drive, and they had obliterated Wexler's cloud storage account just to be certain.

But were there additional copies he had *not* been told about?

"It might have been a bluff," said Allen. "You can listen to the recording and make your own judgment. But from what I heard, Rourk was taking the guy very seriously. I even got the sense that Rourk had pre-knowledge that such a flash drive existed. He agreed to let the detective go in exchange for it."

"Still could have been a bluff. Rourk had to explore the possibility it was real. Just because he pretended to be willing to free the PI means nothing. I doubt he had any intention of keeping his word."

Cargill wondered whom he was trying to convince, Allen or himself. If the private eye had been telling the truth, this was an unmitigated *disaster*. Cargill realized he was grinding his teeth, a subconscious manifestation of his tension.

How had that fuck-head Knight gotten to Rourk, anyway?

Cargill turned his head toward the window and the dark skies beyond, deep in thought. He then turned back toward Allen and locked his eyes onto his subordinate's for what seemed like an eternity, not blinking for an inhumanly long period.

Could he trust this man? He had thought he could trust Rourk, after all. And while Edgar Knight had always been a strange duck, he had trusted him as well. Until he learned otherwise—the hard way.

Men were snakes. If God himself could be betrayed by an angel in Heaven—an angel named Satan, whom he was forced to cast out—certainly any man could be betrayed by any other man at any time.

He continued staring at Allen, who met his stare calmly, although he was forced to blink half a dozen times.

When Cargill had first learned that the men extracting Wexler had been ambushed, he had asked Allen point-blank why he should trust him, and Allen had reminded him of their history together. But now Cargill had even more reason to continue to trust this man. Hadn't Allen found Argent's phone? If he, too, were in league with Knight, he could have ignored the recording on the phone or deleted it. Instead, he had brought the recording to Cargill's attention, fingered Rourk, and given him Argent's phone.

And Allen's earlier response had been on point, as well. Cargill *had* known him longer than any of the other men now under his control. Allen *had* proven his loyalty time after time. Which were the very reasons he had chosen him to be his second-in-command. If Cargill had to choose someone to trust, he couldn't do better than Joe Allen.

Cargill finally broke eye contact with the man seated across the small table from him. "Is that everything?" he asked, breaking the long silence. "I assume Rourk and the PI both marched off into the night so Rourk could check out this supposed flash drive. Or did Rourk cap this unlucky bastard right after he got the drive? Have you looked for this PI's body in the woods?"

"No. Believe it or not," said Allen, shaking his head in wonder, "I'm all but positive the guy *escaped*. He was apparently throwing the flash drive to Rourk when a gunshot sounded. *Loudly*. Had to have been fired from the PI's gun, since the shots Rourk fired to kill Argent were silenced. And then Rourk cursed, the kind of screamed profanity you might expect out of someone who had just been shot."

"I assume you looked for Rourk's body as well."

"Yes. There was no evidence of either body anywhere within a half-mile radius of Argent's phone. My guess is that the PI escaped and Rourk got the flash drive."

"But you can't be certain of this."

"No."

Cargill paused to consider what he had just learned. Whoever Jenna Morrison had hired was very good, and the more he thought about it, the more convinced he became that the man was not a private investigator. He wasn't sure how the girl had dug him up, but he was quite formidable.

Argent and Rourk were seasoned pros, and being able to generate a brief distraction and then take advantage to turn the tables on each of them in turn demonstrated a level of skill, of real-world experience, that was even greater than theirs.

The range of skill between practiced experts and novices in every human endeavor was immense. A weekend tennis enthusiast could play a hundred games against Roger Federer and lose every point, every time. An average private investigator could try to slip the noose when held at gunpoint by the likes of Argent and Rourk, but he would lose every time, just as surely. He wouldn't have the practiced movements, the speed, the decisiveness, the boldness. This man had to have been supremely well trained and extremely experienced.

"Okay, Joe, good work," said Cargill finally. "I'm going to listen to the recording myself and do some thinking."

Allen nodded to acknowledge this dismissal and swiveled his chair around, locking it into place facing the same direction as his boss.

Cargill listened to the recording with great interest. He had to acknowledge Allen had done a good job of extracting all of the salient information.

Cargill had wanted to find Jenna Morrison, but this had been a low priority. Nathan Wexler had been critical. Jenna Morrison was simply a bystander who happened to be screwing the wrong genius at the wrong time.

But now things were very different. If Wexler's work really had survived, and his live-in girlfriend knew how to get her hands on it, that was a game-changer.

Knight having it was bad enough. But Knight having it without Cargill having it was *unthinkable*.

And this might explain one of Knight's recent moves. Cargill had sent e-mails to both the UCSD physics department and to Dan Walsh, pretending that Wexler was still alive, so he would have more time to clean up after himself.

But later, another message had been sent to Dan Walsh, also pretending to be from Wexler. A message which must have been sent by Edgar Knight. The message had reported that Jenna's computer was infected, and had warned Walsh to block any e-mails coming from her address. Knight must have known Cargill still had men on the UCLA physicist and was trying to make it harder for Cargill to reacquire the girl.

Cargill hadn't understood why Knight would go to the trouble. But maybe now he did.

Maybe Knight had known that Jenna had not only survived the attack, but also had access to another copy of her fiancé's work.

Now all Cargill could do was hope like hell that the flash drive Rourk now had was not legitimate. Either way, he had no other choice but to operate under the assumption that Jenna still had a copy of Wexler's work.

So Cargill either had to find her, immediately, or find a copy. It was his only hope.

His number one priority was still finding and eliminating Knight, as always. But finding Jenna Morrison had now been elevated to a close second.

And this private eye, or whoever he really was, seemed to be the key.

Cargill decided to play this out in his head, what the scientists he had worked with during his career called a *thought experiment*. He decided to pretend he was Jenna Morrison, being taken from her home Sunday night along with Nathan Wexler. Not being told why. Then being ambushed and escaping.

She had been very clever not to go to the cops. Hiring someone out of Cargill's easy reach, instead—a PI, or a mercenary, or whoever this guy was—was inspired.

But regardless of who she went to, or where she found him, she would need to explain what had happened to her. Would he believe her? And what would be his next moves?

Cargill imagined Jenna Morrison describing what had happened, reviewing that night from her perspective. If Cargill had just heard this story without any prior knowledge of the situation, he would want to investigate the scene of the ambush. And her PI had done exactly that.

What else would he have done? What else about her story could he explore?

Cargill's eyes widened as one interesting possibility presented itself. If the man was as good as Cargill now believed he was, he would want to pull street camera footage of the area near Wexler's home in La Jolla. He'd want to see the Hostess truck. Confirm it really was in a residential neighborhood at midnight on a Sunday. Hope to get lucky and see a license plate or a clean shot of the driver.

Cargill had made sure this footage had been doctored immediately, since he insisted that Q5 needed to be fanatically thorough when they cleaned up after themselves. And then he had forgotten all about the footage.

But the man now working for Jenna Morrison wouldn't know this was a dead end. So he would try to get the video. For Cargill to find the PI in this way, the man would have had to come up with the idea and then have the necessary connections to be able to obtain the footage. This was unlikely, but well worth following up on.

Cargill undid his seatbelt and walked the short distance to Joe Allen, whose eyes were now shut. He might have just been resting, or he might be sound asleep, but Cargill couldn't have cared less. "Joe," he said loudly, pausing until Allen's eyes slid open, which they did almost immediately.

"Yes?" mumbled Allen.

"I need you to find out if anyone asked for street camera footage around Wexler's home the night of the extraction. If anyone did, I want to know who they are, and everything about them. Everything."

He paused, and a fiery expression came over his face. "And Joe, it goes without saying this is extremely urgent, and extremely confidential. I don't want you to bring anyone else on the team in on it."

Allen nodded grimly. "Roger that," he said.

21

Jenna spent the rest of the drive to Blake's apartment bringing Walsh fully up to speed on all the events that had taken place since she had returned from Chicago, just the night before.

It was just so fantastic. Walsh struggled to wrap his mind around it all, and the news of Nathan's death continued to hit him hard, as he hadn't had any time to internalize it.

Jenna had been operating on precious little sleep for some time now, and even though it was before nine she was already in danger of flaming out. Blake made a pot of instant coffee, heavy on the caffeine, and Jenna readied herself to drink the entire pot if this was what it took to keep her awake. Given that the entire pot was meant only for her, since neither of her companions were coffee drinkers, this was a real possibility. Walsh elected to nurse a bottle of spring water, and their host chose no beverage at all.

Blake printed out three copies of Nathan's e-mail message from Walsh's cloud account, so they could easily refer to it, and they each took a seat around his kitchen table.

"All right, Dan," began Jenna when they had settled in and had each reread the e-mail, extraordinary as it was. "We have to assume that Nathan was on to something, and that he's right in every regard, agreed?"

"I think for the sake of discussion this makes sense," replied the physicist.

"And let's take it to the extreme," said Jenna. "Let's pretend he'd be able to send something back a full half-second." She whistled. "An entire half-second. Let's go crazy. Doesn't really give you the chance to witness the birth of Christ or see a dinosaur, but I guess the universe makes the rules."

"Let's definitely use the half-second," said Blake. "Trying to think in terms of . . ." He paused in mid-sentence to consult the text of Nathan's e-mail. "Forty-five microseconds," he added, "is impossible for me. It's just too short a time to understand." He looked at Dan Walsh. "So I guess if a millisecond is a thousandth of a second, a microsecond is what, a millionth of a second?"

"Exactly right," said the physicist. "Nathan seems absolutely certain he can push back forty-five millionths of a second in time. And *nearly* certain he can repeat these increments to get to just under a half-second. So I agree with Jenna, let's assume a half-second is feasible."

"So why would anyone care?" said Jenna. "That's the million-dollar question."

Time travel stories were legion, she knew. It was one of the most popular categories of literature ever, especially during the last few generations. The number of stories, novels, TV shows, and movies in which time travel was used seemed infinite. Time travel had once been the purview of hard science fiction, but it was now not only featured in adventures and mysteries, but in comedies, and most surprising of all, the romance genre.

She had never really thought about it, but what was it that made this category so versatile, so universally popular?

The answer came to her the moment she formulated the question. First, time travel played into fantasies shared by every living human being. Who wouldn't want to go back in time and correct a mistake, right a wrong, change how things turned out? Who wouldn't want to have another chance to win the girl, or hit the home run? To kill Hitler, or invest in Apple or Facebook when they were just emerging?

The possibilities for redemption, for profit, and for revenge were endless and profound.

And then there were the paradoxes. Each story could be written to blow minds, as Mobius strip pretzels lovingly constructed and twisted with glee to intrigue and delight an audience. Twists upon twists upon twists, with intricate and startling reveals.

Time, like gravity, was a barrier thrown up by an unyielding universe. Mankind had always railed against both of these barriers, forever fantasizing about their eventual defeat.

But with respect to pushing back against the inexorable flow of time, it now seemed this wasn't a fantasy any longer.

"Nathan was right, of course," continued Jenna. "Even a half-second is far too short to make good use of. Five minutes, sure. You could do a lot with five minutes. Win the lottery. Avert a disaster. But half a second?"

"I know Nathan thinks time travel will harness this immense, um . . . quintessence energy safely," said Blake, "but can we be sure of that? What if this really could be turned into the ultimate bomb? Could this be what's driving all of the interest?"

He paused. "I read a novel when I was a kid called *The Weapon Shops of Isher*. It was science fiction, yes, but if Nathan's discovery doesn't verge on the science fictional, nothing does. In the novel, a man ends up traveling ages and ages back through time. But for every year back he goes, he accumulates more and more energy, until it grows to *incomprehensible* levels. Finally, when he arrives billions and billions of years in the past, this energy is released—*explosively*."

"I read that one, too," said Walsh enthusiastically. "Talk about paradoxes. If I'm remembering correctly, he doesn't just explode, he's carrying so much energy he actually causes the *big bang*. So this time traveler turns out to be responsible for nothing less than the birth of the universe."

Blake smiled. "That's the one," he said. "Anyway, I know this is taking it to extremes, but Nathan acknowledged that he'd have to use crazy amounts of energy to pull this time travel thing off. Enough to shred the planet. He says his calculations show all of the energy will be used up safely, but what if he's wrong? What if it works like in this science fiction story?"

Jenna drained the last of her coffee and considered this possibility further. "It's an interesting thought," she said. "And I'm drawing a blank on any alternatives. But my gut tells me this isn't it. First, the guy at my house, the one I held off with some wine, he told me this was potentially dangerous, but that it was *not* an explosive. He could have been lying, but for some reason I believed him. And Nathan wouldn't have written he was sure this was safe, unless, well . . . unless he was sure it was safe. And would those after this really be so zealous about something they couldn't even be sure would happen?"

Jenna shrugged. "I'd also argue that we already have bombs that can destroy the world. So even if time travel could result in an even greater explosive force, so what?"

"I agree with Jenna," said Walsh.

Blake nodded. "I don't see any flaws in her reasoning myself."

Jenna rose and poured herself another cup of coffee. It was keeping her awake for now, but she knew that she would pay later for this artificial boost to her wakefulness.

Meanwhile, Blake and Walsh were lost in thought, and from their expressions neither were reaching any epiphanies.

"Okay, so we're dealing with a half-second," mumbled Blake, his hand stroking his chin absently. "*We* can't react in any meaningful way in this amount of time. But what about computers? For a computer, a half-second is a huge amount of time. So say you programmed a computer to see an uptick in a stock's price, send this information back to itself a half-second earlier, and put in a buy order."

"I'm not a stock expert, Aaron," said Walsh, "but I'm still pretty certain this wouldn't work. Your computer would be fast enough to take the information from a half-second in its future and put in a buy order, but you could never *fill* the order in time. Even if you could, second to second variations in stock prices are minuscule. And even if you could catch these minuscule upswings, the price could easily go down during the *next* half-second."

Temporarily out of ideas, they decided to read Nathan's e-mail once again. Jenna was nearly finished with yet another cup of liquid stimulant, but yawns were beginning to come periodically and she knew she was ultimately fighting a losing battle.

Jenna finished rereading the e-mail and turned to Dan Walsh. "Nathan mentions something called Hawking's chronology protection conjecture," she said. "Do you know what he means by this?"

"I do," replied Walsh. "For much of history scientists believed time travel was absolutely impossible. But over the last several decades, some prominent physicists from elite universities are beginning to believe it is possible, at least theoretically."

"Why the change of heart?" asked Jenna.

"Well, just so you know," replied Walsh, "it's been clear for quite a while that the laws of physics work perfectly well in either time direction: forward *or* backward. In the 1940s, Richard Feynman showed that anti-matter—which is a real thing, by the way—is identical, mathematically, to ordinary matter traveling backward in time. He used this insight to develop a tool, called Feynman diagrams, that revolutionized nearly every aspect of theoretical physics. So much so that he was awarded the Nobel Prize for this work."

"So time travel may be possible," said Jenna, "in *theory*. But has anyone ever generated any experimental evidence?"

"There's some evidence that the future can affect the present. It's called retrocausality. The experiments are largely in the realm of quantum physics and are too complicated to describe. But Yakir Aharonov and Jeff Tollaksen came up with what I think is a great way for the layman to think about this. Basically, it is known that if you take two radioactive atoms, absolutely identical in every conceivable way, they will decay randomly. The first might decay immediately, while the second doesn't decay for an hour. But they are *identical*, and there is no way to predict when this decay will occur. And scientists have never identified any possible causes that would produce these effects. So Aharonov reasoned that if the information that controls the particles' behavior doesn't come from the past or present, maybe it comes from the future. Retrocausality. Cause and effect in reverse."

"This is all mind-blowing stuff," said Blake. "But one thing I'm confused about." He stopped and grinned. "Okay, I'm confused about *all* of it, but there is one thing I'm *most* confused about. You said the laws of physics work equally well backwards or forwards in time. If this is the case, why does time seem to have a direction?"

"Good question," said Walsh. "There are a number of reasons. One of them you just hit on: our perception. We only ever experience time moving in one direction. But probably the most cited reason is something called entropy, also called the second law of thermodynamics, a concept that has tremendous utility in physics. This principle basically states that things tend to go from being ordered to disordered—in one time direction only. The universe has been running down, in a single direction, since its birth. For example, people have witnessed a crystal goblet being thrown at a brick fireplace and shattering into a thousand pieces. The glass goes from ordered to disordered. But it never goes the other way. No one has ever seen a thousand pieces of glass hurled at a brick fireplace spontaneously assemble into a crystal goblet."

Jenna and Blake tried to digest what they were being told, with limited success.

"This is all fascinating," said Jenna to the physicist. "But you were trying to answer my first question, and I got you off on a tangent before you got there."

"Right," he said. "You asked about the chronology protection conjecture. As I mentioned, serious scientists have begun to take time travel seriously. But Kip Thorne and Stephen Hawking aren't buying it. Thorne says his studies suggest that all time machines would self-destruct upon activation, perhaps the universe's way of eliminating all those fun, head-scratching time travel conundrums. Hawking believes that while the equations of quantum mechanics suggest time travel is possible, the universe will refuse to allow it, since this would be its unraveling. He half-jokingly called this the *chronology protection conjecture.* The conjecture basically states that the laws of physics will conspire to prevent time travel. Which has the effect, as Hawking puts it, of 'Keeping the world safe for historians.'"

Jenna and Blake both smiled at this.

"A broader definition of this conjecture *allows* time travel," continued Walsh, "but only if it doesn't create a paradox. So let's examine a classic paradox. Say you go back in time and kill your mother when she was a little girl. If you did that, then how were you born? But if you were never born, how did you kill your mother?"

Walsh took a drink from his plastic bottle of water and let his companions ponder this for a moment. "But if you couldn't kill her because you were never born," he continued, "then you *would* be born. So now you *could* kill her. It's a circle with no beginning or end."

Walsh arched one eyebrow. "So the broader version of the chronology protection conjecture would say you could go back in time to when your mother was a little girl. But if you were intent on *killing* her, one of two things would happen: One, time travel would suddenly stop working for you until you decided matricide wasn't a good idea. Or two, it *would* work, but something would prevent you from succeeding. Has always prevented you. Will always prevent you."

"Believe it or not," said Blake, "I've actually read a story about Hawking's conjecture. You jogged my memory. It was called *The Chronology Protection Case,* and it was in an anthology of detective stories. A physicist hires a detective after a fellow physicist dies in mysterious circumstances. Before too long they discover that a large group of physicists, who all collaborated on a paper, are dropping like flies, each dying in freakishly unlikely ways. Eventually, the detective comes to realize it's the chronology projection conjecture in action. Seems the entire group was about to publish results on time travel, and the universe was acting to protect itself. The detective, himself, has two freak accidents that put him near death, and begins to realize the universe is nudging him to convince the last remaining physicist to lie about the work, and discredit it, to stay alive, ensuring time travel never happens."

"Great idea for a story," said Walsh. "Apparently, you do *not* want to piss off the universe," he added with a broad grin.

Jenna smiled as well. She never thought she'd see the entire universe compared to a mob enforcer, protecting its interests. "Could this be why a half-second is the limit?" she said thoughtfully. "Because the universe is making sure we don't have enough time to create a paradox?"

Walsh shook his head. "The half-second limit wouldn't, *necessarily*, ensure that," he said. "I'm sure you've heard the term *Chaos Theory*, often called the *butterfly effect*. This just means there are certain systems for which the slightest change in initial conditions can cause huge effects, huge uncertainty in the end result. Edward Lorenz was one of the early pioneers—by accident. He was modeling weather systems, and he wanted to repeat an analysis he had already done, entering interim results by hand. The computer he used calculated numbers to six decimal places, but to save time he truncated them to just three. Instead of entering .546124, he entered only .546. He never thought in a million years this minuscule change would matter in the least. Only it did. It had huge effects on the end results—changed everything."

Jenna had never heard this story but was fascinated by it. "So you're saying that the reverberations of going back less than a second and making even the smallest change aren't predictable, and could be a lot more profound than we could guess?"

Walsh beamed, a proud professor delighted by a talented student. "I couldn't have said it better myself," he said. "Still, despite this, I believe you're right. A half-second limit may well prevent major paradoxes, so the universe isn't under threat. But even if there is no chronology protection, even if time travel is the Wild West and anything goes, Chaos Theory suggests you can't control it. And you can't know for sure what impact a change might have."

Jenna was utterly spellbound by this discussion, and her body chose to demonstrate her enthusiasm by forcing a prolonged yawn, and then another. She shot Walsh an apologetic look as he continued.

"Just to finish the thought," he said, "let me take an example from the iconic time travel movie, *Back to The Future*. I love this movie, but it revolves around human conception, which provides a perfect example of how you can never replicate history, never step in the same river twice."

Walsh took another quick gulp of water and then continued. "Marty McFly changes the past and has to fix it. He has to be sure his parents still marry so he and his siblings can be conceived. But this is absurd. Even if Marty gets his parents together, they'll fall in love in a slightly different way, with different timing. A billion tiny variables are changed, meaning the orgasm his father had that led to Marty's conception can never happen the exact same way. Even if there were only a single change created, say the proverbial butterfly from Chaos Theory flying through the bedroom window when his parents were having sex, this might cause his father's ejaculation to be delayed by Nathan's forty-five microseconds. Even this minute change would mean that this time around, the sperm that has Marty's name on it won't outrace the other hundreds of millions of sperm to the goal. Some other sperm will penetrate the egg instead. Or maybe no sperm will make it and his parents will have to try again. So even if Marty gets his parents together, he can never put the genie back in the bottle."

Jenna's eyes swam out of focus and she shook her head vigorously in response. She rose and poured herself a third cup of coffee, wrinkling up her nose in disgust at the thought of forcing it down, but she was determined to remain alert until they had exhausted all possibilities.

"Nathan also mentioned something called a block universe," said Blake. "What's that?"

"Time isn't my area of expertise," said Walsh, "but I do know the rudiments. But rather than address the questions Nathan posed in his e-mail piecemeal, I think it would be better if I gave a crash course on the nature of time itself. That way you can both put everything into context."

Jenna glanced at Aaron Blake, who nodded his assent.

"Lecture on," she said, unable to fight off yet another yawn. "We're all ears."

22

"Sorry I couldn't take your calls earlier, Jack," said Edgar Knight, a three-dimensional view of his always-intense face hovering in the air above the phone Jack Rourk had purchased from a store at the foot of Palomar Mountain, fortunately open until nine. "I always seem to be fighting fires."

"I understand completely," said Rourk.

And he did understand, only too well. Which is why he couldn't help but be pissed off at his boss, who had seen his calls come in repeatedly two hours earlier but had chosen to ignore them, deciding that whatever he was doing had to be more important than what Rourk might have to report.

Knight was very smart and had probably decided that for Rourk to escort his private eye down the mountain and to a secure location would be laborious and time-consuming, and would probably include having to knock the hostage unconscious for an extended period before reviving and interrogating him more fully. Knight had assumed Rourk's earlier calls were to provide an interim update.

But this wasn't the reason for the calls at all. Knight could never have guessed that Rourk had found the winning lottery ticket. Had he known, no power on Earth would have prevented him from taking his calls immediately.

Fighting fires, my ass, thought Rourk, barely managing to keep from scowling.

"So what do you have to report?" said Knight impatiently. He leaned in closer, as though examining Rourk's image on his own screen more closely. "What's wrong with your arm?" he asked.

"The private eye that I had in my sights was better than I thought. He shot me."

Knight's lip curled up in anger and disgust. "So what are you saying?" he barked. "You lost him! The perfect link to the girl!"

"I didn't lose him," replied Rourk. "I *let* him get away. And only because I have great news that makes the search for Jenna Morrison irrelevant."

And thanks for asking if I'm okay after being shot, he thought. *I managed a field dressing, and it's heavily bandaged, but I'll be good as new.*

"What are you talking about?" demanded Knight, as though ready to choke the life out of the holographic image in front of him.

"I have the flash drive," announced Rourk triumphantly. "Jenna Morrison gave it to this guy for safekeeping, and I was able to get it. I had the choice of either retrieving the drive or going after the PI."

Knight's hostile expression transformed into a broad smile immediately. "Outstanding work, Jack," he said in delight. "Apologies for doubting you. You made the right choice." He pursed his lips. "Can I assume the drive is undamaged?"

"It is. It's password protected, as you already know, but in perfect condition."

"Bring it in. As soon as you can. Get a few hours sleep and then get it here by eight in the morning."

"I *should* be able to make that," said Rourk. "But I can't guarantee it. I need to ditch this car and get new transportation, since I have no doubt my ex-comrades are searching for me by now."

"I understand. I guess you won't be getting any sleep, after all. Don't steal a car. We don't want any more heat on you. Find a car rental place that's still open. If there isn't one around you, I know the ones at the San Diego airport are open until eleven or midnight, so drive there if you have to. I assume you have alternate ID you can use for the rental?"

"Yes."

"Good. So get a car and get your ass, and that flash drive, over here. And be sure to drive at the speed limit. Got it?"

"Understood."

"Great. And Jack . . . fantastic work."

Knight was about to end the connection when he noticed Rourk's arm once again. "Oh, and Jack, try not to lose too much blood. I need you to make it here. I'll be sure to have a doctor standing by to patch up your arm when you arrive."

"That would be helpful," said Rourk, not exactly overwhelmed by Knight's concern for his health.

23

"Time is a nightmare," began Dan Walsh simply. "No subject is so utterly intuitive, and also counter-intuitive, at the same time. It's a subject that really messes with your head. And the more you know about it, the more this is true. The intuitive perception of time for most of us is that we are trapped in an instant of time, but one that seems to be moving. This moment, the precise instant I'm telling you about this, is *now*. But this *now* becomes the past an instant later, before I've even finished my next word. We're the needle on a record player. We stay in an infinitesimally thin band we call *now*, while the past and future are continually unreachable on either side. At least until the future decides to intersect with our infinitesimally thin needle and play a note."

Blake blew out a breath. "Wow. You just started, and I'm already getting a headache."

Walsh laughed. "Don't worry, it will get much worse."

He gathered his thoughts and continued. "As far back as five centuries before the birth of Christ, a Greek philosopher named Zeno was already assembling a host of thought experiments to try to understand time. My favorite that addresses the meaning of the ever-frozen, but ever-moving, *now,* is called *the arrow*.

"Imagine two arrows, one shot from a powerful bow, and one held horizontally and dropped straight down from above. Now imagine a time when the dropped arrow is precisely above the shot arrow. Take a snapshot of just this instant, frozen in time."

Walsh paused for a moment to let Jenna and Blake visualize this in their minds. "Okay, your photograph will show two arrows, perfectly still, one above the other. And they will look identical in every way. In this precise instant of time, they *are* identical in every way. So how do they get to the next instant of time? And how does one arrow know to move toward the target in the next frame, and one arrow know to begin falling straight down? If time really is divided into infinitesimal moments, infinitesimal *nows*, and in each one the arrow shot from the bow isn't moving at all, what is it about the passage of time that informs the arrow where to be at the next moment?"

Jenna groaned. "Please tell me you don't want us to really try to answer that," she said.

"No. I'm just trying to give you a sense of some of the questions that have been asked throughout history. To ease you into the subject," he added with a smile.

"But if we forget about Zeno for a moment," continued Walsh, "time is the most intuitive concept there is. Right? At least if we don't think too hard about it. Who doesn't know what time is? We get it. Einstein once quipped that time's only purpose was to make sure that everything didn't happen at once.

"But when you really think about it, time is also the *least* intuitive concept there is. How fast does time travel? And *does* time travel? Or do you travel through *time*? And if you do travel through time, at what rate are you moving?"

The physicist shrugged. "After all, speed is about how far we move in a given *time*. You drive your car at sixty miles . . . *per hour*. You walk to the store at two feet . . . *per second*. But how fast does time *itself* move?" asked Walsh, throwing out his hands in a gesture of helplessness. "At one second per second?"

He rolled his eyes. "That's like saying you're walking at a mile per mile. It's absolutely an absurd and useless concept."

"Well, take the Einstein quote," said Jenna, proud that she could still channel semi-coherent thoughts in her state of weariness. "The one you just cited. He said time exists to prevent everything from happening at once. Which implies that time is change. A car moves forward. The hand of a clock ticks. And time elapses, moves on."

"Excellent. This is called the *relational theory* of time. People who believe this believe time can only be gauged with respect to change. It's an absolute requirement. Without change, time can't exist. *With* change you have *befores* and *afters*. First you weren't watching TV.

Now you are." Walsh smiled. "If you believe this theory, then you believe time could not exist before there was a universe."

Blake thought about this for a few seconds and shook his head. "I get why this would be," he said. "But my gut feel is that time still passed, even before the birth of the universe."

"I would tend to agree with the relational theory," said Jenna. "Without a universe, there can be no change. Without change, no time."

"There are those on both sides of this issue," said Walsh. "But already you can see how tricky time can be. And it seems fairly clear to me that change is also a requirement for humans to perceive the passage of time. We lay down memory. Our memory changes, and we know that time has passed. Even if we're just thinking with our eyes closed, we have certain thoughts that didn't used to be there, but are now. Before and after. Imagine you were given drugs to knock you out for an eight-hour surgery. No dreaming, no thinking, no observing. Did you experience time during these eight hours? If I told you I gave you the wrong dose of anesthetic and you were really only out for eight *minutes*, would you know I was lying?"

"I doubt it," said Blake. "You make a very interesting point."

"Newton thought time was an absolute," continued Walsh. "Dependable. But Einstein turned this on its ear. He realized that space and time could not be separated. They form the fabric of what he called space-time. Not three dimensions, but four. Newton thought you and your friend would always—always—agree on the timing of an event, agree on when something happened. But Einstein proved this was wrong. *You* might see event A happen *before* event B, while I might see the exact opposite, depending on our velocities and positions. The faster something moves through space, the slower it moves through time. If you were traveling at the speed of light, time would stop altogether."

Jenna nodded. "Nathan explained to me that this has been proven over and over. That Einstein's theory is used to correct the timing of GPS satellites, or they wouldn't work correctly. And particles that decay very quickly take much longer to decay when they're traveling near the speed of light, the precise delay predicted by Einstein's equations."

"Exactly," said Walsh enthusiastically. "It turns out that while objects can move through space and time at different rates, they all move through *space-time* at exactly the same rate: the speed of light. Always."

"I'm not following," said Blake. "You can't mean to say that right now, sitting at this table, we're all moving at the speed of light."

"Through space-time, yes, that's exactly what I'm saying. When you're not moving at all in space, you're moving at the speed of light, so to speak, through *time*—the fastest the universe allows you to do so. When you're moving at the speed of light through *space*, you stop moving through *time*. It stops completely. It turns out that your speed through space, combined with your speed through time, always adds up to the speed of light."

"You've lost me," said Blake. "How do you add your speed through time, which I thought we decided wasn't even measurable, to your speed through space?"

"Good question. It's a bit complicated, and not important at the moment. What is important is what this theory says about the nature of time. It suggests that just like all of space is laid out at once, so is all of time. This is called the *block universe*, which you had asked about, Aaron. In the theorized block universe, everything that *has* happened, or *will* happen, is already set in stone. And no particular 'now' is privileged."

"What does that mean?" said Jenna.

"It means that when you're here and your friend is in New York, you believe that both places are equally real, right? Both exist, and neither location has a better claim to being real than the other."

Jenna and Blake both nodded.

"The same should be true of time. Why is this instant, this now, privileged? Why is it any more real than the instant you experienced years ago, or will experience years in the future? It's all there, all of time, already laid out in its entirety, our consciousness just isn't designed to see it. Einstein wrote that for physicists like himself, the distinction between past, present, and future was only a stubborn illusion. And we're talking about the entire life of the *universe*. From the big bang to the universe's death, it's all laid out. Every point in time existing in a block with every other point, simultaneously. All equally real, and all with an equal claim to the designation of *now*."

Blake shook his head, as though not wanting to believe this could be true. "So what does that say about free will?" he asked.

"Great question. Doesn't bode well, does it?"

"I used to tape football games on occasion for later viewing," said Blake. "I'd watch knowing that whatever I was about to see happen, had already happened. I just didn't know what that was. I could gradually watch it unfold, and it would be a surprise to *me*, but it was already set in stone, like you said."

He tilted his head, remembering. "Once I watched a replay of a game after someone accidentally told me the Saints had won. So I'm watching, and with nine minutes left in the game the Saints are down twenty-three points. So even though I know how it ends, it seems impossible to me that this could be right. Surely there's been some kind of glitch in reality. Surely the universe will now correct for this. But, of course, it didn't. The Saints scored a quick touchdown, followed that up with a pick six, recovered an onside kick, and so on. They kicked a winning field goal with one second left in the game."

A troubled look crossed Blake's face. "So is this really what the universe is? A preordained game that has already been played? We can cheer however we want to, but we can't affect the outcome."

"Very possibly, yes," said Walsh. "There are many brilliant scientists who believe this, just as Einstein did. And many who don't. I love the football analogy. Another good way to think of the block universe theory is to compare it to an old-fashioned movie. A movie made up of thousands and thousands of frames that are quickly moved through the projector to create the illusion of motion. We're like players in this movie. We experience the frames sequentially, but the full movie has already been made, and is already loaded into the projector. The last frame exists every bit as much as the first, even if we can't see it. But the movie plays out as it has to. Inexorably. Inevitably. It's all there on the reel, unchangeable."

"Sounds pretty horrible," said Jenna.

"It really does," said Walsh.

Blake wore a dour expression. "But like you said, we aren't *certain* this is the case, right?" he asked, looking for reassurance.

"Right. Einstein's work supports this view, but we can't be sure. Sometimes I think the block universe theory is correct and I'm quite troubled by it. But I've also found the idea comforting at times. If I'm struggling with a problem, I tell myself, it doesn't matter, either I solved it, or I didn't. Either things worked out, or they didn't. But either way it's already happened. It's already locked in. Just as the past has already been laid down and I have no power to change it, so has the future. I just don't know it yet."

Jenna sighed. "I have to agree with your first statement, Dan," she said. "Time is a nightmare. This must be why Nathan seemed so excited that he could use his discovery to perform actual experiments and test these ideas."

"Exactly," said Walsh. "Nathan's work could help us get a handle on time, and time travel, potentially leading to major breakthroughs we have yet to imagine."

"But would people really get this excited, this quickly?" said Blake. "Enough to kill haphazardly? Just so they can do some experiments?"

"You wouldn't think so," agreed Walsh.

Jenna knew she was now just minutes away from falling into a coma. She had continued to yawn periodically as Walsh had spoken and had choked down all the coffee she could bear. She just hoped she could fight through it just a little longer.

She turned to Walsh. "So what are some of the time travel theories he'd be able to test? In Nathan's e-mail, he mentioned branching timelines and so on. Could you run through the possibilities?"

"I'm far from an expert on time travel theory," said Walsh. "But I have read and seen my share of time travel stories. I can't imagine there's any soil that hasn't already been tilled by a century of science fiction writers." He shrugged. "I'm sure you two know as much about this as I do."

Blake sighed deeply. "That may be, Dan, but I have no doubt you'll do a better job of analyzing and organizing all of it. So why don't you start us off."

"I'd be happy to," said Walsh.

He paused for a long moment in thought. "We've already discussed one idea. That the universe won't allow the past to be changed. It will protect itself. The other end of the spectrum is that it will allow it, and the tiniest change is amplified through time and has profound effects. There's a famous story by Ray Bradbury about a group who goes back in time sixty-five million years to the age of the dinosaur. They have a discussion about the possible ramifications of killing a single mouse there. One character thinks it's no big deal, but the other explains that killing that one mouse also kills all of its future descendants, possibly billions of future mice over millions of years. And for want of mice, other species up the food chain die off, finally leading to a cave-man dying for lack of food, one who wouldn't have died otherwise. A critical cave-man at a critical juncture in human development, when mankind was hanging on by a thread. So killing one mouse sixty-five million years ago can lead to the extinction of the human race."

"Good thing we can only go back half a second, then," said Blake with a smile.

Jenna laughed. "Yeah. Even mice can't breed *that* fast," she said wryly.

"There is also a possibility that is basically the opposite of this," continued the physicist. "That time absorbs changes, big and small. That it has an inertia, and it absorbs blows and quickly returns to its course. Like throwing a large rock into a raging river. The rock might change the course of the river slightly, and briefly, but its effect downstream is virtually zero."

"So what about branching timelines?" asked Blake. "I think I have a feel for them from the movies, but I'd like your take."

Walsh paused in thought. "It seems to me that there are two major possibilities," he began. "One, there is only one timeline. If you change your past, you change events after this, either dramatically or with great difficulty. In this case, provided the universe lets you change things, you get endless paradoxes, which is why this one is the more interesting for time travel stories. You can get all kinds of cool circular stuff. Man A sends instructions for an invention to man B in the past. But the only reason man A knew the instructions is because B had already invented it. But the only reason B invented it is because he received instructions from A. So how was it invented in the first place?"

"So the cleaner alternative is the multiple timeline one," said Blake.

"I think that's right," agreed Walsh. "Because you really can't get any paradoxes. The moment you change the past in any way, at that point, time splits, and you have two different universes. One in which the change happened and one in which it never did. So if you kill your mom before you were born, a new timeline branches off. You went back in time and killed your mom, but *not* the mom on *your* timeline—so you could still be born. You killed your mom at the very start of a *different* timeline. On this new branch, most everything in the universe is the same, except you aren't born. Still, as far as you, the murderer, are concerned, the original branch remains intact, and your life and timeline remain unchanged."

"So how could Nathan's discovery be used to differentiate between the two possibilities?" said Blake.

Walsh opened his mouth to reply when he noticed that Jenna had lost her battle and was dead asleep on the chair, her head lolled to the side.

"Maybe we ought to finish this discussion another time," said Blake, being careful to keep his voice to a whisper, although, given Jenna's state of exhaustion, he probably could have screamed this out without waking her.

Walsh nodded. "We all have a lot to sleep on. Maybe while we're sleeping one of us will have an epiphany and figure out what we're missing."

"Maybe," said Blake, but he said it in such a way that it was clear he didn't believe it for a moment.

24

As the ground continued to streak by far below him, Lee Cargill had out an old-fashioned college-ruled notebook and jotted notes with an actual pen that spread ink, something that was increasingly rare in the digital age.

He needed to be well prepared for his meeting with President Janney. He had to report what had happened and insist that a new base be built just for Q5, one designed to his strict security specifications, ensuring they wouldn't need to scurry from underground base to underground base like cockroaches after a light was turned on.

Having Q5's Palomar Mountain headquarters blown, his people temporarily scattered, and their semis hurriedly relocated, was humiliating. So he also needed to recommend a temporary headquarters, knowing he would need to decapitate the remaining snake in the weeds before the move to a more permanent location.

And he had to get Janney to agree to let Q5 become the blackest of Black Ops organizations. Which meant that Janney would be the last president to know of it. Whoever followed him into the White House would not be read in.

Presidents could be fickle and arbitrary. Each new one with wildly different visions and priorities. And when all was said and done, they were nothing more than civilians who managed to get donors excited enough to give them money, and then win a popularity contest. They weren't the smartest or best trained that humanity had to offer, and they didn't have the best judgment. The truly brilliant, truly gifted, wanted little to do with politics.

Cargill scowled. Besides, this was *his* ship. *He* was the captain. Which meant he was the ultimate authority, certainly not a flavor-of-the-week president.

So far, he had let the current resident of the White House maintain the illusion that he was in control, making pilgrimages to the man like a supplicant, a beggar, dancing for coins. Cargill had too many other worries to let this illusion lapse at the moment, but he wasn't about to assent to letting another politician interfere, another commander in chief who knew less about the realities of actual command than the greenest new recruit.

Cargill was still organizing his thoughts for his meeting the next morning when Joe Allen swiveled his chair around to face his boss once again. Cargill looked up from his notepad. "Yes?"

"Someone did pull video footage from street cameras near Wexler's home," reported Allen. "A woman named R. Sylvia Tagert. She's CIA. Reporting through the Directorate of Intelligence. She's a civilian, but has considerable field experience. Was stationed in Yemin, Afghanistan, and Syria as part of counter-terrorism operations there. Worked with select spec ops individuals and groups when necessary. Excellent performance reviews." He paused. "I've already sent her full dossier to your computer so you can read in whatever depth you'd like."

"She sounds like the type our guy might know. So who did she send the video to?"

Allen frowned. "I woke up a top computer guy at Langley, since you wanted me to stay away from our own people. He hacked into her computer, but she had left no traces of where she sent the video. We tried to get her phone records, but she's high enough in the CIA pecking order to have a phone that shields this information."

"So you're telling me she left no traces, and you don't have any idea who she pulled the video for?"

Allen nodded unhappily. "Yeah, I'm afraid that's what I'm telling you."

Cargill digested this for several seconds. "Is *she* stationed at Langley?"

"No. She's currently based at a facility at Palm Springs, California. One disguised as a think tank."

"California?" said Cargill, rolling his eyes. "Really?"

Allen shrugged. "The CIA has a number of offices in California."

"I know that, Joe. I was just thinking this was bad luck for you."

"How so?"

"I needed you for a few projects in DC, but this takes priority. And until I have more confidence in the trustworthiness of our current team, I need to lean on you more heavily than ever. I need you to get the information from her. *Yesterday*. And we can't be sure that pulling rank over the phone will do it. We need you to be in her face, an intimidating presence who won't take no for an answer."

He gave Allen an apologetic look. "I'm afraid when we land in DC, I'll need to have a jet standing by to take you back to California immediately."

Allen sighed. "Not a problem," he said. "I can get a few hours sleep on the way back. And it isn't exactly as though I'm flying coach with a screaming infant behind me."

"I know I'm losing time by sending you there instead of one of our team already in California, but this is too important to send someone whose loyalties aren't absolutely certain. I need you to find out who she was helping, and get the information to me immediately. I don't care if I'm in the powder room with the fucking president—interrupt me."

"Roger that," mumbled Allen.

"While you're flying back, I'll randomly activate a team on the West Coast. One we haven't worked with before, so we're sure they haven't been contaminated by Knight. I'll have them standing by so I can field them at a moment's notice."

"Can I assume you'll want me to lead this team on whatever op you end up assigning them to?" said Allen.

"Yes. And one more thing. Once you have the identity of our private eye, or private eye impersonator as the case may be, you obviously can't let this Sylvia Tagert tip him off that we're coming."

"Obviously," repeated Joe Allen grimly.

25

"Jack Rourk is at the outer perimeter of the property," said the deep, masculine voice of Edgar Knight's personal digital assistant, responding to his command that he was to be informed when this happened.

"Throw him up on the monitor," said Knight to his PDA, which he had named Lazlo.

Lazlo did as requested, and a car appeared on a three-dimensional screen that filled up an entire wall of Knight's twenty-second-floor penthouse office.

"Welcome back to Lake Las Vegas, Jack," whispered Knight excitedly under his breath. The flash drive couldn't get there fast enough.

Security around Knight's spectacular Lake Las Vegas headquarters was as impenetrable as it was invisible. The sprawling campus appeared harmless, even tranquil, but it was anything but.

Even the outermost perimeter, miles from the island and its numerous buildings, was secure. If this was crossed without the proper wireless signal having first been received from a bracelet or ring that his people all wore, indicating whoever was crossing was authorized to be doing so, electronic and human eyes would lock onto the trespasser immediately. Cameras were everywhere, and facial recognition was state of the art.

And this was only the beginning. Once through the second perimeter, even those whose jewelry had broadcast the proper codes were scanned for authenticity. Knight's Brain Trust had recently come up with dramatic advances in biometric scanning that would have been worth billions if Knight had any interest in sharing this technology with the world.

Like highway scanners that could collect tolls electronically as cars rushed by, these biometric scanners could detect retina prints, heart rate, and even brain activity from passengers in closed vehicles moving at up to five miles an hour. Since cars proceeding to the island were forced to slow to a crawl to pass a series of the most treacherous speed bumps ever constructed, this wasn't an issue.

If security ever had a question about an approaching person or vehicle, the interlopers could be stopped and queried by other people and vehicles that would seem to appear as if by magic. Friendly people, driving friendly vehicles.

But security also had a decidedly less friendly side, and the street could be made to come alive. Steel beams could punch up from the pavement to send cars tumbling, and automatic munitions emplacements could be made to reveal themselves.

Finally, there was only one approach to Knight's island in the middle of the desert—a quarter-mile land bridge that crossed the lake Knight thought of as his personal mote. While this route over the lake wasn't a drawbridge of old, which could be raised to protect a castle, the land bridge concealed the heaviest armaments of all. It was also mined, and could be rendered impassible by a single command.

While security had been forced over the months to shoo a few strays away, there had been no major incidents and they had always been able to discourage unauthorized visitors with a smile. They hadn't yet had to bare their teeth, or deploy weapons systems that could take down a small army.

Knight wanted to keep it that way, taking great measures to be sure suspicions were never aroused. Their security was intended to be used as a measure of last resort, since turning their little stretch of heaven into a war zone would raise more than a few eyebrows, although having unlimited money to throw around would certainly help induce amnesia if such a situation did arise.

Lake Las Vegas had the most checkered of pasts, and had died and been reborn several times before going into yet another death spiral in 2020, enabling Knight to swoop in a few years later and purchase his island headquarters for a song.

In 1980, Transcontinental Properties had acquired over three thousand acres of land and associated water rights, seventeen miles east of the Vegas Strip, adjacent to the Lake Mead National Recreation Area. This would later become the Lake Las Vegas Resort, an audacious and fantastically expensive project.

In September of 1988, construction began on the Lake Las Vegas dam, an eighteen-story structure almost a mile long that had required more than two years to complete. The lake itself was created by filling a canyon in the high desert countryside with three billion gallons of water, an eight-year ordeal that had resulted in a lake that spanned three hundred and twenty acres, by far the largest man-made body of water in the state, running to a depth of one hundred and forty-five feet.

The concept of a vast lake resort community this close to the Vegas strip had attracted billions from giddy investors, most of whom eventually lost their shirts. And while the developers had grossly overestimated the allure and potential of such a resort, they hadn't skimped on vision or shied away from massive construction projects.

Once completed, the Lake Las Vegas resort featured ten miles of shoreline, premier residential facilities, golf courses, luxury hotels, spas, a full-service marina, a large retail enclave, fifty acres of open spaces with hiking and biking trails, and numerous other fabulous facilities and amenities.

But when demand fell far short of expectations the resort community failed in spectacular fashion, and quickly fell into disrepair. The Ritz-Carlton and other premier tenants shuttered their doors. The area became a ghost town, and lawsuits abounded as everyone pointed fingers at everyone else for this catastrophic failure.

The resort experienced several rebirths over the years, but the 2020 bust was perhaps its most profound. When Knight was considering headquarters locations he learned about this debacle and realized this could be the perfect location. He had snapped up the entire resort for only two hundred million dollars nine months earlier, through third parties that couldn't be traced to him. He had moved quickly to park his shell corporation in the center of the resort, on the island, while leaving all other properties abandoned.

So here he sat, in desert splendor, while Lee Cargill continued to search for him underground, in all the wrong places.

Not many of the buildings were currently occupied, as Knight's group was still fairly small. The ones that were occupied were in the center of the island, ringed by outer buildings that contained sensor outposts, electronics, security personnel, and more armaments. Even if scores of attackers somehow managed to reach the island, they would have to fight their way to its center.

In the brief time since he had split from Cargill, he had assembled the greatest collection of human ability the world had ever seen, what he affectionately called his *Brain Trust*, a group so important he insisted these words be capitalized. He provided these geniuses with unlimited funding, the ability to interact with the best people in the world, state-of-the-art equipment, and treated them like gods. Not surprisingly, his Brain Trust had paid dividends already, and the prospects for a steady stream of game-changing breakthroughs were excellent. And this had all been accomplished in only nine months.

It was spectacular progress if he did say so himself. If he had been God, he dared say he would have been able to rest on the fourth or fifth day instead of the seventh, which would have really screwed up the calendar.

Rourk finally passed through the security gauntlet fifteen minutes later and entered Knight's penthouse floor, looking like shit. Bloody, dirty, and bleary-eyed. But Knight didn't care about Rourk's appearance. All he cared about was the flash drive he had brought, which the returning soldier produced from his front pocket and handed to him.

"Well done, again, Jack," said Knight, holding the flash drive up to the light with such euphoria it could well have been the Ten Commandments handed down from Mount Sinai, rather than a simple memory stick handed down from Mount Palomar.

"I'm guessing Dr. Jackson can crack this in minutes," said Rourk.

"Actually, I won't be using Jackson or anyone else from the Brain Trust. I've hired a consultant who is due to arrive in two hours."

Rourk squinted in confusion. "I don't understand. Isn't Gary Jackson the most accomplished computer expert in the world?"

"Yes, but this won't require his level of brainpower. Why use a nuclear missile to swat a fly? Also, Jackson claims he's completely loyal to us, but this is too important to take any chances. I can't risk sabotage. So using someone who doesn't know why this is important makes the most sense."

"Understood," said Rourk.

"I'll keep you posted on our progress," said Knight, gesturing toward the door. "In the meanwhile, a doctor is waiting for you in the infirmary. A new hire, Dr. Susan Schlesinger. She'll take good care of that arm."

"That would be nice," replied his injured subordinate. "It's been a long night."

26

Jenna Morrison awoke and wiped the sleep from her eyes. She seemed to be in an oversized conference room, with a large center table and a few couches and chairs thrown in for good measure at points along the perimeter. In fact, she realized that she was lying on one of these couches, with a white blanket covering her.

Plants, tables, and upbeat framed posters decorated the room. She continued taking it all in as her eyes came into clearer focus. At the far end of the table, as far away from her as the room would allow, Aaron Blake and Dan Walsh were engaged in a whispered conversation.

She rubbed her eyes again and then removed her hands, expecting the room to disappear and for her to return to reality. Remarkably, the same scene greeted her eyes.

She pulled herself up from the couch and noticed that both men had caught her movement from across the room and were now watching her. "Guys," she called out. "Uh . . . where, exactly, are we? And how did we get here?"

Blake laughed as she walked over to them along the ridiculously long table and sat at an empty chair.

"Welcome to the party," said Blake, moving a large nylon duffel bag on the floor beside him so she would have more leg room. "It's just after eight Tuesday morning. Dan and I have been up for over an hour, but we didn't want to wake you."

"*Thank you*," said Jenna in sincere appreciation. She had never needed an extended slumber this desperately.

"To answer your questions," continued Blake, "we are now in my apartment complex's community center." He waved a hand to encompass the large room. "Not bad, huh? Residents can sign up to use it from eleven in the morning until nine at night for kids' parties, adult parties, wine tasting, pot lucks, arts and crafts fests, whatever. It's a board room slash party hall."

He grinned. "When you live in an apartment complex as swanky as this you can expect top-of-the-line amenities. There is a pool and Jacuzzi just outside of the door, and a weight room about twenty yards the other way."

"And, what, you just happened to have a key?" asked Jenna.

Blake smiled crookedly. "More or less. Let's just say that disabling alarms and breaking and entering are some of the things a good private investigator needs to master. As to how we got here, I carried you."

Jenna shook her head. "I have absolutely no memory of that."

"Yeah, you were out pretty cold," said Walsh.

Her eyes widened. "Was there trouble?" she asked in alarm. "Why did we need to relocate?"

"No trouble," said Blake, but a second later he added, "at least not yet. After you passed out, it occurred to me that the guy named Rourk saw me clearly on Palomar Mountain. Once he got the flash drive, I'm confident we fell off their priority list. But still, it never hurts to err on the safe side. I think we would have been okay last night in my apartment, but why take the chance? And we'll be back on the radar very soon, no matter what."

"Right," said Jenna. "When they break through the password and discover it's a decoy."

"Exactly. When this happens, they are *not* going to be happy. May have happened already, but whenever it does, Rourk will be examining the photos of every PI in California and beyond looking for me."

"I think changing locations was a wise move," said Jenna. "From here on out, I don't think sleeping soundly in your apartment will be great for anyone's health."

"Agreed," said Blake. "Turns out this was a perfect place to relocate. No windows to the outside, with several buildings between us and my unit. We're so tantalizingly close to where we were, yet so far away. If they did breach my apartment last night and discovered we had left, I'd bet my life they'd never think we relocated here."

Walsh grimaced uncomfortably. "You pretty much did bet your life," he observed.

Blake smiled but didn't reply.

"I took down Aaron's website," said Walsh, "and did my best to remove all traces of his image from the Internet. This should buy us some more time, but not forever. Information once on the Internet is stubbornly difficult to remove for good. Like a bad penny, it keeps resurfacing."

"I checked the cameras in my apartment and outside of my door remotely when I awoke this morning," said Blake. "And I reconned the entire complex on foot. With great care. In my practiced opinion, no one came calling last night, and no one is staking out my apartment now. But we'll have to be careful when we leave in case this changes."

He lifted a small cardboard box from an empty chair beside him and extended it toward Jenna. "Granola bar?" he offered. "You can have as many as you'd like, but since we had these for lunch yesterday, I don't want you getting spoiled. I can't let you have these gems *every* meal."

Jenna laughed and removed one of the bars. "I understand. And after this, I'm prepared to forgo these for the rest of my life if it will help our cause," she added wryly.

A wave of guilt passed over her for allowing herself to laugh, to be momentarily happy in the wake of Nathan's death. She had made great efforts to push this event from her mind, pretend it hadn't happened, so she could have the best chance to survive and exact revenge.

But had she been too successful at this?

After another moment of consideration, she decided that she had not been. If she continued to ping-pong between feelings of crushing remorse and feelings of guilt for temporarily *not* feeling remorse, she would lose her mind.

She took a deep, cleansing breath. The need for sleep could be a terrible burden, but she was glad sleep existed. If it didn't, one would never get any real downtime. This way, no matter what happened the night before, you could wake up and feel like you had a new lease on life, a clean slate, that a chapter had ended and a new one had begun.

"So this is what it feels like to be almost human," she said with contentment.

"Glad you finally managed some real shut-eye," said Blake. "But just so you know, you faked being human really well, even under duress and sleep-deprived."

"Thanks," she replied.

Walsh nodded his agreement. "Aaron and I discussed it while you were still sleeping. We both saw you yawning and nodding off occasionally while I was walking through a very complex subject, and yet you'd miraculously pop up with a relevant observation or insight, or a great question. We decided you're impressive even when you're half zombie."

"Probably the strangest compliment I've ever received," she said. "But, thanks. I'll take it."

She bit off a big chunk of granola bar and began chewing. After she swallowed she gestured to the nylon duffel bag on the ground beside Aaron Blake. "So what's in there?" she asked.

"Weapons, ammunition, a bug detector, night vision equipment, a set of lock picks, bolt cutters." Blake shrugged in mock innocence. "You know . . . the usual."

"Right," said Jenna with a smile. "So what now?" she asked. "A visit to your friend Greg?"

Blake nodded. "Exactly. He should have Nathan's file accessible by now, and also set up in the cloud with a trigger we can use to release it if we decide to."

"I'll review Nathan's work as quickly as I can," said Walsh. "With luck I'll be able to grasp it sufficiently to understand its full implications. If not, I'll be able to determine which academics would be able to help. My vote would be to visit one of these people immediately. The faster we know why this is so important to the people who killed Nathan, the better, in my opinion."

"I agree," said Blake. "So let's get moving." He turned toward Jenna. "In addition to breaking in here, I broke into the pool locker rooms, men's and women's. Dan and I have already showered, but we can wait for you if you want to take a quick one. I brought a few new toothbrushes and some toiletries with me from my apartment as well."

"You just happened to have unopened toothbrushes just lying around?"

"Absolutely."

"I have no idea what to even think about that," said Jenna playfully.

"I see," said Blake with a smile. "You can understand complex physics and mind-bending time-travel logic, but a man with a stash of new toothbrushes has you totally stumped."

Jenna laughed.

Blake let her enjoy this bit of levity for several more seconds and then said, "As much as I hate to spoil the mood, we really do need to get a move on. I haven't even discussed this with Dan, but we can't take my car, which will cause a further delay in getting to Greg."

Jenna nodded. "Of course. Because if they identify you, they identify your car."

"Right."

"We can take mine," offered Walsh helpfully.

"Thanks, but I'm afraid we can't," said Blake. "They have to be wondering where you disappeared to last night. Your car is a hot potato, also."

"Rental car?" said Walsh.

"No. That's traceable."

"I see," said Walsh, nodding sagely. "We physicists don't know much about cloak and dagger, but I get it now. You're suggesting that we'll have to steal a car."

Blake laughed. "*No!*" he said emphatically. "If you want to stay off the radar screen, *stealing* a car is a really bad move." He nodded toward Jenna with a grin still on his face. "Besides, we already have *one* stolen car."

Before she could misinterpret these words as a criticism rather than an attempt at humor, he hastened to add, "Not that Jenna had any other choice. She did the exact right thing. But in this case, we *do* have a choice."

"Okay," said Walsh. "I give up. What's our other choice? Public transportation?"

"Really?" said Blake. "A full professor of theoretical physics at UCLA, and you can't get this one?"

Walsh continued to blink at him stupidly.

Blake shook his head in amusement. "We *buy* a car," he said. "I guarantee I can find dozens listed online that are being sold by their owners within five miles of here. I'll find one for a few grand, take a cab to the bank so I can pay cash, and then take a cab to the car. We'll be on our way to visit my friend in no time."

Walsh looked disappointed. "Right. Buy a car. I guess I've watched too many movies. I have to admit, I was looking forward to seeing how you would go about stealing one."

"Uh-huh," said Blake playfully. "One adventure through a maze of steam tunnels and you're ready to go over to the dark side. Maybe that sign we saw in the tunnels had it right—maybe we *did* travel through Hell."

Walsh laughed, but Jenna's expression remained grim. Because she had little doubt that her own journey through Hell was far from over.

27

R. Sylvia Tagert wasn't a morning person. She needed to get herself going, get the blood flowing. She could stay out all night without feeling the least bit tired, but when she first awoke she felt like a slug.

And that was when she had gotten the duration of sleep she expected.

On this morning she had been rudely awakened earlier than usual, and barely had enough time to brush her teeth and throw on a white terrycloth bathrobe.

The doorbell rang, right on schedule. It was a little before seven and she had yet to take the first sip of her first cup of coffee, which explained why she was in the mood to kill someone, preferably the man she saw on a small plasma screen waiting impatiently at her door.

"Hold up your ID to the red camera indicator light," she shouted through the closed door.

She relished the annoyed look on his face. "Didn't your superior just contact you and tell you I was coming?" he shouted back.

"He told me someone with proper ID was coming, yes."

The man all but snarled as he pulled out his wallet, opened it, and held it steadily in front of the camera. The ID showed he belonged to a government agency that she was sure didn't exist, and that his name was Nathanial Lubbers, which she doubted was true, either.

She unlatched the door and swung it open. "Make this quick," she said. She gestured to her robe. "And thanks for the short notice."

Sylvia knew she was being less than hospitable, that this could well be very important, and that this man was just trying to do his job. But dammit, she couldn't help being wired the way she was wired. Early mornings and lack of coffee made her grumpy. She was normally pleasant, cheerful, and well liked, but even her closest friends knew better than to wake her early.

The man entered her small home and shoved his wallet back into his back pocket. "Sorry about the lack of notice," said Joe Allen, trying to be friendly. "And this should be very quick."

She sat on a chair in her family room and gestured for him to take a seat across from her on a small black leather sofa. "So what can I do for my friends in Black Ops?" she asked when he had seated himself.

"You pulled some footage Monday morning of a residential neighborhood in San Diego. In La Jolla to be precise. I just want to know who you sent this to."

She wasn't sure what to expect, but this wasn't it. Aaron Blake had told her he needed this footage for a new case he was on, but couldn't tell her the details. She had been happy for him, since at least it wasn't another divorce case, and no one deserved success more than Blake.

"What?" she said, feigning confusion. "Why would you possibly ask that?"

"Not to put too fine a point on it, but your superior did tell you to give me your full cooperation, correct? So let me worry about my motivations, and you can worry about answering my questions."

Sylvia's agile mind had come awake in a hurry. She needed to come up with a strategy, and quickly. She had experienced any number of tricky situations, and one didn't get far in the CIA without being able to think their way out of a box.

But what was *in* this box? What had Blake gotten himself into?

Whatever it was, she knew only one thing: Aaron Blake was a good man. Whatever he was involved with, he was the guy wearing the white hat. But that didn't automatically make the man across from her the bad guy. She decided she needed to test the situation further before she would give him anything. See how he reacted.

"I didn't send it to anyone," she replied as innocently as she could. "It was for a project I'm working on, by myself. What made you think it was for someone else?"

"And what project would that be?" said Allen dubiously.

"Classified. You have *your* secret projects and I have mine. Until I'm told to read you in, I'm afraid I can't comment."

"Look," said Allen, "I know you're lying to me. I *know* it. Which means you must be trying to protect someone. But here is the thing. Whoever you're protecting isn't in any trouble. I just need to speak to him or her. Ask some questions. This person is just a stepping stone in what is an investigation vital to the security of this country. When a nuke goes off in Chicago because you wanted to play games, how are you going to feel then?"

Sylvia considered. If she refused to cooperate after being given a direct order, this would not go well for her. And she thought it likely he was telling the truth. Because why would they want Blake? So maybe delaying this guy *would* lead to the type of disaster he had described.

But just in case it was all bullshit and they *were* after Blake, she could warn him the moment this man left. Let her friend know someone was coming.

Aaron Blake could be taken if he was surprised. But if he knew you were coming, she liked his chances against anyone. Or any group. She had seen him in action. He had a rare talent for survival. Survive a few ops that go south when other men don't, maybe you're lucky. But when a man like Blake keeps beating the odds, time after time, you have to chalk it up to skill.

"Okay," said Sylvia. "You're right. The man you're looking for is named Aaron Blake. I worked with him pretty extensively when I was stationed in Yemin. He was spec-ops counter-terrorism. Ballsy, brilliant, and heroic. And very tenacious. Very popular with everyone, inside and outside of the service. But also self-reflective. Did a lot of soul-searching. The sort who never stopping worrying about turning into a monster, becoming *too* good at killing."

Allen nodded as if her description of Blake's skills and background didn't surprise him in the least. He raised his eyebrows. "What's he doing now? Is he still in the service?"

"No, he left. Recently. He runs a private detective agency in LA. He said he needed the video footage for a case he was working on."

"Interesting. And that's all he told you?"

"That's everything."

Sylvia paused and stared intently at the man across from her. "Just know this, if you were bullshitting me, and Aaron Blake *is* in your cross-hairs for whatever reason, you've got it wrong. He's a good man. And he is fully on our side. His loyalty is absolute. So whatever intel you think you have, if it suggests he's working at cross-purposes to the interests of the United States, the intel is shit."

Allen rose from the sofa. "Thank you for your help. And also for giving us this perspective."

"Just don't forget what I told you about him," said Sylvia bluntly.

But as she finished this sentence she found herself staring into the barrel of an automatic pistol, pointed at her chest.

Sylvia's heart accelerated madly. "I told you the truth," she insisted desperately. "You can check on it and you'll see. There is no reason to threaten me."

"Sorry about the gun," said Allen politely. "But I can't help but worry you might contact Aaron Blake the moment I leave. You know, warn him that I was here and wanted to talk to him. I can't risk him going to ground. This is too important."

Her eyes widened in horror. "So you're going to kill me?" she said.

R. Sylvia Tagert had been in any number of dangerous situations, but she never thought she would die in her own home, in a white terrycloth bathrobe. A part of her mind, unbidden, came up with a stray thought that if she had to die, being killed at seven in the morning before she had any coffee was the best time for it.

But her visitor shook his head. "Of course I'm not going to kill you," he said. "I really am grateful for your help. And what would your boss say if he helped a fellow organization and they returned the favor by killing one of his best people?"

He removed two small yellow capsules from his shirt pocket. "Swallow these," he said. "They will put you out for about eight hours. That way I can be sure you won't issue any warnings. And you'll be fine. I've tried these on flights, and while I'm giving you a stronger dose than you need, I always wake up feeling like a million bucks."

Sylvia took the offered pills, put them in her mouth, and swallowed. She knew she didn't have a choice, and they could still be on the same side. She couldn't blame him for not wanting to take any chances with Blake, a critical lead.

"Open your mouth and lift your tongue," said Allen pleasantly.

She did as she was asked and within minutes already felt a pleasant drift toward sleep, although the man in her house wasn't about to leave until he was certain she was sleeping like the dead.

On the other hand, this was infinitely better than *being* dead. And her visitor had robbed her of sleep, after all. Maybe this was just his way of returning what he had taken, with interest.

* * *

Joe Allen left a sleeping Sylvia Tagert and returned to his car. After half an hour of pulling strings and scanning through Blake's file, he felt he was prepared enough to call Lee Cargill and answer whatever questions he might have.

Cargill answered the audio-only call on the first ring. "Good timing, Joe. The president is over two hours late for our meeting," he said, his words dripping with barely contained rage. "But I've just been given the five-minute warning, so you'll need to make it quick."

"I had no trouble with our CIA agent," said Allen. "She pulled the street video for an ex-special operator named Aaron Blake, who has seen enough action for ten men."

"No surprise there," noted Cargill.

"And get this, at the moment this Blake really is a PI, working and living out of LA. He left the service to try to make a go of it as a gumshoe. I've had his file pulled and I've sent it to your computer. He's as formidable as we expected. I have his address, know what car he drives, and have people working to learn where he is right now."

"Well done," said Cargill. There was a long pause. "The team we spoke about on the plane is standing by. But let's not be too hasty. Jenna Morrison and her PI aren't the goal, after all. We need to find out if the flash drive exists, and then find it. Nothing else matters. So I want to know where this guy is now, but just as importantly, I want to know everywhere he's *been* since Sunday night, and I want deep background on anyone he's spoken with. If he went to a gas station to buy a candy bar, I want to know when this happened and the life story of the gas station attendant."

"Understood. I'll pull street camera and satellite footage of his past travels right away."

"While you're setting the wheels in motion, get your ass to San Diego, to Camp Pendleton, so you can lead the team I have waiting there when we decide to act. Report in as soon as you've gathered the information I've asked for."

"Roger that," said Joe Allen.

"I have to run. Time to meet with President Janney," said Cargill, with all the distaste most men reserved for a visit to the proctologist.

28

Jack Rourk was resting in a seated position on a bed, watching a movie on the room's main monitor. While the nineteenth floor of the twenty-two-story building was simply called the infirmary, it was as sophisticated as any hospital and just as well equipped.

He looked out a window at the lake off in the distance. It was hard to imagine he was in the middle of one of the most brutal deserts in the world, and less than an hour away from the neon lights, gaming tables, glamorous shows, and hookers of Las Vegas.

Dr. Susan Schlesinger had wasted no time patching up his arm, stitching the wound as neatly as a seamstress, and hooking him up to an IV drip for meds, hydration, and nutrition. She had no idea what was really happening on the man-made island, but she was being paid a fortune not to display unnecessary curiosity, or complain about the lack of cell phone coverage or outgoing Internet. She had been told to care for every patient as though he or she were a head of state, and since she had only been there a week, and Rourk was her first patient, she had maintained a bedside vigil while he slept.

She had left a few minutes earlier, after Rourk had awakened, and when he heard someone approaching he assumed she was returning.

But he was wrong. It was not Susan Schlesinger.

It was Edgar Knight.

Knight didn't make personal visits to wipe the noses of his underlings, so it must be something important. And one glance at his boss's face made it clear it was something *bad*.

"The flash drive is shit!" barked Knight immediately, not one to prolong suspense. "We cracked it, and it's a huge data file of baseball statistics through the ages. Just in case the real file was somehow hidden, encoded, the consultant turned over every last possible stone."

He glared at Rourk with an intimidating intensity. "That asshole on the mountain played you, Jack. Like a fucking fiddle."

Rourk blew out a long breath. "Shit," he said softly, embarrassed. "I don't blame you for being pissed, Edgar. But the guy was good. It was the exact same brand and style of memory stick the real file is on. I had to assume it was real. If I'd have gone after this guy, while Cargill's men were figuring out I killed Argent, I could have lost both the PI and the flash drive."

"Which is what happened, anyway, isn't it?" snapped Knight caustically.

He paused and made a visible attempt to calm down. "I'm not saying it's your fault, Jack," he added in more controlled tones, "or that you made the wrong choice. But I thought we had it, the holy fucking grail, and learning otherwise has put me in a foul mood. So quit lounging around and find me this private *dick*."

"You know he probably isn't really a PI?"

"Thanks, Jack. Any other brilliant thoughts you want to share? I know he probably lied. But where else are we going to start? So assume he really is a PI. When you've finished looking at photos of every PI on earth, then we'll think of something else."

"I'll get right on it."

"See that you do. It goes without saying that if you find him, I want to know about it seconds later."

29

Joe Allen stood in a secure conference room within Camp Pendleton, a Marine Corps Base in Oceanside, California, halfway between San Diego and their target in Orange County. Retracing Aaron Blake's steps had proven quite valuable. When they discovered he and Jenna Morrison had visited a computer expert, one he had served with in the military, their purpose in so doing had been obvious.

Allen's tablet computer was wirelessly synched with a sixty-inch monitor hanging like a picture from the wall, capable of displaying images and video in three dimensions without the need of glasses.

His four-man team, who knew nothing about Cargill or his black project, looked on in anticipation, having wondered why a team of Army Green Berets had been flown into a Marine base. The only conclusion they had come to was that they were about to conduct an op on US soil, and this was a nearby staging area, a prospect they found troubling.

Allen swiped the tablet computer with his fingers and an image of a soft-looking blond man hung in the air, as though he was personally in attendance, just in front of the monitor.

"This is Gregory Soyer," began Allen. "He's a civilian now, and looks like he'd be a pushover, but don't be deceived. He spent six years with the Rangers and is extremely dangerous. He specialized in computers and electronics, hardware and software, and left the military a few years ago. Since then he has built a thriving computer consulting practice."

He slid a finger and the next image appeared. "This is his home in Orange County. He's wealthy enough, and quirky enough, to have bought a home that is fairly isolated, which is ideal for our needs.

The house is one-story and relatively small, but it is secluded, and backed up against a canyon."

Allen sent several images to the screen in quick succession, close-up and panoramic satellite photos of the back of Soyer's house, as crisp and clear as if they were taken by an expert photographer standing twenty yards from the residence.

"Notice that the back of the house abuts a forty-foot cliff," said Allen. "Soyer has a backyard we judge to be eleven yards wide, then a wrought iron fence so no one accidentally falls, and then an immediate and sheer drop off into the canyon below."

The men took in everything he said but remained expressionless.

"Soyer is known to mostly work from his home, and satellites show his car, a white Mercedes C300 sport sedan, is still there, even as we speak. We believe he will remain at home for at least the next few hours. I know you've been assigned to me on a temporary basis and haven't been read into the bigger picture. I'd love to do that for you—but I can't. Just know that your actions are serving the national security and will be instrumental in averting one of the gravest threats this country has ever faced."

Allen paused to let this sink in, his face grim. After several seconds he continued. "Our objectives today are three fold. First, and most importantly, we believe Soyer has a flash drive on premises that is vital to national security. I need to retrieve this drive, undamaged. Which is what makes this mission tricky. Because if we fail to nullify Soyer quickly, we run the risk that his first action will be to destroy the drive. So he can't have any indication that we're coming. He has to be taken out of the equation the moment he knows that we're there."

Allen frowned. "The problem is that he's experienced and fairly well prepared. We've pulled the plans for his house and studied satellite images. He has video and sensors protecting the lead up to his house in the front. Given he's now a civilian living in Southern California, he isn't too worried about anyone scaling the short cliff in his backyard, so he doesn't have any monitors pointed in this direction, and no alarms. It's his only real blind spot. At least electronically.

When he's in the office, he does look out through a large sliding glass door, so anyone coming this direction has to be mindful of him spotting you the old-fashioned way."

Allen gestured to the leanest member of the team, who had short black hair and Hispanic features. "Lieutenant Recinos, this is where you come in," he said. "I understand you've done some competitive bouldering?"

Ricardo Recinos nodded. "Yes, sir, I have," he replied.

There were different types of recreational and competitive rock climbing, but bouldering was the climbing discipline in which participants didn't use safety rope typical of other styles. Instead, bouldering required the ascent of relatively low routes, with at most a cushioned bouldering pad below the climber to protect against injury.

"What's the most difficult outdoor climb you've flashed recently?" asked Allen.

Recinos was impressed that Allen knew this term. *Flashing* a climb meant completing it on the first try.

"I flashed a V12 two weeks ago, sir," replied Recinos, now confident Allen would know what this meant. Bouldering climbs were rated from V0, for beginners—although even these could confound strong athletes with no climbing experience—to V16 for the elite of the elite.

"Excellent," said Allen. "I've had a climber pore over dozens of close-ups of different sections of the cliff below Soyer's backyard. In his judgment, if this were a bouldering climb, he'd rate it a V4, maybe a V5. You'll have time to study the photos yourself. Impossible for a beginner, but fairly comfortable for you. Except that it's forty feet up, so you'll have no choice but to flash it. And you'll be carrying a backpack, which will add weight and change your center of gravity."

"What equipment will be required, sir?" asked Recinos.

"You'll need a gas grenade launcher, about twice as large as your current weapon, but no heavier. It can shoot a baseball-sized canister of highly compressed gas through Soyer's sliding glass door in the back. The gas is colorless, odorless, and has dispersal kinetics that are off the charts. Non-lethal, but will knock him out within seconds of a single breath."

"I see," said Recinos. "So scale the cliff, quiet as mouse, and shoot the gas canister through the slider?"

"Yes. Wait until you're certain Soyer is in his office. But also make sure he doesn't see you."

"And if he's not in his office?"

Allen chewed his lower lip. "Give it five minutes. All of his computer equipment is in there, so he won't be anywhere else for long. If he doesn't show after five, shoot multiple canisters through as many different windows as you can. If he's anywhere in the house, the gas will reach him in seconds."

"So I assume I'll also need a gas mask," said Recinos.

"Yes. So you can confirm that he's down. Sorry, I know this will add extra weight and bulk to your ascent, but it won't be too bad."

"I'm sure I'll manage," said Recinos.

Allen gestured to one of the other men before him, a balding man with a wide face. "Captain Thompson will be piloting a—let's call it an experimental helicopter—with the rest of the team inside. A helo that runs so quiet you could set it down in a library without attracting attention. We'll be at high altitude and out of sight, but minutes away. So fire the canister, Lieutenant Recinos, and call us down. Soyer's front lawn is large enough for us to land there. We'll gather up his unconscious body for later interrogation and I'll do a methodical search of his house for the flash drive I'm after."

"Is that it, sir?" said a lieutenant named Akke Wilmes, correctly wondering why he and Lieutenant Brandon Laub were required for this mission. Recinos and Thompson would seem to be all the manpower required.

"Not quite," replied Allen. He pulled up two additional photographs, which now appeared to hover in the air behind him, side by side. "You're looking at Aaron Blake, ex-Army Ranger with considerable combat experience, and Jenna Morrison, a genetics graduate student at UCSD. We have satellites monitoring Blake's car. While it's still parked at his apartment complex in LA, we think the chances are reasonably good that he'll visit Soyer later today. We'd ideally like to capture these two as well, alive and unharmed. That's why I've opted to go with a slightly larger team. I'll brief you on how I want to play that portion of the op after we've completed the higher priority half of the mission."

The men nodded their understanding.

"Recinos, I'm afraid you're the man of the hour," said Allen. "Study the photos. If you aren't certain you can flash this climb, I need to know it, because we're only going to get one chance at this." He shrugged. "Not to mention that a fall from this height onto jagged rocks will almost certainly be fatal for you."

"Thank you, sir," said Recinos with just the hint of smile. "Believe it or not, that thought had already occurred to me."

30

Lieutenant Ricardo Recinos was flown by helicopter to a staging area near Soyer's home, where the latest model Ford Raptor, known for its off-road tenacity, was waiting for him. The vehicle's GPS was already programmed with the best route into the canyon, and he drove as close to Soyer's home as he could before hiking the remaining short distance to his destination.

Once he arrived, he achieved a Zen-like state of calm and studied the wall face before him—and above him. He had studied close-up images and had also brought a scope to plot out his route up the rock face.

He laid out three crash pads at the foot of the cliff, wondering just how helpful these would be if he fell. He had to admit there was a good chance they would save his life, but this wasn't something he was keen on putting to the test, because if he fell from near the top, he would require hospitalization at the very least.

He didn't mind risking his life. He wouldn't have undergone the insanely brutal and arduous training necessary to join the Green Berets if he was afraid of hard work or risk. But he liked to know what he was risking his life *for*.

Say what you wanted about terrorists, but fighting them was nicely black-and-white. They harbored an ideology that would tolerate no dissent. If you didn't subscribe to Sharia Law, to Islamic justice, you needed to be erased from existence. Period. They couldn't be reasoned with. They believed their god wanted them to kill you, and it didn't matter how they had come to this belief—only that it was either kill or be killed.

When a stampeding herd of cattle were coming your way, it didn't much matter what had caused the stampede. You only had to know that no argument would alter its course, no persuasion would save your life if you were standing in its path.

Recinos was willing to risk his life to battle extremists, to attempt to prevent barbaric zealots from slaughtering as many innocents as they could manage.

But having this Joe Allen assigned as his temporary CO, knowing the man was part of an off-the-books Black Ops group with incredible power and little accountability, was something he found very troubling. Conducting a mission on US soil even more so.

What was on that flash drive?

There was no way of knowing. Maybe it was as important as Allen had said. Maybe it listed the locations of thirty nukes hidden in the thirty biggest cities in America, set to detonate later that night.

On the other hand, just because Allen suggested it was vital didn't make it so. It could just as easily contain evidence that Allen's girlfriend was cheating on him.

Allen seemed like an upstanding guy, but tyrants could pretend to be saints when it suited their purposes. So the motives of his temporary CO might be heroic, but they also might be treacherous. For all Recinos knew, the world would be better off if he *did* fall from the cliff.

And he didn't like the fact that two Rangers were part of this. Why did Allen want them? Recinos vowed to make sure this operation went by the numbers so Soyer and Blake were taken cleanly. Rangers and Green Berets were both Army Special Forces, and he felt a kinship with these men almost as great as if they had been Green Berets themselves.

Joe Allen's voice whispered through his earpiece, informing him that the chopper was in position, hovering far above him, just out of sight, and ordered him to begin his climb.

The lieutenant took a deep breath and launched himself off the canyon floor, his hands locking onto a five-inch-wide handhold that was as secure as the rung of a ladder. It was good that the lower part of the climb was the easiest so he could get used to the added weight of his backpack and his new center of gravity.

Climbing wasn't just about strength. It was about training fingertips to cling to small crevices with superhuman tenacity, about making them bleed so often they grew calluses as tough as Kevlar. It was about turning tendons into steel. About wedging the tips of shoes into the tiniest of imperfections in a smooth wall and hanging upside down when this didn't seem possible. And it was about balance and body control.

The lieutenant gained confidence as he continued to climb. Halfway up he hung from one arm while he worked the kinks out of the other, and then calmly and methodically worked out the next necessary moves as though solving a crossword puzzle at his kitchen table.

His focus was as absolute as the life-and-death stakes required, and minutes later he finished his ascent, grasping the wrought iron fence at the back of Soyer's yard.

He peered through the fence to be sure he wouldn't be seen, and then silently, effortlessly, pulled himself over and onto Soyer's lawn.

* * *

Greg Soyer sipped a Piña Colada and wondered idly what kind of ribbing he would receive from his fellow rangers had they spied him nursing such a girly drink. Not that he would care. He liked what he liked, and the best thing about having been a ranger was that his masculine self-image could not be brought down in the slightest, even if he were wearing a pink tutu and high heels while preparing a scented bubble bath.

He had finished work on Aaron Blake's project the night before, which had been even more straightforward than he had expected, even given the care he had used. He had opened the file and confirmed that it wasn't gibberish, but only because there were a few recognizable English words between the unrecognizable math symbols and diagrams. Once he had succeeded, he then set about protecting the file once again, only this time far more securely, and setting up a secure copy in the cloud.

He checked the time on the bottom of his computer monitor. It was already after ten. He had expected Blake and his female client to return the night before, or if not, at the crack of dawn. Not that it was time to panic. Not yet. He would give his friend another few hours and then he would be forced to take steps to investigate.

If it was anyone other than Aaron Blake he would have been more worried, but after having served with him for several years and traveling through hell and back, he had decided that when the world self-destructed, the only creatures remaining would be the cockroach and Aaron Blake.

Boom!

Soyer was blasted from his reverie as a thunderous explosion rang in his ears, and he jumped as if hit by a cattle prod. This was accompanied, almost simultaneously, by the sound of shattered glass as a large hole appeared in his sliding door, created by what could have been a small cannon ball from the look of it.

He instinctively dived for cover while pulling out the H&K he had armed himself with after Blake's visit. He came out of a roll searching for an intruder, his eyes frantically scanning his office and just beyond the slider, but instead of an intruder, he spied a small canister that had bounced against one wall and had come to rest in the middle of his office, five feet away.

At that instant he realized two things, just before his world went black.

First, his instincts had betrayed him. Diving for cover wasn't any help against a fast-acting gas. He should have held his breath the moment he heard the crash of glass, but it was too late: he had already inhaled.

And second, the bluff the girl had advised, an insistence that the data on the drive would be released if he were killed, would not work.

A bluff only had a chance of working if you were alive to deliver it.

31

Joe Allen and the three other members of the small team descended from the heavens as inconspicuously as possible. The large helicopter incorporated two breathtaking new experimental technologies, one that eliminated noise and one that camouflaged the craft. These technologies worked so well that unless one was expecting to see the helo, it could easily fail to register in the conscious mind.

Captain Jason Thompson landed on Soyer's front lawn as Recinos stood a safe distance away with his mouth hanging open. How in the world had someone managed to camouflage something so big? To completely silence a machine that was thunderously noisy by its very nature? Was there anything science wouldn't eventually enable mankind to do?

"Well done, Lieutenant Recinos," said Allen as he stepped from the just-settled aircraft. At his orders, Laub and Wilmes carefully gathered up Greg Soyer from the floor of his home and carried him into the helicopter, and then remained outside to alert Allen if anyone happened to approach the house.

"Recinos and Thompson," said Allen, having remained inside, "just sit tight. I need to get what I came here for," he explained, and then he proceeded to tear through Soyer's office like a spinning Tasmanian devil out of a Looney Tunes cartoon, leaving no drawer, painting, or piece of furniture intact.

While he was careful to avoid shards of glass, halfway through his demolition he was stabbed by a piece and began bleeding far more excessively than the minor damage it had caused should have warranted. He was more annoyed that he had to steal a hand towel from Soyer's bathroom to staunch the flow, delaying his efforts, than by the actual stab wound itself.

After fifteen minutes he had found a half-dozen flash drives, but only one that was password protected. He put this one in a special steel case and then all six in his pocket.

Joe Allen then gathered the entire team on Soyer's front lawn, next to the parked helicopter, his hand still wrapped in the towel.

"Okay, here's the plan going forward," he said. "Lieutenants Wilmes and Recinos will stay inside the house, out of sight. Captain Thompson will fly me and Greg Soyer out of here. We'll deposit Soyer somewhere safe and then return as soon as possible, landing a few minutes away and awaiting a signal."

Allen turned to the hulking soldier on his left. "Lieutenant Laub, I want you to conceal yourself outside, watching all approaches to the house. Aaron Blake's car is still in LA, but we've learned that he isn't in his apartment, either, so I wouldn't be surprised if he's in a car unknown to us and on his way here. If you see the UPS guy or a few girl scouts selling cookies, let them ring the bell, and make sure they leave when no one answers. If you see Aaron Blake or Jenna Morrison, alert Lieutenants Wilmes and Recinos immediately and stay out of sight."

Allen paused. "I should also mention that Soyer has a live-in girlfriend, Alisa Bonesteel, but we'll be monitoring her and don't expect her to be a factor. Obviously, if this changes, we'll alert you immediately."

He faced Wilmes and Recinos and removed two gas canisters from a rucksack, each the shape of a soda can, except almost three times larger in every dimension, and handed one to each man. "Using both of these would be overkill. Even a single one is overkill given the size of this house. But since overdosing isn't a problem with this particular gas, don't be shy."

Recinos examined the canister he had been given. Its operation couldn't be simpler. Pull the pin and throw or roll the canister.

"Once you two get the word from Laub that he's spotted your targets," continued Allen, "open the front door a hair, put on your masks, and get out of sight. Make sure the door to Soyer's office remains shut, so they can't see it was tossed. When they enter to investigate, give them some time to make it to the center of the house. Then activate the canisters."

He paused to be sure they were with him. "Signal us and we'll be here in a few minutes. I'll want to spend more time tearing apart the rest of the house, including every last couch cushion, mattress, and drawer, just to be sure I have the flash drive I need. But after this we can all haul our unconscious cargo back to base."

Recinos sighed inwardly. It was bad enough having a temporary CO with questionable motives, but even worse when he was of questionable competence. To be fair, Allen had done well planning the attack on Soyer, but maybe he had just been lucky.

"Sir," he said, "with all due respect, this plan won't work."

Allen's eyes narrowed. "Why do you say that, Lieutenant?" he asked evenly, and to his credit, he sounded interested rather than defensive.

"Given Blake's background and record, he won't fall for it. Leaving the door slightly ajar is too obvious a trap. When he sees this, the *last* thing he'll do is enter the house."

"Do the rest of you agree?" said Allen.

They all nodded yes.

"So what do you recommend, Lieutenant Recinos?"

"We have to make him work for it. At least a little. We want him to think we struck here and are now gone, so he'll feel comfortable doing a post mortem on the house. Let him figure out we were here on his own. If he's half as good as his file says, it'll be obvious enough to him without us purposely making it *too* obvious. So keep the front door closed and locked. When he realizes we were here, he'll recon the perimeter. When he comes to the slider in back, he'll see that it's been smashed and the office tossed. We'll stay out of sight inside. Since it won't seem to him like we're inviting him in, he'll come in on his own."

Allen considered. "Thank you, Lieutenant. I believe your analysis is correct. Please proceed accordingly."

Recinos was surprised by how well he had taken this. "Yes, sir. Thank you, sir."

Since Allen appeared to be so receptive to his recommendation, perhaps he would try his luck again. "And one other thing," he added, gesturing to Allen's hand. "Before you use the first aid kit in the helo to bandage that up, how do you feel about donating some of that red liquid for the cause?"

Allen raised his eyebrows questioningly.

"And don't worry, sir," added Recinos. "We can make a little of that go a long way."

32

Blake turned from the busy street and began to wind his way up the twisted quarter-mile path to his friend's home, hoping the aging, dented 2008 Kia Optima he had bought for two grand had enough power to make it up a short incline without collapsing. He hadn't exactly had the time to give it a proper test drive, and the guy he had bought it from seemed about as trustworthy as . . . well, as a used car salesman.

"I sense you're a little tense, Jenna," said Blake.

"I thought I had disguised it better."

"Are you worried about Greg's trustworthiness?"

"Not at all. I'm just nervous about finding out what's really on that flash drive. Whatever it is, it's been the cause of so much violence, so much tragedy."

"This is true," said Blake solemnly. "But we already know the nature of the discovery from Nathan's e-mail. We'll just be getting the nuts and bolts, which only Dan will have a hope of understanding, anyway."

Jenna simply nodded as they reached their destination.

Blake pulled up beside Soyer's car and the three passengers walked the short distance to the door in silence.

Blake couldn't put his finger on it, but something wasn't right. When he reached the front door he spun slowly around. When his eyes came to rest on the middle of Soyer's front lawn, his stomach tightened.

This is what he had noticed in his peripheral vision, what had alerted his subconscious. Either his friend had just been visited by a dragon, or something else had landed on his lawn and left telltale indentations in the soft ground.

Other than this, there wasn't a hair out of place anywhere. Given the chopper was no longer there, the assault team that had visited Soyer must have already come and gone. Blake felt bile rise in his throat as he imagined his friend lying in a pool of blood, his death entirely Blake's fault.

Jenna was oblivious to these concerns and raised her hand to push the doorbell. Blake snatched her wrist with surprising speed, startling her. Fortunately, she didn't let out any sound. He leaned closer to his two companions. "Someone was here," he whispered. "Probably gone, but let's take a look around before we go inside."

He considered sending them back to the car but decided against it. The odds were that the safest place for them was by his side.

"Follow me," he whispered, even softer than before, his mouth just inches from their ears. "Be alert. I'll be looking in windows. I need you to scan the real estate away from the house when I do. Tread silently, and no speaking. Tap me if you see something noteworthy." The corners of his mouth turned up into an almost undetectable smile. "Unless we're about to be shot," he added, "then scream for all you're worth."

Blake began circling the house, his gun drawn, cautiously peering through windows as he came to them. When he reached the back of the house the wounded slider made its presence known, with half of an entire pane now obliterated.

Blake's jaw clenched tightly. Along with pieces of glass, Soyer's office was a wreck. Someone had put it through a blender. They were too late. The attackers had almost certainly gotten what they were after.

His friend's body was not in sight, nor could he detect any blood. Not that this necessarily meant anything. Greg Soyer could well be lying dead elsewhere in the house, somewhere that couldn't be seen from a window.

Blake motioned for the two civilians to follow as he carefully pulled a few large shards of glass from their moorings to enlarge the jagged hole enough for them to enter without becoming impaled.

When all three were inside, Blake spent several minutes inspecting the office and listening for hostiles, but was not rewarded in either endeavor. Finally, he cautiously opened the door into the main house. Seeing no one, he motioned yet again for Jenna and Walsh to follow.

Blake began searching the house methodically, his gun always leading the way. When he reached the family room he threw open the door to the closet, prepared to fire, but only found a few light jackets hanging inside.

As they approached the half-open door to the kitchen, Blake spied remnants of a bloody handprint near the handle, further sharpening his already heightened sense of alertness. When he reached the entrance, he rushed through, crouching low as he did, but the room was empty, and the door on the opposite side leading to the dining room was fully closed. Jenna and Walsh followed him in, and their mouths hung open as they saw hints of a trail of blood leading to Soyer's massive refrigerator, as though the blood trail had once been extensive, but a hasty clean-up hadn't quite managed to get it all.

All three walked zombie-like toward the refrigerator in horror.

Blake, who was in the lead, shot up a hand to call a halt, but his companions missed this signal and continued walking, only stopping when they ran into him.

Blake's intuition was sending him an alarm once again. This didn't feel right. Either the assault team wouldn't care about leaving tracks, or they'd be sure to clean up perfectly. There should be no middle ground. And why would a group this sophisticated stuff Soyer's body in a refrigerator?

The appliance was probably booby-trapped, Blake realized. The tiny lightbulb wouldn't be the only thing that was activated when they opened the door.

A loud thud sounded as something large crashed onto the kitchen's glossy black cooktop, landing among four large circles etched into the ceramic. Blake wheeled, prepared to fire toward the small center island, and spotted the newly arrived canister.

The instant he saw it, he instinctively resisted the urge to draw more air into his lungs. If the gas was largely benign, this would buy him time. If not, he was dead already.

Regardless, he couldn't hold his breath for long.

Jenna Morrison and Dan Walsh reacted the way any civilian would. They gasped, and their hearts accelerated explosively, causing them to suck in even more air than usual. Both collapsed in heaps beside Blake.

Blake darted behind the half-open door leading from the kitchen to the family room, from which the canister had been tossed. He flattened himself against the wall and waited, his gun still drawn. His only chance was that he could hold his breath until whoever was responsible entered the kitchen to inspect his handiwork.

But after only thirty seconds, Blake's lungs were already *on fire.* Perhaps he had joined the wrong Special Forces unit. Had he been a Navy SEAL he could have held his breath until the sun set, but breath-holding wasn't his strong suit.

At last, fifteen seconds of agony later, a man walked cautiously through the door, and Blake struck, clocking him in the skull with his gun, but it was only a glancing blow and the man retained consciousness. Blake knew he could only hold his breath for ten or fifteen seconds more, if that. Every cell in his body was now screaming for oxygen, and only his battle-tested will prevented him from succumbing to this ultimate, irresistible need.

As the man chopped at Blake's arm, forcing his gun to fly into the middle of the kitchen and clatter around the floor, Blake slapped desperately at his mask, dislodging it from his face.

The man's eyes widened in panic, but as he moved to replace the mask over his mouth, Blake jabbed him in the stomach, causing a reflexive exhalation, followed by a reflexive *inhalation.*

The gas took effect instantly.

As the man folded to the ground, Blake stripped his mask from him and brought it to his mouth. He gasped a breath, barely clinging to consciousness. The infusion of air sparked him back to life, and his vitality returned in a rush as he gulped down several more rapid-fire lungfuls while securing the mask in place.

His mind began hitting on all cylinders. Were there more hostiles?

If this was his op, he would have assigned *two* commandos. He would wait until his quarry was in a contained room, without windows, as they had done. But this kitchen had two entrances. So he would man *both*, in case a man like Blake managed to hold his breath in time and race for a window, crashing through to breathable air. So Blake reasoned there would be another man in the dining room, one who had the sense to wait longer before entering the kitchen.

Blake scooped up his gun and darted to the opposite entrance, once again pressing himself flat against the wall, but this time masked and able to breathe.

Just over a minute had passed since the canister had been thrown, but it seemed like ten. He was vaguely aware of time compressing, of his mind being able to operate at superhuman speed, of events proceeding in slow motion—one of the reasons he was such an adrenaline junkie.

Then, right on cue, a second man opened the door from the kitchen to the dining room and entered the kitchen.

"Freeze!" snapped Blake, pressing his gun into the intruder's back.

He considered tearing off the man's mask and rendering him unconscious, but decided against it. "Drop your gun," he barked though his mask, but even as he said this he realized the man wasn't holding one. "Get your gun with two fingers and toss it to the other side of the room," he amended.

The man did as he was told.

"Who are you?"

"My name is Recinos."

"How many?" barked Blake.

"Just two of us," said Recinos, nodding toward his fallen comrade on the opposite side of the kitchen.

"Lie to me again and I put a bullet in your head. How many?"

"Just two," repeated the man without hesitation.

Blake spotted a small, nondescript tattoo on the man's neck, just above his shoulders. Kermit the frog, only half an inch high.

Blake understood its meaning immediately. The man was a special operator. Green Beret.

Despite what was often depicted in movies and television, special operators were severely discouraged from getting any unit identifying tattoos. Often these soldiers sported long hair and beards on missions overseas to blend in. Being recognized as military in any way could spell disaster. If a mission went wrong, wearing a tattoo of a SEAL Trident or Special Forces arrowhead wasn't the best way to pretend you were a student, simply visiting your captor's spectacular third world country.

But some soldiers took to wearing tattoos they believed only other commandos would recognize. Terrorists wouldn't connect Kermit the Frog, if they had any idea who that was, with the Green Berets. But Blake did. The frog's catchphrase said it all: *It's not easy being green.*

So what the hell were an Army Ranger and Green Beret doing warring in a civilian home in Orange County? It was all insane.

But Blake had no time right now to reflect on the absurdity. He still had plenty of work to do.

"Remove your mask," he ordered, "and take a breath."

"Not going to happen," said Recinos. "You'll have to shoot me first."

Blake sighed. "Look, I know you're a Green Beret. Are you aware I was a Ranger?"

"Yes."

"Then what the hell are you doing attacking me?"

"I wasn't told why. And I was assured you weren't going to be harmed. If not, I wouldn't have been a part of this op, regardless of orders, until I was convinced you were an enemy of the state."

"You're being played," said Blake. "I don't know what's going on, but I'm one of the good guys in this drama. So take off your mask and breathe. I promise you, you'll awaken good as new. I swear it."

Recinos stared long and hard into Blake's eyes, weighing his soul. "Okay," he said finally, reaching for his mask. "And if my superiors *did* get it wrong, as you say, I wish you the best of luck."

"It would help if you would tell me if there are any men outside."

Instead of replying, Recinos removed his mask, took a deep breath, and collapsed to the floor, unconscious.

Blake verified that Jenna and Walsh were still alive and then rushed to the front door. He opened it halfway, but stood to the side in case this attracted gunfire. When none was forthcoming, he crouched low and screamed as loudly as he could through the opening. "Both of your comrades are unconscious. Recinos told me you were out here. Surrender in the next ten seconds and everyone lives. Stay where you are and I put bullets into the heads of your two friends."

Blake hoped his acting ability was holding up. For one, he could well be talking to himself, since there was no guarantee there was anyone outside, and further, he wouldn't hurt the helpless men lying unconscious in the kitchen under any circumstances.

"Okay then!" shouted Blake. "Your mistake! You'll miss them when they're gone. Especially knowing *you* killed them."

With that he began to swing the door fully closed.

"Wait!" screamed a man, bolting out from behind Soyer's Mercedes, his hands raised over his head. "I surrender."

"Good choice," said Blake, pushing the door fully open once more. He was a little surprised there had actually been another hostile. Good for Recinos. He had protected his teammate under threat of begin shot, never once flinching. Blake was aware there could well be more men lurking about, but at this point it was a risk he had to take.

He ordered the newcomer inside the house. As he slowly moved forward, the man shot a quick, furtive glance over Blake's head and skyward, but Blake was locked onto his eyes like a laser-guided missile and easily caught this.

He understood the significance immediately. They must have signaled their ride to return. Which meant his time was running out. "*Move it!*" he demanded, now aware the man was stalling.

Blake shot several rounds within inches of his captive's head to make his point, and the man's pace picked up considerably. Seconds after he was marched deeper into the house, Blake forced him to breathe the invisible gas that had yet to fully dissipate, and he joined his friends on the floor, unconscious.

Blake hurried to the kitchen and used a fireman's carry to haul Jenna, and then Walsh, back to their newly purchased car, studying the sky periodically.

Just as he deposited both passengers into the backseat and finished seat-belting them in as tightly as he could, he saw something far off in the distance. It was as if a small portion of the distant sky was blurry, and the blur was moving. He tilted his head in confusion, not sure what he was seeing, when it finally occurred to him that it was the helicopter he was looking for.

It was whisper quiet and somehow tricked his eye into ignoring its presence for several seconds. *Unbelievable.*

But Blake had no time to gawk. Astonishing or not, the pilot had no doubt spotted him, and the aircraft was accelerating in his direction with terrible purpose.

He started the car and tore down the hill toward the crowded street as the helo swooped down from above, a hawk having spotted helpless prey.

33

Joe Allen ran through options in his mind as the pilot beside him streaked toward Aaron Blake below.

How the hell had Blake done it?

Allen had been texted less than five minutes earlier that the targets had taken the bait, and he had been certain Blake and his two companions would soon be in dreamland on the floor.

But for someone who was unconscious, Aaron Blake sure could operate a car effectively. And none of the three men tasked with capturing him were responding to his calls.

Blake was tearing down the road at a rate that required massive balls and impressive driving skill, spurred on by the terror anyone on the ground would be feeling when under the guns of a military aircraft. He was approaching a portion of the drive that would be partially hidden under a canopy of trees, and soon thereafter he would hit the main road.

"Abort!" shouted Allen, his face showing nothing but disgust that he had actually uttered this word. "I repeat, break off."

"Break off, sir?" said Jason Thompson, pulling back on the yoke to slow his meteoric descent, but only a little, unwilling to fully retract his talons.

"Yes, break off!" repeated Allen. "Now!" he shouted, and Thompson finally pulled up into a hover.

"What would you have me do, Captain," said Allen miserably, "chase him along a busy shopping district in a Black Ops helicopter that's so futuristic it might be mistaken for a fucking UFO? It tricks the eye, but not forever. How many more chances am I going to take with technology that isn't supposed to exist—in domestic airspace!"

He shook his head. "Even if this were standard-issue equipment, I couldn't make a spectacle in Orange fucking County. And unless we want to kill him, we can't stop them anyway."

"Yes, sir," said Thompson, who had been gradually taking the helo to a higher altitude as his temporary CO was speaking.

"Land at Soyer's house again," said Allen.

He needed to learn what had happened. See if any of the men were still alive. And he still needed to conduct a more thorough search.

Allen clenched his hand into a fist and his features hardened. "But mark my words, Captain, we'll get this guy. We now have photos of the car he's driving. We can call in law enforcement and satellites. He won't stay at large for long."

"You really think so, sir?" asked Thompson.

Allen gritted his teeth. No, he didn't think so. How could he? Blake had proven himself too smart and resourceful too often for Allen to believe standard techniques would snare him. He wasn't even sure why he had said something so stupid, and then realized it was probably because he didn't want Thompson to perceive him as impotent after he had called off the attack.

So what would he answer? Would he tell Thompson the truth, that of course he didn't think they'd get him this way? Or would he feign confidence, and thus appear to be even more the naive idiot?

"Just land the helo, Captain," said Allen finally. "I thank you for your assistance, but in a short while, Aaron Blake will no longer be your concern."

34

Blake careened down the road as though the car's brake lines had been cut, now knowing how a field mouse felt when under attack from above. Totally overmatched, and totally helpless.

He half expected to receive a rocket-propelled suppository at any moment, but none came. He shot into the main street, tires squealing, and risked looking back for the helicopter, since his sense of hearing wasn't the guide it should have been, ignoring the honks, shouts, and extended middle fingers of motorists not pleased with his driving etiquette and the burnt rubber he had deposited on the road.

The aircraft was no longer behind him.

Blake blew out a long breath, his heart still pounding away in his chest. He had hoped the men after him wouldn't pull a stunt like attacking him on a crowded road in broad daylight. But given the resources of the group hunting him, he had an hour, at most, before they'd be able to divert a satellite from others duties to attend to him. He had to ditch the car, and every minute counted.

"Myla," he said to his PDA. "I need to know the largest parking structure within ten miles of here."

Seconds later his phone provided the answer to his question. There was a five-story structure four miles distant. He asked his PDA to call out directions, and his phone did so in a pleasant female voice.

His mood darkened as he drove. Yes, he had managed to pull off a minor miracle at Soyer's house, although it could be argued that his own incompetence and hubris had put him in this situation in the first place. But Nathan Wexler's flash drive had been taken, and Greg Soyer also. If he wasn't already dead.

And Blake had been responsible. It had been *his* decision to bring this good man into the middle of a situation he had known couldn't have been more dangerous.

He let out a primal scream that had been bottled up for some time, so loud and long he half-expected his two passengers to regain consciousness.

Provided Greg Soyer was still alive, Blake vowed to extricate him from this mess no matter what it took.

He made one stop at a convenience store, where he purchased two oversized blankets, before entering the busy parking garage. He was now hidden from satellites.

He parked in the farthest reaches of the structure, his car an island in a sea of empty spaces, and turned the front and back seats into couches for his two sleeping passengers, stretching them out and hiding every inch of them with a blanket, while relieving them of their money.

Jenna had two twenties, along with the five hundred dollars she had withdrawn from the ATM the night before, and Walsh had almost two hundred. Blake had five twenties, giving him a total of just over eight hundred dollars to work with.

He left the parking garage on foot and called a cab company, asking them to send a cab in fifteen minutes to a location seven blocks away. After walking for five minutes he came to a small grocery store, and used an ATM inside to withdraw five hundred dollars from his account, pushing his total to thirteen hundred. This would be the last money they would have for some time, as he was confident their accounts would be frozen very soon, and any attempts to access their money noted with great interest.

While he waited for the cab, he had Myla call up a list of cars for sale within a few miles. This time he decided his car budget could only be a thousand dollars, so they would at least have three hundred going forward. The kind of clunker he would get for this price would have over two hundred thousand miles on the odometer and make the dented Kia look like a *Ferrari*.

His goal was to buy a car and return to the parking structure for his two companions within forty-five minutes, hopefully even sooner. With luck, he could have them loaded into the new vehicle and on their way in half an hour.

The clock hadn't yet struck noon, but it had already been a very long day. And he knew it was about to get longer.

35

Jenna Morrison and Dan Walsh finally regained consciousness at about four p.m., within five minutes of each other, almost an hour after Blake had carried them inside the ratty motel he had paid for in cash, the Best Border Inn, a name that was surely meant ironically.

The motel was located in San Ysidro, a San Diego district bordering Mexico to the south. No one would expect them to remain in Southern California, and if they did, certainly not in one of its least glamorous locales, home to arguably the world's largest land border crossing, where the highway branched into twenty-five lanes, each with a booth, to accommodate almost twenty million vehicle crossings, and ten million pedestrian crossings, into the United States each year.

Blake was playing a shell game, and hiding his peas under a shell in San Ysidro was an unlikely move, and one that should help keep them all alive for a little longer.

He brought his groggy companions up to speed on what had happened after they had collapsed onto Greg Soyer's kitchen floor, and how they had ended up in a seedy motel in San Ysidro. Both were duly grateful and expressed awe at the skills that had allowed him to slip a nearly perfect trap.

Blake had walked to a nearby sub shop while they were sleeping off the knockout gas and was able to offer his two companions an assortment of sandwiches, chips, and drinks, which they gratefully devoured. Being knocked unconscious apparently stoked one's appetite, although Jenna playfully complained that she was making too great a sacrifice having to eat a meal that didn't come out of a box of granola bars.

When they had been fed and had recovered their clarity of thought, Blake said, "I'm not going to sugarcoat it. We've lost this round big.

The only positive news is that I checked, and before they got to him, Greg did manage to copy the contents of Nathan's file to a cloud account, and I was able to access it with the password. So *they* got a copy, but at least we have one too."

"So where do we go from here?" asked Jenna. "We could still have Dan study Nathan's work and then make decisions from there like we planned."

"Not yet," said Blake grimly. "Before I do anything else, I intend to get Greg back. And I have to be honest with you, I don't care what it takes."

"How?" asked Walsh.

"By talking to the bastard who took him," he replied, holding his phone out in front of him.

Jenna nodded appreciatively. "I forgot about that," she said.

"Forgot about what?" said Walsh.

"Sorry," replied Blake. "I told you about my run-in with a killer named Rourk. But I should have mentioned that I recovered his phone. He had called his superior, and Jenna put this number into my phone."

"I see," said Walsh.

"I didn't want to use it just yet," said Blake. "I wanted to wait until we understood more about what we were dealing with. The nature of Nathan's discovery and some sense of the players and their motivations."

A dark, intense scowl came over his face. "But this timetable has changed," he growled. "They know who we are. And they have Greg."

Blake nodded at Jenna. "So let's call this guy. And do what we have to do."

"Can he trace the call?" said Jenna.

"No. When I first set up shop as a PI, Greg modified my phone. I can put it in a mode that Greg guaranteed can't be traced."

"That's good enough for me," said Jenna.

Blake turned to the physicist. "Dan," he said, "I want you to listen in, but I don't want to reveal that you're with us. They know Jenna hired me and that we're together. They almost certainly know you're involved, but why confirm it? And they can't be sure we didn't split up. So let's not give them any more information than we need to."

"I understand," said Walsh. "I won't make a sound."

"Okay then," said Blake. "Let's do this. It's time to find out what the hell this is all about."

36

Blake set his phone to speaker, audio-only, and had Myla tie it into the microphone and sound system of the motel's television set. This way, he and Jenna could speak normally in the direction of the television and their voices would be picked up easily, and all three in the room could hear and see audio or video coming from whoever answered.

As expected, Blake was forced to leave a message, since whoever they were calling wouldn't recognize an incoming call from the PI's phone, and would let it go to voicemail. But also as expected, Blake's phone rang minutes later.

He had a feeling his call would get attention in a hurry.

Blake and Jenna had taken up positions sitting on a solid beige bedspread at the end of the king-sized bed, facing the television, and Walsh sat to their side, at a small desk, facing the same direction.

Blake glanced at Jenna, who nodded her readiness.

"Aaron Blake here," said the private detective as he accepted the call.

"I got your message," said a baritone male voice. The video was also off at the other end, so this had become an old-fashioned audio-only call. "I have to say the timing couldn't be more ironic, since we didn't know who you were until about an hour ago."

"Sure you didn't," said Blake skeptically. "And who are *you*?"

"My name is Edgar Knight. Do you mind if I call you Aaron?"

"How very polite," growled Blake icily. "Sure, call me Aaron. And while you're being polite, I have an idea: stop trying to kill Jenna Morrison and everyone she touches."

"It was never my intention to hurt Jenna or anyone else involved. Can I assume she's there with you?"

"She is," said Blake. "But let's cut the bullshit already. I'll tell you why I called. You have Greg Soyer. Keep the flash drive, which is all you've ever cared about anyway, for reasons that escape me. But return Greg unhurt. You don't need him. And I have a copy of the information on that drive also. It's stored in the cloud and rigged with a fail-safe. If a week ever passes without both me and Jenna Morrison having entered a code, it's automatically released into the wild. And we can also proactively trigger it at any time."

He leaned closer to the television and its microphone. "So I'll offer an exchange. You give me Greg Soyer. And in return, I won't blast Nathan Wexler's findings to every last corner of the Internet."

There was long silence. "I honestly have no idea what you're talking about."

"Don't play stupid!" thundered Blake. "It won't help you. You sent a team of Green Berets to retrieve Nathan Wexler's thumb drive, and to capture my friend Greg."

"Oh shit!" said Knight, as though he had just been informed he had an inoperable brain tumor. "You've got the wrong guy. I had nothing to do with this. A man named Lee Cargill is behind this. Which is exceedingly bad news," he finished grimly.

"Who is Lee Cargill?"

"Look, Aaron," said the caller, "you're right. It is time to cut the bullshit. It's time for me to explain everything. Because there's a lot going on here, and you're operating under some very false assumptions. As a first show of good faith, I'm going to start sending video from my end."

A moment later the man's image appeared on Blake's phone and the motel's thirty-inch television monitor. He was dressed casually and looked to be in his forties, with receding brown hair, parted down the middle, and eyes that were an intense dark blue. He had the look of a man long used to being in charge, and one who didn't suffer fools gladly. His narrow face showed the hint of several pockmarks, perhaps acne scars from his adolescence. He stared calmly at the camera and didn't speak, as if knowing his audience would appreciate a brief pause to study his appearance.

"I trust you can see me," said the image on their television after a few seconds had passed. "Let me say again, in no uncertain terms, that I don't have your man, this . . . Greg Soyer. In fact, I have no idea who that is. And while I do want Dr. Wexler's flash drive, I don't have it."

"Why should we believe anything you say?" snapped Blake.

"Look, I understand how you feel," replied Knight. "And I have some sense of what you've been going through. Especially you, Jenna."

"No you don't!" hissed Jenna, chiming in for the first time. "Don't even *pretend* that you do!"

Knight nodded gravely, but Blake also had the sense that he was pleased to get this confirmation that Jenna was on the call.

"I know it's been a nightmare for you," said Knight, "and I apologize for that." He paused. "But let me start at the beginning and lay it all out for you. And hopefully you'll begin to understand the whys of the past few days."

Dan Walsh remained perfectly silent but quietly moved his chair forward a few feet so he could be in line with his companions, see their expressions, and gesture to them if he felt this was useful.

"To begin with," said Knight, "I am an experimental scientist. In my not-so-humble opinion, the best who ever lived. I have an intuitive sense of how things should work—and what technical goals might be achievable. Think of me as akin to an autistic savant, those strange people able to memorize phone books or calculate square roots as fast as a computer. Or a chess prodigy, able to see all the pieces as lines of force, able to remember the positions of thirty games simultaneously and win them all while blindfolded."

"Okay already," said Blake, rolling his eyes. "We'll stipulate you're good at what you do. Is this going anywhere?"

Knight smiled, either not offended, or doing his best to pretend to be affable no matter what was thrown at him. "By the time I was thirteen, I had come up with inventions that netted me millions. The media was calling me the next Edison. Long story short, the head of Black Ops R&D got wind of my abilities and plucked me right up after I graduated MIT. They made an offer I couldn't refuse. Full access to a dizzying array of expensive toys—many of them being kept secret from the public—an unlimited equipment budget, and a chance to work on the most interesting problems in all of science and technology. And royalties on any tech I developed once it was declassified for commercial use, which could ultimately be worth billions. As I proved myself over the years, I was eventually given unlimited freedom to pursue whatever was of interest to me."

He paused and then leaned in toward his unseen audience. "Four years ago, I joined a group headed by a man named Lee Cargill, who had a brilliant track record of assembling teams in such a way as to produce extraordinary results. In this case, he was working on finding practical uses for dark energy."

"There are no practical uses for dark energy," said Jenna. "Nathan told me that repeatedly."

"This was certainly the going wisdom when I began, that this energy field could never be harnessed. Still, with something this leading edge, I was eager to apply my particular genius to the problem. As is sometimes the case with Black Ops projects, Cargill had fabricated the footprint of a large tech company as a front, which he named Q5 Enterprises."

"Is the Q for quintessence?" asked Blake. Given what Jenna had told him about this being considered the fifth force, Q5 seemed an appropriate name.

"Very good," said Knight, nodding approvingly at this demonstration of Blake's knowledge.

"So I joined Q5," he continued. "And Cargill. If this were a *real* tech company, you could think of him as the chief executive officer and me as the chief technical officer."

Knight sighed loudly. "I know most people believe everything the government does, especially within Black Ops, is all about war mongering, for military uses only. But this isn't true. Yes, the military gets first dibs and can elect to keep findings secret for a time, but many of the greatest tech advances in history came about as military projects that were initially covert. Secret research during World War II on radar spawned numerous non-military applications, including the microwave oven, initially called the Radar Range. Efforts to crack Nazi codes led to much of the foundation for modern computers. Military rockets led to the space program. Jet engine research led to . . . well, jets. And both the Internet and GPS were initially developed by the US Department of Defense."

"We *get* it," said Jenna disdainfully. "Once the military skims off anything that can be used to kill and destroy, they sometimes allow their technology to be used constructively. So you worked in secret, on a Black Ops team, but you gave your little speech just now so we would know that your giant heart has always been in the right place," she spat, her tone dripping with acid.

"That was the point I was trying to convey," admitted Knight calmly, "although without the sarcasm. But just because what I said paints me as more humanitarian than monster, this doesn't mean it isn't true."

"Sure it doesn't," said Jenna skeptically. "But go on."

"Let me cut to the chase. After years of effort, I succeeded—almost two years ago. I won't go into details of how I cooked up the apparatus, or why my intuition told me it would work, but it did. And not in the way anyone expected. Turns out I could safely harness quintessence—but only to one end." He paused for effect. "To send matter back in time."

The silence that seized the motel room was profound, but only lasted a few seconds. "You mean to say you've actually done this?" blurted out Blake in disbelief.

"I have," said Knight. "Believe me, it took some time for us to realize what was happening, and months for us to gain enough understanding to apply this routinely." He arched one eyebrow. "Anyone want to guess how far back in time I'm talking about?"

Jenna's mouth fell open, and she was too stunned to speak.

"A little more than forty-five microseconds?" whispered Blake.

"Excellent," said Knight. "That was a little test. It appears you *are* familiar with Nathan Wexler's work. Yes, forty-five millionths of a second."

"So what are you saying," asked Jenna, "that Nathan just stumbled upon work you had already done?"

"Yes and no," said Knight cryptically. "But allow me to table that question and get back to it later."

"It's your show," said Jenna.

"So I could send matter back in time," continued Knight. "Whatever I could fit inside my device—my time machine for want of a better term—which was about the size of a Rubik's cube. But soon I expanded this device to its theoretical maximum. The largest time machine possible is about the size of your typical buried treasure chest from the movies, or say a Coleman cooler you'd use to keep drinks cold at the beach."

"Impressive scientific precision," said Jenna caustically.

"I could give you the exact number of cubic inches out to five decimal places, but I thought I'd try to give you a visual image that would give you a better sense of it."

"So is that where you are now?" asked Blake. "Anything you can fit inside your time travel suitcase, you can send a fraction of a second into the past?"

"A little more complicated than a suitcase," said Knight, "but essentially correct. Forty-five microseconds."

"So a split second in the truest sense of the phrase," said Blake. "You are, literally, splitting a second into millions of pieces. But so what? Why is this information something you're so willing to slaughter innocents to protect?"

"I reject your use of the word slaughter," protested Knight vigorously, "along with your implication of just how willing I am to hurt people. But I'll wait to defend myself until I'm through bringing you up to speed."

"The question remains," said Blake, "how does sending something back an instant help you?"

Knight allowed the corners of his mouth to turn up into the slightest of smiles. "Almost no one grasps the implications right away," he said. "It does seem useless to go back in time less than the blink of an eye. But it's not. You're thinking about the effect the wrong way. Don't think of it as a *time* machine."

He paused once again for effect. "Think of it as a *duplication* machine."

37

All three residents of room twenty-seven of the Best Border Inn stared at the screen as if they hadn't heard correctly.

"What?" whispered Jenna and Blake at the same time.

"A *duplication* machine?" repeated Blake stupidly.

"Yes," said Knight. "You heard me. A duplication machine. You'll understand better if we forget about microseconds for now. Just imagine for a moment that you could send your cell phone back in time a *week,* to your earlier self. Wouldn't the *you* from a week earlier now have *two* cell phones?"

There was a pause in the conversation as all three inhabitants considered this scenario.

"Well, sure," said Jenna. "But that's a week. If I could only send my phone back a millionth of a second, I'd have two cell phones trying to inhabit the same space. Wouldn't that lead to an explosion? Like a matter-antimatter explosion, I guess, only bigger?"

"Not at all," said Knight smugly. "You've been misled by the science fiction you've been fed all of your life. Science fiction gets half of it right, but not all. When you travel through time, you travel through time only. *Not* space."

"I have no idea what that means," said Blake.

"Say you're in California today. You board a plane and arrive in Australia tomorrow. Once you're down under, say you activate a time machine and go back a day. Where are you?"

He didn't wait for an answer. "Science fiction would have you believe you'd be in Australia a day earlier. Right? You wouldn't end up in California, just because you happened to be there the day earlier. You don't retrace your actual steps. You would move through time, but not space. Wherever you activate the time machine is where you end up, just at an earlier time."

"And you're saying this isn't correct?" asked Jenna.

"No. I'm saying this is correct. You maintain your precise position in space. The only thing that changes is your position in time. But it's not that easy. And this is where science fiction tends to get it wrong. Because Australia, *itself*, moves. If it didn't, you *would* end up there. But the Earth doesn't stand still. You'd be pinned in space. But a day earlier, Australia wasn't anywhere *near* your pinned position. You activate your time machine and go back a day. You arrive without changing your spatial position in the universe. The only trouble is that yesterday, the Earth was millions of miles distant from where it is today. Wouldn't you find yourself in outer space?"

He was right, thought Blake, his eyes wide. And from the expressions on the faces of his companions, this was blowing their minds as well. When Knight got no response to his question, he continued.

"The Earth rotates at roughly a thousand miles per hour. It revolves around the sun at sixty-seven thousand miles per hour. Our solar system whips around the center of our galaxy at four hundred and ninety thousand miles per hour. The galaxies in our neighborhood are also racing toward something called the Great Attractor, which has a mass one hundred quadrillion times greater than our sun, and is a hundred and fifty light years from us."

Knight paused. "So how do all these motions add up? In 1989 we launched the Cosmic Background Explorer satellite, which measures something called the cosmic background radiation. Because this radiation pervades the entire universe, but not uniformly, scientists were able to get an exact measure of the Earth's speed and direction. Turns out we're moving with respect to the cosmic background radiation at two hundred and forty-two miles per second. Per *second*," he repeated.

Blake glanced at Dan Walsh, who nodded, confirming this figure.

"So I'll confess," continued Knight, "my time machine can only hit the first electron orbital, so to speak, the first landing platform Nathan spoke about, forty-five microseconds in the past. But in that amount of time the Earth has moved. I'll spare you the math and just tell you: approximately fifty-eight feet. So I can put my phone in my time machine and press *send*. And while it does travel back through time to a split second before, it stays pinned in space. But a split second earlier, the Earth was fifty-eight feet away. So in this earlier time, there are now two identical cell phones, separated by this distance."

Walsh left his seat and seized a pad of paper on the desk. He hastily scrawled on it and held it up for Blake to read. *Wouldn't it materialize in mid-air?*

"Wouldn't it materialize in mid-air?" asked Blake.

"Good question," said Knight. "By rights it should. We're not entirely clear on exactly how this works. Our best hypothesis is that while it doesn't fully move in space, only time, gravity plays a role as well, that we haven't fully characterized, such that it ends up fifty-eight feet away, but the same distance off the ground as when it started. We also shouldn't be able to achieve any directionality. The Earth moves through the universe the way it moves, and we should have no control. But we do. By adjusting the polarity of the time travel field and the directionality of the field itself—which we can do by positioning the device in a certain orientation combined with a certain field dynamic—we can more or less point the effect."

Walsh's face wrinkled up in absolute confusion, and he looked at Blake as though Knight had just told them that two plus two was five. If the UCLA physicist was confused, what hope did Blake have?

"This makes no sense at all," said Blake.

Knight actually smiled. "I don't fully understand it either. We've figured this part out empirically. Guess-and-check, over many months. Time travel doesn't seem to cut across the space-time axis, per se, which would be through the fourth dimension, but rather through a fifth dimension. Movement through this dimension translates in unexpected ways through our own, so we get results that aren't intuitive, to say the least, and don't even seem possible."

"I'll take your word for it," said Blake, giving up.

"But you've actually done this?" said Jenna. "You've actually sent matter back through time?"

"Many, many times," replied Knight. "It's become routine."

Blake looked at another scrawled question from Walsh and repeated it, even though he didn't understand what Walsh was getting at. "And what if you decide after you've sent something back, *not* to send it back?"

Knight grinned in delight. "Outstanding, Mr. Blake. You have an excellent scientific mind. No wonder you're a good detective. For Jenna's benefit, who probably isn't on the same page as you are, let's pretend again we can send something back an hour, just because thinking in microseconds messes with one's mind, and makes everything harder to understand.

"So Aaron's question is this: Say I decide that in an hour from now, I'm going to send my phone back in time an hour. The hour passes and I press the button, as planned. Because I did this, an hour earlier, a cell phone magically appears in front of my earlier self. To make this as easy as possible to picture, imagine the phone appears right next to the earlier version of itself. *Cool*, the me in the past thinks when the phone appears. I must have sent it back from the future like I was planning. Now I have *two* phones."

Knight arched an eyebrow. "But now, what if the me in the past changes his mind? What if he now decides *not* to send it back, after all? *Now* what happens? Does the second phone disappear the moment he makes this decision, like a photo of Marty McFly and his siblings? Or does it stick around? And what if the hour passes and I really *don't* send my phone back? Do I still have two phones? And if so, how is this possible? After all, in this version of reality, I never sent it back, so how is it still there?"

"Which would be the single timeline theory of time travel," said Jenna. "The one in which this type of paradox is possible. However, if a version of the chronology protection conjecture were operating, the phone would never appear in the past in the first place, as long as the universe *knew* you were going to change your mind and not send it. Or, if it did appear, you *would* send it back after an hour passed. Nothing could prevent you from doing this, including changing your mind."

Knight shook his head in wonder. "I have to say your grasp of time travel theory is truly impressive."

"So what's the answer?" said Jenna, ignoring him. "What happens?"

"What happens is that you *can* change your mind," said Knight. "And the second phone remains anyway, even if you never send it back."

"Which proves that timelines branch," said Jenna.

"Yes and no," replied Knight. "I see how you would think this is the only alternative left. That this is the answer to more than a century of time travel speculation. The instant you change the past, time branches into two separate and distinct realities. The you on the original timeline always sends the phone back. The you on the new timeline has two phones, forever, and can decide to send a phone back, or not, without affecting this."

"But you're saying this isn't really how it works either?" said Jenna.

"That's right. Turns out to be a combination of the two theories. I won't describe the experiments that led us to this conclusion. Just suffice it to say that when you change the past, you get a new timeline. But the old timeline no longer exists. No branching occurs. You reset the universe from the point of the change onward."

"You *are* planning to walk through an example of this, right?" said Blake.

"Yes. So you press the button and send your phone back an hour. Now, in the past, you have two phones. But whatever had happened before in the upcoming hour is wiped out. The universe is reset to where it was an hour earlier and then proceeds forward again. The original timeline is erased. And there is no branching."

"Which gets us back to your original question," said Jenna. "If this original timeline is erased, and you decide *not* to send the phone back this time, how do you have two phones?"

"Yep," said Knight. "It's a head-scratcher. Nonetheless, the second phone remains, and the universe just moves on from there, as if you've always had two phones, not caring about paradox. The universe would rather live with paradox than infinite timelines, I guess. Which may explain why there is a half-second limit. So it doesn't have to reset too far back, and have to wipe out too much forward history. But the bottom line is this, once a timeline affects its own past, even though it erases itself in the process, the effect it had still remains."

"So if you go back in time and kill your mother," said Jenna, "history is rewritten from the moment of her death forward. Your own history as you knew it no longer exits, and never existed. You are never born. But the universe doesn't care that you shouldn't exist, and couldn't have killed her. It just accepts the reality of a universe in which you exist anyway and she is dead. It ignores the paradox and continues forward from that point."

"Outstanding," said Knight, beaming. "There are world-class physicists who couldn't catch on this quickly."

Jenna just sneered at the television screen as he continued. "I hate to keep treating the universe like it is a living being, but the way I think of it is that the universe wants to deal with changes in time in the most efficient way possible. And it wants to maintain a single timeline, as infinite timelines aren't very efficient."

"And no doubt give the universe as much of a headache as they give me," said Blake wryly.

Knight smiled. "Exactly. Another way to think of it, which removes some time travel confusion from the analogy, is this: Say you're writing a novel, and you can only publish one version of it. You finish the novel and realize that you gave two characters names that are too similar: John Doe and John Dode. Too confusing. So you decide to go back in your novel and change John Doe's name to Steve Smith. So you tell your word processor to find every instance of John Doe in the novel and change this to Steve Smith. You hit the button and instantly, wherever you had John Doe, you now have Steve Smith."

He paused to give his listeners a chance to imagine this scenario.

"Now you want to save the file for publication," he continued. "First, to be efficient, the computer doesn't bother resaving the entire novel, since the vast majority is the same. It only saves the new name wherever it appears. Second, once this new version is saved and published, it's as though the original version never existed. Steve Smith is just Steve Smith. There is no record of him ever being John Doe. A reader would have no idea what had led to the name Steve Smith having been chosen, could never tell that this was due to a different version of the story that no longer existed."

Jenna nodded thoughtfully. "So in this analogy," she said, "the writer is God, and the novel is the universe."

"Yes. Or perhaps the universe is both the writer and the novel. Either way. I admit the analogy is tortured and incomplete, but hopefully also a little helpful."

Blake thought that it was, although he also decided he would never fully grasp how this worked. That no one ever would.

He glanced at Walsh and he could tell the physicist was ecstatic. He was receiving the kind of answers to fundamental questions of physics the likes of which might be revealed only once in a generation, if that.

"All of this may be fascinating," continued Knight. "But also a potential problem for us. Because when you alter the timeline, the universe makes as few changes as possible. You have two phones, but everything else remains unchanged."

"Right," said Blake. "You just change a name, the rest of the novel is untouched and unfolds exactly as before."

"Yes. A tiny ripple is created exactly where you changed history, but the rest of the mighty river rages on, unchanged. Just because a split second of history is wiped out when I send my phone back, everything else in the universe, not directly influenced by this event, goes forward the same way it did."

"So you send your phone back a split second," said Jenna, "and the universe starts over from this point. But if a man had an orgasm during the forty-five microsecond period that got erased, when the universe goes forward again, he'll have the exact same orgasm, and the exact same sperm will outcompete all the others in a race to the egg."

Knight's mouth dropped open. "That's right," he said. "Great example to really drive the concept home. Although I must say it isn't exactly the first one most people think of," he added in a way that made it clear this was an understatement. "But unless the phone I sent back smacks the man in the head when he's about to . . . ejaculate . . . his ejaculation, and everything else in the universe, would unfold the same way."

"So why is this a potential problem for you?" asked Blake.

"I'll have to explain with more examples. Say it's eleven a.m., and I program my device to send my phone back an hour in time, exactly when the clock strikes noon. Noon arrives and the device sends it back to eleven. So the me at eleven now has two phones, and the universe does a restart from there. The old future no longer exists. But . . ." he paused once again for effect, "because the rest of the universe unfolds as before, my original phone is still in the chamber, and the device is still programmed to send it back at noon. That hasn't changed. So even though I now have two phones, if I do nothing, the computer will send the original phone back *again*."

"But once you see you already have two phones," said Blake, "you can just cancel these instructions."

"Easy to do when you have an hour to play with," said Knight. "But in forty-five microseconds you don't have *time* to cancel your instructions. So boom, you have two cell phones, and in the new reality you continue to have two, no matter what else happens. But the time machine exists in this new reality, cocked and ready to go. So you move forward forty-five millionths of a second and, boom, the button is triggered again, and an instant earlier you now have *three* phones. And *these* three are here to stay on the new timeline, no matter what happens. But then, boom, the machine is triggered again and an instant earlier, now you have four."

There was a long, stunned silence in the motel room.

Knight waited patiently for his audience to wrap their minds around this.

"So it isn't just a duplication machine," said Blake finally. "It's a duplication machine that makes infinite copies."

"Yes, in theory. Fortunately, in practice, here is what happens: The original phone sent back ends up fifty-eight feet away from itself, on its own private real estate. But the *second* time the original phone is sent back, the second time it runs through the loop, the phone arrives at the precise location in space as the first time it was sent back. While this could result in the mother of all explosions, as Jenna suggested, it doesn't. Nuclear repulsion prevents this. Matter exerts such a strong repulsive force that other matter trying to occupy the exact same space is deflected away to a more receptive location. Like forcing two opposing magnets together. The instant you let go, they will push each other away. The third time through the loop, the new incoming phone has to be deflected even farther away, since it has to bypass two phones. And so on.

"Eventually, the phone has to be deflected such a great distance from its arrival coordinates that time travel stops working. The system doesn't have the energy to send something through time that has to be deflected so far away. Which is why your phone can't materialize in a wall or a mountain. For a wall, it will take the path of least resistance and appear just beside the wall, in open space. For a mountain, assuming no open space is near enough, time travel just won't work."

"So eventually the endless loop stops," said Jenna, "but how many phones do you end up with before this happens?"

Knight shrugged. "I'd have to do the math, but basically you can fill a space about eighty times the size of your time machine. So I can send whatever fits inside my—call it a large suitcase-sized device—and fill a space about eighty times this much volume with phones before time travel fails."

"So there isn't a way to just make a single copy?" asked Blake.

"No, there is. You can make as many as you'd like. Humans can't operate at the microsecond level, but computers can. So I have the computer send the phone back forty-five microseconds. From a location I would call the *sending station*. At the receiving station the phone appears in the past. Now there are two phones, fifty-eight feet apart. The receiver is rigged so that the instant a sensor records the phone has appeared, it signals the sending station, fifty-eight feet distant, to abort sending the original phone back. So what happens in practice is you send the phone back, get two phones, and then turn the system off."

Blake shook his head. "How can any of this even be possible?" he asked. "How can the universe work this way?"

"How can anything be possible?" replied Knight. "How did our universe of more than a hundred billion galaxies, each with hundreds of billions of stars, arise from a single point smaller than an atom?"

"This has been fascinating . . . *Edgar*," said Jenna. "Truly. But no more time travel theory. Let's get to the part where Nathan comes in. Why is he dead? Why have we been hunted?"

Knight sighed. "I understand your impatience, Jenna, I really do. But I promise you, I'm almost there."

38

Blake had studied Edgar Knight ever since his video image had appeared on the Best Border Inn's television, trying to employ what he had learned about reading body language while taking specialized courses at Fort Benning. This was not an exact science, in the best of times, and it was made harder by the fact that his mind kept either getting blown by the utterly fantastic nature of Knight's revelations, or getting fried as he tried to understand concepts out of his depth, which required a diagram, at minimum, to truly understand.

Even so, he believed that much of what the man was saying was the truth. He seemed genuine. He didn't come across as hiding an evil or sadistic streak. At least not in a way that was obvious. But innate human nature could be hidden, and truth skillfully adhered to yet distorted at the same time. So the jury was very much out on the man.

As for Jenna, she had stab wounds to her psyche that couldn't be more raw, and Blake could tell she was desperate to uncover Knight as a villain, as someone against whom she could target her venom, extract her revenge.

And poor Dan Walsh. Blake still believed asking him to sit out this call had been the right choice, but the man was jumping out of his skin he was so eager to join in.

Now that he thought of it, it was lucky the physicist *wasn't* involved. Blake could only imagine how long the call would take, and how much further over his head it would get, if Walsh and Knight were allowed to discuss these advances in scientific depth.

"At first we thought time travel was utopia," continued Edgar Knight, his pocked face slightly tilted and his dark blue eyes gleaming. "The answer to the world's prayers. Take nearly infinite dark energy, harness it to push something through higher dimensions, just a hair, and end up with a matter generator. A matter duplicator. Think of all the good it could do humanity."

"Why do I have the feeling there's a *but* coming?" said Jenna.

"Because there is. Nearly free duplication, and the ability to make massive quantities of whatever you want, has a dark side as well, as do most things. Markets would collapse. Gold bars could be duplicated until they filled stadiums. Diamonds could become as common as sand. Oil and Rolex watches. Rare stamps. And most disruptive of all, computer chips and electronics."

Knight cleared his throat. "Imagine that Apple releases its next great electronic gadget that it's spent billions developing," he continued, "or Intel a chip it's spent *tens of billions* to develop. And then, boom, a single one is purchased and duplicated millions and millions of times over a few day period, at virtually no cost, since the energy used is siphoned from a nearly infinite pool. Why purchase when you can pirate? When you can duplicate?"

"And why kill yourself trying to innovate when you know you'll just be pirated?" said Blake.

"Exactly," said Knight. "But most ominous of all is the production of super pure uranium. Uranium enrichment is difficult, time-consuming, and a key step in the construction of nuclear bombs. The difficulty of obtaining this enriched element is the only thing that keeps every terrorist on the planet from having their own nuke—and let me tell you, they wouldn't hesitate to use them. But what if a microscopic bit of enriched uranium could be turned into a *mountain* in a single day?" He paused to let this sink in. "What about heroin? LSD? Difficult to manufacture chemical toxins?"

Blake had been thinking this truly was utopia, that the world would adjust, economies would adjust, and that the good outweighed the bad—until Knight had mentioned uranium. Blake had dealt with the fanatics enough to know that if they could magically duplicate weapons and uranium the human race would be extinct soon afterward. He was beginning to see what the fuss was about.

"I'll give you one last example," said Knight, "a theoretical non-nuclear explosive. One that some believe could ultimately prove more dangerous than uranium if duplicated in the device. Carbon can form bonds at a number of different angles. In diamonds, for instance, the carbon atoms are linked by bonds angled at one hundred and nine degrees. But it's possible to force carbon into even tighter, ninety-degree angles. Possible, but brutally difficult. So you can synthesize a cube of carbon, with eight carbon atoms each forming a vertex of the cube. This is called *cubane*. This molecule is far and away the highest energy form of carbon and is under a tremendous amount of strain. Add in some nitrogen and oxygen in the right places and you get a wonder explosive. Octa-nitro-cubane," he said, emphasizing each syllable.

"The problem is," he continued, "chemical synthesis to get the tiniest whiff of this substance is a forty-step process, and most of these steps are treacherous. Despite efforts in military labs for years, no one has been able to synthesize enough octa-nitro-cubane to even test it, which is what has kept this molecule theoretical for so long."

"Until now," said Blake. "Now you could whip up a mountain of it in no time."

"I'm afraid so," said Knight solemnly. "The more we thought about the potential to use duplication for ill," he continued, "the more Lee Cargill and I decided we had to go even blacker. We had to enlist President Janney's support to make Q5 the ultimate stealth program, and to ensure this discovery never saw the light of day. Not easy, given the temptations of unlimited wealth. But we agreed we would use this discovery to help fight terror. To duplicate gold and diamonds to buy weapons for third world fighters helping us in the global conflict. And we formed another shell company that claims to specialize in the manufacture of drugs that pharmaceutical companies have given up on, simply because they can't find a way to make them."

"Is that common?" said Blake.

"It isn't uncommon," replied Knight. "There are drugs that are extremely effective, but turn out to be impossible to scale up, to make in quantity. Many decades ago a highly effective anti-cancer drug was discovered, Taxol, that could only be obtained from the bark of the Pacific yew tree, killing the tree in the process. After twenty years of effort by chemists, and hundreds of millions of dollars invested, a process was finally found to make the drug from the needles of the tree rather than the bark. Ultimately, years later, a synthetic route was discovered so that chemists could synthesize this molecule on their own, without need of the tree."

Blake rubbed his chin thoughtfully. "So you're saying you go to companies and say, give us your wonder drugs that you can't make, and we'll supply them for you?"

"Exactly. We can't tell them how we do it, of course. But we take the drug and allow runaway time travel, runaway duplication, to take its course. The companies can't argue with our success and assume we've come up with some sort of super-secret miracle chemical process."

"But if you send something back repeatedly," said Blake, a disturbed look on his face, "aren't you resetting the universe tens of thousands of times? Millions? Just to scale up a drug."

Knight shrugged. "Yes. But this has almost no impact on the rest of reality. You can try a thousand different names for a character in your novel, but it has little impact on the novel. The reader doesn't know, or care, that there are nine hundred and ninety-nine versions that led to the final name. Versions that no longer exist."

Knight opened his mouth to continue when Jenna interrupted.

"You said you were getting to where Nathan comes in," she said icily. "That was five minutes ago."

"Just a little more background and we're there," said Knight. "So we established our new Black Ops group," he continued hurriedly, "so secretive it made Area 51 look like public access television. And in addition to using the device for what we considered noble purposes, we had to make sure no one else ever developed the capability. The US did the same in the early days of the atom bomb. Imagine after World War II some college graduate student publishing easy-bake oven instructions for how to make a nuke—instructions that actually worked. You think the government wouldn't move mountains to suppress it?" Not waiting for the obvious answer he added, "And rightly so."

Knight sighed. "So we monitored the leading physicists of our generation," he said, with an expression suggesting he felt guilty about doing this. "Hundreds of men and women around the globe we thought might have the ability to one day stumble upon time travel—or duplication, if you will—on their own. I'm not proud of this. But in our defense, we had computers monitoring for key words, so human eyes never invaded privacy unless we had reason to worry someone had replicated my work. Again, imagine if this were published and everyone in the world began working on it?"

Jenna nodded at this revelation, now knowing how Nathan had come into the picture, but didn't interrupt.

"A year ago," continued Knight, "I learned that Cargill had gone off the reservation. He was using the technology to enrich himself, to gather power. He had become unstable. I confronted him on this, and he tried to have me killed. The only thing that saved me is that I had confided in several of his team, who had seen the evidence of this themselves. He couldn't be trusted with the technology. I tried to go to the president, but Cargill had beaten me to it, painting *me* as the one who had gone off the reservation."

Blake considered. He was an avid fan of the Marvel universe, and this sounded a lot like a Hydra, Shield situation. Two organizations that would ultimately be bitter rivals initially housed together.

"So we broke off from Cargill, literally and figuratively. I took a number of people with me, and a number of my devices. I duplicated enough wealth to build a world-class think tank, and a world-class team of mercenaries, and keep it all private. But Cargill is intent on finding and destroying me, because he knows I'll never stop trying to do the same to him."

Knight nodded slowly to his unseen audience. "At long last, Jenna, we're getting to you. Fast forward to a few nights ago. Nathan Wexler e-mailed a summary of his findings to Dan Walsh at UCLA. And Cargill's computer issued an alarm that was loud enough to wake the dead. Because Dr. Wexler didn't just *conjecture* about time travel. He didn't just claim to have a groundbreaking theory. No, he wrote the magic words: *forty-five point one five microseconds*! No way he arrives at this precisely correct figure if his theory is wrong."

"Okay, so that would explain why Cargill sent a team to Nathan's house," said Blake. "But if it was all about suppression, why not destroy everything immediately and kill Dr. Wexler? Why take the drive and kidnap the man?"

"Because it's not only about suppression. Not in this case. Dr. Wexler arrived at the forty-five microsecond figure from *theory* alone. This is *huge*. Extraordinary! Cargill and I would both give our arms and legs to get a look at it. Who knows what vistas this might open up?"

"Why is that such a big deal?" said Blake. "You've already perfected your device."

"I told you I'm an experimentalist. Not a theoretician. I designed my device based on experiments and intuition, and discovered that I had sent something back forty-five microseconds. But Nathan Wexler *derived* this period of time. He *understood* this at a fundamental, mathematical level. This could revolutionize the process. Who knows what insights it could give us? I made the system work, but I was driving blind. It's like the difference between solving a complex equation using the guess-and-check method, and using a tool like calculus."

Knight couldn't contain his excitement. "This is exactly analogous to the Michael Faraday, James Clerk Maxwell situation," he said, his eyes as wide as a kid in a candy store. "With me as Faraday and Nathan Wexler as Maxwell."

"Is that supposed to mean something to us?" said Blake.

The question visibly pulled Knight out of his own world and back to sobriety. "Einstein was known to have photographs of only three scientists hanging on his study wall," he explained, "Isaac Newton, Michael Faraday, and James Clerk Maxwell. Until I came along, Michael Faraday was the greatest experimentalist in history. He had almost no formal mathematics education, yet his experiments with electricity and magnetism paved the way for the electric motor, and the marriage of electricity and technology."

Knight paused. "But as amazing as this feat was, Maxwell took this to an entirely new level. He was able to translate Faraday's experiments into *theory*. Into a set of equations that showed that electricity, magnetism, and light were manifestations of the same phenomenon, and which predicted the existence of radio waves. His genius, his theoretical insight, paved the way for every major discovery in modern physics, including relativity and quantum mechanics, which in turn were the basis for a huge percentage of modern technology."

Blake glanced at Dan Walsh, whose nod confirmed the accuracy of what Knight was saying.

"I'm proud to play the role of Michael Faraday," said Knight. "But a few nights ago, Nathan Wexler likely emerged as the next *James Clerk Maxwell*. Who knows where his insights might lead?"

"Okay," said Jenna evenly, the typical disdain in her voice blunted by the unmistakable esteem in which this man held Nathan, "so Cargill was drooling when he read Nathan's message. Because he knew Nathan had hit the jackpot. So he sent a team to our house. But how did *you* find out about it?"

"I had a mole in his organization. Jack Rourk. The man Aaron met, and shot, by the way, on Palomar Mountain."

Blake nodded slowly, happy to have another piece of the puzzle fall into place.

"Jack Rourk provided intel," continued Knight. "I knew Cargill had relocated to an underground base on Palomar Mountain, and I knew the route they were taking to bring Dr. Wexler to him. So I staged an ambush. Very poorly done, I'm afraid."

"Poorly done!" screamed an outraged Jenna Morrison. "Poorly done! That's all you have to say about it?"

Knight winced. "It was supposed to be a surprise. My men had planned to use gas and other non-lethal weaponry to pry you and Dr. Wexler from Cargill's forces and bring you both to me. I would have explained the situation. I would have treated Dr. Wexler like *royalty*. I had planned to offer your fiancé the keys to the kingdom if he'd join me."

"But when it went to hell," said Jenna, "Cargill's man decided that if *they* couldn't have Nathan's discovery, no one could, least of all you. So they killed Nathan's hard drive, and then *him*."

"I'm afraid so, yes. Tragic doesn't even begin to describe it. And I take responsibility. The raid was obviously poorly designed, or maybe Cargill has someone in *my* camp. All I know is that it was a disaster."

Knight appeared genuinely distraught. And for good reason. To him, Nathan Wexler was nothing short of the Messiah, the second coming of James Clerk Maxwell.

"After this I sent a man to watch your house," he continued. "To bring you in. But when he discovered you had another copy of Dr. Wexler's work, he took matters into his own hands. And he has been severely reprimanded. But at that point, if he had just explained he wanted to talk to you, that we were the good guys, and offered to bring you in, I doubt you'd have done it. Not after what had happened."

"No. I wouldn't have cooperated," admitted Jenna.

"So Cargill's team scrubbed the ambush site at Palomar," said Knight, "and Jack Rourk was forced to reveal himself when one of Cargill's men captured Aaron. Jack did kill that man, yes, but those loyal to Cargill are driven only by greed and power, and are absolutely ruthless and despicable. They may not seem that way at first glance, but trust me, I know what they're capable of. And Cargill has the President of the United States utterly conned."

Blake decided he had only one more loose end to clear up—at least for now. He caught the eye of the physicist who was sitting nearby and nodded slowly. "So Nathan's message to his friend at UCLA is what triggered all of this, correct?" he said, turning back to face the television and Edgar Knight's image.

"Right. His message to Dr. Daniel Walsh."

"Aren't you worried that Walsh has seen this e-mail? What if he duplicates Nathan's work?"

"Dr. Walsh is a very talented man," said Knight, "but from this e-mail alone, he has no chance of recreating Dr. Wexler's results. This isn't a concern at all."

"So you aren't going to take him out? To prevent this dangerous secret from eventually becoming public?"

Knight shook his head adamantly. "Again, Walsh is harmless. Even after having read the e-mail. Rourk had told me that Cargill was monitoring the man, to get a handle on Jenna if she tried to contact him. Long story, but I actually sent a message to Walsh, urging him to block any e-mails from Jenna to make it harder for Cargill to do this. But apparently, Cargill was able to zero in on the two of you in another way, so I'm sure he's lost interest in Dan Walsh."

A kaleidoscope of emotions danced across Walsh's face. Blake couldn't tell if he was slightly offended by being called harmless, horrified that he really had been monitored, or relieved that he probably wasn't being monitored any longer, not that he still wasn't neck-deep in the muck with them, anyway.

"So say we believe what you've told us," said Jenna. "Where do you propose we go from here?"

"I'd love for you and Aaron to come in. So we can meet in person, and so you can see duplication in action. You'd be under my protection and completely safe from Cargill."

Knight sighed. "Then, *I can't tell you* how much it would mean to me to see a copy of your fiancé's work," he added, like a little girl gushing about a unicorn. "The fact that Cargill has it is a disaster, but this way he and I could at least maintain parity. If not, he's sure to be unstoppable, something this country, and ultimately civilization, will come to profoundly regret."

Blake glanced at Jenna but was unable to read her expression.

"And just to circle back to the beginning," said Knight, "I don't have the guy you say was taken. I don't know who he is. And I only learned who *you* were about an hour ago, when Jack Rourk was finally able to identify you from a photo. We were surprised you really are a PI like you said. Somehow, Cargill was able to deduce some things that we weren't."

"Jenna and I have to talk this over," said Blake. "Do some thinking. We have your number. So if we decide to take you up on your proposal, and pay a visit, we'll give you a call."

"Fair enough," said Knight. "And if you have any questions or concerns, or if there is anything else I can do to demonstrate my goodwill, don't hesitate to ask. If you'd like, I can prepare a demonstration of the technology for you and walk you through it over the phone."

"We'll keep that in mind," said Blake noncommittally, and then ended the connection.

39

"That was un-fricking-believable!" exulted Dan Walsh the second Knight was no longer on the line.

Blake grinned. Forcing Walsh to remain silent, to bottle up his questions and enthusiasm, had almost turned him into a mass of the octa-nitro-cubane explosive Knight had described.

"It's like, how can this even be real?" said Walsh, his excitement turning his dialect into that of a giddy teenager. "How can I not have dreamt it all?"

"Good question," said Blake. "*Do you* think this was real? Does everything Knight said make sense to you?"

Jenna stared at the physicist intently now as well, eager to hear his response.

"*Yes!*" said Walsh unreservedly. "If it's made up, he's spent *a lot* of time thinking things through. Because he knew his stuff. The complexities are immense, and he navigated through them flawlessly. And his Faraday, Maxwell comparison seems dead accurate to me also. I'd bet my last dollar that everything he said, at least the science part, was true."

Blake nodded thoughtfully. "What about you, Jenna?" he said. "Thoughts? Impressions?"

Jenna sighed. "I don't know. I agree with Dan. I'd be easy to fool, but the science sounded right. The logic of his interest in Nathan sounded right. And his explanation of what happened also. If I had to bet, I'd bet he's completely on the level, as much as I wanted to hate him."

She gestured to Blake. "But what about you, Aaron? What did you think?"

"I don't know what to think," he replied. "It's all crazy. Yet it sounds so plausible."

The PI shook his head. "I used to believe in God," he continued, "but after losing my close friends and staring into the face of true evil, I've become much less sure. But if there is a God, how could he allow for such an utterly insane universe? The universe resetting to where it was a split second earlier every time Knight uses his device. Runaway duplication. And how could God allow a species as flawed as humanity to control such universe-altering power? To develop a capability with this much potential for misuse, this much potential for destruction?"

Walsh frowned. "Why would God, or the universe, allow for the hydrogen bomb?" he said grimly, "which could easily wipe out our planet. The answer is that fusion is a force required to power stars. So if you want the sun, you have to live with the destructive potential of the bomb. Maybe this is the same. Maybe time travel of less than a second is part of the fabric of the universe, and if it wasn't possible, maybe the universes couldn't exist."

"Maybe," said Blake, unconvinced.

"Or maybe God thinks this makes for a more interesting universe," added Jenna.

"He'd definitely be right about that one," said Blake. "But I begin to wonder if he also doesn't have a demented sense of humor, and thinks it's fun to throw wild shit our way. I guess he's already hit us with the gem that most of the universe is made up of matter and energy invisible to us. We already know time slows down the faster you go. So why not this? Why not time travel that allows a phone from one frame in our movie to jump to the previous frame, and join its earlier iteration?"

"The concept of this is messed up," said Jenna, nodding toward Blake. "It's hard to deny that. But forgetting the science for a moment, what did you think of Edgar Knight?"

"I'm not really sure. I wouldn't be surprised if he turned out to be everything he says he is. And I wouldn't be surprised if he wasn't."

"The real question is, do we take him up on his offer?" said Jenna, turning to each of her companions in turn.

"Are you including me in this?" asked Walsh. "He didn't know I was here, so I wasn't part of the offer."

"You've become a critical part of our three-man army," said Jenna with a smile. "Which in my book makes you part of the offer. You're free to go back to your life, or you can um . . . hang out with us. Your choice."

"Are you kidding?" said Walsh eagerly. "I'm in. I'm with you whatever you decide."

Both turned to Blake and raised their eyebrows.

"I'm afraid we can't take him up on his invitation," he said. "At least not yet. Greg Soyer still isn't safe. But now we know the score, and who has him. And why. So before we do anything else, we have to pry him from Lee Cargill."

"Maybe Knight could help," said Walsh.

Blake shook his head. "Maybe, but we can't ask him. I'm still not sure I trust him. But even if every word he said was true, his camp might be infected with a spy or two. He admitted as much. Moles within moles. The only thing we know for sure right now is that we can trust ourselves."

"It's hard to argue with that," admitted Jenna.

"So we need to get your friend back," said Walsh. "But do you have any ideas as to *how* we do that?"

Blake smiled. "As a matter of fact," he replied, nodding in satisfaction, "I do."

40

Lee Cargill and Joe Allen had both made it to Cheyenne Mountain in Colorado Springs at almost the same time more than three hours earlier. Cargill had raced there immediately following his meeting with President Janney, and Allen had arrived just after his triumphant campaign to retrieve Nathan Wexler's flash drive.

Cargill was well aware that his second-in-command had failed miserably in his attempt to recover Jenna Morrison and her PI friend, but in the scheme of things, retrieving the flash drive had been of such paramount importance it was difficult for Cargill to characterize Allen's actions as anything but a complete success.

While the base inside Palomar Mountain was blacker than black, a secret kept from even the highest ranked military, the one within Cheyenne Mountain was the most famous underground facility in the world. First conceived as a cold-war defense against Soviet missiles in the late 1950s, construction of the underground city within the granite mountain was completed in 1967, beginning its life as the operations center for the North American Aerospace Defense Command, commonly known as NORAD. Although the facility was later quadrupled in size, a project that was this time kept hidden from the public, the details of the initial construction had been widely disseminated.

The facility, carved out under a ceiling of granite that stretched seven football fields high, was designed to withstand a thirty-megaton nuclear explosion. Inside was a series of twenty-five-ton blast doors, a water-storage lake, and state-of-the-art air and water purification systems. Fifteen three-story buildings were initially constructed and placed on a system of giant springs, ensuring they were protected from earthquakes and explosions. Even in the sixties it had included a medical facility, store, cafeteria, fitness center, and living quarters, and the four-fold expansion had added so much more.

Cargill never stopped marveling at the engineering capabilities of the human race. The longest tunnel ever constructed, the Delaware Aqueduct, had been completed in 1945, and ran eighty-five miles through solid rock, delivering half of the water used in New York City each day.

Since the time when projects such as this and Cheyenne Mountain had been completed, the technology used for tunneling and the construction of underground facilities had advanced by the same leaps and bounds as most every other technology. By the late eighties, boring machines weighing millions of pounds were employed to drill a thirty-mile train tunnel, over ninety feet in circumference, between the UK and France, most of which was cut deep below the English Channel, and advances made since this time made these machines look feeble.

But of all the underground bases that had ever been built, using techniques that earlier generations could only dream of, the most famous continued to be Cheyenne. The idea of such a base built under a third of a mile of solid granite captured the public fancy like nothing else, as did photos of the facility, which most often evoked a single word: *cool.*

So Cheyenne Mountain was featured in movies such as *War Games* and *Independence Day*, and in television shows such as *Stargate SG-1*, among others.

Despite its fame, Cargill had chosen it for his temporary headquarters because no place on Earth was more secure, more impregnable. And while his group would have its own wing, so to speak, they would be only one of a number of military groups, black or otherwise, calling the mountain home. This meant that security was redundant, handled by so many separate groups that a cancer within any one of them couldn't weaken the security organism as a whole.

Cargill and Allen were the only two members of Q5, now about eight hundred people strong, currently within the granite embrace of Cheyenne, but twenty others would soon join them—the twenty with the most complete knowledge of their operation, although no one other than Cargill knew it all, including his second-in-command.

Later that night, a dozen of their top scientists would move in to begin work on unlocking the secrets recorded on Nathan Wexler's flash drive. And within a few days, eight of their highest ranked and most trusted lieutenants would follow, all of whom had been recalled from assignments and asked to stay at hotels of their choice in Colorado Springs until their accommodations could be readied inside the mountain.

These men, whom Cargill collectively called the Inner Circle, all had considerable commando experience in theaters around the world, and were all intensely loyal. At least they had been at one time. This could well have changed for one of them.

There had been seven more in the Inner Circle only a few days earlier. Five of these had been among the casualties of the Palomar Mountain ambush. Jack Rourk was the sixth. And the man he had ruthlessly murdered, Mark Argent, completed the tally of devastating losses.

The other odd seven hundred and eighty members of their group, whose knowledge of the big picture was severely limited and whose activities were varied and compartmentalized, would continue to stay at the Palomar site. They would be relocated to Cheyenne in a few weeks time, and remain there for six to eight months until their new facility was ready, one President Janney had wholeheartedly supported. These other, lesser members had no idea Q5 had anything to do with sending matter a split second back into the past.

As Cargill was streaking through the sky on his way to Colorado Springs, he had sent a bulletin to every member of his group, providing the details of the new arrangement. If Knight had declined to attack the Palomar base when Cargill and Allen and his top fifteen lieutenants were there, it was inconceivable that he would do so now.

And Cargill's bulletin had been purposely misleading in one regard. He had said that he and Allen were staying at an undisclosed location, and they would be interacting with the team as needed through secure messaging and video channels, whereas the truth was that they would also be based inside Cheyenne. The hollowed-out city was large and labyrinthian enough that they could reside in a remote section, with its own exit, without fear of being seen by anyone else from Q5. Knight and his mole would be searching for them elsewhere, ensuring the rest of Cargill's team would remain unmolested.

Cargill knew that Knight would keep his powder dry until he was sure he could eliminate him. Cutting off the head of a snake was an overused cliché, but it was overused for a reason. And in this instance, it could not be more apt: Edgar Knight and Lee Cargill were the only two who really mattered.

After Cargill and Joe Allen had arrived at Cheyenne, they had toured their new digs and checked into their living quarters. Then, once the effects of the quick-acting gas had lifted, they had spent almost two hours of quality time with Greg Soyer, both giving him their undivided attention, and Cargill was convinced that no two hours had been better spent.

After they were done with Soyer they had moved to Cargill's new office, from which he would be directing Q5 for a while, although it was as much war room as office, large and high tech, with all communications untraceable.

"So I never had the chance to ask," began Allen when they both were seated around a small oval conference table, "how was your meeting with Janney? I know he agreed on your base proposals, but what else happened?"

"I got *everything* I wanted," reported Cargill triumphantly. "Most importantly, he agreed that we're too important to risk interference from future presidents. So after he leaves office, we'll be completely self-contained, a law unto ourselves."

"Perfect," said Allen.

Cargill was about to reply when his phone rang. He glanced at the caller ID. "It's a woman named Amy Adams-Vanliew," he explained. "From Homeland. I asked her to call the instant she had any credible leads on Aaron Blake or Jenna Morrison."

"Hi, Amy," he said, putting the call on one of his larger monitors. A three-dimensional image of an attractive blonde appeared. "What can you tell me?"

"Just got word that Aaron Blake accessed an ATM machine in San Ysidro, California," said the caller. "Less than ten minutes ago."

"Outstanding," said Cargill. "Where is that?"

"In southern San Diego," replied Adams-Vanliew. "It borders Tijuana, Mexico."

"Thanks. How long until you have the video of this transaction?"

"In minutes, if not seconds," came the reply. "I'll send it to your phone the moment I get it. I've asked for five minutes of footage on either side of the transaction."

"Perfect. Thanks again, Amy," he said, ending the connection.

A smile spread across Cargill's face. "This is the break we've been looking for," he told his second-in-command with great enthusiasm. "I know this Blake is good. I know you weren't surprised he managed to stay off the radar after he left Soyer's house. But nobody's perfect. He finally made a mistake."

"I'll believe that when I see it," said Allen, unconvinced.

"He's not Superman," said Cargill. "How fast can we get a team to San Ysidro?"

"San Diego is riddled with military bases," said Allen. "I could scramble a team and have them there in five or ten minutes."

Cargill was about to reply when his PDA informed him he had received the message he had been waiting for, with the video file attached.

He ordered his personal digital assistant to throw the footage on his primary screen and play it in real time, four minutes in from the beginning.

The ATM's cameras initially showed no one in front of the device, which Cargill had expected. But about thirty seconds later, a short Hispanic boy, his hair jet black and his clothing old and worn, approached the machine cautiously. He couldn't have been more than twelve.

"What the fuck?" said Cargill.

The boy slipped a colorful plastic card into a slot in the front of the ATM. He carefully consulted a piece of paper in his hand and entered a password. The instant this was completed the name Aaron Blake appeared in the corner of the video, indicating the boy had entered a correct password and the ATM's computer had now identified him as the ex-Army Ranger they were after.

Next, the boy attempted to withdraw five hundred dollars, which the ATM denied him. He grinned impishly—as though he had been told this wouldn't work but couldn't help but try anyway. The boy tried to withdraw a lesser amount, with the same result. Finally, satisfied that he wouldn't be getting any money from the machine, he requested an account balance, which the ATM dutifully printed on a small slip of paper that it spit out into his hand. He pocketed this and then turned the piece of paper he had brought with him over. He held it in front of him, facing the camera.

A message had been written on the paper in neat capital letters.

LEE CARGILL, WE NEED TO TALK.

This was followed by a phone number.

Finally, the message ended with the words, AND FEEL FREE TO SEND A TEAM HERE. YOU WON'T FIND ME.

The boy threw down the paper and ran off, no doubt to collect his spoils for a job well done.

"Maybe this guy doesn't make mistakes, after all," said Cargill, unable to hide his admiration.

Allen nodded. "The way he slipped the noose inside Soyer's home was as impressive as anything I've ever seen."

"So you've told me."

"Are you going to call him?"

"Of course," said Cargill. "But let's do some war gaming first. Let's look at this from every angle, consider the various directions in which this call might go, and plan accordingly."

"He'll be expecting you to call back immediately."

"That's okay. He'll keep." Cargill tilted his head and stared at the ceiling thoughtfully. "And maybe it's time we stop doing the expected."

41

Jenna Morrison was reclining against the headboard of the Best Border Inn's low-rent king-sized bed, her blonde wig thrown unceremoniously on an end table. Her eyes were closed, but she was wide awake. Dan Walsh was tapping his fingers rhythmically on the desk. And Aaron Blake was pacing like a caged lion, which was not easy to do in the seedy, cramped room.

It had been over thirty minutes since the kid had returned, assuring Blake that he had accomplished his mission.

So where was Cargill?

"Is it possible Cargill wasn't alerted when the boy entered your ATM password?" said Walsh.

"No," replied Blake decisively. "I may be willing to believe time travel is possible. But I'm not willing to believe Cargill would ever be so sloppy as to fail to monitor our accounts. The only reason I got away with using an ATM earlier today was that they were scrambling after our escape from Greg's house. But once they had a chance to think, this would be one of the first things they'd do."

"And you're certain the kid didn't screw up?" said Jenna.

"Not certain, but confident. He brought me an account balance like I asked, so I know he got into the system as me. He insisted he held up the paper with my message facing the camera. My Spanish isn't perfect, but it's good enough for me to be sure that *he* was sure. Maybe Cargill is out of reach, or can't be disturbed. Although I'd be surprised if he didn't leave orders to be interrupted if he got a bead on us, no matter what."

Blake sighed. "Let's give it another hour. If we don't hear, we'll try something else."

He continued pacing and checking the time. Another fifteen minutes passed, and he thought he would lose his mind if he had to wait another forty-five.

His phone rang.

Blake had already instructed his PDA to set up the call through the motel's television as before, audio-only. Cargill must know what he looked like by now, but giving him a peek at the motel room would give him clues to their location that Blake wanted to avoid.

All three assumed the positions they had taken earlier, with Blake and Jenna on the edge of the bed and Walsh seated in the desk chair.

Blake answered the call, and confirmed that it was, indeed, Lee Cargill on the other end. Unlike Knight, the man was broadcasting video from the very start. He was seated at a desk in an office that looked like a high-tech nerve center from which a military or business chieftain could conduct far-flung operations. Cargill appeared to be in his early fifties, with salt-and-pepper hair, brown eyes, and a world-weary face.

Blake introduced himself and informed Cargill that Jenna Morrison was also on the call.

"Can I assume Dr. Walsh is still with you as well?"

Blake thought about this, but saw no point in denying what had to be obvious to the man. "Yes."

"I have to say you've been most impressive, Mr. Blake. And I don't impress easily."

"Good to know," replied Blake dismissively. "But this isn't a social call. You have Greg Soyer," he said, his tone now ominous. "I want him back. *Immediately!* If not, I make sure Nathan Wexler's discovery goes viral."

Cargill let out a heavy sigh. "Fine," he said. "You can have him. He's unhurt."

His speed of capitulation made Blake certain that the man had expected this demand.

"But first let me tell you what this is all about," added Cargill. "No one was supposed to get hurt. I don't blame you for not trusting me, but let me explain what's really going on."

Jenna's expression turned feral. "Was it *you* who ordered your men to kidnap me and Nathan from our home?" she spat. "Were those *your* men in the Hostess truck?"

"Yes," said Cargill. "But let me explain."

"*Let you explain what?*" she screamed. "That one of your men shot Nathan in the face at point-blank range? Is that what you need to explain? Are you going to tell me I imagined it all? Because I was there. I saw it happen!"

Cargill's face fell. "Everyone on that exfil team was killed," he said despondently. "I didn't know for sure until just now that this is what happened in that truck, although I have to admit I suspected it. And this is on me. I know that. I was in charge of making sure you were both brought in safely, so his death is my responsibility."

"His death isn't your responsibility because you were in charge of safety!" screamed Jenna. "It's your responsibility because *your man killed him!*"

"This is far bigger than you know. Let me start at the beginning, and then—"

"No!" barked Blake. "No stories. No long conversations. I don't care what you have to say. I want Greg Soyer."

"But once I tell you what's going on, you'll see things differently. And I need you to come in so I can protect you. You're in great danger."

"No shit!" said Blake. "We're in great danger from *you*."

"Not from me. From a man named Edgar Knight."

Blake arched one eyebrow. "Yes," he said. "We've had the pleasure of speaking. How do you think I know you have Greg?"

"Shit!" said Cargill, shaking his head. "Tell me you didn't give him Dr. Wexler's file."

"I don't have to tell you squat," said Blake derisively.

"Look, given what I know about you and your prior actions, I have to assume you were prudent enough not to give this up right away. Which means Knight is moving Heaven and Earth to find you, so he can get it. You can't trust him, although I'm sure he said the same thing about me. But let me tell my version of the truth—which is the *actual* truth—and you can decide for yourself."

"After I have Greg Soyer."

"But I'm the only one who can give you adequate protection."

"Look," said Blake, "I don't know who to trust, and I'm not in the mood for another lengthy conversation about forty-five microseconds of time travel. But once I have my friend back, I'll humor you. You can give us a call and delight us with your storytelling abilities, okay?"

Cargill shook his head in obvious frustration. "You're making a mistake not listening to what I have to say. And you're putting far more at risk than just yourself."

"I'm willing to take that chance," said Blake.

Cargill sighed. "It looks like I don't have any other choice," he said in resignation. "So you win. Looks like we're going to play it your way."

42

Brian Hamilton sat alone in a booth at the Colorado Springs Outback Steakhouse and sliced off a small piece of the twenty-ounce prime rib he had ordered, intending to savor every last piece. He brought the fork to his mouth, already salivating from the aroma. As the flavor washed over his taste buds his phone buzzed, indicating he had a secure text coming in, from none other than Lee Cargill himself.

He glanced around the room, out of habit, to ensure there were no prying eyes, but this was unnecessary as he was in a booth with his back against a wall.

He shoved another piece of steak into his mouth and began reading:

This message is for members of the Q5 Inner Circle only. We have recently come to learn the whereabouts of Jenna Morrison and Aaron Blake. You are familiar with Jenna Morrison and why she is important, but I've been purposely keeping you out of the loop, so Aaron Blake is a name you haven't heard.

Blake is an ex-Army Ranger she recruited, and from our experience, elite even among this elite group. He has also proven himself highly capable, creative, and quite competent at the art of deception. While we think recovering these two will now be routine, we've made this mistake before. When we first tried to bring in Jenna Morrison and Nathan Wexler, we were also confident it would be a cake walk. Until we ended up losing over a dozen men, including five from the Inner Circle.

For this reason, even though acquiring these two targets should require very little manpower, I want all eight of you to join me and Joe Allen on this op.

Along with Morrison and Blake, a scientist named Dan Walsh is with them at a motel, at an address and room number provided at the end of this message. Joe Allen and I are flying to Cheyenne Mountain now, since we know all of you are in the vicinity. Two hours from when I send this, at eight tonight, we will all meet at runway three, where an aircraft will be gassed up and ready to go. I'll provide an extensive mission briefing while we're en-route to their motel.

I need to tell you we suspect we have a mole in the organization. We don't think it is one of the eight of you, but we can't rule this out. This is one reason we're taking all of you along, because if one of you do decide to cause trouble, he will be hopelessly outnumbered. For this reason, I must ask you to keep your eyes open and watch each other. And Joe and I will be doing nothing but watching all of you during the mission.

I hate to do this, since nothing impairs a mission more than not being able to trust every one of your teammates with your lives, but I have no choice. Again, I can't imagine the mole, if he exists among you, would dare reveal himself given this warning and the numbers involved, but understand that this is still a possibility.

That was everything. Beneath this was Lee Cargill's electronic signature, and below this the address of the motel at which their targets were staying.

Hamilton shook his head in wonder. Perfect!

He forwarded the message to Edgar Knight's highest priority address, one he had never used before, and one whose misuse was not taken lightly, since Knight's PDA would wake him from the dead if it ever received a message on this channel. If Knight later decided the importance of a message didn't warrant this pulling of a fire alarm, heads would roll, or in this case one head: his.

But Hamilton knew that Knight would not consider this a false alarm.

He would consider it one of the most important messages he had ever received.

***

Hamilton finished his meal in total contentment. He had plenty of time to reach the rendezvous point at Cheyenne mountain while Cargill was flying in. He finished his last bite, smacking his lips in satisfaction, and then leisurely ordered and finished a large wedge of cheesecake.

Finally satiated, he left his pretty young waitress a big tip and drove back to the Colorado Springs Hilton, where he had chosen to stay while awaiting the assignment of permanent quarters inside the mountain.

He was resting in his room, thirty minutes before he planned to leave for the base, when his cell phone indicated he had received another priority message from Cargill. He quickly pulled it up and began to read.

To members of the Q5 Inner Circle. Belay my last orders. I had negotiated a handoff with Aaron Blake, which you would have been briefed on, but it turns out this was yet another test, another deception. I mentioned Blake was slippery, and careful. It turns out that he isn't at the motel he said he was, and now has insisted on a new rendezvous point and set of procedures.

Given these changes, and given his painstaking caution, I've decided not to take any chances. For this reason, Joe Allen and I will be handling this by ourselves, after all.

Apologies for the change of plans. I will be contacting you soon to give you details about your new quarters and assignments.

Lee Cargill.

"God-dammit!" thundered Hamilton in disgust. So much for getting lucky.

He quickly forwarded this message to Edgar Knight using his highest priority channel once again. His boss would know these events were out of his control, and that he had proceeded precisely as he should have, but he would not be happy.

43

As he watched Greg Soyer exit the small commercial helicopter in the waning light of sunset, Aaron Blake felt a crushing weight lifting from his throat. He had been suffocating since his friend was taken, and finally felt as if he could breathe freely again.

Soyer looked unharmed and in good spirits, as advertised.

Blake had sent Cargill's pilot to two other locations, changing the drop-off point to the Torrey Pines helipad at the last moment, ensuring they couldn't set up a team on the ground to keep tabs on him. He also had a clear strategy for getting out from under satellite surveillance once he picked up Soyer.

Jenna and Walsh were safely back at the Best Border Inn in San Ysidro, waiting for him to lose any surveillance and return for them.

Jenna had suggested the Torrey Pines helipad for the handoff since it was in an area considered part of La Jolla, where she lived, and she knew it well.

The area was heavily wooded with its namesake tree, the Torrey pine, which basically only grew on this narrow strip of coastline, making it the rarest species of pine in the US. In addition, the Torrey Pines area was home to a prestigious hospital and a thriving biotech community, a spectacular golf course situated along cliffs overlooking the Pacific, and a two-thousand-acre natural reserve, with eight miles of trails.

The helipad was surrounded by the location's namesake pine, which provided both shade and isolation, but was also near a frequently traveled street. The air was fresh and cool, and Blake's surroundings were tranquil and beautiful, but he was focused only on his friend and the small helicopter.

As Soyer moved quickly away from the helo, heading due north as Blake had instructed, the helicopter rose into the air and flew off toward the east. Blake watched it carefully until it was out of sight.

Not that he had any real concern Cargill would make a play for him. He had made sure the man knew he had separated from his two companions, so that if anything happened to him they could still release Nathan's work, the very threat that had secured Soyer's release in the first place.

Blake was sitting in the driver's seat of a rusted yellow Chevy Impala, the second car he had purchased that day, parallel parked on the street between a Mercedes convertible and a Lexus sedan. When Soyer was within twenty yards of him he exited the vehicle and waved him over. His friend quickly closed the distance between them and they exchanged a heartfelt bear hug.

"I am so sorry I got you into this," said Blake.

"Don't be," said Soyer. "You did warn me what might happen."

This did little to assuage Blake's guilt, but he needed to move on. "Are you bugged?" he asked.

"I don't think so. But knowing you, you're prepared to check."

Blake grinned. "You know me too well, Greg," he said, removing the same bug detector he had used to clear Dan Walsh. Within a minute, he had cleared his friend as well.

They both got into the car and shut the doors, but Blake didn't start the engine. "So what happened after you were captured?" he asked. "Did Cargill tell you anything about what's going on? Was he able to crack the flash drive?"

Blake also wondered if Cargill had used torture, or had threatened such, in order to get Soyer to reveal the password, but decided Cargill was too smart for this tactic. For all Cargill knew, Soyer had set up a password that would initiate an immediate self-destruct, so any password that was coerced out of him could blow up in Cargill's face. Better to crack it on his own.

"Before I tell you what happened," said Soyer, "can I assume we'll be reunited with your friend soon? You know," he said in amusement, "Jane Smith."

"Not immediately," replied Blake, "but soon enough. I have all kinds of fun planned to be sure we shake any human or electronic eyes on us before I go anywhere near her."

"Where is she?"

"At the Best Border Inn in San Ysidro. Nothing but the best for my clients."

"Yeah, I noticed the word *best* in the name of the inn."

"And for good reason," said Blake with a grin. "It's the finest one-star motel money can buy."

Blake started the car to begin taking his pre-planned counter-surveillance measures. He was wedged in between the two luxury cars surrounding him with only inches to spare on either end.

The car was so old it didn't even have a rear-view camera, so he studied his mirrors to begin to extricate himself from the spot, as optimistic as he had been since this whole affair had begun. Maybe things were finally turning in their favor. Knight had made a gracious offer for them to align with him, and to protect them from Cargill. His friend was safe and unhurt. And they now had leverage that had proven its value.

Blake continued to bask in positive thoughts, right up until he heard a loud spitting sound and felt a dagger in his gut at the same instant.

He clutched at his stomach, but instead of finding a gaping hole, he found a tranquilizer dart imbedded there.

He had just enough time to glance up to see Greg Soyer with a gun in his hand.

In a rush, he realized what had happened. He had been shot at point-blank range by a man he considered to be his closest friend.

He had no time to consider this betrayal further as the drug hit his bloodstream and he slumped over against the steering wheel, unconscious.

PART 3
Pandora's Box

"I myself believe that there will one day be time travel because when we find that something isn't forbidden by the over-arching laws of physics, we usually eventually find a technological way of doing it."

—David Deutsch (Oxford Physicist who laid the foundations for quantum computing)

"Technology . . . is a queer thing. It brings you great gifts with one hand, and it stabs you in the back with the other."

—Carrie Snow

"Beam me up, Scotty. There is no intelligent life on this planet."

—Unknown (often printed on T-shirts)

44

Blake awoke, having no idea how long he had been out. He was unbound and found himself in a room the size of a small classroom, with several conspicuous cameras pointing at him from above. Jenna Morrison and Dan Walsh were lying on the floor beside him, unconscious, but apparently unharmed. Jenna had cleaned the eyeshadow from her face after he had left the motel, and whoever had deposited her here had done her the favor of leaving the hideous blonde wig behind.

His memories returned and he pieced together what had happened. Soyer had shot him with a dart and he had been taken here—wherever *here* was. He had told Soyer where Jenna and Dan were staying, which explained how they had been gathered up, surely a simple exercise without him there to protect them.

Had Soyer been working with Cargill all along?

It seemed impossible.

But then so did so many other things he had learned of recently. His definition of the word *impossible* was certainly getting a work out.

He looked down and saw a page of unruled printer paper affixed to his chest by a piece of clear tape, with a message neatly scrawled on it in blue ink.

Touché, he thought. Apparently, one low-tech, hand-written message deserved another. He began to read:

To: Aaron Blake

From: Lee Cargill

Since you are reading this, you have no doubt recently awakened. We expect you to be the first, but we tried to time things so your friends will also awaken fairly soon. We gave you enough of a dose that you would sleep through the night, so it is now Wednesday morning.

Given that you are unbound in an innocent-looking room, you might be tempted to escape, but let me discourage you from such an attempt. You've no doubt noticed the cameras. The door is locked and there are men as highly trained as you guarding it.

In case this isn't enough of a discouragement, you should know that you are now in perhaps the most secure military facility in the US, Cheyenne Mountain. If you aren't familiar with this base, and haven't seen it in any movies, it is a tiny city carved out of a granite mountain in Colorado Springs. Trust me, as formidable as you are, you have no chance of escape.

Sorry about having to proceed in this way, but you refused to let me explain things over the phone, so I felt I had no other choice. As soon as your friends are awake, though, I promise to bring you all up to speed and answer your questions.

I look forward to meeting you in person.

Lee

Blake glanced once again at the cameras facing him, and then at the door. As much as he was tempted to try to escape, he believed Cargill's message. After all, the man could have easily chained him to a wall. He didn't need to bluff.

But Blake had to admit, being held prisoner within America's premier fortress was the last situation in which he had ever expected to find himself.

He sighed. Maybe cheating spouse cases weren't so bad, after all.

45

True to Cargill's word, the moment all three prisoners were awake a man named Joe Allen arrived to escort them to a large conference room within the mountain.

Blake couldn't help but gawk at a site he never expected to see, and Jenna and Dan were doing the same. They first passed a wide tunnel protected by a famous twenty-five-ton blast door that was only shut in times of crisis. Blake estimated that the steel door was over three feet thick, ten feet tall, and slightly more than ten feet wide.

After this they continued on through several sections of the complex, including a glossy paved concrete road as wide as a runway, claustrophobic corridors dotted with doorways, and expansive brown, unfinished caverns, in which the mountain ceiling and walls had been smoothed but left natural and uneven, in case anyone had any doubt where they really were.

They finally arrived in a standard conference room that would have been at home in any Fortune 500 company in America. Opulent leather chairs surrounded a never-ending lacquered redwood conference table, so smooth and shiny it almost seemed radioactive. Oversized plasma television monitors covered the walls, and a clean, overturned drinking glass had been placed at each spot around the table, waiting to be filled by one of several evenly spaced pitchers of icewater perched on large lattice coasters.

When the three prisoners had taken a seat next to each other near the center of the table, their armed escorts left, and Joe Allen took a seat across from the trio. Seconds later Lee Cargill entered and extended his hand.

Blake ignored it, focusing instead on the man who had entered next to him: Greg Soyer.

The PI shot up from his seat and looked ready to leap over the table, causing both Cargill and Soyer to reflexively step backwards.

"You son-of-a-bitch!" hissed Blake at his former friend. "Were you with them from the very *beginning?*"

Soyer shook his head and looked physically ill. "How could I be, Aaron?" he barely managed to croak out.

Here was a man who had battled vicious terrorists with courage and calm, but seemed to be unraveling when confronted by a friend he had betrayed. "I knew nothing about this until you brought me into it."

Soyer took a deep breath. "But after they captured me," he continued, "they were very persuasive. You'll see. I don't blame you for hating me right now. But everything I did, I did with your interests at heart, and with good intentions."

Blake bored deep into Soyer's eyes and saw nothing but hurt and sincerity. He unclenched his fists. He had been too close to this man not to at least hear him out. And he would believe almost anything before he would believe Soyer would purposely do him harm.

He sat back down beside his two companions, who had been tensely observing the altercation and who seemed relieved that this powder keg had not gone off, at least for the moment.

Cargill gestured to Soyer, still standing by his side. "I know what you must think of this man," he said to Blake. "But put yourself in my shoes, in your friend's shoes. Edgar Knight is good enough to convince you that he's Mother Teresa and I'm Darth Vader. I have no idea what he told you, how much he's poisoned you against me. All I know is that you refused to even let me make my case."

"You could have told me you'd won Greg over. *He* could have told me. That would have changed things."

"Maybe. I considered this. But over the phone, you might have convinced yourself he was being coerced. Or that we had fed him nothing but lies, and he was being duped. You had no idea who to trust. You still don't. And Greg Soyer was my ace in the hole. If I would have let you know he was siding with me, and you refused to come in, I couldn't have used the tactic that *did* get you here."

Blake glared at Soyer once again, but remained silent.

"Edgar Knight is the wrong man to underestimate," said Cargill. "I've made that mistake several times now. He's brilliant, competent, and has unlimited resources. Believe me, there is no doubt he was closing in on you fast. If he found you, as I said, the consequences for you, and the world, would be catastrophic. For all I knew he was minutes away. I explained the danger you were in, and Greg believed me."

Cargill finally took a seat next to Joe Allen, facing the three prisoners, and Soyer followed suit.

"So if you were in his shoes," continued Cargill, "what would you have done? You believe that your best friend might be one step away from a landmine, but has been lied to and isn't in the mood to trust anyone, or anything. Do you risk taking the time to try to win him over to your point of view, while he continues to traipse through the minefield? Or do you tranquilize him before he can take another step and airlift his ass to safer terrain?"

As Cargill finished, Blake noticed that Soyer's eyes had moistened, indicating he was experiencing emotions too powerful to fully contain. Apparently, Soyer's betrayal had been as hard on him as it had been on Blake.

But this still didn't mean his friend hadn't been duped.

"You've made an interesting case," said Blake, "but it all hinges on how real or imaginary this minefield is. So I'll postpone judgment—for now." He waved a hand at Cargill. "You wanted to tell your story. Okay, you have the floor."

"Before I begin," said Cargill, "I need to know everything Edgar Knight told you."

"And if we refuse?" said Blake.

"Then you refuse. I won't try to coerce you. But knowing what truths, and untruths, you've been told will allow me to proceed more efficiently, and I'll be able to tell which parts of his story I need to demonstrate are lies." He shrugged. "But it's your choice."

Blake glanced to either side of him, and both Jenna and Walsh nodded their approval. "All right, we'll do as you ask," he said. "Why not?"

The three prisoners took turns covering the tenor of their conversation with Edgar Knight, as much as they could collectively remember. Soyer appeared fascinated, while Cargill and Allen remained poker-faced throughout.

"So that's everything," said Blake when they had finished.

"Thank you," said Cargill.

"So now I suppose you're going to tell us it was all lies, right?"

Cargill smiled wearily. "No," he replied, "because it wasn't. What Knight told you about going back in time forty-five microseconds is accurate. So is his depiction of Q5's initial mission, and how this changed once he found a way to tap dark energy and send matter back in time."

He shook his head adamantly. "But it was *Knight* who went off the reservation. Not me. He broke off from Q5, killing some very valuable people on the way out the door. He had become paranoid, with delusions of grandeur, although I didn't recognize this until later. He is no doubt brilliant, every bit the inventive genius of a Faraday, as he told you. But there can be a fine line between genius and insanity. Years ago there was a guy named Ted Kaczynski, a brilliant mathematician accepted into Harvard at sixteen, who became a crazed recluse, killing three and injuring dozens in bombings over several years."

"Was he the guy they called the Unabomber?" asked Blake.

"Exactly. And Bobbie Fischer was considered the greatest chess player who ever lived, and he ended up losing complete touch with reality. John Nash, a brilliant mathematician who developed game theory, was debilitated by paranoid schizophrenia. There are numerous other examples of brilliant people becoming deranged."

"So what?" said Blake bluntly. "I can give you more examples of *stupid* people becoming deranged. This doesn't prove anything."

"I didn't say this *proved* anything. I just thought I'd point it out."

"And now you have," snapped Jenna. "So Knight says you're the rogue, and you say *he* is. So how do we know who's lying, and who's telling the truth?" She shook her head, a dark scowl on her face. "The only thing I know for sure is that your side killed Nathan in cold blood."

"For one, I have a video of Knight trying to convince me of his perspective, before he took matters into his own hands. The video that, among other things, convinced Greg Soyer. But even without that, from what you've told me about your conversation with Knight, I know he lied about several other things, and I can *prove* it."

"And these things are?" prompted Jenna.

"First, he lied about the maximum physical dimensions of his time travel devices. You can construct them as big as a room. Second, he lied about his reason for wanting Dr. Wexler's work. He didn't want it to improve the process. It's already seamless."

"So why then?" said Blake.

"Because he's only ever been able to get his device to push back forty-five microseconds. But he *desperately* wants it to be able to go back the full half-second Dr. Wexler indicated should be possible."

"I still don't get it," said Blake, shaking his head. "Why does any of this matter?"

"I agree," said Walsh. "How did lying about these things help Edgar Knight in any way?"

"Because it allowed him to accomplish exactly what he accomplished," said Cargill. "As always, he did a brilliant job of it. He managed to freak you out about the possibilities of time travel, of duplication, to justify why this discovery needed to stay hidden forever, and convince you my actions were due to megalomania and greed."

Cargill leaned forward, and his voice took on a new intensity. "But Knight didn't even *scratch the surface* of what is possible. He made you think the device was the size of a suitcase, and limited his examples to cell phones." He paused. "And he did this for a very important reason."

"What reason?" said Blake, still not seeing it.

"To distract you. Like a great magician, he focused you on the small so you'd never consider the big. Why? Because a *human being* can't fit inside a suitcase," pointed out Cargill. "If he started you off thinking the device could be as large as a room, you would soon ask the question: can you send *people* back in time? In essence, can you duplicate not just phones, but *human beings?*"

Blake's jaw dropped, and his two companions both reacted with equal dismay.

"In case you were wondering," continued Cargill, "the answer to both questions is *yes*. If you think duplicating octa-nitro-cubane, enriched uranium, and complex electronics opens up some serious cans of worms, spend a few days thinking through the implications of copying *people*."

All three prisoners remained absolutely dumbfounded, too much in shock to attempt speech.

"And, yes," said Cargill, "I can show you a device much bigger than Knight said was the theoretical maximum, and give a demonstration, *proving* that he lied."

Walsh was beginning to recover his mental equilibrium, and his shrewd scientific mind was coming back to life. "Okay, this explains why he had to pretend the device was small," he said. "But why the half-second? This doesn't help him duplicate matter any better than forty-five microseconds does."

Cargill raised his eyebrows. "One word," he said evenly. "Teleportation."

46

This word hit the room like a fifty megaton bomb. Blake's mouth hung open once again as he tried to steady himself.

Teleportation?

Of course, teleportation, thought Blake. How had they missed it?

Because Knight had done a brilliant job of misdirection, as Cargill had said. Getting them to think small, and solely about phones, really had prevented them from taking the next logical leap. As magicians had learned many ages earlier, human beings were easy to misdirect.

"The Earth moves through space at a rate of two hundred and forty-two miles per second," mused Walsh, as if talking to himself. "So in *half* of a second, we'd be looking at . . ." The physicist paused, reluctant to even finish.

"About a hundred and twenty miles," whispered Jenna, completing his sentence.

All three newcomers to Cheyenne Mountain began speaking at once.

Cargill held out his hand as if it were a stop sign. "Before we get too far ahead of ourselves," he said loudly to be heard above the clamor and to stifle the excited cross-talk, "let me start at the beginning."

"Good idea," said Blake after the commotion from his side of the table had died down.

Blake rose and poured himself a glass of water from a nearby pitcher, and then poured one for each of his companions. Walsh took a long drink immediately, with an expression suggesting he wished it were alcoholic.

"We began with the goal of tapping dark energy, as you know," said Cargill. "And then Edgar Knight made his discovery, and we started considering the possibilities. Including human duplication.

But before we wasted any time discussing this further, we conducted a series of experiments."

"Right," said the UCLA physicist, "because you couldn't be sure anything could live through the time travel process."

"Correct. We had no idea what effect this might have on life, and especially sentience. So we began by sending back an assortment of bugs, one by one. A pill bug, an ant, a spider. We ended up with perfect copies, and none seemed to be any worse for wear." He paused. "And just to be clear, the words *copies* or *duplication* are just used for convenience."

"We understand," said Walsh. "You aren't making a copy, per se. You're taking an older version of something and sending it back in time to join a version that is a split second younger."

"Exactly. So after we tried this on bugs, we sent back hamsters. They did fine, also. Finally, we made a copy of Joe's dog, a black cocker spaniel and poodle mix named Dash," he explained, nodding toward Joe Allen seated beside him. "It was the most important test of all."

"Why?" said Blake.

"Because if anything had changed in Dash's brain," guessed Walsh, "it would manifest itself behaviorally. And a man knows his own dog. Joe would know if there was anything different about him."

Cargill nodded. "That's right."

"You'll be happy to know," said Allen, "that Dash made it through with flying colors. The trip through forty-five microseconds of time had absolutely no effect on him whatsoever."

"And the duplicate is still alive?" asked Jenna.

"Absolutely. Dash and Dash have become the best of friends with himselves."

Jenna couldn't help but smile. "This isn't the first time you've used that line, is it?" she said.

Allen grinned. "You caught me. But I still find it amusing every time."

Walsh turned once again to Cargill. "So did you then try it on a human?" he asked.

"No," said Cargill. "That's where Edgar and I stopped seeing eye to eye. My feeling was that duplicating a person wouldn't be stepping onto a slippery ethical slope, it would be rocketing down an *ice-cliff*."

He paused. "Imagine there were two of any of you. Two exact copies, both of them *you*, just taken from different frames of your life. Since forty-five millionths of a second is too short to even notice, it's as though two of you budded off into identical copies in an instant. So what if one of you commits a murder and leaves a fingerprint behind? Can *you* get off, claiming your other self did it? And who has signature authority? Which one of you owns your money and car? Your kids? Your girlfriend or wife? Who is the real Daniel Walsh, or Aaron Blake, or Jenna Morrison?"

Blake whistled. "I can see where this could be tricky," he said. "And I'm sure the more you think about it, the more complexities arise."

"Absolutely," said Cargill. "Imagine making *ten* copies of yourself. Just as easy with Knight's process as one."

"But you're saying Knight wanted to try it anyway," said Jenna, "despite these issues."

"Yes. He acknowledged the issues existed and needed to be addressed. But he became obsessed with the *promise*. His intuition told him that he should be able to configure the device to go back further than forty-five microseconds. He saw that as the holy grail. When he realized that Nathan Wexler had almost certainly cracked this nut, he must have been *ecstatic*."

"But it's still only half a second," noted Walsh. "And, apparently, Nathan's equations show that this is an absolute limit."

Cargill shrugged. "He'd like to be able to go back even further," he said, "meaning, of course, a greater distance, but a little more than a hundred miles would still suit his interests perfectly. He was a *Star Trek* fanboy as a kid, and of all the technology on this show, the transporter machine ignited his imagination the most. He fantasized about perfecting a technology that would allow him to beam from place to place. He spent years working on such a device, but decided it couldn't be done, at least not for hundreds of years."

"Until this came along," said Blake.

Cargill nodded.

"But this device *isn't* a *Star Trek* transporter machine," protested Walsh. "Yes, you can send yourself a hundred miles away, but you *duplicate* yourself in the process. So every time you beam yourself to the grocery store, you create the pesky problem of having another you with a claim to all of your possessions."

"I agree," said Cargill wearily. "But Edgar didn't. He envisioned a machine that would do time travel and incineration in one fell swoop."

"Is that supposed to be a joke?" said Jenna.

"I'm afraid not. Let me explain how he envisioned this working. Say this room is a time travel device. Imagine you stand here with an electronic transmitter in your pocket. One that is programmed to trigger the instant it detects that you're no longer at the GPS coordinates of this room. Now you send yourself a half-second back in time, which effectively moves you over a hundred miles in space—although it's really the Earth that's doing the moving through space, not you."

"Yeah, we get that part," said Jenna impatiently.

"When you arrive," continued Cargill, "your transmitter knows you aren't in this room anymore, and instantly transmits a signal to the time travel device here. The signal does two things. It tells the computer to cancel the time machine's upcoming operation so it won't send you back in time yet again. And," he paused for effect, "it causes the device to flash incinerate the *old* you, the one waiting to go back in time."

He arched an eyebrow. "There are some complexities that would need to be worked out. And Knight would have to make improvements in incineration technology, but he didn't think this would be all that challenging."

Blake knew he wasn't following all the intricacies involved, but the take-home message was clear. And horrifying. "So basically, teleportation creates a copy of you, and Edgar Knight's *solution* to this," he said incredulously, "is to *kill* one of the copies each time?" He shook his head in disgust. "Really?"

"Really," repeated Cargill.

"That's awful," said Jenna, aghast. "*Beyond* awful. I don't even have words for it."

"I couldn't agree more," said Walsh.

"I feel the same way," said Cargill. "But Knight didn't. He argued this was exactly the way the transporter machine worked in *Star Trek*, which never seemed to trouble anyone."

"But this *isn't* how it works in *Star Trek*," said Blake. "We've just been over that."

"I'm afraid it probably *is*," said Cargill. "I didn't realize this either before Knight brought it up. Physicists have analyzed a number of episodes of the show, and most agree this is how the transporter machine works, more or less. How such a device would *have* to work. You step onto the *Enterprise's* transporter pad. Your information, your *pattern*, is scanned into a computer. And then you're *destroyed*, basically melted down. And a second later a copy of you is reconstituted on the planet below."

"That can't be right," said Blake. "It's still the same *you* on the planet."

"No it isn't. A number of episodes reveal this. Episodes in which a crewmember's information is trapped in the pattern buffer, and there is a delay in reconstitution. Or in which *two* copies of a transporting crewmember are produced. Or in which the transporter errs and creates kid versions of adults." Cargill shook his head. "So even in the show, the person standing on the planet isn't the same *you* who was standing on the ship. That *you* was disintegrated."

"Wow," said Jenna, dumbfounded. "No wonder Dr. McCoy had such an aversion to the damn thing."

Cargill smiled. "Amen to that," he said. "And while it seems pretty horrible for the one getting flash fried, Edgar argued that in practice you would say to the computer, 'I want to go to the grocery ten miles away.' It would calculate the right number of forty-five microsecond intervals it would need to send you back in time to get there. And the correct polarity and orientation of the field to move in the exact right direction. You would give the order, and the next thing you would know, you'd be at the store. The budding off and incineration of your alter ego would be all but simultaneous, and *you* wouldn't have any awareness of it at all."

"But the other you would feel the pain of being fried," said Blake.

"Not if you did it fast enough. No pain. Just disillusionment, like on *Star Trek*. It really would be the same. All you know is that you're standing on the transporter pad one moment, and the next you're standing on the planet—or inside a grocery store."

"Could you really signal your arrival from a hundred miles away before the time travel device triggers a second time?" asked Jenna. "We *are* only talking half a second."

"Easily," said Cargill. "Modern cell phones can take your voice, digitize it, bounce it off satellites, and reconstruct it, so your friend a thousand miles away hears you say hello, with much less than a half-second delay. Admittedly, the cell phone industry was having problems with conversational latency several years ago, but the improvement since then has been dramatic." He shrugged. "Not that you would use a cell phone for this, anyway. But bottom line, a half-second to communicate an instruction a hundred miles is child's play."

"So Knight was convinced such a teleporter was feasible," said Jenna.

Cargill nodded. "Working out clean, instant incineration was the only real hurdle, and Knight estimated he could clear this within five years."

"So was this his utopia?" she asked. "A world with *Star Trek* transporter devices that eliminate cars and congestion, but with just one *tiny little* unfortunate side effect—you have to die every time you use it."

"This is part of his utopian vision, yes," replied Cargill. "But he also envisioned a world of free energy, unlimited food, and unlimited wealth. You can see the potential for this even with the suitcase-sized version he described."

Cargill paused. "But there was so much more he wanted to do. He also saw a world with unlimited copies of Einstein. Of Mozart. Of Da Vinci. You think a tennis final between the two greatest tennis players in history, Federer and Nadal, would be a close match. Knight wondered what a match between Federer and *himself* would be like."

"It's demented," said Jenna, "but I can't deny the benefit of a thousand Einsteins. But if you could make endless copies of the best people in every field, where would everyone else fit in? How would they get jobs?"

"That's just one of a multitude of ethical issues you run into," said Cargill, taking a page from Blake's book and pouring himself and the two men seated beside him glasses of ice water.

"Another is who gets to make these calls," said Walsh. "Who decides how many copies of Einstein to make? Who decides which people in the population are impressive enough to warrant being copied?"

Blake marveled at how quickly they had all started thinking of the process truly as duplication, and not time travel.

"I'm guessing Knight wanted to be the one making these decisions," said Jenna.

"That's for sure," said Cargill. "If someone had to play God, he figured he had as good a case for it as anyone. He *is* one of the most brilliant people of his generation, and he did invent the device."

"So what do *you* want to do with this technology?" asked Blake. "*You* meaning Q5. What would you plan to do with Nathan's work?"

"What Edgar said I wanted to accomplish is largely true," said Cargill. "Other than the part about me being evil and greedy and wanting to use it to gain more power and line my pockets."

Cargill took a drink of water from his newly filled glass and then continued. "It was my idea to start the shell company to make pharmaceuticals that were impossible for the industry to manufacture, by the way. But the part about using the devices to duplicate wealth and weapons, to help with the war on terror, is correct. And what Knight didn't mention, because he couldn't let the conversation go there, are the possible military uses of teleportation, even if human teleportation is prohibited."

"Right," said Blake, nodding slowly as he considered the possibilities. "You could teleport explosives behind enemy lines. You'd just have to set your bomb on a short delay, so you'd have time to turn *your* version off once you've verified the time-traveling version arrived. You could teleport bombs inside fortresses, inside the homes of terrorist leaders, anywhere."

"You got it," said Cargill. "But once again, Knight wanted to push the military uses of this technology to its limits. Imagine if sending humans back in time, copying them, didn't trouble you? Imagine what you could do? You could teleport hundreds of copies of SEAL Team Six behind enemy lines, or into a terrorist leader's residence. They'd even be somewhat expendable, since the originals, so to speak, would be back at headquarters, lounging by the pool."

Walsh's eyes narrowed. "But you'd have to set up your device at the exact right distance and direction," he pointed out. "You know, field orientation, polarity, the stuff that Knight told us was required. Which means you'd have to get close enough to your target for it to work."

"We have mobile units as well as stationary," said Cargill. "This wouldn't be a problem."

Jenna nodded. "You build the devices inside semis, don't you?"

"Yes. This was Knight's idea. To get mobility and directionality. And also to get to within fifty-eight feet of a potential target, which is our current limit. We haven't used it as a weapon in this way before, but it made sense to have a number of devices in tractor-trailers to provide maximum flexibility."

He paused and took another drink. "But getting back to the much more aggressive military use Knight favored, he also wanted to push the intelligence possibilities. Beam a guy into Kim Jong-un's bedroom in North Korea when he's asleep. Keep him that way with chloroform or gas. Then teleport a copy of him back out."

Blake nodded in appreciation. "When the fearless leader wakes up the next morning, he'd have no idea you were ever there. Meanwhile, you'd have a copy of him. You could torture him. Learn all his secrets. All his passwords and codes. Everything. And yet no one in the world would suspect how you were doing this, and no one would be looking for him. Because he *wouldn't* be missing."

"That's right," said Cargill. "The possibilities are nearly endless. Knight argued that we should do this sort of thing. And while you can do a lot more with a hundred-mile range, much of what he proposed would be possible, even limited to fifty-eight feet."

"So weren't these arguments a clue that he was developing delusions of grandeur?" asked Blake.

Cargill frowned deeply. "Yes, but not as much as you might think. He argued his case in a lighthearted, intellectual, abstract way. He lobbied for what he thought best, but he pretended that he was mostly on the fence. Basically, he played me like a violin."

"In Lee's defense," said Joe Allen, "he did express concerns. We discussed them. And Lee began secretly videoing Knight during their sessions, the ones in which Knight was pushing to exceed the bounds the rest of us supported."

Greg Soyer now came to life as well. "These two explained the situation to me, at length," he said. "I didn't believe a word of it. Until I saw demonstrations of duplications that couldn't have been faked. They also played the videos of Knight they just mentioned. I'm sure they'll do the same for you when we're through here. But the bottom line is that I've verified everything they've been telling you."

Blake extended a hand across the wide table. "Looks like I owe you an apology, Greg," he said earnestly. "I'm sorry for doubting you."

Soyer shook the offered hand. "Thanks, Aaron. But no need to apologize. Who could blame you? And even though I had my reasons, I did betray your trust. And I did shoot you with a tranq dart from two feet. I'm guessing that didn't tickle."

Blake grinned. "No. That pretty much sucked," he said. "But you had compelling evidence to believe we were in danger, and that this was the best strategy."

With this said, all eyes turned once again to the head of Q5.

Cargill cleared his throat. "Knight always told me he enjoyed our little debates as intellectual exercises," he continued. "He said he knew he'd never really persuade me, and that it was probably lucky I was in charge, because he was aware of the Pandora's Box he might be opening. Even so, after a short while, in addition to taping our sessions, I kept a close watch on him."

"Apparently, not close enough," said Blake.

Cargill's jaw clenched. "No. Not nearly close enough," he said in disgust. "I failed to realize that what he was pushing me to do with the technology was just the tip of the iceberg. He had far grander plans for himself, once he decided to set out on his own. And I was unaware that he had won over some of my best people to his way of thinking."

"When the people you have spying on someone are actually in that person's camp," said Allen, "you don't get great intel."

"So the reports all came back that he was behaving," guessed Blake, " and was as harmless as a baby chick, right?"

"I'm afraid so. Until he and his recruits waged a civil war, took many of the mobile units, and killed many of my best men. That was almost a year ago."

"You mentioned that his plans were even bolder than he had let on," prompted Blake.

"Yes. During our little civil war, we captured some of the people who had sided with him, so we know what he's been gearing up to accomplish since he split from us."

Cargill paused as though even *he* couldn't believe what he was about to say. "Basically, Knight wants to take over the world. Become the ultimate global authority."

Jenna shook her head as if her ears weren't working properly. "Do you know how *ridiculous* that sounds?" she said.

"Yes, I do. But do you know how *possible* it is? Especially with Nathan's work likely making a half-second possible. Brainpower isn't an issue. Want to field fifty different project teams, each with its own Jobs and Edison and Zuckerberg and Einstein? No problem. Money isn't an issue," added Cargill, ticking these points off on his fingers. "Even if Knight couldn't duplicate wealth, which he can, he could duplicate the richest men in the world, torture them for their passwords and bank account information. He could force them to withdraw funds from their accounts. While other versions of these people go about their business in blissful ignorance. And he could do the same to *any* dictator, terrorist, or world leader, *including* the President of the United States."

"President Janney has been read into this, right?" said Blake.

"Yes," replied Cargill, "but I've been treading carefully. I limit the information he has, in case Knight does manage to obtain a duplicate of him. Q5's responsibilities are too great, and too profound, to have an obvious target like a president involved. And we need to stay above political whims. Fortunately, President Janney agrees with me, so he'll be the last president with any knowledge."

"Leaving you with absolutely no oversight," said Blake.

Cargill blew out a long breath. "I'm well aware of the need for someone to be a check on me. On us. I'm trying to figure out how to do that. But as it stands right now, my goals are to push the genie back into the bottle as much as I can, and be ready in case Q5's unique capabilities are needed to ward off a disaster."

Blake wanted to discuss checks and balances on Cargill's power at length, but for now, Edgar Knight posed the more immediate problem. "Let's get back to Knight," said Blake. "I have to agree with you that he really could take over the world, given time. The darkest secrets of any leader are potentially accessible to him. And manpower, an army, isn't an issue either. It's a lot easier to build an army when you can, you know, literally, *build* an army."

"And what an army," said Cargill. "He can duplicate the modern equivalent of five hundred Sun Tzus. A thousand Pattons. Five thousand MacArthurs. Ten thousand copies of the best sniper on Earth, the best commando, the best pilot."

"All this," said Blake, "and he can make them magically appear anywhere. Hardly seems fair."

"And that's really the point," said Cargill. "These capabilities are so profound he probably would never need to use them in this way.

Just threaten to. He could pull strings from off-stage to build his world government. He'd just need to demonstrate to world leaders what he can do. You teleport a commando team inside a world leader's bedroom and he'll never feel safe again. At that point you own him. Not to mention that Knight could have duplicates of world leaders that he, almost literally, *does* own. With the right combination of money, power, intimidation, and coercion, he can get leaders to gradually work their way toward consenting to a global government, with himself at the helm. Without firing a single shot."

"What I find the most insidious about this," said Joe Allen, "is how fervent, how zealous, his followers seem to be. Even if they don't always like his personality, they believe in his cause."

"His cause?" said Jenna in disgust. "Ruling the world is a *cause*?"

"No. He claims this is only a means to an end," explained Cargill. "Stabilizing the world. He'll be a benevolent ruler. He'll wipe out terrorism in a single fell swoop, which is appealing to more and more people as this problem continues to build."

Blake had to admit this *was* an appealing prospect. Ridding the world of this blight could well save all of humanity.

"He'll tear down totalitarian regimes," continued Cargill. "Democratize the world. Well, to some extent. Everyone will have the illusion of self-rule, but he'll be the ultimate authority. The followers we captured claim that he wants to exert as little power as possible. Well, that is after he makes the entire globe a single nation under his domain, destroys terrorism, reduces crime, and returns society to civility. And the technology breakthroughs his teams of duplicated geniuses will be able to make will revolutionize industry after industry. This, and his ability to duplicate food, water, precious metals, what have you, will vastly increase the wealth and quality of life of every person now alive."

"I can see why his vision would have a certain appeal," said Walsh.

"If it weren't for all the eggs he'll need to break to make this omelet," said Cargill, "it doesn't sound all that bad. Except that he also believes that the least intelligent people in our world are reproducing far faster than the most intelligent."

"Idoiocracy," whispered Jenna under her breath, but too softly for anyone to hear.

"Because of this belief," continued Cargill, "Knight also plans to sterilize everyone not in the top ten percent in intelligence, and limit population growth in general."

"Why not?" said Blake, shaking his head in disgust. "He has to make room for all those copies of Albert Einstein, after all."

"Yeah," said Cargill. "That, too. Everyone has a different definition of utopia. Knight could do a lot of good, which is one reason his followers are so passionate. Unlimited wealth, an end to terrorism, and the world populated only by brilliant, educated people. Sounds great, if it weren't for the sacrifices *others* would have to make. And if we didn't have to rely on his good nature and benevolent disposition. When Ted Kaczynski goes nuts and turns into the full-on Unabomber, you don't want him ruling the world at the time."

The room fell silent as everyone considered what living under the rule of an unstable genius might be like.

"Would he also force people into using his transporter machines?" asked Walsh finally. "You mentioned this was a long-held fantasy of his."

"Actually, no," said Cargill. "He was excited about this in the beginning, but he knows he has to keep time travel technology a closely guarded secret. He would keep the supply of his devices limited, and knowledge of their capabilities known only to a select few."

"Won't people catch on when they see a thousand Pattons?" said Walsh.

"Eventually, but they won't know how he does it. They'll suspect cloning before time travel. And they won't know where he keeps the devices. He'll also wield an iron fist to be sure no one else ever comes up with the technology." Cargill paused. "Which it goes without saying, is something we're dedicated to doing as well."

"About the only thing you both agree on," noted Blake.

"This makes sense no matter who controls the technology," said Cargill. "Would you rather have one man with his finger poised above a nuclear button, or ten thousand men? With ten thousand you just multiply the chances that someone will push it."

"So who does have access?" asked Blake.

"With respect to Q5, only me. I'm the only one with the proper codes to activate any of the devices. Knight invented the technology, and I was his boss. So we saw to it that the software that controls the devices was inextricably intertwined with instructions that limited access to the two of us. Period. I'm sure Knight didn't change this. He has to protect his own power, and if his underlings could use these devices without him, what would stop them from freelancing? He needs control over his people. Some are true believers, but some are just in it for the money and power. And most, of course, have no idea what this is really all about, as is the case with Q5."

"So I'm guessing there are no duplicate Edgar Knights out there," said Blake.

"Hard to imagine," said Cargill. "A megalomaniac like him would never be able to, um . . . trust himself."

"Right," said Jenna. "So maybe Roger Federer doesn't want to play Roger Federer for the title, after all."

Blake gestured to Cargill. "Can you still activate *his* devices?" he asked.

"Almost certainly. And he can still activate mine. Tearing out either of our accesses from the software can't be done without compromising it. You'd have to redesign very complex control systems. Why tamper with success? He can use his own devices whenever he wants, so why would he use mine?"

"And vice-versa," said Blake.

"Yes," said Cargill. "Even if he did take my access away somehow, I had a backdoor engineered in without his knowledge. I wanted to be able to control it, even with respect to Knight. To override him. I suspect he's built or duplicated additional devices, but each of these would also retain this backdoor access."

"Have you ever re-captured any of his devices?" asked Blake.

"Not yet. They give off a telltale radiation signature—call it dark energy residual—but you have to be within a mile or two to pick it up. It's very faint."

"Any other major pieces of the puzzle?" said Blake. "Or are we pretty much up to speed?"

"You're close. I've told you all the key facts."

"I have to admit," said Jenna, "as absurd and horrible as this all is, it does seem to explain everything that's happened since I got involved." She paused, remembering, and a veil of sadness settled over her. "So Knight was right about how Nathan and I came into the picture, wasn't he?"

Cargill nodded, looking distinctly uncomfortable. "Yes," he said. "We've had computers tasked with monitoring any scientist who might have even a slight chance of reproducing Knight's work, or in this case, explaining and extending it. When Nathan wrote about forty-five microseconds, he may as well have triggered a nuclear-powered siren. But we never wanted to hurt him," he insisted. "We wanted to show him our set-up, tell him about Knight, and recruit him."

"But Knight had a mole," said Jenna, "and was just waiting for you to find someone like Nathan."

"Yes. I was asleep at the wheel. It was unforgivable carelessness. Knight had been absolutely quiet since he left. I assumed he was building his team and capabilities, making sure to stay well under my radar while evading my considerable efforts to locate him. I let myself believe he wouldn't risk taking any actions that might give himself away. I got soft and stupid. In short, he lulled me to sleep. It goes without saying," he added, his eyes now blazing, "that I am now very much awake."

"But at the cost of Nathan's life," said Jenna.

Cargill lowered his eyes. "Yes. Knight's people must have been closing in on Dr. Wexler during his ambush. My men knew if Knight got to him, there would be nothing to stop him from ultimately achieving his goals."

There was silence in the large conference room for almost a full minute, as everyone digested all that had been discussed.

"So what now?" said Blake, finally breaking the spell.

"I'd love for all of you to join our efforts," replied Cargill.

He turned toward Greg Soyer and nodded, making sure he knew he was included in this invitation. "Part of this is because you now know the score, and not many do. People who do are valuable. Since I want to limit this number, having you join the team would kill two birds with one stone."

"And the other part?" said Blake.

"You've impressed the hell out of me, Mr. Blake. I wasn't just blowing smoke when I told you this over the phone. I could use a man like you. As the number three man here, just behind Joe."

Blake stared at Cargill thoughtfully, but didn't respond.

"And we would love to add another world-class physicist like Dr. Walsh. Greg's computer and Arabic language skills are also extremely impressive and would be very useful to us. And while Jenna is in genetics rather than the physical sciences, she is brilliant, and given the depth of her knowledge about what is really happening here, she could make significant contributions. Who better to study the ethics of our situation, and to find ways to keep me honest?"

Aaron Blake exchanged glances with the other three in question. "I'm sure I speak for us all in saying that we'd need to consider this a while before making any decisions. And learn more about your operation and goals."

"Of course," said Cargill. "Perhaps we can convince all of you to stay with us for a few weeks while you're considering. Think of it as a trial period. We can pull strings so you have cover stories that keep your options open, and your employers happy."

"Maybe," said Blake noncommittally. "You've given us a lot to think about. We just have to decide how much we trust you."

"I understand," said Cargill, rising from his chair and motioning for the rest of the group to do the same. "So let me give you a tour, and demonstrate duplication. Then you can review tapes of Knight pushing for more aggressive use of the technology. And then of some of the men we captured who were in his camp. I'm not sure I painted Knight as being as much of a monster as he really is, but when you hear firsthand accounts of what he really wants to accomplish, I think you'll find it very eye-opening, and very disturbing, "

"You want to do all of this right now?" said Jenna.

"Absolutely," replied Cargill. "The faster I can get you comfortable, the better."

He blew out a long breath. "Because we're dealing with a resurgent Edgar Knight. And we have a lot of work to do."

47

The tour of Cheyenne Mountain—at least three quarters of it, since Cargill had said they couldn't venture into the south quadrant and risk certain people there seeing them—had been as fascinating as any tour Jenna Morrison had ever taken. And yet only half of her mind was taking it in.

The other half was darting around like an over-caffeinated hummingbird, flittering madly from thought to thought. She had been drinking from a firehose since Sunday night, a period of less than seventy-two hours into which ten lifetimes of agony and trauma and revelation had been crammed. Her world had been destroyed, she had feared for her life on numerous occasions, and her horizons had been expanded in unimaginable ways.

And now she was being given a tour of the most remarkable facility in the US by the man who headed the group that had killed Nathan. Could she really work with this man? Just bury the hatchet and forgive? Should she say, "Sure I'll work with you. Ever since you killed my fiancé, I've become a lot more flexible."

She hated herself for not hating Lee Cargill more.

But he seemed genuine, and a good man. A man striving to help protect the world, a man who agonized over many of the things he had been forced to do in service to this goal. A man who was forced to weigh innocent lives and make impossible choices.

But she had thought the same of Edgar Knight, proving how easily she could be fooled.

The difference was that Lee Cargill was offering proof. And she was helpless, entirely in his control, and he had done nothing to take advantage of this. At least not so far.

Even if she came to believe that killing Nathan had been the only option under the circumstances—still a big if—could she ever forgive? And could she really change gears, abandon the years she had spent working toward her dream of becoming an experimental geneticist? And did Lee Cargill really mean it when he said one of her jobs would be to find ways to guard against abuses of power—by him and Q5? While this wouldn't be her only responsibility, it was sure to be a treacherously difficult task, with no obvious solutions.

But wasn't working with Q5, especially on this assignment, more important than anything else she could do with her life? And although they would be part of a larger team, the number of people within Q5 who knew what was driving this group was relatively small, so she would have ample opportunity to socialize with, and work with, Dan Walsh and Aaron Blake, something she found immensely appealing, much to her own surprise.

She had heard of the unbreakable bonds forged between brothers-in-arms during times of war, but never thought she would experience this. But she had. The level of affection, loyalty, and friendship she now felt toward the two men who had been with her through the past days' trials and tribulations was extraordinary.

"So now that we're done with the tour," she heard Lee Cargill saying, as though through a fog, "it's time for the demonstration."

These words brought Jenna back from her reverie. If a time travel demonstration wasn't worthy of her total focus, nothing was.

Cargill led the group through a reinforced door into a large room, a perfect square of maybe twenty-five yards on a side. The ceiling was unfinished mountain granite, but almost close enough to jump up and touch, especially for Cargill, the tallest of the group.

Walsh glanced up and winced. "Is it just me, or is having such a low ceiling that weighs as much as . . . well, as a mountain, a little disconcerting?"

Jenna and Blake both nodded their agreement, while Cargill exchanged a glance with Joe Allen and smiled. "I'm not going to lie to you," he said, "while that feeling gets a little better, it never fully goes away."

"Good to know I have company," said the physicist.

Cargill led them to a rectangular structure against one wall, about the size of a small apartment bathroom, made principally of what looked like two-inch-thick clear Plexiglas. The Plexiglas enclosed inner walls of four-inch-thick white plastic. A recessed viewing window had been cut into the plastic about chest height. The chamber's floor and walls were crisscrossed with red grid lines and several arrows. The most interesting feature of the structure was the thick Plexiglas door with a bank-vault handle, which needed to be turned or spun to gain access.

Next to the structure was a table on which sat a sophisticated desktop supercomputer and several monitors.

"If this is your time travel device," said Jenna, "it sure doesn't look very impressive. Shouldn't there be lasers and generators and cool spinning helices?"

Cargill laughed. "You forgot about electrical discharges and blindingly bright lights," he said. "I'm afraid we're a disappointment compared to Hollywood's vision of time travel."

"Not to mention," said Greg Soyer, "that people in the movies tend to go back in time more than forty-five millionths of a second. You know, just a hair."

"All kidding aside," said Jenna, "you would seem to need much greater complexity to make something this impossible work."

"The plastic is hiding all kinds of electronics and power grids," said Joe Allen. "The device does generate a field, and it does have means to change the polarity and orientation of the field to achieve directionality. But once you know the secret to making it work, it's surprisingly simple."

"Which is what makes this even more dangerous," said Cargill. "At least nuclear weapons have the decency to be difficult to construct in one's basement."

"Think of it this way," said Allen. "The quintessence field powers it, and this is everywhere. The trick is to tap into it and let it provide the incomprehensible energies required. It's like standing under the world's most powerful magnet before the discovery of metal. You would think that tapping this mysterious magnetic force would require some major generators and complex electronics, when the truth is, a simple hunk of metal is all you'd need."

"Good analogy," said Jenna.

Cargill waited for further questions. When none were forthcoming, he said, "So let me demonstrate. Does anyone want to volunteer something to send back through time?" he asked. "A shoe? A piece of jewelry?"

Blake pulled a well-worn brown leather wallet from his back pocket. "How about this?"

"Perfect," said Cargill. He took the wallet and entered the chamber. He placed it in a precise location and orientation on the floor, using the grid lines as a guide, and then placed a small glowing disk on top of it, one that was about the size of a very fat quarter and clearly electronic in nature. He then exited, spinning the door handle until a buzzing sound from the computer indicated the room was once again airtight.

He walked the short distance to the table and sat before the computer. "Joe, show them to the destination area. I'll set this to fire one minute from now."

Cargill's hands flew over the keyboard while his second-in-command escorted them to a position fifty-eight feet away, along a diagonal. An X, about the size of a stop sign, appeared on the floor, made from red duct tape.

Jenna took her place with her companions, roughly encircling the X, and shook her head. The fact that she was about to witness one of the most extraordinary scientific and technological achievements of all time by watching a handmade X on the floor was absurd beyond measure.

Cargill began bellowing out a countdown from twenty yards away. "In five. Four. Three. Two. One. Now!"

There were three gasps as Blake's wallet appeared in the center of the X, with the electronic disk still on top of it.

Greg Soyer, who had seen a few demonstrations already, simply grinned, and Joe Allen didn't display emotion of any kind.

Intellectually, Jenna had expected this to happen, but it was still insane, still unreal. There had been no discharge, no fanfare, no sound. One moment the wallet wasn't there, and the next it was.

"Notice that we only see one wallet," said Allen while the three newcomers were still gawking. He lifted the electronic disk and held it up. "Which means this transmitter did its job. The instant it realized it was no longer at the coordinates we programmed in, it signaled the computer, which aborted the firing of the device."

He picked up the wallet and handed it to Blake. "Follow me," he said as he began walking back to Cargill.

When they arrived at the apparatus, Cargill turned the handle and held open the door, gesturing for Blake to enter.

His wallet was still on the floor, just where Cargill had left it. He brought it back out and set both wallets on the table. There could be no doubt they were identical. Every discolored spot, every worn-down edge, every nick was the same.

He opened both wallets to reveal the same contents, laid out identically. He removed a thin sheath of bills from both wallets, and compared the top one on each, a five. They were identical in every way. Their serial numbers, of course, but also creases, dirt, coloration and everything, down to the last atom.

Cargill asked for one of the sets of bills. When Blake handed them to him, he produced a lighter and set them on fire, tossing them into a steel trashcan by the desk when they became too hot to handle. "We tend to frown upon having bills with the same serial numbers in circulation," he explained.

"Can you repeat the demonstration," said Blake, "so we can watch the sending chamber this time?"

Cargill laughed. "We can do that, but it won't do any good. I don't know how much of this Knight covered, but you never actually see something get sent back through time. You never see it disappear. Because the universe starts all over again, reboots, after it arrives in the past. So the future universe it came from never comes into existence. And then it sends a signal to turn off the system."

"So the universe with the wallet in the chamber *waiting* to be sent still exists," added Allen. "But the universe from which it is actually sent never does."

"That is just so messed up," said Blake in exasperation, and Jenna, Walsh, and Soyer nodded their agreement.

"Here is my advice to all of you," said Cargill. "The best thing to do is ignore time travel, and don't think about the paradoxes too hard. If you do, your head really will explode," he added with a wry smile. "Just think of it as duplication and teleportation. But always keep in mind that the universe seems to go out of its way to ensure that infinite alternate timelines aren't allowed. So no matter what, we only ever get this one universe."

He sighed. "So we'd better make sure we don't screw it up."

48

Brian Hamilton hated Cheyenne Mountain. Sure, it was one of the most interesting places in the world to visit, but *living* there only worked if you were a bat. The Palomar facility had also been underground, but nothing like this. It had a much larger security perimeter, so trips to the surface were easier to make happen.

Not that it really mattered. Soon enough he would be traveling on another assignment anyway, living in a hotel room somewhere. But what he really wanted was to work side by side with Edgar Knight, toward their common goal. He was tired of being Knight's designated spy, having to watch Lee Cargill squander Q5's vast resources and capabilities. Watching him crawl like a wounded baby when he could be soaring.

Cargill was an idiot.

He could transform the world, but he was too weak to do it. He could wipe out the asshole terrorists who wanted nothing more than to butcher the helpless. If you have the ultimate cure for cancer, you use it to wipe out the disease once and for all. You don't wield your cure only as a last resort, when the cancer has all but choked the life out of you.

Edgar Knight, on the other hand, was a man with *vision.* He was able to make the tough decisions. If you were captain of a life raft with a maximum capacity of ten people, choosing to take five passengers of a sinking ship on board was an easy decision, not a heroic one. But what about when there were fifty passengers? Was it heroic to take them all, dooming *everyone* to death? Or was the heroic move using force, if necessary, to limit this number, to ensure some would survive?

Sure, from the outside this looked coldhearted, while the converse seemed compassionate. But watching the world circle the drain because you were too much of a pussy to make the hard decisions was the real crime.

Survival of the fittest was harsh reality. In the animal kingdom it was eat or be eaten. If you saw a group of fuck-nuts just itching to nuke the world back into the Dark Ages—who believed the Messiah equivalent, the twelfth Imam, would only come out to play when Israel was destroyed, and worldwide Armageddon unleashed—you *wiped them out*. To a man.

Or else they'd do the same to you.

It had been three days since Cargill had reported that he was on the verge of acquiring Jenna Morrison and Aaron Blake. Since then, Hamilton had heard almost nothing from the man. He assumed Cargill had been successful, since all attempts by Knight to locate Blake and Morrison had failed. If they were on the run, they would have at least made one mistake by now, no matter how good they were.

Hamilton and his comrades on Q5's Inner Circle had been assigned quarters within Cheyenne, in the south quadrant, but they were restricted to this quadrant alone. Bad enough having to be trapped in a claustrophobic base. Worse still when you were restricted to just a fraction of it.

Edgar Knight had made it clear that Hamilton's number one, and *only*, priority was to get a copy of Nathan Wexler's work, and Knight was willing to unleash unlimited manpower to do it.

If only they had this information already they wouldn't have to dick around. They could beam a team inside the fucking mountain and take down the entire Cheyenne facility if need be. But to do that now, they'd have to get their eighteen-wheelers within fifty-eight feet, not just of the mountain, but of their destination inside. Since Cargill ringed every base with sensors that would alarm if they detected the unique energy signatures of the devices, they couldn't get nearly this close.

Hamilton was reflecting on this while he lifted weights in a small gym on site, and attempting to strategize as to how he could carry out the mission that Knight had assigned to him. The file was better protected than the gold in Fort Knox. The physicists Cargill had assigned to digest its contents had been moved to an undisclosed offsite location, and were no doubt heavily guarded and as tightly sequestered as a hung jury.

Without interaction with Cargill, Hamilton had little hope of learning anything. And the fact that Cargill seemed certain there was another mole on the inside, and wasn't in the mood to confide in anyone, made his job all the more difficult.

So Hamilton was basically in a holding pattern. Waiting for something to happen. Anything. It was as if Cargill had vanished. Hamilton would sell his soul to the devil to hear from this pussy again.

Right on cue, his cell phone buzzed, indicating an incoming message from Cargill.

Ask and you shall receive, he thought happily.

The message ordered all eight remaining members of the Inner Circle to meet in an hour inside one of the largest meeting rooms on the Cheyenne campus, which was about the size of a school gymnasium. It didn't say why, or anything else for that matter.

Very interesting.

Upon entering the room, Hamilton was frisked and relieved of all weapons. He was alarmed by this request, thinking he had been discovered, but was told that everyone was getting the same treatment, at Cargill's orders.

Once all eight remaining members of the Inner Circle were inside, Lee Cargill and Joe Allen entered the room, shutting the door behind them.

Hamilton watched Cargill closely, wondering what game he was playing.

The room was stark and utilitarian, with a shiny concrete floor that a finished garage might have, and some wooden chairs spread here and there throughout. At one end was what looked like a steel voting booth, or a portable closet.

Hamilton and his seven comrades were bunched loosely together in the middle of the room, and as Cargill and Allen walked through this group and to the other side, all eight turned to face them.

"I hope everyone is enjoying their new quarters," began Cargill, "and getting a feel for this facility. I'm sure you've been a little bored, and wondering why you haven't heard from me."

His audience looked on with great interest.

"As you know from the last message I sent, three days ago, I have reason to believe Edgar Knight has a man who is loyal to him within Q5. I'm not sure the mole is within the Inner Circle, but until I can be sure, our entire program is paralyzed.

"But have no fear," continued Cargill. "Good fortune has shined upon us. We're all familiar with the classic polygraph test, and we all know that any of us worth his salt can beat it. But one of our sister Black Ops science groups has had a team working on dramatic improvements to the test, working toward perfecting a foolproof system. So I checked with them." He shot the group a broad smile. "You guessed it. It turns out they've recently made a breakthrough. Not as impressive as being able to send matter forty-five millionths of a second back in time, of course," he added, "but not bad."

Cargill paused, and the room was now perfectly quiet.

"They weren't keen on letting one of only two available prototypes out of their sight," he explained. "But I made it clear this was an emergency. And President Janney made sure this was a request they couldn't refuse. So lucky us. We now have a polygraph system that is unbeatable. Today we get to find out, once and for all, who is ready to stab us in the back. Who is ready to drink the Kool-Aid that Edgar Knight is serving. Who wants to sabotage us and help this madman build a global government and take the helm."

"Assuming the mole is in our Inner Circle, of course," added Joe Allen from beside him.

"Right," said Cargill. "Which I hope like hell isn't the case. But either way, we'll finally be confident we can trust each other, and we can move forward on that basis."

Cargill's face hardened. "So none of you are leaving this room until all of you are tested. You should be honored to know that this will be the first use of the new test under field conditions. So when I call your name, come with me into our little chamber, and let's make history."

49

Brian Hamilton's heart pounded away inside his chest, but he was happy to note that outwardly he appeared no different than any of his comrades, who all showed signs of stress at Cargill's announcement. And *they* were all innocent.

One of their group, Chris Entwistle, appeared particularly nervous, and Hamilton wondered what sordid secrets he was hiding, not that he had anything to worry about, since Cargill's questioning would be focused on one transgression only.

Hamilton knew he was out of options. They were locked in the room and the door was certainly being guarded. Only Cargill and Allen were armed. Besides, the fucking Incredible Hulk would have trouble escaping from this mountain once an alarm had sounded.

He had no other choice but to take the test. The question was, was everything Cargill just said bullshit? The more Hamilton thought about this, the more convinced he became that it was.

The timing was a little too convenient. A sister group just happening to develop an unbeatable polygraph just when Cargill needed it most. Doubtful.

Cargill was clever, with a reputation for guile. Surely this was yet another example.

Contrary to popular perception, polygraph tests were notoriously inaccurate, and if one knew what one was doing, easy to beat. Those administering tests were skilled in the art of deception, which ensnared many perps that the test would not have.

The test administrator might tell a subject to wash his hands thoroughly with soap, to avoid false perspiration readings, and then monitor a hidden camera in the bathroom to see if the suspect washed or not. If he didn't wash, this would speak volumes, since an innocent man would wash his hands raw, wanting to avoid an inaccurate reading at all costs.

The polygraph test had great utility as a psychological ruse that could be used to extract confessions. And the best way to provoke a confession, or a mistake, was to convince subjects that the test was all but infallible. Those who truly believed they were about to be discovered tended to react in very impulsive, and very stupid, ways, which is what the testers were counting on.

This is why the current situation was likely a ruse. This fantasy story of a foolproof test was designed to intimidate Hamilton into making a mistake. Cargill was hoping to flush him out without need of asking a single question.

Well, Hamilton wasn't falling for it. He would take it as if it were a standard polygraph, and use techniques he had been trained on to beat it. If Cargill wasn't bluffing after all, then he was fucked. But he was betting he'd slide right through the trap.

Two long hours passed as three other members of the Inner Circle went before him. And then Lee Cargill exited the steel booth and called out the name Brian Hamilton.

The moment of truth had arrived.

Cargill led Hamilton back inside the makeshift testing room, foolishly turning his back on him and letting him get very close. If only they weren't deep within a fortress, Hamilton could have snatched Cargill's gun and escaped without working up much of a sweat. For a clever man, Cargill was exceedingly stupid at the same time.

He entered the booth, bigger than it looked from the outside, and took a seat before a glass table. Cargill and Allen both took their places behind the table, facing him. Allen carefully hooked him up to the device, attaching leads to his fingers, forehead, and chest, while Cargill studied a large monitor, nodding periodically.

And then the testing began. Allen had a script in his hand and saw little need to diverge from it. Which was perfect, Hamilton realized. After all, he knew exactly what they were after, making the test even easier to beat, because it was obvious which questions were the controls—being used to establish baseline breathing, pulse, blood pressure, and perspiration readings—and which questions were the real deal.

The trick was to keep answers short. And when being asked control questions, to delay taking breaths, taxing your system, and to imagine yourself in highly stressful situations, being burned alive or smothered by fire ants. If you could stress yourself out while answering control questions, the minor stress reactions to lying wouldn't differ from the "normal" state. There were also tricks to convince yourself you were telling the truth, even when you weren't.

Allen walked him through thirty minutes of questions while Cargill studied the monitor, not showing any reaction. The longer the test wore on, the more confident Hamilton became. If the test was as good as Cargill had said, he would have been discovered by now.

Finally, it was over, and Cargill instructed him to join the others until all were through being tested. A few of his comrades were engaged in idle conversation to pass the time, but Hamilton didn't join in.

Next up was a man named Joe O'Bannon. After him there were only two more. The mood in the room had improved considerably as the majority had now passed the test, although Chris Entwistle, who had appeared to Hamilton's practiced eye to be anxious, now seemed even worse, as though he might vomit at any moment. Perhaps he had food poisoning. Hamilton wondered how a stomach flu would affect the results.

Once O'Bannon was done, Entwistle's name was finally called. Cargill came out of the booth and led him back in, as he had with all the rest.

They were ten feet from the steel room when Entwistle moved—with a purpose.

The man became a blur of motion, tearing Cargill's gun from its holster and backing away, pointing the weapon at Cargill's chest before anyone in the room could even begin to react.

An instant later the others all reflexively reached for their own weapons, reacting with instincts that had been honed over many years, only to remember that they were no longer armed.

But Entwistle now was.

Several in the Inner Circle began moving toward him, silently and with deadly intensity, but Cargill quickly waved them off.

Only a few seconds had passed since Entwistle had made his move.

"Fuck you, Lee Cargill!" the gunman hissed. "So I sympathize with Edgar Knight," he said. "So the fuck what? Any sane man would. That doesn't mean I haven't served you faithfully."

"Put the gun down," said Cargill, struggling to remain calm.

"Kiss my ass!" roared Entwistle. "I don't take orders from you anymore. Edgar Knight came up with technology that could stop bloodshed around the world. Could save the lives of thousands of our brothers who are fighting barbarians. Could spare the lives of *heroes*. And all you do is shiver in the dark and squander the gift Knight gave us. You're a *disgrace!*"

"Look, Chris, let's talk about this. You know you can't escape."

"We'll see about that," said Entwistle defiantly. "Joe Allen!" he shouted, turning toward the makeshift steel room they had been about to enter. "If that door opens as much as a millimeter, Cargill is *dead*. If anyone in this room even *thinks* about making a move, the same goes."

"I've heard enough," said Cargill, his voice suddenly taking on a command tone once again. "Thanks for playing, 'flush out the traitorous cockroach.' It's a little game I invented. See, Chris, this polygraph is standard issue, dressed up a little for show. I was just hoping to stress you into making a mistake."

Entwistle stared at him in disbelief, but only for a moment. "Congratulations, *asshole*," he said. "But now I'm going to use you as a shield to get out of here. Not too smart now, huh genius?"

Cargill slowly began crouching down. "You don't really think I'd let you steal a loaded gun, do you? It has blanks for weighting, but it was bait. And you took it."

At that moment, several things happened all at once, at a speed that would have been impossible for most men to follow with the naked eye, although Hamilton was not most men.

The door into the booth began to open at the same time that Cargill lunged for a gun in an ankle holster, and Entwistle fired three times at Cargill's head. The blanks exploded with the sound and fury of real ammunition, but Cargill had not been bluffing when he said the gun wasn't live.

Entwistle's recognition of the situation was immediate and decisive. He rushed Cargill as he was lifting his gun from the ankle holster and in one fluid move used an advanced martial arts technique to twist Cargill's arm in such a way that he had to release the gun into Entwistle's hand or have his elbow destroyed.

As Entwistle was replacing his decoy gun with a live one, he spun Cargill around so the leader of Q5 was between himself and the door, turning his ex-boss into a human shield as Allen emerged from the polygraph room with his gun drawn.

"Drop it or he dies!" screamed Entwistle, freezing Allen in mid-motion.

Before Allen could comply, Cargill dropped to the ground, exposing the man behind him, and betting his life his second-in-command would react before Entwistle did.

It was very close, but Allen reacted first, pumping three bullets into Entwistle, two in the chest and the last in the head. Entwistle got off one shot after he was hit, but it missed Allen by several inches.

The moment Entwistle hit the ground, his face now hamburger, four guards burst through the door, automatic pistols drawn.

"Stand down!" Cargill shouted at the four newcomers.

The four men took in the scene and then lowered their weapons as ordered.

"Thanks for your quick action," said Cargill, "but we have the situation under control."

As the guards exited the room, Hamilton noticed the horrified expressions around the room. He planted the same expression on his own face, but he desperately wanted to grin, or maybe even dance a jig.

The loss of a man who shared his disdain for Lee Cargill was unfortunate, but Entwistle's grisly death was nothing he hadn't seen before.

Hamilton had been hoping simply to avoid being snared in Cargill's trap, but something even better had happened. Entwistle, a talented soldier, had been sympathizing with Knight, had probably been thinking of ways to reach out to him and offer his services. But he had stupidly let Cargill panic him into making the most idiotic of blunders.

Cargill's ploy had not been an exercise in futility, as Hamilton had expected. Quite the contrary, the man had trapped his one and only mole, after all.

Hamilton had thought Cargill was an idiot for letting the men get so close to his gun as he led them to take the test. But he had been too hasty. Cargill had done this on purpose.

He had been more clever than Hamilton had given him credit for.

As it turned out, *too* clever.

Because he had flushed out the wrong man. And now he would return to his old, trusting self, confiding in his Inner Circle once again. So now the real fun could begin.

50

Six days had passed since Cargill's stunt with the polygraph, and this entire time Hamilton had been tasked with an assignment off base, and had only just returned, ordered to a meeting in a conference room within the mountain. During this time Knight's patience was wearing thinner and thinner—as was Hamilton's own. He was still no closer to figuring out how to obtain a copy of Wexler's breakthrough than he had been before.

Hamilton arrived at conference room D with some half-baked ideas of how he could worm his way closer to Wexler's work, but hadn't arrived at a concrete strategy. He was joined by three other members of Q5's Inner Circle, Joe O'Bannon, Tom TenBrink, and Eric Beal.

Lee Cargill and Joe Allen entered shortly thereafter, and everyone took a seat around the large conference table.

Cargill wasted no time on pleasantries. "I've called you in today for what is a very important assignment, but one that should be routine—even boring. Nine days ago, as you no doubt recall, we were in position to acquire Jenna Morrison and Aaron Blake. Even though I now have full faith in all of you, I still like to keep information on a need-to-know basis, so I didn't mention that we were successful in this task."

"Congratulations," said both TenBrink and Beal in unison.

Ass kissers, thought Hamilton in disgust.

"Thank you," said Cargill. "A few other things I haven't told this group. First, Joe and I have been staying in the north quadrant of this base all along. We didn't want anyone to know until we weeded out our remaining mole." He paused. "And along with Blake and Morrison, we also acquired two additional men, a physicist from

UCLA named Dan Walsh, and a computer expert named Greg Soyer. All four have now been fully briefed on Q5's activities."

"Fully?" said O'Bannon in a tone that indicated he hoped this wasn't true, and didn't approve if it was.

"They all know as much as you do," replied Cargill. "We extended an invitation to all four to join us. Walsh, the physicist, has been off-site with the team studying Wexler's work. He's like a kid on Christmas morning. The other three have all been staying here, at least until today."

"What happened today?" asked TenBrink.

"Greg Soyer has a live-in girlfriend. We've provided cover for him, telling her the military recalled him for a classified mission and making up a lame story to account for the mess their shared home was in. But he wants to get back to her. He is being returned home even as we speak. The good news is that he's agreed to consult with us whenever we need him."

"Does Knight know about him?" asked TenBrink. "And more to the point, will he go after him?"

"We don't think so," said Joe Allen. "Knight only cares about Nathan Wexler's breakthrough, and Soyer can't help him with this. Soyer did save the file to the cloud, very securely I might add, and put in a fail-safe mechanism. Unless Jenna and her PI friend both enter correct passwords every week, the data will be automatically made public, which neither we nor Edgar Knight can let happen. If anyone tries to break in or delete the file, the same thing happens. Originally, Soyer could also access Wexler's file, but he's had his two friends change the codes so even he can't get in."

"Which means that only Jenna Morrison and Aaron Blake have any value to Knight at this point," added Cargill.

A surge of electricity coursed through Hamilton's veins. Had he heard correctly? It seemed impossible. "I don't understand," he said. "You said these two have been staying here for over a week. But are you saying the file in the cloud still exists? That the fail-safe mechanism still exists?"

Cargill frowned. "Yes. Q5 killed the man Jenna Morrison loved, and Aaron Blake has had some bad experiences with politically driven military decisions, which make him slow to fully trust the judgment of his government. We've tried to get them to destroy the file, but they've refused until they're certain they can trust us."

Hamilton couldn't believe his ears. What a pussy this Cargill was. Even more so than he had known.

"With all due respect," said Eric Beal, "if this file gets into Edgar Knight's hands, or out into the public, the world is pretty much fucked. If this doesn't warrant enhanced methods of . . . persuasion . . . to get these two to take it down, *nothing* does."

Hamilton almost grinned. When a pussy like Eric Beal thinks you're a pussy, then you're *really* a pussy.

"Valid point," said Cargill. "First, until it's taken down, my highest priority is to make certain that they reset the fail-safe every week, which they just did. Second, I have every reason to believe these two will come around, because I've been truthful with them, and both really will make valuable members of the team. But if I use force to get them to disable it, they'll never join. Yet they'll know all about the most classified black program in America. So what then? Kill them? Hasn't Jenna Morrison been through enough? Wasn't killing Nathan Wexler, *in front of her*, enough abuse for her to take?"

Cargill surveyed the men across from him, but none chose to respond.

"So far," he continued, "Jenna sees no reason not to join us. But she wants to reserve judgment for two more weeks. During this time she wants to continue to get to know us, and spend more time with me and Joe."

Cargill sighed. "But not here. She's feeling a growing sense of claustrophobia. Knowing there's an entire mountain poised a few feet over her head is getting to her. And living here, without getting any natural light, is making her more depressed than she already is—and believe me, that's saying something, since she did lose someone she loved deeply."

"I see," said TenBrink. "So can we assume you've agreed to relocate her?"

"Yes. And also Aaron Blake. He's very loyal to her, and wherever she goes, he's going to be there to protect her."

"We've chosen a nearby military base for her two-week sojourn," said Joe Allen. "Very close so we can visit often and continue to get her comfortable. Schriever Air Force Base, to be precise."

"There are a number of bases fairly close by," said Cargill, "but Schriever is only thirty miles from here. For those unfamiliar with this base, it's home to the 50th Space Wing, which controls satellites. Warning satellites, navigational, communications, spy—you name it. There are almost six thousand personnel based there. Schriever is also where the GPS master control station is located, as well as the Master Clock used to synchronize all GPS satellites."

"Schriever is perfect for our needs," said Allen. "It's in the middle of nowhere, with miles of mostly flat, barren ground all around, so there's no way to sneak up on it. No one there will know who these two are, or why they're important, but they'll have security that a visiting president would envy."

"This is where all of you come in," said Cargill. "We'll move out at 0700 tomorrow. We'll take a midsize truck, one so reinforced it could take a missile strike and not slow down. The outside will read, *Colorado Carpeting Discounter*. I'll be driving, so I can show our two guests around once we arrive. The four of you will be in the trailer minding them. Once we arrive on base, you'll also be stationed there, as added protection for Morrison and Blake."

"Will one reinforced truck and five men be enough for this transfer?" asked O'Bannon. "Knight would give his left nut to capture these two. Shouldn't we put them in a convoy of tanks with a fighter jet escort?"

Cargill shook his head. "No. Knight has to know we have them, but by now he also has to believe they no longer have access to Wexler's file, so they aren't useful to him. And he's run out of moles, so he has no way to know where they are. So the goal is to make this casual, to not draw attention to ourselves. It is virtually impossible for us to run into trouble this time. It will be one of the easier assignments you've ever been given." He smiled. "But that being said, make sure you're armed to the teeth."

"While we can't imagine Knight still wants them, " said Allen, "or has any idea where they are, just to be paranoid, we'll still ring the base with dark energy sensors. That way, in the unlikely case we're wrong, he won't be able to get any mobile time travel units within the fifty-eight feet he would need to infiltrate the base."

"So we'll be babysitting for two long weeks?" complained Tom TenBrink .

"Don't think of it as two long weeks," replied Cargill with a smile. "Think of it as fourteen short days."

TenBrink didn't return the smile. "I know you're sure Jenna Morrison will eventually join us," he said. "But what if she doesn't? What if she decides to get back to her life and leave the fail-safe in place?"

"I'll just have to convince her that she can't," said Cargill. "That she'd be too exposed to Edgar Knight. Even if he doesn't think she has access to Nathan's work anymore, I know him too well. If she was that unprotected, he'd never leave this stone unturned."

"And if *that* fails?" said O'Bannon.

"Enough!" barked Cargill, having suddenly lost his patience. "She's going to join us! But be assured that if I'm wrong, I'll do what I have to do. Even if it isn't pretty. So no more questions. Just be ready tomorrow morning."

Hamilton's comrades all wore grim expressions, but he was *ecstatic*. This transfer was the exact break he needed. This was his chance. Not only to be a hero, but to finally end this double agent shit.

In just one more day, Hamilton could finally begin fighting alongside Edgar Knight to forge a glorious future.

51

Jenna Morrison and Aaron Blake sat with their backs against the wall of the trailer compartment of the midsized truck, facing the doors at the back of the vehicle. Cargill was just a few feet away from them, driving, but the cab compartment was separate from the trailer and he couldn't be seen. Hamilton and O'Bannon sat against the right wall, and Beal and TenBrink against the left. Other than its human cargo, the small trailer, proudly proclaiming the false identity of a carpet discounter, was empty.

Hamilton was tingling with anticipation. He studied the girl carefully and noticed that she looked almost ill.

"Are you okay?" he asked Jenna, deciding it couldn't hurt to play the role of the concerned Samaritan.

She forced a smile. "Sure. It's just being in the back of a semi with a bunch of soldiers brings back memories I'd rather not have. Last time, it didn't work out so well."

"Don't worry, ma'am," said Eric Beal, "I promise this time will be very different."

"I know it will be," she said with a sigh. "Thanks."

They drove in silence for ten more minutes. Hamilton and his three comrades had rucksacks beside them, filled with weapons, just like the team that had been assigned to extract Jenna Morrison and Nathan Wexler originally. And just like this team, they had been instructed not to carry any weapons that would be visible to their guests, so as not to panic them.

This just served to further reinforce Hamilton's low opinion of Lee Cargill. If the girl saw that each of them had an M5 on their lap, it would make her feel *less* panicked rather than more.

As for Aaron Blake, Hamilton was familiar with his file, and this man never panicked. Even now he seemed hyper-alert, hyper-vigilant.

The truck rolled to a stop. Almost a full minute later, Cargill activated a microphone that broadcast his voice into the trailer compartment. Apparently, this wasn't just another red light.

"There's a minor fender bender blocking the road," he explained. "But a tow-truck is already on site, so we should be on our way in less than five minutes. This is not an ambush. The drivers of the cars in question, as well as the tow-truck driver, are harmless civilians, and I'm watching them closely. No suspicious vehicles or pedestrians are approaching. Finally, I have a good field of vision, and can get around them if I need to."

Hamilton's eyes narrowed. "What are the odds there'd be an accident blocking our path?" he said, posing the question to no one in particular.

"I'm thinking maybe one in a million," said TenBrink uneasily.

"It is an unlikely coincidence," said Joe O'Bannon, "but Cargill obviously knows this, too, and he isn't worried."

Hamilton could tell TenBrink was biting his tongue, wanting to express how he felt about Cargill's judgment in these matters, but not wanting to do so in front of their two guests.

"Even so," said Hamilton, unzipping his ruck and removing an H&K .45 caliber handgun. "I'm gonna check it out. Just to be sure."

"Good idea," said Blake, whose instincts were obviously also screaming at him that this had to be trouble, despite Cargill's assurances.

The trailer had two doors that met in the center and opened outward. Hamilton opened one a crack and looked out. He turned back to face the others. "The coast is clear, and it looks calm. When I return, I'll knock twice, pause, and then three times, so you'll know it's me."

Not waiting for a response, he exited the truck and shut the door. He moved rapidly to the passenger's side of the cab and motioned for Cargill to lower the window.

Cargill glared at Hamilton as he powered the window lower. "What are you doing?" he snapped angrily. "Get back in the trailer!"

Hamilton began screwing a silencer onto the end of his gun, doing so below window level and out of Cargill's sight. "I just wanted to check things out," he said innocently. "You know, make sure this isn't an ambush."

"I told you it wasn't!" said Cargill. "Sometimes an accident is just an accident. And Knight has no idea we're even here."

"Wrong on *both* counts, *jackass*," said Hamilton, raising his weapon and depressing the trigger three times in quick succession, sending three rounds ripping through Cargill's chest.

Before he had fired he had surveyed the area, and was satisfied that no one would witness this long overdue execution. Knight had paid the most harmless-looking civilians he could find a king's ransom to stage this accident, and others on his team had put up barricades out of sight to limit the number of possible witnesses.

Hamilton walked to the back of the truck and took a deep breath. From one pocket he removed a reinforced padlock, and from the other a small canister of gas. He knew for certain his comrades—soon to be *ex*-comrades—hadn't packed any masks.

He knocked. Rap Rap. Pause. Rap Rap Rap.

He waited another few seconds and then began opening the door, secure in the knowledge that no weapons would now be pointing in his direction. He pulled the pin on the canister, tossed it inside, and slammed the door shut, padlocking it firmly closed.

He returned to the cab, pushed Cargill's lifeless body to the passenger's side, and checked the time.

Right on schedule.

Now all he had to do was take a detour into the woods to meet with others on Knight's team tasked with transporting Hamilton and his two prisoners back to Lake Las Vegas, taking care to exercise appropriate surveillance countermeasures, including a few that Knight's Brain Trust had only recently developed.

Hamilton turned to Cargill's blood-soaked corpse as the truck began rolling forward, happier than he had been since he could remember.

"Mind if I drive?" he said with a broad grin.

52

Jenna and Blake were given shots to reverse whatever knockout agent had been used on them, and the effect was immediate and dramatic, bringing them back to full alertness.

Their wrists were locked together with hardened plastic strips, ratcheted into place, and they were led at gunpoint to the room they had seen on their television screen at the Best Border Inn, the office of Edgar Knight.

The building they were in was twenty-two stories tall and it was magnificent: modern, bright, and reeking of opulence. Once a luxury hotel, several of the floors had been converted into luxury offices and apartments. Many others had been torn out and turned into havens for scientists, complete with individual offices, conference rooms, virtual reality rooms where inventors could immerse themselves in virtual 3D representations of their work, and expansive labs—biology, physics, chemistry, electronics, artificial intelligence, and so on—each packed with the most advanced equipment and technology money could buy.

Along with an office that appeared to be the electronic nerve center of an empire, far more extensive than they had glimpsed during their call, Knight's twenty-second-story residence was a lavish penthouse apartment that took up the entire floor, thousands of square feet in space, and one that would satisfy the most spoiled of high-rollers. The outer wall of the entire floor was a single seamless window that looked out upon several shorter buildings nearby and a land bridge that carved a path across a soothing blue body of water. The floor plan was open and expansive, with magnificent arches leading to bedrooms, a kitchen a professional chef would envy, and even a small indoor pool and Jacuzzi.

Knight's lackeys led them to four steel chairs at one edge of the office area, spaced at about five-foot intervals, bolted to the floor. The chairs clashed horribly with the modern decor, introducing a psychopathic prison-warden vibe into the otherwise sophisticated elegance.

They were seated, their legs were tied firmly to the chairs with unbreakable nylon straps, ratcheted tight, and their hands were freed. Knight thanked his four underlings and they quickly exited, leaving him alone with his two prisoners.

Knight studied them thoughtfully for several long seconds. He was most fascinated by the Army Ranger turned PI. He didn't look special in any way, but his file suggested he could not be more formidable. Appearances really could be deceiving.

"Jenna Morrison and Aaron Blake," he said in delight. "It's nice to finally meet you. I can't help but be disappointed that you didn't accept my generous offer and come in on your own. But I guess you're here now anyway."

He gestured to the chairs on which they were bound. "When I knew you were coming, I had these built especially for you."

Blake nodded toward the two empty chairs beside him. "Having a problem with your math?" he said.

Knight shrugged. "You never know when two extra chairs might come in handy."

"How long were we out?" asked Blake.

"Six hours."

"Where are we?" demanded the PI.

Knight considered. Since he had made certain they were checked for bugs and homing devices, there was no reason not to tell them. "You're on an island in the center of Lake Las Vegas."

"Lake Las Vegas?" said Jenna. "Is that some kind of weird joke?"

"No. Why shouldn't there be a giant man-made lake in the middle of a desert?" he said wryly.

Jenna and Blake exchanged confused glances, but this wasn't the time to get a real estate lesson.

"So Hamilton was working for you all along?" said Blake.

"Yes. I hadn't been all that impressed with him, actually. Until today."

"Where are the others we were with?" said Jenna.

"I'm afraid they're all dead," replied Knight matter-of-factly. "Including my old friend Lee Cargill," he added, this time with great satisfaction.

"No!" whispered Jenna in horror. "All of them? But why? They were *helpless*."

"I didn't want to be Q5's enemy," replied Knight. "After all, I'm the person who created it." He shook his head. "But they've made it their mission to kill me. So forgive me for not getting all weepy about it."

He pulled up a chair and sat down, six feet away. Banks of large monitors around the room displayed the whereabouts of various members of his organization, security perimeters, and other information in a never-ending barrage, but he only had eyes for Jenna and Blake.

"I was not happy to learn you had sided with Q5," he said. "A poor choice."

"Who told you we were on their side?" asked Blake, as if this couldn't be further from the truth.

"Brian Hamilton."

"Then Cargill lied to him," said Blake without hesitation. "Cargill was trying to convince us to join him, but we were keeping an open mind. We actually wanted the chance to speak with you, get your side of the story, before we made up our minds. If you would have told us the score on the phone instead of lying to us, we might have been more receptive to your point of view."

"Butchering helpless men isn't winning you any brownie points either," spat Jenna.

"First of all, I don't care anymore if you come to my side or not. I intend to get Nathan Wexler's file from you, willingly or otherwise. And I would never butcher helpless men. When you're being stalked by a lion and you chance upon him sleeping, you kill him.

The difference between me and Lee Cargill is that I'm willing to make tough choices, own up to tough realities."

Knight rose and put his arms behind his back, causing him to take a forward-leaning posture. "Compassion is great. I'm all for it. But if we let it paralyze us from making rational, logical . . . *necessary* decisions, we deserve to go extinct as a species."

"Just the opposite," said Jenna. "Compassion will make sure we *don't* go extinct."

Knight laughed. "Spoken like a true head-up-your-ass idiot," he said. "If *everyone* were compassionate, this would be true. But there are ruthless people in this world. People who relish the idea of Armageddon and are moments away from having the means to make this happen. Compassion in the face of that is suicidal, which is the exact path we're on. You're like a stalk of wheat in a wheat field saying to your compatriots, 'compassion and love are the answer. If we just show that approaching cloud of millions of locusts how caring we are, I'm sure they'll leave us alone.'"

"I agree with you in many ways," said Blake. "I do. But the answer isn't setting one man up as absolute dictator."

"Why not? Right now we have democracies in the world, but we also have any number of countries run by dictators and worse. Irrational, power-hungry people, with only their own interests at heart. At least with me running the show you'll have rational decisions."

"Like sterilization of anyone below a certain intelligence level?" said Jenna.

"Yes. First you wipe the barbaric, destructive extremists from the planet. Simple decision, just like I made with your friends in the transport truck. Kill them, or they'll kill you later. These terrorist types are great at begging for *your* mercy, appealing to *your* compassion, until the moment you're stupid enough to let them off the mat, when they destroy you with a ruthlessness you can't comprehend. Believe me, they won't show you any compassion or mercy, even a second after you spare them."

Knight sighed. "As for controlling the coming swarms of unintelligent, ignorant masses, it's been said before that the Earth is a spaceship, and we're its passengers. Our planet is a tiny lifeboat in a vast ocean universe. But our boat is getting overcrowded and taking on water. When the crewmembers who aren't capable of bailing any water reproduce ten times faster than those who can, it doesn't take a genius to see that the boat will eventually sink. It's only a matter of time. And I'm not advocating throwing these crewmembers overboard. Just making sure their endless progeny don't overwhelm and eventually suffocate the able-bodied members of the crew."

Knight was surprised that Jenna Morrison didn't have a visceral and immediate negative reaction to this view, shouting out her objections. Perhaps, on some level, she knew he was right.

"Rational decisions and compassionate decisions are often at odds with each other," he continued. "Sometimes rational decisions seem cruel. I can't help that. As a compassionate society, we thin herds of animal species, because we see the perils that overpopulation presents to them. We burn overgrown forests in a controlled manner to save them from the devastation of an *uncontrolled* fire. But we refuse to treat our own species with the rationality with which we treat others."

"I'm sure the Unabomber prided himself on his rationality too," said Blake bitterly.

Knight laughed. "The difference is, I know I'm rational. The truth is, not many people are. They think they are, but they're fooling themselves. People like you are horrified because I make decisions based on logic rather than emotion. For me, it's all in the math. A train is about to hit and kill five innocent people. Say you have the power to divert it at the last second, saving these five, but this diversion will kill your mother. Do you do it?"

Knight waited for several seconds. The strained look on the faces of both prisoners, and their failure to answer immediately, was telling.

"Of course you do," he said. "One versus five. The logic is simple. I can make this kind of decision easily, so I'm a monster. You can't, which is why you need someone like me running the show."

Blake sighed. "I have to admit, I don't entirely disagree with what you're saying."

"Good try, Mr. Blake, but I just wanted to give you my side of the argument. I'll never believe you agree with me at this point. Your hesitation in answering my train question gives me all the information I need. I'm willing to do what I have to do to save spaceship Earth. If that means dicing a thousand innocent people into tiny cubes, then that's what I'll do. I won't enjoy it. I'll wish it wasn't necessary. But I'll always keep the big picture, the math, in mind. Kill a thousand, save the world."

"Cargill told us you were suffering from delusions of grandeur," said Jenna disdainfully. "He was dead on about that."

"My grandiosity is a fact, not a delusion," said Knight in amusement. "I *am* extraordinary. And I'm under no delusions about the fate of our species if drastic measures aren't taken. It's easy to bury your head in the sand, think compassionate thoughts while the world burns, avoid making the tough choices. It's hard to face up to the ugly truth, and the unpleasant decisions this forces on you."

"So what do you want with us?" said Jenna.

"You have a copy of Wexler's work in the cloud. I want you to open it, give it to me, and then destroy it, along with your fail-safe."

"That cloud file doesn't exist anymore," said Jenna. "We destroyed it when we joined Cargill."

He raised his eyebrows. "That's interesting. I could have sworn you began this session by telling me you still weren't a part of Q5."

Jenna remained silent.

"I know the file still exists," said Knight angrily. "Hamilton wouldn't have exposed himself to get you here if he didn't know it was still active. Seems that Cargill was very clear on this at his recent briefing. You know, the one he had the day before Hamilton blew him away."

"So does cruel taunting count as rational?" said Jenna. "Maybe killing him is rational, if you're convinced he's determined to do the same and it's preemptive—maybe. But how does sadistic gloating, rubbing salt in our wound, count as rational?"

"Because *everything* I do is calculated," replied Knight immediately. "Taunting can be used to intimidate, to make you fear what I might do. To make you believe I probably am sadistic, so you'll cooperate with less resistance."

"Well calculate *this*," snapped Jenna with a fierce glare, "we're not getting that file for you. Period. We're both prepared to die before letting that happen."

Knight smiled. "She didn't really check that with you first, did she, Mr. Blake?"

"That's because she knows me well enough to know I agree."

"Yeah, I know you well enough, too. You're obviously the strong link in this chain. But Jenna here . . ." He shook his head. "Not so much."

Jenna couldn't completely hide her fear but managed to maintain her resolve. "With this much at stake, I'm going to prove you wrong. We all have to die sometime," she added stoically.

"So let me guess, you're prepared to die a thousand deaths in support of your cause."

"Yes," said Jenna.

Knight issued a command to his PDA and less than a minute later two guards entered his penthouse suite, leading two additional prisoners into the room, their hands bound and both of their mouths sealed with gray duct tape.

Jenna's eyes nearly burst from their sockets.

The first prisoner she recognized immediately: Nathan Wexler. Alive and looking surprisingly well.

The second prisoner was a woman, one she realized she knew, but whom she couldn't quite place.

When she did, bile rose in her throat, and the world began to spin around her.

Because the second prisoner was Jenna Morrison.

53

"Nathan?" said Jenna, turning to the first prisoner.

He nodded, and this was all it took to send a flood of tears streaming down her cheeks.

"Let's hold off on the joyous reunion until I get these two situated," said Knight. He motioned to his men, who deposited the new prisoners in the two empty chairs and bound their legs as well.

"Should we remove the tape from their mouths?" asked one of the men.

"No, leave it," Knight commanded, and then waved them away. "Thanks, that will be all."

As the guards left the room, Jenna turned to Knight, tears still dripping down her face. "How?" she asked simply.

"Come on Jenna. See what emotions do to a person. You are so much smarter than that."

"You duplicated him. Duplicated *us*," she added in horror. "But when?"

"Now that is a more intelligent question. About three months ago. He's part of what I call my Brain Trust. It's a little initiative I've developed to duplicate the best minds in the world."

Blake frowned. "Cargill told us you fantasized about copying the Einsteins of our age. We should have known you wouldn't wait to get started on this."

"No time like the present," said Knight with a grin. "That's a bit of a time travel joke, in case you didn't catch it," he added.

Both prisoners continued to glare at their captor, in no mood for humor.

"The truth is," said Knight, "my Brain Trust initiative has already paid huge dividends. These people have made breakthroughs that are truly stunning."

"But how did you manage to copy us?" said Jenna, finally regaining full control of her tear ducts.

"Carefully," said Knight. "Very carefully. I've built a collection of eighteen-wheelers with time machines inside. We deploy two trucks for each target, one with a device and one without. My men mark off range and distance in the nearest empty field or parking lot. You two were sleeping like babies when they broke in and gassed you. Once you were completely out, they put you in the truck containing my device and parked fifty-eight feet from the other truck, in the proper orientation. I triggered the device remotely, and voila, a copy of each of you."

Blake nodded slowly. "Then your men just returned them to their beds, and they awoke, none the wiser."

"Obviously," said Knight, "since she clearly had no idea any of this happened. My men are supremely talented at this task and have done this repeatedly around the country, with equal success. Right now the operation is limited to North America, but so many brilliant scientists from overseas visit this continent this hasn't posed much of a limitation."

Knight sneered. "I'm sure Cargill told you all about duplication strategies such as this," he added, "no doubt using his favorite example, Kim Jung-un. The difference is, Cargill is too weak to actually do it. Another idiot who blathers on about slippery slopes while our ship is hitting an iceberg."

Jenna stared into the eyes of her double, into her own eyes, and shivered—both versions did so at the same time. "I get why you wanted Nathan. But why did you duplicate *me*?"

"I'm nothing if not practical," said Knight. "I want these scientific titans to have the best work environment possible, the most conducive to clear thought. Men and women both tend to perform better when they're getting laid, genius or no. And when a man is in love, like Nathan, forcibly removing him from the object of his affection almost guarantees lack of cooperation. Members of my Brain Trust are prisoners, yes, but their cages are gilded. Most love being here despite themselves. Where else can they focus their genius without need to raise money, and with absolutely no distractions? Where else can they work with others as brilliant as themselves? I've gathered the most brilliant minds, working on the most challenging problems, with unlimited access to any equipment they desire, and within the best lab facilities in the world."

Jenna turned away from her double and locked her gaze on Nathan Wexler. "I've missed you so much," she said, her eyes becoming moist again. "I love you," she finished.

Wexler's glance shifted from Jenna to the gagged version of Jenna—the woman with whom he had lived the past three months—and back again. His eyes were now moist as well and he nodded his acknowledgment of this sentiment, unable to speak, and clearly unsure how to process this impossible situation.

"So if you have Nathan Wexler," said Blake, "why do you need his file? Your Wexler has the identical mind and capabilities of the other. Surely this Nathan Wexler can come up with the same discovery."

"You'd think," said Knight, showing a flash of anger. "But apparently not. And I even have the advantage of being able to put more than one of him on the problem."

"How many others of him are there?" whispered Jenna in horror.

"Eight," said Knight. "Each with their own Jenna Morrison to screw at night," he added bluntly. "I wanted more, but I have to be practical, and if eight aren't doing the trick, more probably won't either. And because they each know the importance of what I'm after, and each are head-up-their-ass pacifists, they have more incentive to escape than any of the others. You know, nothing drives one like a grand cause."

"And none of the eight have solved it?" said Blake.

Knight frowned. "No. They are all Dr. Wexler, possessing the same extraordinary genius of the man who made the breakthrough, but none of them experienced whatever random catalyst set this brilliance on such a revolutionary path. I've come to appreciate that this isn't all that surprising. Because creativity is a fickle bitch. Who knows what one random occurrence sparks a eureka moment. Alexander Fleming discovered penicillin because one of his plates of bacteria accidentally became contaminated. A million Flemings couldn't have discovered antibiotics without this key event."

He paused. "If you copied a hundred Einsteins, only one would have come up with relativity. Why? Because the others would be in different environments. Any Einstein in a university environment would have worked on other problems, and would have been restricted in his thinking by the status quo, would have been discouraged from ideas that seemed insane.

"Only Einstein the patent clerk would have come up with relativity. First, he was free of academic shackles. Second, it just so happened that he worked on patents having to do with the transmission of electric signals and electrical-mechanical synchronization of time. Both of these are key ingredients in the thought experiments that led him to his radical conclusions."

"So you can access endless Nathan Wexlers," said Blake, "but not the one you need. Ironic isn't even the word for it."

Knight ignored this jab. "There was a chance they weren't really trying," he said, "or had found what I was looking for but didn't want me to have it. So I tortured a few of them to death, just to be sure. Turns out they were telling the truth."

Nathan Wexler couldn't move his mouth, but his eyes conveyed absolute revulsion.

Knight smiled. "That's the beauty of having different versions of a person," he said. "It really lets you be creative. Some you can treat like kings. Others you can bully and torture. And you get to see what inducement is more effective. This man here has been treated like a king and had no idea there were other versions of himself working on the problem, or getting tortured to death."

"You are a sick, demented sadist!" spat Jenna, acid dripping from her every word. "You don't know what sparked Nathan's breakthrough, but you know for *certain* it wasn't torture. Yet you did it anyway. But I'm sure you had a rational reason for what you did, right? Because you aren't a pathetic psycho, you're the paragon of rationality."

"I wasn't trying to spark a discovery. I was making sure they weren't holding out on me."

Blake shook his head in disgust. "But in that case—"

"*No more discussion!*" interrupted Knight, rising from his chair. "It's time to cut to the chase." He faced the Jenna he had captured that morning. "So what do you say, Jenna? I need that file. But I'm willing to make this easy on all of us. I'll offer you the deal of a lifetime. Get me that file, and I'll reunite you with the man you love."

"This is all so . . . wrong," said Jenna. "What you're doing, what you're planning to do . . ." She paused, searching for the right words. "It's atrocious. It's *grotesque*. I'm more certain than ever that I won't help you."

Knight turned toward the gagged version of Jenna Morrison, drew a gun, and shot her twice in the chest. She fell forward, held to the chair by her legs, as blood poured from her body and collected in a widening pool around her chair.

Jenna and Nathan Wexler both screamed at the same time, although Wexler's screams were muffled by the duct tape covering his mouth.

"That's better," said Knight calmly. "No one wants to share their man, after all. Even if the person they're sharing with is themselves. So now that he's all yours, Jenna, how about it?"

"You are the sickest bastard who ever lived!" screamed Jenna, on the edge of hysteria.

"I'm just a man willing to do what's necessary to save the species," said Knight, as though he expected to be congratulated. "And as for you," he added ominously, "you did say you were willing to die a thousand deaths before you would help me."

He nodded at Jenna Morrison's dead body. "Well, good news—you just might get that chance."

54

Knight seemed completely untroubled by the presence of a cadaver slumped over in a chair nearby, and the sickening amount of blood she had left on the wood floor below her feet.

"You see how this works," he said to Jenna. "You can't win. I can make a copy of you and then torture you to death. If you won't help me, I'll try something else with the copy. Eventually, I'll find the key."

Knight gestured to Nathan Wexler. The physicist's face was now as tear streaked as Jenna's and he looked like he had been hit by a train. "In fact, why don't I start the festivities by torturing this man, this new widower, while you watch. The man you love more than life itself. The man you thought you lost forever. Then I can fetch another copy of him and try again." He smiled. "Isn't time travel fun?"

Jenna's tears had stopped, almost as though she had run out, and she looked as emotionally spent as Wexler. "I'll help you," she said. "I will. But under one condition: you let Aaron Blake and this version of Nathan go. Once they call me and tell me they've made it to safety, I'll give you what you want."

Knight shook his head in disappointment. "Yeah, that's not going to happen. Sorry. I'm willing to bet you'll break sooner rather than later using the other methods I just mentioned. But isn't it interesting how irrational you've become. You're convinced I'm a monster and will destroy the world. And yet you're suddenly willing to sell out all of humanity in exchange for just two men. You'd never catch me doing that."

"Yeah, you're a real hero," growled Jenna through clenched teeth.

She paused for several long seconds, taking deep breaths to calm herself. "I'm not willing to sell out humanity," she added finally. "But part of me thinks your actions may be as necessary as you say. That without a psychopath like you running the show, the world will self-destruct. Saddam Hussein was a psychopath, too, but at least he maintained order in the most volatile region on Earth. So I *am* doing the math. I have to admit, my love for Nathan Wexler does factor in heavily, but maybe you really are the answer, God forbid."

Her face hardened. "So I'll make one last offer," she said. "Remove their restraints and let them exit this building. Then give them a thirty-minute head start. You can have dozens of men guarding this room so they can't circle back. But give them thirty minutes. After that they're fair game, in the truest sense of the word *game*."

"Your proposal is for me to hunt them like animals, and you think *I'm* the one who's sick?"

"I have confidence in Aaron Blake's skills. Do you have confidence in your security? And you get to win twice. You get your holy grail without having to spill more blood on your office floor. And you get to test your security arrangements. You seem to be a big fan of survival of the fittest. This would pit one unarmed man against hundreds. Thousands. Surely your people can stop a single ex-Army Ranger and an egghead physicist from leaving your little lake, right?"

"Just so you know," said Knight, "they won't be able to get a message out to your allies, if that's your plan. I have some of the most brilliant minds in history here, many of whom no doubt want to escape. So I hired consultants to block all communication off the island, from landlines, cells, or computers. Cells can't get voice, text, e-mail, or Internet."

From Knight's bearing, it was obvious he was quite proud of this accomplishment. "Ninety-nine percent of the people here have no knowledge of our activities," he continued, "so I've maintained the fiction that the island never did get coverage. It's a hardship for employees here, and they know the cover story is bullshit, but they're paid too much to complain. So if anyone who is here against their will ever does manage to steal a phone, they can't call for help.

"And Internet is incoming only," continued Knight. "Brain Trust scientists, and others on this island, can enter terms into a Google search bar, but that's the only way they can interact with the outside world. The results of their searches can be opened and downloaded, but it's one-way traffic only." He smiled. "None of this was easy to do, but it is quite foolproof."

Knight paused. "But don't you worry, Jenna. I know you'll have to enter codes to retrieve the file I need. But on this floor and the one below—both the most heavily guarded real estate on the island—Internet and phone communications are unrestricted, so you won't have any trouble."

"Thanks for clearing that up," said Jenna, rolling her eyes. "But I couldn't care any less. So let me repeat my offer. Give them a thirty-minute head start," she continued, gesturing toward Blake and Wexler. "In exchange, I'll give you the breakthrough you want. The work of the second coming of James Clerk Maxwell."

"Fifteen minutes."

Jenna was silent for several seconds. "It has to be a fair head start."

"Of course. Other than this floor and the one below, I'll have security in this building stand down for the full fifteen minutes, unless they're attacked. Not only won't my men here go after them, they won't alert the security apparatus on the rest of the island." He shrugged. "Not that they'll need to."

Jenna paused in thought once again. Finally, she nodded. "Agreed."

"Why would you do this?" said Knight.

"Were you not listening? I told you, there is a chance what you're planning to do is a necessary evil. Giving you this information might actually save the world. And I have confidence in Aaron Blake. He'll find a way to get Nathan out of here to safety."

"You are suffering from some pretty severe delusions," said Knight. "But why not? I'm truly looking forward to identifying any weaknesses in my security. The farther Blake gets, the more he'll be helping me."

He smiled. "You have yourself a deal."

55

Knight issued commands to his PDA and soon various members of his organization snapped into action. Within minutes the lifeless body of Jenna's doppelganger was removed from the office and what seemed like gallons of blood cleaned up with very little trace.

Two heavily armed men led Nathan Wexler and Aaron Blake from the room. Once they had left, two additional guards were stationed by the twenty-second-floor elevators, and four more just outside the entrance to Knight's suite.

Knight instructed these men not to interrupt him under any circumstances, and he explained to Jenna that the inner walls of the penthouse floor were reinforced and virtually impregnable, so she shouldn't expect any heroic rescues from Blake.

The office area of the suite was ringed with eight plasma screens, each larger than the last, and one of them was on the wall over Jenna, who was still strapped to the steel chair. Knight had his PDA display video feeds on it, two views of the twenty-second floor, just in case: the bank of four elevators and the entrance to his lair.

On a different screen, one that he and Jenna could both see clearly, he had his PDA display the progress of Aaron Blake and Nathan Wexler as they were led to the ground floor and escorted outside.

"Okay, Jenna," said Knight. "You're getting your wish. None of my men in this building will molest them for fifteen minutes, unless *they* initiate. Security elsewhere on the island has not been alerted in any way. I'll leave it to them to figure out that these men are on the loose and do something about it."

"Aaron Blake is going to beat your security and survive," said Jenna confidently.

Knight laughed. "Aaron Blake and a small army couldn't get off this island alive," he countered. "But I believe we had an agreement.

I've held up my part." He gestured toward her expectantly. "Now it's *your* turn."

She studied the monitor as Blake and Wexler disappeared around the edge of the building.

"Okay, get to a computer and I'll tell you what to do," said Jenna. "But not until the full fifteen minutes have gone by. It's not that I don't trust you to give them their full head start," she added, "it's just that I don't trust you to do *anything* you say."

Knight smiled, unoffended. "Fair enough," he said, moving to a computer ten feet away. "You have just over thirteen minutes."

***

"Purse your lips," Blake instructed Wexler the moment they were left alone at the foot of Knight's building.

The physicist looked confused.

"Are they pursed?" said Blake impatiently, and got a nod in the affirmative.

Blake reached up and ripped the tape from Wexler's mouth with considerable force and speed.

The physicist let out a squeal of terror and discomfort but then blew out a long breath in relief as he realized his lips were still intact, thanks, no doubt, to his companion's advice.

His eyes reflected a deep anguish, and not just due to their current circumstances. He had seen the woman he loved killed in front of him. Knowing there was still a Jenna Morrison alive was some consolation, but the woman who was shot was the one he had spent the past three months with on Knight's island.

"We need to get back inside," said Blake, pointing toward the building they had just left. He shoved the piece of duct tape he had removed into his pocket. "Come on! Quickly!"

"Why?" said Wexler.

"They'll expect us to move as far away from here as we can, as fast as we can. But we're sitting ducks outside. I'm sure we're on camera right now. But once inside we can raid a bathroom, storage closet, or lab and get a broom or plunger or something else we can use to knock out the cameras on as many floors as possible before our fifteen-minute head start is up. Once we do that, there are lots of rooms in which to hide and plan. They'll have to do a floor-by-floor search."

"Why bother?" said Wexler as they reentered the first floor of the building and Blake hit the button for the fifth. "I'm glad Jenna made this arrangement, since Knight would have gotten what he wanted anyway, and now at least she won't be tortured. I love her even more for trying to protect us. But I've been here three months and have a taste of the kind of security this madman has in place. Believe me, escape is impossible."

They arrived at their floor and Blake looked up and down the long corridor, ringed with office doors and what looked like labs. The coast was clear. "Come on," he whispered, stepping from the elevator.

"Didn't you just hear what I said? Knight is going to win. We should just surrender. What's the point of this?"

"I'll tell you the point," said Blake. "But listen well and fast, because I don't have time to repeat myself."

* * *

The fifteen minutes had ended three minutes earlier, making Blake and Wexler fair game, but Knight continued to stare at his monitors. "I'll be damned," he said. "He's as impressive as you say. They've reentered this building, and he's managed to blind us on the first, fifth, seventh, and ninth floors already. Not to mention all four elevators. Nice."

Knight finally turned from the monitor, which showed various members of building security cautiously making their way through the stairwells toward the floors in play. Just before he completed his turn, a red warning light appeared once again, indicating they had lost video feed on the eleventh floor as well.

"As interesting as this manhunt is," said Knight, "It's time to see that file. Time to learn how to extend my reach." He frowned. "I wish the universe would allow for time travel of a minute or two—which would open up some truly staggering possibilities—but I guess beggars can't be choosers. I'll have to settle for the nearly half-second that Dr. Wexler will make possible."

Jenna provided instructions for how to access the file in the cloud, and how to get it open. It was a lengthy process, and she walked Knight through it step by painstaking step.

* * *

Nathan Wexler was in awe of his companion's resourcefulness and speed of decision making. The man hadn't had time to give his background. Wexler only knew that he was working for someone named Lee Cargill and a group dedicated to bringing Knight down.

Blake had listened with rapt attention as Wexler told him everything he knew about the layout of the twenty-two-story structure.

Blake ushered the physicist into yet another elevator and pressed the button for the nineteenth floor.

"They've had plenty of time to mobilize," said Wexler. "So why are we using the elevator and going to a floor that still has video?"

"Even though I knocked out video in the elevators," Blake explained as they began their ascent, "they'll expect us to be taking the stairs. And they'll think what you just thought. That we'll be sticking to the floors that are blind."

"So why not go directly to the first floor? I told you that's where we need to be."

"You also described the security there. We have to improve our situation first. And I have something else I need to do beforehand. You're sure nineteen is the medical wing?"

"Positive."

The elevator door opened and no one was in sight.

"If anyone is even watching this floor now," whispered Blake, "which is doubtful, they'll be looking for two men together. So we need to split up. I'll go first. Wait about a minute and follow. Don't look up at any cameras and move slowly, like you have all the time in the world. Find the suite of doctor's offices. I'll be in one of them. Look for duct tape on the door and you'll know which one."

Without waiting for a confirmation, Blake sauntered down the hall, staring down at his hands, which he held together near his chest as if he were holding a phone and studying the screen.

Wexler waited a minute, his heart racing, and followed. He passed two random strangers in the hall as he did, nodding hello, before coming to a hall with three offices belonging to doctors in Knight's employ.

Even though three doctors served the medical needs of the island, only one was usually on duty, and this person often had little to do. The piece of gray duct tape that Blake had removed from Wexler's mouth was hanging near the bottom of the door to the far left, which a nameplate indicated was the office of a Dr. Martin P. Fricke.

Wexler took a deep breath and entered. The room was empty except for Blake, who had no doubt forced his way in. Blake put a finger to his lips to motion for quiet. His other hand was clutching a scalpel with a two-inch blade that tapered to a lethal, stainless steel point, which he must have stolen from a storage closet.

Blake set the scalpel on the desk and hastily began rifling through every drawer in Fricke's office, his scowl indicating he wasn't finding what he was looking for.

"Wait here," he whispered, lifting the scalpel once again. "There's another empty doctor's office down the hall. I'll break in and mark it again with tape. Leave here in one minute and join me."

Wexler waited the full minute and then located Blake once again, this time in the office of a Dr. Allene Rohrer. Once again he was tearing through her drawers, on a mission. His eyes lit up when he came upon a flash drive, which probably hadn't been used in months, if ever.

He shoved it into Rohrer's computer and accessed the Internet.

"Knight wasn't lying," whispered Wexler. "You can type inside a Google search bar, and download files, but can't send anything else through cyberspace, including passwords."

"Won't need to," whispered Blake. "Two doors down is the office of a Dr. Susan Schlesinger. I heard her in there with some guy doing a check-up. Sounded like it was almost done. While I'm finding and downloading what I need, open the door a crack and watch for him to leave."

Wexler nodded and did as he was asked. Only two minutes later he reported that the patient had left and the doctor had returned to her office. Blake hurriedly finished up, shoved the flash drive into his pocket, and exited, with Wexler in tow.

He moved quickly to Dr. Schlesinger's door and rapped twice. The woman opened the door halfway and looked troubled when she didn't recognize either of her unexpected visitors. "Can I help you?" she said.

"Sorry to bother you, Dr. Schlesinger," said Blake pleasantly, "but we're with security here. We have reason to believe someone was searching through your office earlier today. Can we come in and take a look?"

She opened the door wider, an anxious look on her face. "Why would someone do that?" she asked.

"I don't know," said Blake, entering the room.

Once inside his friendly demeanor turned distinctly menacing. "I need you to stay very quiet," he said, lifting his right arm from behind his back to reveal the scalpel he was holding. "If you scream or make any loud noise, I'll kill you where you stand."

"What's this all about?" she whispered, barely managing to croak out the words.

"I don't want to hurt you," said Blake. "But I need you to do something for me."

She nodded, not trusting herself to speak.

"Call security," he said. "Tell them you saw two men who looked suspicious near your office five minutes ago. Give them our descriptions. Tell them they both exited to the stairs, but you think they were using your computer."

"And you won't hurt me?" whispered Schlesinger, trying not to panic.

"I can't tell you how much I don't want to hurt you," said Blake earnestly. "So just pull yourself together, do this, and we'll be out of your hair."

She lifted her phone while Blake repeated what she needed to say.

"Deep breaths," said Blake, trying to calm her down.

The doctor took a few deep breaths, as instructed, and then dialed zero, asking for security. Her voice was shaky, but she was calling to report possible intruders so it wouldn't be unreasonable for her to be a little rattled.

When the call had been transferred to security she gave her report as instructed, listened for several seconds, thanked the man at the other end, and hung up.

"What was his reaction?" said Blake. "Did he sound excited or bored?"

"Excited," said Susan Schlesinger. "He promised to find the men I reported."

"That's all?" said Blake.

She nodded.

"You sure he didn't also say he would send someone to check on your computer?" asked Blake. "After all, you did report we used it."

"Positive," she whispered.

Blake sighed. "Look, who could blame you for withholding something like this? I've given you reason to be afraid for your life. I get that. But I still promise I won't hurt you if you cooperate. So I'll ask one last time, are they sending a man here now?"

"Yes," she said, fighting back tears. "Yes, you're right."

"Thank you," said Blake, sounding almost relieved.

Wexler continued to marvel at his companion's skills. Blake had spread the building's security forces thin checking every nook and cranny for them on a number of blind floors, and after the doctor's report they would be scrambling to check the floors above and below the nineteenth.

But Wexler realized Blake had *wanted* security to send a man to Schlesinger's office. This is what he had been after all along. Wexler decided that if the stakes weren't what they were, this Aaron Blake would have been fun to watch operate.

"When the man knocks," Blake said to the doctor, "don't make a sound. You're almost at the finish line," he added, "so hang in there."

Blake opened the door a few inches and stood ready near the entrance. He handed the scalpel to Wexler. "Stay back with the doctor," he said. "Out of sight of the door. If she makes a sound, kill her."

Wexler had to remind himself this was all an act, but it was a role that could not have been more out of his comfort zone. He strained to come up with a response that was in character. "Roger that," he said, wondering if people said this in real life or just in the movies.

Less than a minute later a member of security arrived and grabbed the handle to the door, still slightly ajar. "Dr. Schlesinger?" he called out.

Getting no response, he opened the door wider and entered, an extended gun leading the way, even though he had been told Blake and Wexler were long gone.

Aaron Blake moved with astonishing speed and dexterity, using the man's slight momentum to pull him farther into the office with one hand while chopping at his Adam's apple with the other. Not waiting to be sure the man had blacked out, Blake grabbed his head and ran him a few yards to the doctor's desk, slamming his head down hard on the unforgiving surface.

The man dropped like a lead weight.

Blake didn't waste a moment. He relieved the guard of a semi-automatic pistol, combat knife, and cell phone.

He rose from the floor and used the combat knife to sever the cord of Schlesinger's landline. Since her cell phone was useless here, she would be unable to call security a second time.

"Thanks for your help," he said.

Wexler was still holding the scalpel, wondering if he looked like as much of an imposter as he felt. Blake gestured to him. "My colleague will wait outside your door for five minutes to make sure you don't exit, to give me time to do what I need to do. After five minutes, you can leave unmolested. When you do, feel free to tell security what happened. But since you've already put them on our tail, I wouldn't waste time on this. I'm urging you to leave this island as quickly as possible. Trust me, you do not want to be in this building right now."

She nodded meekly but didn't reply.

Blake motioned for Wexler to exit the office and then closed the door behind them.

"Go to the elevators," he whispered to the physicist. "I'll wait thirty seconds and join you there."

"Didn't you want me to guard the door?"

Blake grinned. "Really?" he whispered. "You thought I meant that? Trust me, she won't peek her head out of that office for the next five minutes no matter what."

Blake waved his hand toward the corridor. "Go," he said impatiently. "And don't look up at any cameras."

56

Edgar Knight paused just before opening the file now on his computer. If it really was *the file*, this would be one of the most monumental moments of his life. He knew once he began digging in he would be unable to focus on anything else.

So before he opened it, he needed to check on things. He put in a call to the man leading the search for Blake and Wexler, David Robinson. Unlike the rank and file, members of security had cell phones that had been programmed to act as walkie-talkies on the island.

"What's the status on our two bogies?" he asked.

There was a brief hesitation at the other end. "We still haven't found them," reported Robinson, his voice strained. "We've now searched every square inch of every floor that Blake blinded, but nothing. We had a report that they were spotted on the nineteenth floor and exited into the stairwell. They may have used one of the computers in a doctor's office. We've sent someone to check on this office, and others to search the stairwells and nearby floors."

"Any chance they left the building?" asked Knight.

"Hard to imagine," said Robinson. "The outside cameras are still operating, and we haven't seen anything. But it's also hard to imagine they're still at large, so anything is possible. I'll make sure we're paying attention outside as well."

Knight frowned. Blake was giving his security team a workout, just as Jenna had promised, but it was only a matter of time. And Knight was now only seconds away from getting information that would ensure his success, that would change the world forever.

"Okay, don't contact me unless you have good reason to believe I'm in personal danger. No matter what." Knight smiled with great satisfaction. "I'm going to be very busy."

***

Blake and Wexler traveled to the fifth floor, one of those that was no longer subject to video coverage.

The doors opened and a member of security appeared two feet away, facing them as though he had been waiting for the elevator. Blake and the man raised their guns at the exact same time and stopped, both with their weapons now trained point-blank at the other's head.

Neither took their eyes off the other, or even blinked, and both ignored Nathan Wexler completely.

"Looks like we have a standoff," said the man, still staring at Blake with the intensity of a predatory cat.

Blake pulled the trigger and the man's head almost exploded from his shoulders. His body fell to the ground along with his gun.

Idiot, thought Blake as he exited the elevator.

Standoffs were for the movies. Even if a gunman was a hair away from exerting enough trigger pressure to fire, human reflexes weren't nearly fast enough to react if another gunman decided to go first. It was like spreading your thumb and forefinger an inch apart and having a friend hold a pencil in between, choosing when to drop it. If you waited until you detected it being dropped, you would never be quick enough to catch it.

The same was true in a supposed standoff. Whoever fired first would win, unscathed.

Blake retrieved the man's gun and cell phone, giving him two of each. He pushed the last button on the phone and someone answered.

Blake focused on mimicking the voice of the man he had just killed. "I've been shot," he said, deepening his voice and rasping out these words, knowing that pretending to be near death would help pave over any differences in vocal tone. "Overhead them," he croaked, as though seconds away from bleeding out. "They plan to kill Knight. Nothing else matters to them. They're taking elev . . . "

Blake allowed his voice to trail off and he dropped the phone. He then entered the elevator on which they had arrived and pressed the button for the twenty-second floor, stepping back off before the doors closed.

"Come on," he said to Wexler. "We'll take the stairs to the first floor. Hopefully most of the men stationed there will be flocking to protect their boss."

* * *

Edgar Knight studied the contents of the file in silence. This was it! Part of him had almost believed it was all a dream, that something would always stop him from putting his eyes on this holy grail, but here it was.

He only had to read the introduction to know it was Wexler's work. He had familiarized himself with his previous work, and he had read physics and analysis done by other Nathan Wexlers as they attempted to replicate the first one's breakthrough.

The equations were elegant and the thinking profound. Wexler's insight was to look at the ways a fifth dimension could be forced to interact with the other four in an entirely novel way. Knight knew it would take years for him to fully understand all the mathematics, if ever, but already the logic of it was making sense.

He was euphoric.

And unlike Nathan Wexler, he knew much about how time travel worked in practice. So while Wexler wasn't entirely certain he could extend this effect from forty-five microseconds to almost half a second, Knight now was. It might be as simple as initiating certain patterns of vibrations in the field when it was activated.

Knight read on in fascination as the wheels in his head continued to turn.

* * *

"Through these doors," whispered Nathan Wexler, "and then left."

Blake nodded, hoping like hell his diversion had at least reduced the number of men guarding the room they needed to enter. They had made it to the first floor and to within twenty yards or so of their destination without running into any resistance, which meant that the men who had remained on this level were concentrated ahead of them.

Blake motioned his physicist companion to wait several feet behind him around a bend in the corridor. He threw open one of the double doors and dived through into a roll, anticipating that hostiles were lying in wait on the other side.

The barrage of gunfire that greeted his ears indicated he had surmised correctly, although the shots were all chest high, just missing his body as it knifed lower. He came out of his roll firing, shooting bursts into all three men who were facing the newly opened door, killing them instantly.

Blake retreated a few steps and signaled for Wexler to join him, but as the physicist neared the double doors another gunman turned into the corridor behind them. Blake yanked Wexler down, taking two rounds meant for the physicist, one in his left shoulder, which shattered, and another in his left leg.

Blood coursed down this entire side of Blake's body as he sent a burst of gunfire at the newcomer, but since the man was diving back around a bend in the corridor, he remained alive. Still, he had been severely wounded, and Blake had no choice but to assume he would be unable to give chase.

"Let's go," said Blake. He used the physicist as a crutch and proceeded back through the double doors. The two men went left for eight yards, and then right, following Wexler's instructions.

The pain in Blake's shoulder was so excruciating that the hole in his leg barely registered. He continued to leak blood like a sieve, leaving a trail behind him as if he were a snail.

Wexler half-carried, half-dragged him the remaining ten yards to the door that had been their goal from the very beginning. The door wouldn't open, but Blake removed his right arm from around

Wexler's shoulders and sent a burst through the lock to remedy this situation, steadying himself against the wall.

A dozen men were typically stationed around this room to be sure no one who wasn't authorized entered—so the lock was just a formality. Especially since it didn't matter if anyone entered, anyway. The room could only be useful to one man: Edgar Knight.

They entered the room that housed Knight's stationary time travel chamber. To Blake's eyes, the device was identical to the one inside Cheyenne Mountain. As Cargill had predicted, Knight had seen no need to change a good design.

Wexler managed to get them both to the sending station and Blake slumped into a chair in front of the computer that controlled the device. Blake handed the physicist one of the cell phones he had taken, which would work just fine anywhere but on the island.

"I've programmed Cargill's number," whispered Blake, his voice strained. "Call him . . . instant you arrive."

Wexler nodded. "Got it."

Blake tinkered with his belt buckle and removed an electronic device, about the size of a thick quarter, which began to glow from an inner light. "Put this . . . in pocket," he rasped.

"What is it?"

"When you . . . arrive," replied Blake, continuous speech becoming more and more of a challenge as he continued to weaken. "It signals. Aborts device. So you're only . . . sent . . . once."

"Right," said Wexler, as though this should have been obvious.

Blake was losing blood so rapidly he knew he had only minutes to live. He handed Wexler the flash drive he had taken from Dr. Rohrer's abandoned office, knowing he no longer had the motor skills to insert it into the computer. The physicist found the proper port and shoved it in.

When the file Blake had downloaded appeared on the monitor, Wexler opened it, and it immediately began carrying out automated instructions that required no additional human input.

"Get inside . . . chamber," whispered Blake, his voice weak almost beyond recognition.

As he had already explained to Wexler, Cargill's group had studied the breakthrough the other Nathan Wexler had made, and after only four days had been able to modulate the field, causing it to vibrate in a precise pattern that allowed for an extended range, in time and thus space. And the only change necessary to achieve this result was in the software.

Q5 had hastily conducted experiment after experiment, rapidly climbing the learning curve and perfecting the technique.

The software Q5 scientists had designed was even now working its magic. It would use Cargill's backdoor to take over the computer, and would trigger the device as soon as it detected that someone was in the chamber and the door was sealed. The device would be programmed to send Wexler far enough back in time for him to end up sixty-two miles away, a somewhat arbitrary distance.

Since they didn't know where Knight was headquartered, if sixty-two miles away in a certain direction happened to be inside a mountain, preventing time travel from occurring, the programming would alternate polarity, and thus direction, every second, and try again, until success was achieved.

Wexler spun the crank on the chamber door to open it and lifted Blake from the chair, propping him against the device.

The moment Wexler was safely inside, Blake marshaled his massive will, and the last of his remaining strength, to spin the crank back the other way. The device would fire the moment the door was sealed once more.

Blake wondered what it would be like to have every cell in his body vaporized in an instant. While he hadn't felt the need to tell Nathan Wexler about this, the transmitter in his pocket would serve *two* functions the moment it detected unfamiliar GPS coordinates.

In addition to aborting the device, it would activate the tiny grain of octa-nitro-cubane explosive attached to a detonator inside his belt. Enough to turn two rooms this size into a fireball.

"Thanks," said Wexler from inside the chamber. "I'll never forget this."

Blake nodded, almost imperceptibly.

The door to the room burst open and scores of men shot through. Dozens of bullets drilled into Blake's body.

But as he was falling to his death, in a last monumental effort of will, he kept his hand on the door handle, turning it the last rotation needed to seal the chamber.

57

Edgar Knight radiated such a delighted glow that he could have been mistaken for a lighthouse. Jenna Morrison had come through, and then some.

He decided he would never understand the mathematics involved in Wexler's theory, but he didn't have to. He understood the implications of general relativity without being able to solve the hideously complex mathematics that had taken Einstein so many years to master.

Wexler's guiding ideas—at least the ideas of *one particular* Nathan Wexler, now tragically deceased—were beyond genius, beyond elegant. He had found a way of thinking about higher dimensions that was so out of the box that someone tripping on LSD couldn't twist their mind into the pretzel necessary to arrive there. No wonder none of the other Wexlers, even with identical minds, had found this one extraordinary thread that allowed the rest to be unraveled.

From out of nowhere, an eardrum-shattering boom sounded and slammed into Knight's head with tremendous force.

He nearly jumped out of his skin, feeling like he had been shot from a cannon.

The entire building shook violently.

An explosion was rocking all twenty-two stories, the concussive blast so ferocious it made even the loudest thunderclap seem tame and whisper-quiet. Knight lost his balance and slammed into a nearby wall, his heart almost bursting from the adrenaline his terrified system poured into his bloodstream.

In one instant he had been in Heaven, and the next in a disorienting Hell. It took five or six seconds after the shockwave had pulsed through the room for him to regain any clarity of thought, whatsoever, his mind having retreated into a fetal position.

"What the fuck!" shouted Knight finally as his senses returned. He noticed on a monitor that several members of security who had been guarding the penthouse had now recovered and were clamoring to get in to be sure their boss was okay.

"Lazlo, what just happened?" he said to his PDA.

"There was an explosion in the building."

"No kidding. But where and why?"

"I am attempting to retrieve this information now."

"You don't need your *PDA* to tell you what happened," said Jenna Morrison smugly. "*I* can do that for you."

Knight had been so rattled by the explosion he had forgotten Jenna was even in the room, but he turned to her now. She had weathered the earthquake better than he had, as she had been strapped to a chair that was bolted to the floor.

And from the triumphant look on her face, she wasn't bluffing. She knew exactly what had happened, and why. How could that be?

"Lazlo," he said. "Tell security outside that I'm okay and to maintain watch."

"Complying now," said the PDA.

Knight's prisoner now had her hands clasped together, her right index finger resting lightly on the only jewelry she was wearing, a diamond ring that Knight knew must have been given to her by Nathan Wexler. "You know what that was?" said Jenna as a smile crept slowly over her face. "That was the signal I've been waiting for."

"*What's going on?*" he demanded.

"What's going on is that you're *fucked!*" she hissed, her eyes wild with hatred. "You may be the Faraday of our generation, but Cargill just played you for a *chump*. He orchestrated all of this."

"Impossible."

"Really? Why? Because you had a trusted mole inside, Brian Hamilton? Cargill knew you had a mole. He tricked you into revealing Hamilton's identity before he even had us in his custody."

"How?"

"He sent eight of his most trusted men a text, telling them he had found me and Aaron, and giving our location. And then telling them that the operation to get us wouldn't go forward for several hours."

Knight had fully recovered from the blast, but he still didn't understand where she was going with this.

Jenna saw that he hadn't caught on, and shook her head as though she pitied him. "Are you sure you're smart enough to survive your own eugenics program?" she said derisively. "The eight men each received the same text," she explained, "except for one detail. Each was given a different *location* for us."

Knight finally connected the dots, and he barely managed to stifle a scream.

Cargill *had* outplayed him, at least in this case. Cargill knew that if one of the eight men were working with Knight, they couldn't help but take this bait. The mole would tell Knight immediately that Cargill had found the two people Knight most wanted, and he would scramble a team out to the location given, so he could beat Cargill to the punch.

Cargill had unlimited authority and could direct law enforcement, military, and government agents at will to be his eyes and ears in each of the eight locations. When Knight's team was spied arriving at one of them, and beginning surveillance activities in preparation for an attack, Cargill would know who his mole was: whichever of the eight men had been texted that particular location.

In hindsight it made perfect sense. It explained why Cargill sent this text so far in advance of the planned op, and why he had then sent a second text, explaining that Blake had lied about his location and aborting the op.

"I can tell you're beginning to catch on," said Jenna. "As I told you, Cargill had ferreted out Hamilton early on. But he didn't let on, so he could feed him false information. Manipulate him. The problem was that everyone knew there was a mole, and it would be suspicious if Cargill suddenly pretended to trust Hamilton, or any on his team. So he had to find a way to pretend he had found the mole and was fat, happy, and clueless again. He had to find a justification for trusting Hamilton implicitly again. If not, if he had just begun confiding in Hamilton, you would have been suspicious, and might have guessed your man inside was being played."

Knight's lip curled up into a snarl. "So Cargill staged a polygraph ruse," he said.

Jenna nodded.

As angry as he was at being manipulated, he couldn't help but admire his old friend's ingenuity. The polygraph test was a double ruse, and it was nothing short of inspired. It hadn't been just good fortune that another man had taken the fall for Hamilton, freeing him to operate within Q5 once again.

"Blake and I signed on with Cargill after our second day with him," continued Jenna. "The first thing he had us do was delete Nathan's file from the cloud, by the way. Yesterday, after we had perfected our plan to beat you, Cargill briefed four of his men, including Hamilton, telling them I still wasn't sure I would join. That I had insisted on being relocated. And making it clear that the file in the cloud still existed. Making sure you knew the bait was still on the hook."

She shook her head in contempt. "You didn't think this all played into your hands just a bit too easily?"

"So you expected to be captured," said Knight. "So what? Now you're here. But how has this helped you?" he asked, realizing as he did that he was almost afraid of the answer. He had a sick feeling in the pit of his stomach that there were more layers yet to come, which he was failing to see. The massive explosion was clear evidence of this.

Jenna didn't reply. She remained motionless, her hands still folded together.

Another thought occurred to Knight. "Wait a minute," he said. "If Cargill was the puppet master here, he didn't do a very good job of it. Because I know for certain he's dead, along with a number of his key people."

"Come on, Edgar," said Jenna, mocking his earlier comments to her. "You are so much smarter than that."

Knight shook his head in disbelief. They were all *duplicates*?

Impossible. But what else could she mean?

"Lee Cargill would never allow a human to be sent back through time," insisted Knight. "He would never allow human duplication. He had a bug up his ass about this the size of a dog. It was his fucking Prime Directive. I refuse to believe it."

"*Believe it*," snapped Jenna. "To stop you, he was willing to make an exception. And he'd still never allow two copies of the same person to coexist, but he knew you'd kill everyone but me and Aaron. He and the men involved all volunteered to be duplicated, beginning with Chris Entwistle, the man who pretended to be the out-of-control Knight sympathizer during the polygraph test. They all volunteered to be kamikazes, knowing that one version of themselves would be killed, but their unique consciousness would live on. Joe Allen had strict instructions to execute any of these men you failed to kill."

Knight nodded. Knowing Cargill, this made sense. He would allow duplication as a last resort, but only if he was sure the duplicates would have very short life spans. "Okay," he said, "I believe you. But I still don't see his end game."

"Of course you don't. So let me educate you. Aaron Blake and I knew we would never be safe as long as you were alive. More importantly, the world could never be safe. So I agreed to be the bait. To sacrifice myself to get to you. Aaron volunteered as well. All I asked was that before we completed the mission, we be allowed to do everything humanly possible to try to save Nathan."

"You knew I had duplicates of him?"

"Not for sure, but we thought it was likely. Dan Walsh was shocked when he learned Nathan had been killed. After Nathan's death, he had received an e-mail answer to a scientific question he thought only Nathan could have provided. It occurred to us when we learned the full truth about time travel, about human duplication, that maybe Nathan had sent the e-mail after all. Maybe you had made a duplicate of him and put him up to it. Cargill thought this was likely, given how much time you spent fantasizing about copying geniuses when you were with Q5."

"How did you know I'd bring Nathan into the picture once I had you?"

"We didn't. That was just lucky. My plan was to offer to give you the file you wanted if you let Aaron go and gave him a thirty-minute head start. He would have tried to locate Nathan from there. Cargill assured me you would take me up on this offer. He was sure you wouldn't be able to resist the chance to get the file and test your security. By bringing Nathan here, you made it easier for us."

"If you expected him to be alive, how were you able to weep so convincingly when you saw him?"

"Wow, you really are devoid of emotions and empathy. I thought he was still alive, but I wasn't sure. And I had seen him killed in front of me. Seeing the man I love alive once again was incredibly emotionally charged. The tears were real."

Jenna paused. "As good as Aaron is," she continued, an awed look now on her face, "I thought the chances that he would succeed were one or two percent, at best. But he did it!" she added, beaming. "He is absolutely incredible."

Knight had been caught up in Jenna's narrative like it was nothing more than a fascinating puzzle, but this last brought him back to reality in a hurry. Because it *wasn't* just a puzzle. Somehow it had impacted him, and could well do so again.

But how? Even if Blake and Wexler had managed to cause an explosion somewhere in the building, they still had no prayer of escaping from the island.

Knight gasped as the truth hit him like a pile driver.

"Cargill found a way to extend time travel beyond forty-five microseconds," said Knight. "Didn't he? Q5 used Wexler's theory, and in a week they were able to do what I've spent years working toward."

"That's right," said Jenna. "But there's more. We're just getting to the good part. Cargill guessed your security setup exactly. You two spent dozens of hours over the years discussing security issues, after all. He knew exactly how you would set up cell and Internet coverage. So all Aaron had to do was get to a computer and download a file from cyberspace. One that seemed like gibberish but didn't require a password, so he could get it passively."

Knight felt like vomiting. He had never changed out Cargill's password. So Cargill's people could have easily written a program to take control of any one of his devices and teleport Wexler and Blake to safety.

"How did Blake know where my time travel units were located?"

"He didn't. He hoped Nathan would know where one was. If not, Aaron made sure to conceal a dark energy sensor in his left shoe before our road trip, when we knew Hamilton would capture us. One that Cargill assured us could detect a device within a mile or two. I have no idea if he needed to use it or not."

Jenna paused. "We wanted to give Aaron as much time as possible to succeed, so we made sure we restored Nathan's actual file to the cloud to mesmerize and distract you. Make sure you weren't on your toes."

"What makes you so sure he succeeded?"

"The explosion was the signal. It could only be triggered if the teleportation was a success. Aaron had this ready to go also. We used a little explosive that you actually brought to our attention: octa-nitro-cubane. Ring a bell? The most explosive non-nuclear substance known to science, but impossible to make without a time machine."

Knight saw it all now. Cargill, Jenna, and Blake had played their hand masterfully. And he had no doubt that what he had felt was octa-nitro-cubane in its full glory. It must have come from the ground floor, which housed the only time travel device in the building.

He glared at Jenna in contempt. "Cargill's plan may have been flawless, and it *will* set me back, but he still can't win. I'm sure that the teleported version of Nathan Wexler is telling him where I am, even as we speak. But what Cargill doesn't know is that I've copied the best weapons experts on the planet as well. Half of this building houses my Brain Trust duplicates, and all three buildings surrounding us. And they've made breakthroughs the US military can only *dream about*. This island has anti-plane and anti-missile capabilities more impressive than those of any country on Earth. So Cargill's first attack wave will fail. And I have the means to escape into the night long before he even begins to breach our defenses."

"You still don't get it, do you?" said Jenna scathingly. "Poor megalomaniac, psychopathic asshole." She shook her head. "Here's the thing, *genius,* Blake and I are duplicates also. The goal was to get Nathan out, if possible, and destroy you. We signed on for a one-way mission."

For the first time, Knight considered why Jenna had kept her index finger on top of her diamond ring since this conversation had begun. He had thought it was a nervous habit, but now he knew better. It wasn't a ring Nathan Wexler had given her, after all.

His eyes widened in horror.

"It's finally dawning on you, isn't it?" said Jenna. "You think the explosion *Aaron* triggered was epic? Well, I'm carrying a *hundred times* as much explosive. I push down hard on this diamond and enough octa-nitro-cubane is triggered to flatten this building and at least the three key buildings around it, which house your Brain Trust."

"But you'll die also," said Knight, using the only card he had left. "Horribly. Your body torn to shreds. Are you really prepared for that? Another Jenna may get to live, but it's you who takes the full brunt of the explosion. You who gets vaporized. It won't hurt any less because there's another of you inside Cheyenne Mountain."

Tears began streaming down Jenna's face. "I know," she said. "And I am terrified. I don't want to die. I'm not a hero."

"So don't do it," pleaded Knight. "You said yourself I might be right."

"I only said that to get you to agree to give Aaron and Nathan a head start."

"The world is a fucked up place. The inmates have taken over the asylum. You know it's true. I'm the only person who can save humanity from itself."

"You might be right," whispered Jenna, now sobbing uncontrollably, fear and dread written all over her face. "But let's hope like hell you aren't."

And with that she pushed down hard on her diamond, and a fireball was created that briefly turned the center of the island into the center of the sun, sending shockwaves for dozens of miles in all directions.

Everyone in all four central buildings was vaporized instantly, save for a doctor named Susan Schlesinger who had just left the island, deciding to listen to the advice of a man who had threatened to kill her repeatedly, but whose decency somehow still managed to shine through.

58

Nathan Wexler suddenly found himself in the most desolate place he had ever been. An ocean of desert receded into the horizon on all sides, and he couldn't find a single shred of evidence that humanity had ever existed. Judging only by his surroundings, he could well have been thrust back millions of years in time rather than the just the blink of an eye.

One moment he had been inside the chamber of one of Edgar Knight's time machines, and the next he was here.

He tried not to think of the other version of himself still standing in the chamber, the device now shut down by his transmitter, while armed mercenaries out for blood swarmed into the room like angry wasps.

And he especially tried not to think of Aaron Blake. Whoever he was, the man was absolutely amazing. Creative, bold, and all but unstoppable. Blake's shoulder and leg had been shredded, and yet he had managed to send Wexler off somehow, especially remarkable since Wexler had witnessed a torrent of bullets ripping through the man's body as he turned the crank the last quarter revolution to seal the door.

He checked the phone Blake had given him. Sure enough, despite the desolation surrounding him, the wireless signal was strong. *God bless America*, he thought happily, placing an immediate call to Lee Cargill as he had been instructed.

Cargill was ecstatic to receive his call, and was able to scramble a nearby military helicopter to pick him up only ten minutes after he had traced Wexler's location. After a quick stop at Nellis Air Force Base he was ushered onto a jet and flown to Cheyenne Mountain, arriving less than three hours after he had teleported into the desert.

There were four people waiting to greet him on the runway just outside of the mountain, three men and a woman. Two of the men were unfamiliar, although he assumed one of them was the mysterious Lee Cargill. The other was Aaron Blake.

And the woman he would recognize anywhere.

Jenna Morrison.

She threw her arms around him as tears of joy streamed down her face, and he teared as well, both experiencing impossible emotions never felt by any others in history.

"So it's really true," said Jenna after they had exchanged a prolonged kiss. "Knight really did produce a duplicate. But how? And when?"

"I'll tell you all about it," said Wexler, "but maybe I should meet your friends before I do. Although I do know this man," he added happily, extending a hand toward Aaron Blake. "Or at least one version of him."

Blake shook the physicist's hand. "It's an honor to meet you," he said. "To meet you once again, as it would seem."

Wexler smiled. "To say the honor is all mine is an understatement. I'll tell you everything that happened, but I can say with absolute confidence that no man alive is braver or more heroic than you." He paused. "I'll never be able to thank you enough."

"I appreciate that," said Blake, "but no need. As you know, I'm not the man who managed to get you out of Knight's control."

"True, but we both know you and he have an equally heroic nature and deserve the same thanks."

Blake nodded to acknowledge the compliment. "I'm just happy everything seems to have worked out," he said modestly.

Wexler couldn't help but frown. Yes, it had worked out, at least for *this* version of himself.

But the Aaron Blake and Nathan Wexler he had left behind were surely dead. And Knight still held uncountable members of what he called his Brain Trust on the island, which he could use as hostages to prevent Cargill from capturing him. The first thing Wexler had done was to give Cargill the location of Knight's headquarters, but the man had not seemed to find this of urgent importance for some reason.

Wexler waited until Cargill had introduced himself, along with his second-in-command, Joe Allen, and then said, "Can I assume you're planning to attack Knight's compound immediately?"

Cargill shook his head. "We've sent a mop-up crew to get as many of his supporters as we can. But the octa-nitro-cubane made an attack unnecessary."

"Octa-nitro-cubane?" said Wexler.

"You know, the explosive."

Wexler shook his head. "I have no idea what you're talking about."

Cargill winced. "Why don't we postpone this conversation for a while. We all wanted to meet you and welcome you here, but I know you and Jenna have a lot of catching up to do. And recent events have left us quite busy. Jenna can fill you in and you two can get reacquainted. We can all meet tomorrow for a more complete exchange of information, and so we can all begin to get to know each other. Let me show you around inside the mountain and then let the two of you have some privacy."

"Inside the mountain?" repeated Wexler uncertainly.

Cargill smiled. "Yes. You definitely have some catching up to do."

59

Nathan Wexler reacted to Cheyenne Mountain with the same open-mouthed awe that every other person who had ever made this trip had displayed. After the briefest of tours, Cargill, Blake, and Allen shook Wexler's hand warmly and took their leave.

Jenna knew how badly Cargill wanted the details of all that had happened at Knight's headquarters, but had decided this could wait, that giving her and Nathan some quality alone time took precedence.

She was really beginning to like that man.

She wondered what the other her had thought of Edgar Knight before she had killed him—and herself. She shuddered once again just from the thought of how horrible it must have been for her to trigger the explosive, knowing she was taking her last breath.

When they were alone in her cramped quarters, Jenna melted into Wexler's arms again, hugging him fiercely just to be sure he was real.

"So when did Knight copy you?" she asked again once they had separated, returning to the question she had posed on the runway.

"Three months ago. His men hit us with knockout gas while we were sleeping."

"*Us?*" said Jenna in dismay. "You don't mean to say . . ." For some reason, she found herself unable to finish the sentence.

"Yes. He copied us both." Wexler paused, and tears began to well up in his eyes. "But after you and Blake arrived at Knight's island, he shot the other Jenna to death. The one I lived with for the past three months. Right in front of me."

"I am so sorry," said Jenna softly.

"Thanks. But being here with you . . . I don't know how to feel. I'm not sure the human mind is equipped for situations like this. I just saw the woman I love killed. But then here you are. The woman I love. And it's like my subconscious is trying hard to convince me this other event never occurred. That it was nothing more than a vivid hallucination."

Jenna sighed. Although he didn't know it yet, no one understood how he was feeling any better than she did. It was insane. The Nathan Wexler she had lived with the past three months had been killed in front of her, and the Jenna Morrison he had lived with had been killed in front of him. It was bizarrely symmetrical, in a funhouse mirror sort of way.

And yet they were still Nathan Wexler and Jenna Morrison. They shared every memory until three months previously. And despite having witnessed Nathan Wexler's death on Palomar Mountain, she knew she was in love with this one. Three months of shared memories had been erased, but that didn't wipe out the chemistry between them, the years they had been in love before they had been separated by a madman.

Jenna told him what had happened to him on Palomar Mountain. Explained the circumstances.

For several long seconds after she finished he was too stunned to speak, and she wondered how he would react. Despite what had happened, she knew she could find a way to get beyond it all, to get back the relationship she was certain had been lost. But could *he*?

"Okay," he said finally. "This is all truly horrible. And I don't want to even begin to think of the philosophical and ethical dimensions of it. It's too much for me to handle. The people we lost we loved deeply. And they died loving life as much as we do, and feeling excruciating pain."

He paused and stared deeply into her brown eyes. "Yet the two of us remain," he said finally. "The essential essence of *us* is unchanged."

Jenna nodded. "I've never had so many conflicting emotions. I guess the trick is for us to find a way not to be haunted by what happened. Not to feel guilty about still loving each other."

Wexler sighed and then nodded. "I agree," he said. "So we both saw the other gunned down in cold blood. While this isn't something they probably recommend in couples therapy," he added wryly, a twinkle Jenna knew well returning to his eyes, "you do have to admit, not many couples have *that* in common."

Jenna burst out laughing.

Part of her knew it was too soon for gallows humor, but she also knew they had desperately needed to lighten the mood to retain their sanity in the face of insane circumstances.

And Jenna now had her answer. The man she loved was back. They would always mourn for those they had lost, but it was human nature to compartmentalize, to move on. Months or years from now it would seem like the two of them had never parted. It would all be as distant as a bad nightmare from which they had awakened.

They instinctively began to reminisce about the many shared experiences they did have, and less than ten minutes later they felt almost as comfortable together as they always had. A few months worth of divergent experiences, as traumatic as they had been, had not changed what was at the core of their personalities, nor the palpable magnetism that drew them together.

Jenna wasn't quite sure how it started, but one moment they were talking and the next they were making love with a mindless, animal intensity, unsure if five minutes had passed or five hours.

When they were both satiated, they turned onto their sides to face each other, a sheet pulled over them for warmth. Jenna wanted to just lie there quietly, without a care in the world, basking in Nathan's closeness, but she knew she didn't have this luxury.

She wasn't entirely surprised that Aaron hadn't told Nathan about the explosives they had smuggled onto Knight's island. He had been busy turning himself into a one-man army. She also knew Nathan had guessed what Cargill had meant when he brought it up, but there had been too much to deal with, and Nathan had temporarily pushed it from his mind.

But it was time to bring him up to speed.

Jenna explained what had happened and the thinking behind it. That as long as Edgar Knight was still alive he would be a threat to the world, and no one named Nathan Wexler or Jenna Morrison could ever be safe.

Cargill had made some guesses about what she and Blake would encounter once they were captured, but he couldn't be sure. So they had decided to use a dose of explosive that couldn't miss, even if Jenna had been placed in a lead prison and Knight was in a distant room.

The explosion had destroyed all life in Knight's building and the three that surrounded it, and had caused a number of deaths in buildings even farther away. She explained to Wexler that while he was flying from Nellis to Cheyenne Mountain, Lee Cargill had been working with others in the government to spin the explosion in the media, lamenting the tragic loss of life, keeping the underlying cause a mystery, and making sure it was clear that no radiation had been released and no one else was in any danger.

But before this happened he had sent a number of teams to mop up, locate any time travel devices still on the island, and capture anyone they could who had been working with Knight.

Wexler's expression darkened as she spoke, and it was clear just how saddened and horrified he was to learn about the carnage the other Jenna had unleashed.

"The thought of this makes me sick," he said when she had finished. "There were thousands of people in these four buildings," he whispered. "Thousands. I worked with a number of them. You couldn't have known about all the others Knight copied, in addition to me, but you probably killed every last one of what he called his Brain Trust. They were all brilliant scientists, from every field."

"I know," said Jenna softly. "Before you arrived here, Cargill's early teams had already captured a few key players, and had learned that these scientists had been wiped out."

"It's a huge blow to the world. And I didn't tell you, but apparently, Knight had made a number of additional duplicates of both of us as well, who were also killed."

Jenna sighed. "I don't know, Nathan. In this brave new world of time travel, nothing is easy anymore. Ethics take on a new dimension. We didn't know for sure about Knight's Brain Trust, but we figured if he had duplicated you before your breakthrough, you were probably one of a large number he had done this to. We also discussed the possibility that he would keep them close enough that the blast would kill them."

"And?"

"And we didn't know what to think. Not even what to root for. What if they had all lived? Now what? Do we free them all? And if we do, there are two or more copies of numerous scientists. The legal and ethical issues multiply exponentially. Who owns what? Who's entitled to what job? Do all four versions of a man owe alimony to his ex-wife? Are three identical mothers all legally the parent of one child?"

A troubled expression crossed Wexler's face as he considered these points.

"And could we really just release them?" continued Jenna. "Wouldn't this let the time travel genie out of the bottle?"

"It would," said Wexler. "Scientists around the world would work toward recreating Knight's invention."

"Exactly. And you saw how dangerous this is in the hands of one man. What if it were in the hands of dozens? Or hundreds?"

"You're right. Nothing is simple anymore."

"So if the scientists Knight duplicated hadn't been killed, would we have been forced to imprison them the way *he* did? Turn them into hamsters in a gilded cage producing miracles for the world like so many elves?"

"The ethics are truly impossible," said Wexler in frustration. "Because this really might have been necessary. And I was one of those imprisoned, so I don't say this lightly. But if the imprisonment of a few thousand duplicated scientists would ensure the power of time travel remained largely bottled up, and their collective genius could lead to breakthroughs in science and medicine, improving the lot of billions around the globe, there's an argument to be made it would be unethical *not* to do this."

"I see you're beginning to appreciate what we were struggling to deal with."

"It's a problem as thorny as they come."

Jenna blew out a long breath. "In the end, we decided to eliminate Knight at all costs. If the duplicate scientists survived, we would cross that bridge later. As it turned out, none did. But as tragic as their deaths are, this might just be for the best. Hard to imagine I'm saying this, but maybe it's true. Because all of these people still live. Somewhere else."

Her expression turned even more thoughtful. "I know there have always been those who reject advances. Who think if man were meant to fly, he would have been given wings. As scientists, we've always believed the opposite. That if man were *not* meant to fly, he wouldn't have been given a brain with which to invent the airplane."

"But this case pushes that boundary to the limit, doesn't it?"

"Yes. Because there is just something . . . unnatural about having more than one copy of a person running around. Certain benefits of human duplication are undeniable, but this time I'm not so sure. Maybe this time man really wasn't meant to be able to produce multiple copies of himself."

Nathan nodded. "Three months ago, only a single copy of each of us existed in the universe. And now this is true again. It's hard for me to say this isn't how it's supposed to be."

"Given what happened, we at least don't have to make any impossibly hard decisions right away. We can give this weeks and months of extended thought. Try to come to grips with our new reality."

"And I want to do that," said Wexler, "no matter how complex the issues. But I have to admit, I'm excited to get a look at the discovery my other self ended up making. Knight had me working around the clock, but for the life of me I couldn't come up with what insight I must have had."

Jenna grinned. "Believe me, Q5 is drooling at the prospect of having you involved."

"Q5?"

"We really aren't going to get any sleep tonight, are we?"

"Because of all the sex?" said Wexler with a grin, knowing this wasn't what she meant.

"Sure," she replied, returning the smile. "That and all the catching up we still have to do."

"Q5 is the name of Cargill's group, isn't it? I should have realized that right away. *Q* for quintessence and *five* for the fifth force."

"Good. I was beginning to worry all this trauma had slowed you down," she said in amusement. "Anyway," she continued, "Q5 is dying to have you involved. You'll be the only person who will understand every nuance of the work." Her eyes sparkled in delight. "And just a few days ago, one of the physicists on the team had an exciting idea he needs you to help flesh out."

"I can tell you're pretty enthusiastic about it."

"Absolutely," said Jenna. "Your theory involves using dark energy—an *ungodly* amount of energy—to cause a fifth dimension to push along the time axis of space-time. But this guy asked the question, what if you could leapfrog space-time in the *space* direction instead?"

The physicist in question, Daniel Tini, had been in awe of Nathan's work, and had insisted Nathan would have asked this same question if he wasn't taken out of the picture just as he was finishing the underlying theory. Nathan had never gotten around to an in-depth analysis of the full implications of his theory, nor a consideration of possible extensions, which would have been the next step. Tini, on other hand, had spent more than a week studying Nathan's finished work, a luxury Nathan never had.

"He's convinced this is possible," continued Jenna. "And that practical interstellar travel will be the result. But he thinks the complexities are so great that you're the only one capable of extending the theory to make this happen."

Wexler's eyes widened and he bolted into a seated position on the bed like he had been launched from a catapult. Jenna had never seen him this excited about anything.

"Now *that* is something worth sinking my teeth into," he said excitedly. "I have no idea what to think of all the implications of time travel. But I know for certain what I think about interstellar travel. I'm all for it."

Jenna laughed. "I thought you might be," she said.

"Think about what practical interstellar travel could mean. Humanity could spread to the stars. Spread out to infinity. Survive its adolescence. Even if an Edgar Knight destroyed an entire world, the species would thrive."

"And who knows," said Jenna, "this could be right around the corner. Tomorrow, after you get to know Lee, Joe, and Aaron better, and after a full debriefing, Lee is going to offer you a position on the team." She grinned. "And by *offer*, I mean beg. And by *position*, I mean basically the Chief Scientific Officer of the organization, with unlimited resources."

Wexler nodded thoughtfully.

"Now that Knight is out of the picture," continued Jenna, "we're free to go back to our lives, of course. But I've really begun to like these people. Aaron is flat-out amazing, as a detective, as a commando, and as a human being. I can't wait to hear how he managed to get you out of there, and I have some Aaron Blake stories of my own to tell. As far as I can tell, Lee and Joe are good men also."

"So you would recommend we join them?"

"I would. But I've had a chance to get to know them. So take your time. Do the same. And then decide."

"You have yourself a deal."

"Good. And while you're at it, if you do decide to join Q5, I think we should get married. Make it official."

Wexler's jaw dropped to the floor. "Sounds good to me," he said after he had gotten over his initial shock. "If I'm remembering right, you've always been the one who didn't want to hassle with this. I've been pretending we're already married for over a year now anyway."

"Then it's settled," said Jenna, who realized her new eagerness to finally tie the knot was a direct result of having seen Nathan die. Maybe this *would* be a good technique for couples therapy, after all. "But if we're going to marry, I have one request."

"Anything," said Wexler.

"I get to choose the location of our honeymoon."

"Done," he said immediately. He raised his eyebrows. "Anywhere in particular you had in mind?"

"As a matter of fact," she said, breaking into a broad grin, "I do. Just outside the rings of Saturn. In an experimental spacecraft that we'd beam there. Of course, this will require you to figure out how to use the fifth dimension to push through space, rather than time."

"Of course," said the physicist in amusement. "I was guessing you'd want to honeymoon at a resort in Hawaii. But, you know, the rings of Saturn would have been my next guess."

Jenna laughed. "And just so I don't put any undue pressure on you," she said, "I'm willing to postpone the honeymoon until you've succeeded. I realize that coming up with the most profound breakthrough in human history might take you a while." She shot him a playful look. "But don't take *too* long."

Nathan Wexler grinned. "Yes, ma'am," he said, his eyes dancing. "I'll get to work on that right away."

From the Author: Thanks for reading *Split Second*. I hope that you enjoyed it. As always, I'd be grateful if you would consider putting up some stars on the novel's Amazon page, as this is immensely helpful in getting books noticed.

Finally, feel free to visit my website, www.douglaserichards.com (where you can get on a mailing list to be notified of new releases), Friend me on Facebook at *Douglas E. Richards Author*, or write to me at doug@san.rr.com.

SPLIT SECOND: What's Real, and What Isn't

As you may know, I conduct fairly extensive research for all of my novels. In addition to trying to tell the most compelling stories I possibly can, I strive to introduce concepts and accurate information that I hope will prove fascinating, thought-provoking, and even controversial.

Although *Split Second* is a work of fiction and contains considerable speculation, some of it does reflect reality. Naturally, within the context of a thriller, it is impossible for me to go into the depth each topic deserves, nor present the topic from all possible angles. I encourage interested readers to read further to get a more thorough and nuanced look at each topic, and weigh any conflicting data, opinions, and interpretations. By so doing, you can decide for yourself what is accurate and arrive at your own view of the subject matter.

Before I begin, I have to report there were many times during the writing of this novel that I thought I must be crazy for attempting this particular plot. Thinking about the logic of time travel made my brain hurt, and I pulled out handfuls of hair on numerous occasions trying to wrestle this to the ground.

Time travel is always complex, but when you're dealing with only forty-five microseconds, duplication, teleportation, paradox, possible branching timelines, and so on, it can be maddening to figure out, especially if you're trying to get it as logical and self-consistent as possible. I spent many hours filling pages with diagrams and having to repeatedly change the plot when I realized I had gotten the logic wrong. And if trying to understand the complexities of this particular plot wasn't difficult enough, trying to explain it in a way that had any chance of being understandable in fewer than a million pages was challenging as well.

This being said, since no one really knows how time travel might work, I had to take certain liberties in telling this story that didn't have a firm basis in logic, and I can't guarantee I didn't miss something in my analysis. All I can say for sure is that I did the best I could.

With this out of the way, let me get right to the meat and potatoes:

Idiocracy (or Are We Getting Dumber?): This is a real movie, with the premise I outlined in the novel. I found this movie amusing, but be warned that it isn't for every taste, and many might find it offensive.

As to the accuracy of the movie's premise, this is controversial, and very complicated, so for those who are interested, I would recommend Googling *fertility and intelligence*, *dysgenics*, and the *Idiocracy effect*.

From my research (and, as always, my analysis is not infallible, so I encourage readers to come to their own conclusions) it appears that studies do show an inverse correlation between education and fertility, such that the more educated you are, the fewer children you will have, *on average*. A 1991 study, for example, conducted by the US Census Bureau, found that high school dropouts averaged 2.5 children, whereas college graduates averaged only 1.56 children.

This inverse correlation also seems to exist between wealth and fertility, at the individual level and with respect to nations, which has been named the demographic-economic paradox. To illustrate this point, Karan Singh, a former minister of population in India, famously said, "Development is the best contraceptive."

While there is some correlation between educational attainment and intelligence, IQ isn't entirely determined by genes, and there are other complicating factors, so the higher reproductive rates among the less wealthy and less educated translate into a fairly small reduction of species intelligence (and again, this is quite controversial and still under discussion). Even so, over centuries and millennium, this could have a very noticeable effect.

Critics of this analysis point to something called the Flynn effect, which is the observation that average IQs have actually been slowly rising since 1930, most likely due to better nutrition and quality of life, although new studies have shown this trend slowing or even reversing of late. Proponents of the *Idiocracy* view suggest that these average rises would have been even greater if not for the increased fertility of the less intelligent, and point to the recent reversals.

This last reminds me of a conversation I had with my mother. I was born in the days before women were warned about smoking and drinking while pregnant. (These were also the days in which my sister and I would never wear a seatbelt, would sleep on a platform against the window above the backseat of our car, and in which my sister would slather oil on herself and use a reflecting shield to maximize the amount of sun hitting her body while at the beach).

When I learned that my mother smoked while she was pregnant with me, I teased her about this. She would have none of it. "My smoking obviously had no affect on you," she insisted. "Look how smart you turned out to be." To which I replied playfully, "Yeah, but think of how smart I *could* have been."

Dark Matter and Dark Energy: The information presented with respect to dark energy, dark matter, quintessence, the ancients' belief that the world was composed of four elements (earth, air, fire, and water), that we are totally clueless about the composition of a vast majority of our universe, and so on, is as accurate as I could make it, although highly summarized and not rigorously presented.

The following passage is entirely fictional:

"*Nathan told me that physicists were making some progress identifying this energy, but he was certain there would never be a way to use it. You could tap in—maybe—but even if you managed this, Nathan's calculations, and those of others, showed you'd never be able to control it. It would be all or nothing. Drinking from a firehose. Tap it and the minimum energy you would release would be more than enough to vaporize the Earth, possibly the entire solar system.*"

What I find most fascinating about all of this is how little we really understand our universe. Despite the amazing progress we have made, we may only be scratching the surface. While this is sobering, it is also exciting. Humanity has accomplished quite a lot, but think of what we might be able to accomplish if we could unlock the many mysteries still remaining.

The Nature of Time: I endeavored to make this entire discussion as accurate as possible, but this is a very complicated subject, and I hope I didn't make readers too crazy and confused. The relational theory of time is real, although I'll leave it to readers to decide for themselves if they think time could exist before the universe came into being. The block universe is a real concept that falls out of relativity, and one to which many scientists (including Einstein) subscribe.

I find Zeno's paradoxes a lot of fun, and I encourage you to Google them. I included the one about the two arrows frozen in time, although I'm not sure how clearly I was able to get across the point of this in the limited space I allowed myself for this task.

My favorite of these paradoxes is called *Achilles and the Tortoise*. Imagine a tortoise is given a large head start in a race. Well, before Achilles can catch the slow critter, he has to travel half the distance they are separated. But while he's traveling half, the tortoise is also moving ahead. So now he again must travel half the remaining distance before he can catch the reptile. But again, in the time this takes, the tortoise will have moved forward a small amount. By the time he travels half the remaining distance again, which continues to shorten, the tortoise moves forward again. And so on, forever.

In this way, thousands of years ago, Zeno presented a logical argument that Achilles should never be able to catch up to the tortoise, in a way that was quite difficult to disprove for some time (even though we all know Achilles will, in fact, catch and pass the tortoise).

Apologies if my abbreviated presentation of this paradox isn't clear, and I won't take the time to provide the resolution to it here, but if you're interested, just Google *Achilles and the Tortoise* and you will find all you need.

Time Travel: Feynman diagrams are real. They do model antimatter as going backward in time, and are exceedingly useful. Richard Feynman was a remarkable man, and this is just one of his many contributions to science.

The chronology protection conjecture is an actual concept. The idea of retrocausality is real, and certain experiments with entangled particles in quantum physics suggest that an observation made now can change something that happened in the past. I didn't include these experiments because the background required to understand them is fairly extensive (and I have to admit, I don't fully understand them myself :)).

The logic of duplication and translocation is my own, but it makes some sense, at least to me. Duplication isn't all that controversial, appearing in countless works of fiction. I'm sure we all remember scenes in which two Marty McFlys exist at the same time (one on stage performing and one backstage).

To my knowledge, however, duplication, with or without translocation, has never been presented as the sole point of time travel the way it is in *Split Second*, and all time travel stories with which I am familiar send people and objects back hours, days, and years, rather than millionths of a second.

When I began the novel, I thought I had two basic choices for how time travel would work. Either time travel only affected a single timeline, or time branched whenever time travel caused a change in the past. For a variety of plot-related reasons I won't go into here, I couldn't use the single timeline. But the idea of infinite branching timelines bothered me. The more I thought about this, the more I didn't like it.

If you wanted ten copies of Nathan Wexler, you would get ten different universes, each branch containing a different number of Wexlers, one through ten. And if you repeated this a million times, as you would need to do to scale up an infinitesimal amount of explosive, for example, you'd be creating a million different universes. This just seemed wasteful to me, and if this many universes were allowed, who really cared what happened in the one featured in the narrative.

So I came up with a blended model, which is presented in the book. A single timeline that ignores paradox. A universe that just accepts where it is at, without worrying about how it got there, and moves forward on this basis. And this I came to really like. It brought to mind the way I write novels, and made great sense in this context. My novels are my own personal universes, and sometimes the cause of a change I make no longer exists (because it came from a different universe, a different version of the novel). But even without a discernible cause, the effect remains. The novel goes forward, just accepting the change, and not caring how it came to be.

After I had the rudiments of the *Split Second* plot worked out, I read four books on time travel, *How to Build a Time Machine* (Brian Clegg), *Time Travel in Einstein's Universe* (J. Richard Gott), *Time, a Traveler's Guide* (Clifford A. Pickover), and *Time Machines: Time Travel in Physics, Metaphysics, and Science Fiction* (Paul J. Nahin).

Sadly, while there was some fascinating material here, almost none of it was useful for my novel. It was either too complex, not relevant to my plot, or required engineering impossible even for a species a thousand times more capable than ours (creating wormholes, rotating Tipler cylinders, and so on).

In this case, since I couldn't find anything scientifically feasible that could work, I created my device from whole cloth. Siphon a massive amount of the nearly infinite energy of the dark energy field (which is real), use this to drive matter through the fifth dimension (which could be real, but hasn't been proven), and voila, time travel to 45.15 microseconds in the past (chosen because I thought 58 feet was a good distance).

Earth's Movement: The paragraph detailing the Earth's various movements through space (rotation, revolution, etc.) is accurate, at least according to *Scientific American*. We really are moving through the universe at 242 miles per second.

The *Star Trek* Transporter: Alas, many, if not most scientists believe that Captain Kirk is destroyed and recreated each time he "travels" through the transporter. I find this fascinating. Even knowing this, Edgar Knight would happily use such a device. I encourage you to consider what you would do. I've given it a lot of thought, but haven't firmly decided if I would use a transporter or not.

I considered addressing some of the philosophical implications of this in the novel, but finally decided against it. Here is one example: Basically, the cells in your body are dying and being replaced all the time. It isn't clear if 100% of your cells are replaced during your lifetime, or how long this might take if they are, but a common, albeit controversial figure often cited is seven years (if you Google, "does the human body replace itself every seven years" you will find any number of articles on this subject).

But just to illustrate the philosophical point, let's imagine that this is true, that all of the cells in your body are replaced after seven years.

So are you the same *you* that you were seven years ago?

And what if this only took a single year to happen?

I'm guessing most of us believe that even if every cell that existed in our bodies a year ago was swapped out with a new one, the old us never died, and we are still the same person we always were.

Okay, but what if this happened in a single day?

You see where I'm heading. An argument could be made that having one *you* destroyed on the transporter pad while another *you* takes its place is just an acceleration of this process. If you don't mourn for individual cells that die to make room for the new ones, perhaps you shouldn't mourn for the vaporized Captain Kirk.

I also considered exploring the concept of what makes us conscious beings. Is this an emergent property of our brains? (such that the whole is far greater than the sum of the parts). Or something else entirely?

Randomness of Creativity: Since Edgar Knight could make endless duplicates of Nathan Wexler, it was important for me to explain why he might still need Wexler's work, that events sparking eureka moments are often fickle and random. At first I presented a fictional example from *Back to the Future*, when Doc Brown falls, hurts his head, and randomly comes up with the idea for the flux capacitor.

I decided to remove this example since I had already referenced this iconic movie several times, and there are far more compelling examples from the real world, including the two I presented, Alexander Fleming and Albert Einstein.

I should mention that I find Einstein to be one of the most remarkable people who ever lived, and I find his story endlessly fascinating. If you have the chance, I recommend reading *Einstein: His Life and Universe*, by Walter Isaacson (after you've finished reading all of my books, of course:)).

I am also fascinated by the randomness of our lives, and nowhere is this more evident than the sperm lottery. Each person alive has genetic material donated by a sperm that won a race against hundreds of millions of competitors, a race it could never have won given even the slightest change of circumstances. I couldn't resist using the sperm example in the novel.

Other examples abound. In my own life, I wouldn't be writing this note (or novel) if not for a string of incredibly unlikely occurrences, all of which had to happen in the exact right way. In 2011, I had given up on my dream of writing and decided to go back to biotech. But then one day I randomly decided to get a book to read. Back then, I usually shopped for paperbacks on Amazon, but this time I decided to go to the local bookstore; I have no idea why. While there, a book by Boyd Morrison entitled *The Ark* just happened to catch my eye. I bought it, even though there were dozens of other contenders that I almost purchased instead. And then the author just happened to include a note at the end, explaining how he had published the book on Amazon as an e-book, it had gone viral, and was later published up by Simon and Schuster.

This got me to thinking. Maybe I should put my novel, *Wired*, online, and see if anyone would read it. Boyd Morrison was living proof that good things could happen, so why not? Believe me, I would never have done this if I had not read this note. In 2011, I was barely aware that e-books even existed (although I was filling my house with physical books so quickly I was running out of places to put them).

Less than six months later, *Wired* became a *New York Times* and *USA Today* bestseller and my writing career was off and running. But if I hadn't gone to the bookstore at the exact time I did, or if I hadn't happened to notice this particular book, or if . . .

Octa-nitro-cubane: This explosive is real, although the hyphens are not. I added these for ease of reading, since I stumble over octanitrocubane every time I see it. These cubes of carbon do represent the most powerful non-nuclear explosive known to man, and it is true that this substance is nearly impossible to produce, requiring forty chemical steps to synthesize. In fact, as I note in the novel, there has never been enough of this made to even test (as far as I know).

Taxol and Hard to Synthesize Drugs: The information provided about Taxol is true. I'm not sure how many other drugs are out there that work wonders but can't be made in sufficient quantities (scaled up), but I suspect they exist.

I was once Director of Biotechnology Licensing at Bristol-Myers Squibb, the company that developed Taxol. For many decades the Pacific yew tree could make this drug, but humans couldn't.

While at BMS, I negotiated two collaborations with companies specializing in what is called natural products chemistry. One tried to discover cures from chemicals found in microbes, and one from chemicals found in sea creatures, and I was quoted in an article in the *Wall Street Journal* about one of the deals, saying, "Nature is the world's best chemist."

This is very true. Nature can produce chemicals that we can't hope to match, and a significant percentage of all drugs now in use were first produced in nature (aspirin was first derived from the bark of the willow tree, there is a diabetes drug derived from a chemical found in the spit of the Gila monster, an anti-coagulant used for many years was derived from leech saliva, and so on).

With respect to the shell company formed by Lee Cargill to duplicate difficult to manufacture cures, this would never work in real life. The FDA requires a precise knowledge of every step in the manufacturing process before they will approve a drug, and need to be able to audit manufacturing sites to be sure they are up to standards. Alas, a mystery process (time travel) would never fly with them, no matter how pure the end product.

Faraday and Maxwell: The information about these two icons is accurate. For my plot to work, I needed someone to have invented time travel without fully understanding the theory behind it, and the Faraday-Maxwell comparison worked perfectly. To learn more about these amazing figures in science, I recommend the book, *Faraday, Maxwell and the Electromagnetic Field: How Two Men Revolutionized Physics*, by Nancy Forbes and Basil Mahon.

Polygraph Tests: My research suggests polygraph tests are fairly unreliable, and that testers do try to fool subjects into making mistakes. The strategy for beating the test that I put forth is real, although the improved polygraph test in the novel is fictional (it doesn't exist in real life or even in the novel, as it turns out).

UCLA Steam Tunnels: There is no Kendall Hall at UCLA, but the steam tunnels are real, and my description of them is more or less accurate. The *Welcome to Hell* graffiti did exist at one time, according to my reading.

Originally in the novel, Dr. Dan Walsh was a professor at USC. I knew that many older universities had tunnel systems, and I thought having Aaron Blake use them to bypass surveillance would make for a fun scene. The only problem is that USC doesn't have any tunnels, so I moved Dan Walsh to UCLA :).

Fairly recently, the school's newspaper was offering tours of the tunnel system. Here is an excerpt taken from their website:

"UCLA's underground tunnel system, site of late-night forays by adventurous students and a subject of campus folklore, plays an important role in keeping the university running smoothly behind the scenes. Official tours of the underground tunnels can be arranged with Leroy Sisneros, UCLA Facilities Management's Director of Maintenance and Alterations. Those touring the tunnels should wear closed-toed shoes and be advised that the tunnels are very narrow and hot in some places."

In researching UCLA, I read one reference to a campus joke that UCLA stood for *Under Construction Like Always*. I didn't go to this school, so I have no idea if this is something familiar to most students or not, but I thought it would be fun to include.

Lake Las Vegas: There really is such a place, and while Knight's island doesn't exist nor do his armaments and security, the early history of the resort, its dimensions, the fortunes spent to develop it, and the vast size of the dam that was built to create the lake are all accurate.

This resort came up at a dinner party I attended. A few of my friends were reminiscing about how they had flown out to see it long ago, when it was under construction, but had been unable to invest. At the time they had kicked themselves, but they grew to learn they had dodged a bullet.

When they described the magnificence of the resort and its checkered history, I was absolutely fascinated, especially since I had visited Vegas any number of times and had never even heard of it. I'm still amazed that there is a giant man-made lake in the middle of the desert, surrounded by world-class resort hotels and other properties.

At that moment I knew that this location would have to be a setting in one of my books someday.

Cheyenne Mountain & Other Settings: Cheyenne Mountain is real and in use. My description of the main facility is accurate, although I created a fictional expansion of the base because I wanted more room. Here is a link to a short documentary about the facility: Science Channel Short Documentary on Cheyenne Mountain

Palomar Mountain is real. When my kids were little, I used to take them hiking in the woods there, and they loved it. The Palomar Observatory and Hale Telescope on top of this mountain are also real.

The underground military base at Palomar is purely fictional. In the first draft of this novel, I included some historical information about other underground facilities the government and military had used, but left this on the cutting room floor.

Since I find it interesting, I thought I'd restore a few paragraphs of this deleted section below:

For the most part the Manhattan Project, which led to the world's first nuclear bomb, had been done at secret above-ground sites, but the first ever nuclear reactor was constructed underground, at a small site below the bleachers at Stagg Field at the University of Chicago, and aptly named Chicago Pile-1.

Unlike most reactors built since, this pile had no radiation shielding and no cooling system of any kind. The brilliant physicist, Enrico Fermi, had convinced those in charge that his calculations were reliable enough to rule out a runaway chain reaction or an explosion. Later, the official historians of the Atomic Energy Commission would point out that while the gamble had paid off, these men had conducted "a possibly catastrophic experiment in one of the most densely populated areas of the nation."

This passage is accurate, and a little scary. After receiving my master's degree in molecular biology, I attended the University of Chicago to earn an MBA, and lived just a few blocks from this site. At street level is a sculpture and a steel plaque that reads, "On December 2, 1942, man achieved here the fist self-sustaining chain reaction, and thereby initiated the controlled release of nuclear energy."

The Torrey pine is an actual tree, and Torrey Pines is a famous golf course. I know the Torrey Pines area well since my children both graduated Torrey Pines High School (as did X-games superstars Shaun White and Tony Hawk, interestingly enough).

The information about San Ysidro is accurate, at least to an approximation. The number of border crossings, and even highway lanes, can change from year to year.

Finally, Schriever is a real Air Force Base near Colorado Springs, and it really is home to the 50th Space Wing.

Science Fiction: The science fiction novels and stories referenced in *Split Second* include *The Weapon Shops of Isher*, by A.E. Van Vogt, *The Chronology Protection Case,* by Paul Levinson, and *A Sound of Thunder,* by Ray Bradbury (the one having to do with the possible repercussions of killing a single mouse many millions of years ago).

In an earlier version of the novel I included an excerpt from a haunting story called *The Weed of Time*, by Norman Spinrad, used to exemplify what a block universe would be like if our perceptions allowed us to experience any point in time, instead of just *now*. Here is this deleted passage:

[Walsh speaking] "I read a science fiction story about this concept as a kid, called *The Weed of Time,* that haunted me for weeks after I read it. Basically, this guy ingests an alien weed that frees him to see time as it really is. He is able to see, live, experience every moment of his life, from birth until death, over and over again—any moment he likes. Like being able to visit any frame of a movie, but still unable to leave the reel. In the earlier movie frames of his life, so to speak, people come to believe he knows something of the future." Walsh smiled. "Which he does, of course, since he can experience later frames of his life. But he explains that this will be of no use to anyone."

He gestured to Blake. "You asked about free will in a block universe. I found this the ultimate, most depressing expression of lack of free will I've ever read. If you have a tablet, I'll try to find it."

Blake handed him one of several he had nearby, and after a few minutes of searching through cyberspace, Walsh found the passage he was after and began reading:

"'On April 3, 2040, I am born. On December 2, 2150, I die. The events in between take place in a single instant. Say that I range up and down them at will, experiencing each of them again and again and again eternally.

'For me, time as you think of it does not exist. I do not move from moment to moment sequentially like a blind man groping his way down a tunnel. I am at all points in the tunnel simultaneously.

'I know that it is no use trying to tell any of them that knowledge of the future is useless, that the future cannot be changed because it was not changed because it will not be changed. They will never accept the fact that choice is an illusion caused by the fact that future time-loci are hidden from those who advance sequentially along the time-stream one moment after the other in blissful ignorance. They refuse to understand that moments of future time are no different from moments of past or present time; fixed, immutable, invariant. They live in the illusion of sequential time.'"

ABOUT THE AUTHOR

Douglas E. Richards is the *New York Times* and *USA Today* bestselling author of seven technothrillers, including *Wired*, *Amped*, *Mind's Eye*, *BrainWeb*, *Quantum Lens*, and *The Cure*. He has also written six middle grade/young adult novels widely acclaimed for their appeal to boys, girls, and adults alike. Douglas has a master's degree in molecular biology (aka "genetic engineering"), was a biotechnology executive for many years, and has authored a wide variety of popular science pieces for *National Geographic*, the *BBC*, the *Australian Broadcasting Corporation*, *Earth and Sky*, *Today's Parent*, and many others. Douglas has a wife, two children, and two dogs, and currently lives in San Diego, California.

Made in the USA
Lexington, KY
09 March 2019